The Siren's Scream

Thomas White

Table of Contents

Acknowledgments

It's been ten years since my last novel. No real reason other than facing the daunting task of writing a novel. Simply the hardest thing I have ever done. To anyone who is attempting it, all I can say is to just keep at it. Just when you think you're done, someone will read it and ask a simple question that opens a floodgate of ideas and situations that you will have no choice but to pursue. At the end of the day, you never finish a novel, and you just stop working on it.

In the completion of this work, I received help, inspiration, and encouragement from many different people in my life. As always, Kathleen, my wife and life partner, has been the backbone of my life and work. My two daughters, grown now and living lives of their own lives, are a constant source of pride, and I relish in their success both personally and professionally.

Several friends helped along the way by simply reading it and giving me their honest reader assessments. A grateful thanks to Marion Peacock, a lovely British lady and mother of a friend, who has since passed but was the very first to read the novel and give me feedback. And to Rachal Frank, Karen Garcia, Toni Fleming, Tom Ashworth and Heather

Jagers who are not only dear friends but avid fans, and I appreciate their help and input immensely.

Hopefully, these ten years will fill an afternoon for you as you are engrossed with the work and can't put it down. Fingers crossed.

About the Author

Tom began his career as an actor, which led to a degree from the United States International University School of Performing arts in San Diego. A Cum Laude graduate, Tom was also named to "Who's Who in American Colleges and Universities.

He immediately hit the road and spent several seasons touring across the country with various shows, working as an actor, tech director, stage manager, scenic designer, lighting designer, sound designer, and finally director. Several years later, Tom found himself as an Artistic Director for a theatre in Los Angeles and the winner of several Drama-Logue and Critics' Awards for directing. As Tom's career grew, he ended up doing bigger and bigger projects in the theatre world. He directed and co-produced the world tour of "The Teenage Mutant Ninja Turtles: Coming Out Of Their Shells." The show toured for over two years, was translated into seven different languages, and was seen by close to a million children.

Tom served as President and Creative Director for Maiden Lane Entertainment for twenty-four years and worked on many large-scale corporate event productions that included Harley Davidson, Microsoft, Medtronic Diabetes, and dozens of others.

The Siren's Scream follows up his first novel, Justice Rules, which was a finalist in the Pacific Northwest Writers Association 2010 Literary contest.

Chapter 1

Sausalito, CA – Present Day

Henry Childs led a life of total inconsequence. He had no friends, no hobbies, no guilty pleasures. He had spent his thirty-eight years in the space behind his mother's aggression, lacking the courage to reach for anything more than this pitiless world deigned to dish to him.

Edith Childs screamed at Henry from the other room, "Henry, I'm bored. I want to go for a drive."

Henry's face scrunched in disdain, and the folds in his ample neck turned red. There was no denying her, not that he had ever had the backbone to attempt anything so drastic.

With a stoic exhale, he paused his video game, gulped down his cinnamon roll, lifted his considerable bulk out of the comfort of his reclining chair, and began the routine that would eventually get his mother from her bedroom to her wheelchair and into the car.

He grabbed her yellow sweater to be sure that she would stay warm.

"Henry, I'm not a child. I know if I'm cold or not."

He held up the cardigan and attempted to help her into it.

"I can dress myself, thank you."

Then there was the transfer from her sitting chair to her wheelchair.

"For goodness sakes, Henry, you would think this was the first time you've ever done this. Move the chair closer. I'm not an acrobat."

…the parade out to the porch.

"Henry, don't scrape the wall. You're always so careless. We have gouges up and down the whole hallway."

…down the ramp.

"Don't go so fast. Are you trying to launch me into outer space?"

…across the walkway toward the car.

"Do you have to hit every bump on the walk? Wait, go back, I think you missed one."

…then finally into the car.

"Be careful of my head. I don't want to lose what sense I have left."

By the time the car door was closed, with his disintegrating mother safely ensconced inside, Henry had sweat running down his forehead and was breathing hard. His double chins were dripping from each crevice, and his shirt was beginning to stain from the accumulating moisture.

He dropped her chair into the trunk, wiped his brow on his sleeve, and embraced his final moments of silence before he opened the door and plopped behind the steering wheel of his Nissan Murano.

"Which direction should we go today?" Henry asked, his gravelly voice too crusty for the confines of the car.

"Clear your throat before you speak, Henry." Edith admonished. After brief consideration, she said, "South. Along PCH."

He backed out of the driveway and headed for the Pacific Coast Highway.

"Be careful about the bushes, Henry."

Henry Childs had never lived on his own except for the three months before his father died. Even in college, while taking computer science classes, he was quite content to stay in his room and leave only to go to class. When he was twenty-six, his father had arranged a job at a computer start-up company, and Edith had forced him into taking a small apartment a few miles from their old house. He had hated it. He hated being alone and away from the security of his old room and had quickly fallen into a routine of getting up, going to work, and heading back to the apartment with several orders of take-out. She probably would have made him stay in that apartment had his father not passed away when he did.

"Henry!" Edith screeched, shattering the silence, "don't let that guy do that. These drivers they're always cutting you off. Your father used to do the same thing, and it drove me crazy. Why would he let them cut him off? I never understood."

Henry sighed. Henry had never seen his father lose his temper behind the wheel. As a matter of fact, Henry could not remember his father ever raising his voice. Dead over ten years, Henry still missed him every day. Roland Childs had always been the shoulder Henry would seek out when he had been made fun of by the other kids at school, when a bully had thrown him to the ground, or when his mother had dismissed him without consideration. Where Edith was aggressive and rude, Roland was gentle and polite. For the millionth time, he wondered why he had ever married his mother.

Roland Childs had been a successful attorney, a loving father, and a faithful husband. While arguing a case in front of a judge one afternoon, he simply stopped talking and dropped to the floor. Henry's world collapsed with his father. There was no solace now for the fat little kid with the ugly voice. Nowhere for him to turn for kindness or encouragement. He was trapped between loneliness and his mother. Yet, he remained his mother's son, and upon the death of his father, he moved back into the big house once and for all.

When his father died, Henry had been working on an algorithm that would eventually help connect a server to a remote device. His contribution to the algorithm had vested him in the company, and when he finally cashed out ten years later, he found himself a very wealthy man… who lived with his mother… and drove a Nissan Murano.

Still heading south on PCH, they approached the beach community of Santa Cruz, a cozy burg nestled on the coast thirty miles south of San Francisco. As they entered the city limits, Henry stopped at a red light. Looking up ahead and to his right, he saw a strange cloud formation gathering atop one of the cliffs overlooking the ocean. It appeared to hover, not moving with the ocean breezes or adhering to natural laws. It roiled within its confines and seemed to be attempting to form into some sort of shape. He began to feel a tingle on his inner thighs as they rubbed together under the steering wheel. There was a restlessness building in his heart beating beneath the mounds of flesh resting on his chest.

The sound of car horns pulled him out of his daze, and seeing as the light had turned green, he drove forward through town. Stopping at the next light, he saw the cloud had grown closer and was shifting into what looked like a woman's face. It glided toward him in a menacing fashion. It cast no shadow, and no one in the other cars or on the street showed any indication that they noticed. The face turned toward him, and the mouth moved, "Henry, come to me."

Henry's eyes popped wide, and his jaw dropped. His breath was coming in short bursts, yet it seemed that he wasn't inhaling at all. He turned to his mother, expecting to have to explain why a cloud was talking to him, but she had nodded off in one of her 'eye-resting' moments. He turned back to the cloud and heard her words again, "Come to me." An aura of purpose cascaded around him. He was helpless to disobey this calling. Without consulting his mother, he changed lanes abruptly and prepared to turn toward this vision.

"What are you doing, Henry? Where are you going?" Edith said, starting out of her little nap.

Henry made up a story, unsure of the origin of the inspiration. "I've heard about a place that's not far from here. I've always wanted you to see it."

Edith flinched at the sound of his voice, as she always did, but a small smile appeared on her face. "Henry, do you have a surprise for me?"

Taking advantage of the opportunity, Henry said, "Why yes, that's exactly it. Let me show you a surprise."

He took a right and then a left, and the Nissan began a climb up a very steep hill. The cloud still hung in front of his car, and her eyes followed him, unwilling to let him go. Henry alternated between watching the road and the cloud. It had defined its form and, without question, resembled a face. It had stopped moving and now hung impatient; over what, Henry couldn't tell.

At the summit, he paused and, without prompting, turned toward the cloud. He was being pulled, following an edict he felt in his gut. He coasted to a stop in front of an old, rusted gate. In front of the gate was a weathered realty sign that indicated this property was available.

Popping the gearshift into park, he lifted his considerable bulk out of the car and waddled to the gate. In rusted, corroded letters, the name 'Thornton' was spelled out across the two sides of the twisted, metal entrance. Using his weight as leverage, he pushed it open, and as it swung toward the house, the ancient hinges squealed out a warning that went unheeded.

Pouring himself back into the car, he drove past the stone turrets that stood sentry over this property and glided into the driveway.

"Henry, where are we? Do we know these people? What in the world are you doing?" Edith harped.

Henry stopped the car directly in front of the house. It was a mansion. A stunning mansion that sat deserted on the top of a robust bluff overlooking the Pacific Ocean. Old age had won its share of battles over this grand palace, but Henry saw past the peeled paint and the rotted portico. This house was to be his home; he knew it. He knew it the way a child returning from summer camp knows the peaceful serenity of his own bed.

Chapter 2

The day was wrapped in a gray blanket of an overcast sky. The air hung dull and heavy along the coast. If you looked west, the bleak ocean blended with a bleaker sky obscuring the horizon. All in all, it was a typical midwinter morning in northern California.

Darcy Wainwright sat in her back corner cubicle of The Lewis Real Estate Agency, trying to ignore the hustle and bustle of the office as she intently checked the new listings.

"Come on, there has to be a decent prospect somewhere." She continued to read, "800 square foot studio apartment, ½ bath, partial ocean view, slight fire damage. $1.5 mil. Really? I'm supposed to sell that?"

Two months on the job, and she was getting impatient, along with her boss, and was anxious to close a deal.

Darcy was an attractive, black-haired young woman with green eyes and a winning smile. At twenty-four years old, she had left the waitress life behind and was attempting to start a career in real estate. What she lacked in success, she made up in determination.

Without warning, she was the victim of a drive-by shoulder massage.

"Stan. You really don't need to do that." She shrugged his stubby hands off of her cotton blouse.

Stan Grossman was a short, well-built man with a ring of receding red hair, cut close to the scalp that circled his head like a pomegranate halo. His muscular chest was a transparent attempt to compensate for his height, and he made it no secret that he spent many hours each week at the gym. He sported a pale, red goatee and mustache that made him look like he was constantly screaming. A self-proclaimed ladies' man, he wallowed through the office cesspool of rumor and promiscuity, adding to its debasement with slimy gusto.

"What'cha doin' rook? Closing a big deal?"

"I'm about to, any day now. It won't be long."

"Well, it takes time, kiddo. Work hard and remember...."

"Check the listings. I know. Thanks, Stan. I got it from here." She turned her back to him, wishing that she had the ability to make him vaporize.

"Yep, lots of hard work, and you can cash in that 'V' card."

Darcy stopped typing. "'V' card?"

Stan underplayed a practiced, arrogant chuckle, "Virgin card. You carry it until you make your first sale." He laughed at his own joke.

"Stan, all I can tell you is that when I lose it, you won't be anywhere around." She turned back to her keyboard.

"You know, you're a smart one. You only look like a bimbo."

"It's nature's way of protecting me. Now excuse me, I have work to do," she said, not bothering to look up at him.

"Make a mental note," Stan pantomimed, writing on his hand, "Watch out for Wainwright. Smarter than she looks."

"Make a mental note," Darcy said under her breath, "Introduce Stan to the concept of harassment!"

Re-using his arrogant chuckle, he patted her shoulder one more time, adding what he felt to be an affectionate squeeze, and went off about his business.

Free from further assault, Darcy looked out at the street as the marshmallow fog settled on the cracked, concrete sidewalks. Condensation formed on the edges of the picture window, forming little rivulets of water that streaked the pane.

Then the phone rang.

The phone ringing pushed a dose of adrenaline through her system. Darcy prepared to answer in her most casual, confident, and professional manner. She knew she needed to present a tone that instantly let the caller know she was in the middle of several very important transactions. She prepared an attitude that said, 'Yes, I can help you if it's worth my time.'

With a big inhale, Darcy reached for the phone.

"Lewis Realty, Darcy Wainwright speaking, can I help you?

Good! Nicely done, she thought. That was the perfect tone, with very subtle inflection. She must remember how she did that.

"Stan?" The gruff voice on the other end of the line asked. "Hey, I was looking for Stan Grossman. Is he around?"

"Well, yes, he is, but..."

"Look, girlie, I want to talk to Stan. We're just about to close escrow on this strip mall, and I got some questions. Is he there or not?"

Darcy dropped her head, dejected. Was Stan closing on a strip mall? Can life get any more annoying? "I'll connect you," she said and pushed the hold button to forward the call.

Chapter 3

"So, what I really need from each and every one of you is to make a concerted effort to follow up on leads. It drives me insane when someone says, 'I called the office twice, and no one returned my call.' So, people, let's get with it!" Tim Lewis, the owner of Lewis Realty, preached with absolute conviction. "Now get out of here and sell some properties."

The weekly sales meeting broke up without hesitation on anyone's part. Most of the agents went directly to their phones to see what they had missed while wasting their time listening to the boss. Darcy checked the screen on her phone. All she had was a text from Shelly, the receptionist, about getting a drink after work.

As she started off to her little cubicle, Darcy heard her name, "Darcy, could I see you for a minute?" It was Tim Lewis waving his hand to direct her into his office.

"Shit!"

Darcy walked into the spacious office and sat down in front of Tim's oak desk. Most of the cubicles had glass-top workstations, but Tim had a giant oak desk left to him by his grandfather, the founder of Lewis Realty. It had a carved front that portrayed an elk in the wild, well-crafted, even if it was at odds with the corporate surroundings. Tim was in his early fifties with a full head of brown hair that was just starting to show signs of gray. He had very hairy forearms and was always wearing long-sleeved shirts to cover them up.

He sat down and smiled at Darcy. "So, how are things going?"

Darcy shivered. Anytime she was about to be fired or lectured, it started with that question. "Good, everything's good," she said. Her legs twitched against the front of the overstuffed chair, and her foot began to silently tap.

"I see that you haven't closed on anything yet. You have anything in the pipe?"

She relaxed. It was going to be the lecture. Darcy was sure of it. At least that was better than the alternative, "Well, I'm working at it every day. I came close to a sale with that house over on Maiden Lane, but the buyers didn't qualify. Apparently, they never had a credit card or any kind of credit. The guy got really pissed, I tried to explain that you need to have credit to buy a house, and he started yelling about how he has great credit cause he doesn't owe anyone anything and stuff like that. It was not fun."

Tim Lewis took a deep breath. "Darcy, you understand that it's part of your job to check out the buyer before getting too deep into the sale?"

"Oh, yeah, I do. I know that. It's just that with this guy, he said one thing, and then it turned out that..."

"Darcy." Tim took another deep breath. "Part of checking them out is verifying the things they tell you. You can't take anything at face value because people will tell you anything to be able to qualify. Understand?"

"Yes," she said, holding back the damn tears that always came at moments like these.

"Now, to help you out, I'm going to have you work with someone for a while, you know, to get you started."

"Work with someone? Who?"

Tim shuffled some of the files on his desktop. "Now, hear me out here..."

"No! Don't tell me that you want me to work with Stan? That can't happen, believe me, it's a bad idea."

"What do you mean? He's our top guy, and you could learn a lot from him."

"I don't want to cause any trouble but believe me when I tell you I cannot work with that man."

Tim paused and looked at Darcy with honest concern, "Is there something you want to say?"

Darcy sighed, "No, really, Mr. Lewis, I just want to give this a little more time. I really believe I can get started without help. Please, give me one more week. I know I can do it."

Tim pursed his lips and slowly shook his head. "Okay, but I want to see results in a week, and if it's not going to be Stan, it will be someone else. You have a week. Now get out of here and sell something."

Darcy rose and said, "Thanks. You won't regret it."

She went back to her cubicle and sat down, "Great!" She dropped her head on the desk and banged it up and down. She took a deep breath and sat up straight. "I can do this. I can totally do this."

The phone rang.

It startled Darcy, and she jumped a bit at the sound. Clearing her throat, she picked up the phone. "Yeah, Shelly?"

"Some guys on the line asking for you. Says he wants to talk to you about buying a house."

"Is this a joke? I swear to God, Shelly, if this is a joke, I will kill you."

"Hey, calm down. It's not a joke. This guy said he would only talk to you. Wouldn't even tell me what property he was talking about. I swear."

Darcy looked around the office to see if anyone was snickering in her direction. Not seeing anyone, she said, "Okay, put him through, but I'm warning you, Shelly, you're going to be sorry if this is a joke." She hung up and waited for the phone to ring again. It rang almost immediately, and Darcy answered, "Darcy Wainwright, can I help you?" She heard her annoyed tone, and she took a deep breath to calm herself down.

A grating, strained voice that sounded like wrenching metal replied, "Yes, m-m-my name is Henry Childs. I'm interested in looking at a house. The large one, on the cliffs, overlooking the ocean."

"On the cliffs? The large one?"

"Exactly. I think it's beautiful."

"In Santa Cruz?"

"Yes, right on the cliff."

Darcy scanned her memory for a house matching that description. The only thing she came up with was too absurd.

"You don't mean the Thornton house?" The hair on her arms tingled.

"Are you familiar with it?" Sparks flew from his larynx.

"Uhm, yeah, I'm familiar with it. Would you like to see it?" Darcy said, trying not to make it sound like a question filled with perverse wonder.

"Yes, I would. You see, my mother, I live with my mother, well, we saw that house from, uh, a drive we took into the area, a few weeks back. She thought it was marvelous and a terrific location. She said if someone took the time and trouble to fix it up, it would be a palace."

Doubt surrounded her like a lynch mob. Darcy was sure this was a prank being played on her by the guys, but a quick survey of the cubicles revealed no cliques of middle-aged adolescents gathered around a phone, stifling their laughter.

He explained, "She fell in love with it almost at once. My mother is a willful woman who won't take no for an answer."

She considered asking if dead bodies bothered her because that was all that seemed to fill the Thornton place, but her real estate license, framed so neatly on the corner of her desk, kept her from doing so.

"I'd like to buy that house for my mother as a surprise present," the metal lathe turned in Henry's throat. "I was wondering if I could see it?"

Listening to this voice was like listening to a demolition derby. She imagined large chunks of putrid rust spewing out when he spoke. It reminded her of one of her girlfriends who had been a cheerleader throughout high school. It had been years since she graduated, yet this poor girl still had a low, raspy voice from taunting an unwilling crowd to root for a one and ten football team. The resulting bedroom voice gave her a sultriness that many men found sexy. The man on the other end of the phone had no such advantage.

The hideous uniqueness of his voice pushed her closer to believing that the call was legitimate. She didn't think anyone in the office could create that sound. She tried to hide her growing excitement as she once again did a quick survey of the office staff to be sure this wasn't a setup. "Of course, mister. … I'm sorry, what did you say your name was?"

Without hesitation or any sign of resentment, he replied, "Childs. Henry Childs. I'd like to see it as soon as possible."

"Anytime that's convenient for you is good for me." Her excitement grew with the realization that this inquiry may be legit. "I'd be happy to show you this wonderful piece of real estate."

"Fine!" croaked Henry, "How about now?"

"I can be there in an hour?"

"I'll meet you there. Thank you very much for your time. An hour! Goodbye!" The rusted hinge that had been creaking at Darcy ceased.

A few miles away, a sweaty palm clutched the phone as he disconnected the call. His gaze never wavered from the dilapidated mansion. An hour. An hour was so far away. He would have to wait. He would have to be patient. She was on her way. She would open the door and let him enter his new sanctuary.

Henry had not yet been inside the mansion, but it had been inside him. From that very first day, it had lived in his heart. His mother had given him the business for dragging her up here just to see an old house, but she didn't understand. This was his hearth and his home. From the moment he had driven into this courtyard, his life had begun to change. He felt his very first tinge of confidence. He began to form an opinion. Even his mother was less intimidating. There was no question that he was home.

Chapter 4

Shelly, the receptionist, was a high school dropout with short brown hair, an extra thirty pounds, blue mascara, and matching blue acrylic nails. She had wandered back to Darcy's cubicle to see what was up. The expression stuck on Darcy's face struck her as she hung up the phone. She expected her to be happier.

"What was that? Someone die?"

"No. Matter of fact, it was a great call," Darcy said, looking around to see if anyone else was within earshot. "I have an appointment to show the Thornton place."

"No flippin' way! You're kidding?" Shelly burst out.

"Shhh. Keep it down. I don't want this to get around, so don't tell anyone. Let's see what happens first."

"How'd you do that?"

"He just called and asked to see it. Says he wants to buy it for his mother." Darcy shook her head in disbelief.

Shelly snickered. "I wonder what his mother ever did to him?" They both let out a nervous laugh.

"You know, no one has ever survived owning that place. They all get killed or die in some horrible accidents and stuff. There's probably fifty of 'em so far," Shelly said.

"You don't know that. It's just urban legend. Nobody actually died 'cause of the house," Darcy snapped back, her brow furrowing.

"Oh no? You better bring someone with you when you show this place, someone big, with a gun. It's no lie." Shelly turned away, giving Darcy an expression that said, 'And I'm not kidding.'

Bring someone with me? Yeah, right. And share the commission? I don't think so. "It's just urban legend."

The truth was that there were more horror stories connected with the Thornton Mansion than there were roaches in El Juan's Mexican restaurant on Highway 17. The firm's best salespeople had been trying to dump the eyesore forever, but no amount of open houses or mailings ever generated any real interest. The Thornton flyers have lined every trashcan in the county for years. Only those with a macabre curiosity ever came to look at the shabby, old place.

Darcy didn't believe in ghosts; she believed in luck. This nut wanted it for his mother, so much the better for her. She searched the company database and found very little. Then, she remembered the closet in the back of the office, the place where the old file boxes were kept. She walked into the room and pulled out a huge file from the cabinet. The faded, dog-eared label read "Thor on Hous'." She opened the file and began to read.

Having grown up in Santa Cruz, she was familiar with the legend. They had thrown rocks at the place as kids, trying to taunt the ghosts into showing themselves.

"The Thornton House is a big ol' shed

Go into the house, and you'll wind up dead."

They had dared each other to go in and explore. Darcy had a vague memory of the inside but couldn't remember ever going into the house.

But now, she needed facts. She wanted the square footage, the lot size, and the asking price. She had no intention of telling Mr. Childs about ghosts, goblins, and death. Glancing at the cracked screen on her smartphone, which in her mind, was quickly becoming the newest incarnation of the iPhone, she checked the time. Darcy inputted the factual materials from the file onto her phone and tossed the remainder on her desk. She had all the info she needed to help her close this deal.

Her instinct told her she would be better served wearing something a little sexier than the blue business suit she had finally decided on that morning. Henry Childs sounded like a man who didn't get the full treatment from anyone. She owned a beige linen dress that clung to her admirable figure and thought it would be just the ticket. The neckline scooped down, and with the right body movements, it would reveal a little more cleavage than would normally be acceptable around the office.

Watch out, Mr. Henry... Whatever it is. You ain't gonna know what hit you.

Chapter 5

Darcy's dingy gray Ford Focus pulled into the driveway of the Thornton Mansion fifteen minutes late, spewing smoke and stalling just as she stopped.

She still wasn't a hundred percent convinced that this wasn't a snipe hunt, some initiation prank set in motion by the comb-over boys that trolled the office. Looking through the cracked windshield, she saw an overweight, corpulent man she assumed was Henry ... she-couldn't-remember-his-last-name, standing in front of the house. He seemed frozen in a Zen-like trance. He was a tall, bulky man with ruddy cheeks that barely contained the lavender veins that ran beneath them. Tall and bulky were not two adjectives that she would have thought to ever use together, but they fit this man perfectly. At over six feet tall, his body was blob-shaped with a huge butt and man-tits that no T-shirt would ever hide. His rapidly receding hairline accentuated the unevenness of his scalp and made him look older than Darcy was sure that he was. He was dressed in green pants and a light green shirt with dark green piping. Over the shirt, he wore a dark green sweater vest that stretched across his expansive back like the mainsail on a schooner. She hadn't seen the socks yet, but she would've bet on green wool. She didn't think anyone dressed like that outside of a golf course.

"No, there's nothing creepy about this." She said under her breath.

Darcy grabbed her phone, got out of her car, and walked toward him as the wind whipped across the property. She pulled her coat tight. *"So much for the plunging neckline."*

Vague memories of fear struck her as she approached the house. Probably just the cold ocean breeze that seemed to be targeting her, not this odd man she was about to greet at this haunted mansion.

"I'm so sorry to keep you waiting."

Henry jumped slightly.

"T-t-that's quite all right, Ms. Wainwright. I'm just happy you came," Henry replied, his vocal cords grinding in his throat, creating a sound that was a cross between the braying of a donkey and a car crusher. He was sweating, which she found astounding considering it was February by the ocean.

Henry held out his hand, and she shook it. It was clammy and squishy in an octopus kind of way, and she had to resist the reflex to wipe it on her coat. Instead, she put her hand in her pocket and wiped it on the lining.

Henry's face was pale, tinted with lavender and pink that radiated from his very visible veins. He looked like a pen and ink cartoon character, all squiggles and no dimension. Reddish greasy hair, no depth in his clouded eyes, no character lines; his face was forgettable. Darcy had envisioned a smaller, less formidable man, but she understood better about his voice. The weight of the man seemed to sit on his chest. The flab that encased his rib cage was substantial. It was perpetually bearing down on his lungs, strangling the sound as it passed his lips.

Henry rocked from one foot to the other like a six-year-old who needed to use the bathroom. He looked at her with an awkward squint, and she realized that he was waiting for her to say something. Indicating the lockbox that held the keys, she said, "Why don't we take a look inside and get out of this wind?"

As she walked toward the house, her arms started to tingle, and she had a deep desire to be anywhere else. She didn't want to go into the house, and the disturbing man following her did nothing to calm her apprehension. She reached into her pocket to caress the small canister of pepper spray that she always carried and realized that she had left it in the pocket of her other coat, the one she had worn when she left the house that morning.

She stepped away from Henry and up onto the dilapidated porch. Once on the porch, she could see a window to her left that had been broken out years ago. The weathered, separating piece of plywood that covered it told the tale. The front door was peeling and warped, and she hoped the locking mechanism still functioned.

Her gut told her to turn back and call this whole thing off, but the thought of Tim Lewis having her work with Stan Grossman kept her feet moving. If she could sell this house, it would solve a ton of problems for her. She stepped into the shadow of the house and reminded herself.

It's just an urban legend!

Henry Childs lumbered to the door, once again the six-year-old, this time waiting in line at the Ferris wheel. Standing this close to her, she saw a few rogue hairs extend from his right nostril, and she could hear wheezing in his chest as he breathed.

She felt caught between two evils, a haunted house on one side and a very strange, large man on the other. She opened the lockbox and extracted the house key. She stuck the key into the lock and, with a bit of effort, managed to get the key to turning. She swung open the door with caution, ready to turn and run at the slightest provocation.

Darcy wasn't sure what she expected when she opened the door, ghosts to come running down the stairs, furniture to start flying around the room, shadows to start chasing her? She stood rigid for a moment, and, not unexpectedly, nothing happened. The only thing out of the ordinary was Henry Childs giggling under his breath, sounding like a little boy peeking at his sister in the bathtub.

Henry then brushed past her and lumbered into the house. She waited for a few beats and with trepidation, followed him inside.

The place had been vacant for a long time and presented every day of that vacancy with the unique, musty odor reserved for old houses. The smell seemed oddly familiar to Darcy. She considered unbuttoning her coat to show off her dress but immediately abandoned that idea. This whole experience was taking a bizarre turn, and she wasn't about to add fuel to any macabre fire.

"Mr. Childs, would you like me to show you around?" Henry's eyes glazed with tears, and he said, "Oh yes."

They walked through the foyer, to the left was a very large dining room, and to the right, a spacious living room. Darcy gestured for him to go into the living room, and as he passed, she could see the small collection of dandruff accumulating on the back of his sweater.

The living room was empty except for a broken lawn chair and a stone fireplace. There were no window coverings and the late morning light streamed through the grimy glass. The dust that their movements had disturbed swirled through the vibrant beams. Decades of abandonment had settled over the room, smothering it like a finely woven shawl. Tiny tracks were visible in the dust.

"Of course, you'll need to do some serious renovations, and I bet an exterminator would be a really good idea," Darcy said.

Henry was staring with wonder at each corner of the living room, and then he gazed at her as though she was offering him the greatest gift ever by giving him a tour of this monstrosity. She looked down at the notes on her phone to avert his stare.

The Thornton House was once a beautiful property but had fallen badly into disrepair. It was considered as a "serious fixer-upper" on the brochures and an "abomination of nature" over drinks, a Bates Motel for tree huggers, they had all joked. The house was originally constructed in the early 1900s, and the architecture reflected that period. It was a white clapboard, three-story mansion, there were ten bedrooms on the two upper floors and eight bathrooms, each competing for the privilege to display the most exquisite throne, along with an assortment of linen closets, servants' quarters, and nooks and crannies. Now, it was nothing more than a collection of peeling wallpaper, cracked baseboards, fallen lath and plaster and creaky floorboards, not to mention home to various rodents.

The condition of the house, coupled with the creepy Henry Childs, made Darcy feel as though she was suddenly starring in her own private horror flick. 'The Thornton Chainsaw Massacre 13 starring Darcy Wainwright as the idiot, rookie realtor who stupidly shows the house to a lunatic and is skewered alive.'

She watched him as he moved clumsily around the house. She assumed he was a closet case, a middle-aged man trying to hide his obvious homosexual tendencies from an unsuspecting mother. Still, she felt a tinge of pity because, gay or not, no one was ever going to touch Henry. The thought that maybe he might have been a yell leader in school made her smirk. One look at this man and she knew that he had never belonged to any group like that. He was not someone who would have ever been popular. He was not someone who had ever fit in with the right crowd. This tall, butterball of a man looked like something that came with a Good Humor truck.

"You can see over here what a huge dining room there is with the four picture windows overlooking the shoreline." She said, trying to make this tour seem more normal.

Henry studied the dining room like it was Tutankhamen's tomb. Darcy wondered if he was maybe, just a tad, insane.

She led him around the main floor, not stopping in one place for more than a second or two. Henry followed, not talking, just staring at everything she showed him as though each aspect of the house was a new and tremendous discovery too awesome to be put into words.

"So, to recap, the bottom floor consists of the sitting room, the dining room, two powder baths and, of course, the living room. Each room is much larger than one would expect."

The light from the uncovered windows bounced off of Henry's tear-filled eyes. The uneasy feeling of being in the wrong place at the wrong time clung to her like a lost child.

Then, she had a more terrifying thought than Henry Childs attacking her. Maybe Henry Childs was having a change of heart. Maybe his tears were the tears of disappointment. Maybe he was hoping for something nicer than this pile of rotted cornices. What if he was about to walk away? She refocused on her real objective as she tossed the little lost child aside and pulled out the big guns.

"And of course, the best part. Follow me, I'll show you the kitchen. It's massive. I'm pretty sure it's this way."

Henry skipped ahead and pushed open the oft-painted, swinging door that led to the kitchen. As he did, the last flake of white paint that clung to the old hinges fell to the floor, followed by the door itself. The hinges had separated from the frame. Darcy jumped back and let out a small scream, but Henry caught it and leaned it against the wall in one graceful motion.

"Well, you really have to expect some deterioration in this old house. Nothing that can't be fixed in a jiffy, though." She said.

Entering the room, Darcy was disoriented until she realized why the room seemed so strange. The west wall that faced the ocean had no windows. Light streamed in from the side porch, but where there should have been a spectacular view of the Pacific, there was a solid, grease-stained wall.

Darcy checked her phone where the descriptive realtor dialogue had been entered; she paraphrased, "There's a pantry off the kitchen that has two full walls of shelves and an old-fashioned icebox. Very cool." Darcy let out a nervous laugh.

"Icebox. Cool. Get it?"

Henry did not respond.

"That door leads down to the basement, and there are several smaller rooms down there too."

She wasn't going into the basement with Henry Childs for anything and wondered why she even brought it up. *Isn't that always what the bimbo did in those movies, go into the basement with the creepazoid guy?*

Darcy decided to keep Mr. Cellophane Face in the sunlight at all times. *I don't want this giant Eraserhead flipping and not making an offer or, even worse, ripping my guts out to make a kidney sandwich.*

"Let's take a look upstairs," Darcy said, thinking of the many windows and the open hallways.

She opened the door to reveal a narrow winding staircase that led upstairs.

As they climbed the back stairs, Darcy explained, "There are two stairways that lead to the second level, the grand staircase in the front and these back stairs off the kitchen."

Henry was sweating more as they climbed, he clutched the handrail and pulled himself from step to step, but he exhaled loudly and wheezed his way along.

She noticed that something was changing about Henry. As they had moved through the house, he seemed to get taller for one thing, but it was something else, something in his demeanor.

Finally, on the second floor, Henry continued to examine each room as though he were a boy attending his first striptease. He relished in the texture of the walls, the silkiness of the handrails, and the window frames' wood grain.

"I want to show you something special." She moved toward the master bedroom. Henry was sweating profusely and making very strange guttural sounds.

As they entered the master bedroom, she saw that there were no windows that overlooked the ocean in there either. Ignoring that fact, she turned to share a few more appealing architectural facts about the space and saw him leering at her in a perverse, 'break-in-and-rape-you-in-the-middle-of-the-night' kind of way. She had been leered at before, and there was no mistaking Henry's stare. He took a very confident step forward, his hands rising from his sides.

She held up her hands, stepped backward, and slammed her back into the wall. Panic welled inside and, in a screechy voice, said, "Why don't we look at the backyard?"

Henry's eyes lit up. His expression changed as though a switch had been thrown in the back of his head. He turned away from Darcy and ran out of the room.

Darcy had no time to react. Relieved that he had left, she was still startled by his behavior. She heard him bound down the stairs and heard the screen door on the back porch slam. She instinctively moved toward the window to look out when she was reminded that there were no windows.

Chapter 6

Henry had felt it the second he had crossed the threshold. He had first entered this house as a boy enters his first woman, tentative, excited, and uncertain. And just as a woman passes on her experience to the young man, this house passed along its experience to Henry.

He was lighter in both body and spirit. The feeling of ecstasy had increased as he had followed Darcy from room to room. When they moved into the kitchen, the door had fallen into his hands as he pushed it open, and he caught it. *Any other time and I drop that door on my foot.* But not today. Today, he is an Olympian.

He could feel his fervor increasing as he moved through the house. It was a search. He wasn't certain what he was searching for, but he knew it was somewhere close by. He knew that he had to keep looking. The woman was talking, but he could barely distinguish what she was saying. She ushered him up a staircase and continued talking. As he climbed the stairs, he felt a raw, primitive fire begin to burn inside him. He felt the need for contact, some type of physical interaction that could not be satisfied by his hand alone.

He watched her walk down the hallway in front of him. *Maybe it's her. Maybe she is what I am looking for.*

He walked to the doorway of the master suite and instantly began to absorb the sexual air of past liaisons. He felt virile for the first time in his life. He stared at Darcy. She was young and attractive, her hair cascaded around her shoulders, and the scoop of her dress nicely accentuated her breasts.

"Ahhh." A lusty gasp escaped his lips.

He took a bold, confident step toward her.

Then she spoke. "Why don't we look at the backyard?"

The words hit him like a lightning bolt.

Henry knew in that second that his passion had been misdirected. His calling, his mission, and his destiny were outside. He turned immediately, totally forgetting his lustful impulses, and headed outback.

Through the upstairs hallway, to the stairs, down the stairs, toward the rear of the house, he strode as though he was plowing through an unruly crowd.

In four dynamic steps, he crossed the kitchen and ran through the mudroom, stepping out onto the landing and looking out over the backyard.

There it was. Shimmering and silent. Proud and powerful.

Henry had seen his pool.

Chapter 7

Darcy headed downstairs, and the feeling that she was trapped in a personal Stephen King moment intensified. She headed for the front door, determined to leave this nightmare of a situation. As she ran into the foyer, her phone rang. Caller ID told her that it was Tim Lewis calling from the office. She considered declining the call but then hit answer.

"Hi Tim, what's up?" Her voice was just a tiny bit shaky.

"Darcy, I'm just checking up on you. What're you up to?"

"Well, actually, I am showing a property to a client. It's looking really good. I was just about to do a credit check. Is there something I can do for you?" She turned and looked back toward the rear of the house, tears starting to form.

"Well, that's encouraging. I'll let you get to it then. Let me know how it goes." Tim hung up.

Darcy slowly dropped her hands to her side. She turned around and headed back into the kitchen with a big sniff. She stood at the back door summoning all of her courage. Her hands extended and were ready to push open the back door, and yet she could not step forward and make contact.

The options ran through her head: *Turn and run away!* Sounded like a solid plan, and yet her feet weren't moving. *Call out and see if Henry hears me?* Not a very strong choice, in her opinion. *Wait here for him to return?* It was an option, but it wouldn't help close the sale, and after her conversation with Tim, she knew that was her only choice. Unless she was willing to return to the waitress life, she had to close this sale. Against all logic, against her better judgment, and against the terror rising in the pit of her stomach, she stepped forward and pushed open the back door. She crossed the mudroom and stepped onto the landing that rose above the backyard as though she was sneaking into class, hoping not to be noticed.

It's just an urban legend.

Chapter 8

He was lost. He was found. In the time it took for Henry to look in the direction of the pool, it reached across the vacant backyard and staked its claim on his soul. The Henry Childs that the world had ignored for so long was no more. His pathetic existence had melted away in an instant.

It was no ordinary pool, no cool decking, no diving board or slide. This pool was 60 feet long by 30 feet wide and extended deep down. The lip of the opening was covered in shale rock and stone to give it the appearance of an opening to an underwater cave. It was hard to look at the water because the sun reflected off the surface so strongly it appeared to be glowing. The pool filled the yard like a giant oxymoron. While the yard itself was filled with dead plants and was overrun with weeds, ivy, and small piles of sand blown up from the beach below, the pool sparkled with clear, refreshing water, clean and inviting. Lush vegetation grew abandon on an island in the middle of the pool and yet had not overtaken it, as though it was landscaped and cared for regularly.

Henry crossed the yard with awkward, bounding strides. He was drunk with happiness as he stood at the edge of this talisman of greatness. He could see himself reflected in the stillness of the surface, but he barely recognized what he saw staring back at him. The reflection was not what he had grown accustomed to, a puffy and forlorn blob ignored by most and ridiculed by others. This reflection was of his soul, tall, regal, and handsome. His flabby jawline was now pronounced, his nose sharp, his gaze cut through the horrors of the past and showed him a premonition of things to come, a promise made to bind him.

Henry knelt down and gently placed his hand into the water. He felt a vibration, a buzz of excitement run up his arm and into his chest. He pulled his hand out of the water and placed it on his lips, letting the salty liquid drip onto his tongue. *My first kiss*, he thought.

The surface began to move in a counterclockwise direction. With increasing speed, it turned into a whirlpool, swirling with greater and greater force, the energy dousing him in an aura of contentment, a Jacuzzi for his soul.

On the far side of the pool, rising from beneath the surface, a beautiful rainbow arched out of the water. The pulsating colors glistened in the light the way a fish belly shimmers as it spins and races away. Each color shone in its purest form. He had never seen color so untainted, so alive, so trustworthy.

The rainbow geyser headed toward him like a cosmic divining rod, bending perfectly over the pool. It reached down and touched him, marking him as the pot of gold.

Henry was lifted out of himself and began to float upwards inside the contour of the rainbow. He felt himself rise above the water, climbing inside the arch of effervescent color, slowly spinning like a pig on a spit.

He looked back to where he had been standing and, much to his surprise, saw his discarded body stacked like a pile of horse manure next to the water's edge, a steamy Michelin Man in green polyester pants, empty and disgusting. He had left his physical presence behind and, for the first time in his life, was experiencing his true self, a person unencumbered by that ugly organism.

When he reached the top of the rainbow arch, he slid like melting butter down the backside of the shaft and into the pool. The water rushed over him, cooling his being and salving his many, many wounds. He was weightless and unafraid. The colors surrounded him, entered him, as he sank lower and lower into the blissful depths.

Chapter 9

On the porch, Darcy peeked around the corner of the house.

Henry Childs was standing next to the edge, tipping precariously, appearing to be ready to fall in.

"Mr. Childs?" Darcy yelled. She took the first step down the stairs, testing the tread for its structural integrity. The stairs ran down the back wall of the house to a yard of dead weeds and dirt. The hand railing was loose, and she was wearing heels. *Damn heels! What the hell was I thinking? I thought I could charm this jerk into a sale. So much for my feminine wiles.*

Again, her foot slipped to the next tread, testing it before placing her full weight onto it. *Take off your shoes, stupid, you'll kill yourself.*

Reaching down, she slowly slipped off her right shoe and then her left. She placed them on the stairs. *I can get them on the way back up.*

Both hands gripped the splintered handrail as she slowly lowered herself from tread to tread.

"Mr. Childs. You're really close to the edge. You think you should step back?" She yelled out. Childs didn't move.

Finally, on the ground, she utilized the same caution taking one tentative step at a time. The dry, dusty earth puffed up with each footfall sending dirt between her naked toes. She realized that she was caught between the house and Henry Childs. *Does it matter? It's just an urban legend, and I want this sale!*

She was ten feet from him when she called his name again. "Mr. Childs?"

He didn't move. He stood there frozen. He looked to be part of the landscape, a statue. All he needed was a lantern, and he could be placed at the end of the driveway.

Darcy moved next to Henry, and she could see his face. There was no expression. She touched his hand to get his attention, and it was cold, cold like the hand of a corpse. Keeping one eye on the water's rocky edge, she shook his arm.

"Mr. Childs. Mr. Childs!"

There was no reaction. *Great, I'm this close to a sale, and the guy dies on me.*

Without warning, Henry clutched his stomach, doubling over in pain.

"Oh my God!" Darcy screamed.

Henry fell to his knees and vomited on the dry dirt. Darcy jumped back just in time to avoid being sprayed.

Henry wiped his chin and looked up at Darcy, his eyes glazed and distant.

"Mr. Childs! Are you alright? You look like you're going to faint or something."

Henry's eyes blinked furiously, trying to regain focus. He shook his head and stretched his mouth as though he had been punched in the jaw. With great care, he stood up straight and turned to Darcy.

"I'm fine, thank you." He managed to get the words out, but neither of them recognized the sound. He spoke again, unsure that he had heard himself correctly.

"I'm really quite fine."

The guttural, scraping voice was gone. He no longer sounded like a spoon caught in a garbage disposal. His voice had an angelic quality. This was a voice that should be coming from a Hollywood leading man, not Henry Childs.

"What happened to your voice? It's so different!"

Henry was confused, "Oh, it's nothing. I've been congested lately. The fresh sea air must have loosened it up."

"Must've been nasty. You sounded like crap. Are you sure you're alright?"

"No, I'm quite..."

Without warning, a loud and terrifying creaking noise filled the air, metal wrenching against metal. Darcy jumped, thinking in the back of her mind that it was Henry's voice coming for her. She spun around. On the far side of the pool, she saw an older, stout man entering the backyard through a wooden gate on the far side of the fence. He was sporting three days growth of beard that obscured a goatee and was wearing overalls and a faded gray T-shirt under a green denim maintenance shirt. He had opened the old wooden gate that led to the service road, and it had been the rusty hinges that screeched so loudly. As he moved closer, she saw Frank's Pool Service silk-screened onto his shirt. The smudged area over the left breast pocket told her that this was Frank.

"Hey, what're you guys doing here?" the man shouted.

Darcy was still breathless from the scare. Henry challenged, "I'm buying this house. What are you doing here?"

"Gotta stock the pool. Been doing it for sixteen years."

"I'm Darcy Wainwright, Lewis Realty. I'm the agent. Please just go on about your business." She heard herself and thought that maybe she had acquired Henry's old voice from how hers had caught in her throat.

"Well, that's fine. No problem, ma'am. I hope I don't bother you any. This won't take too long."

Frank grabbed his equipment and headed toward the pool. He dropped a twelve-inch hose right at the edge and moved away without lingering, keeping his eyes on the water at all times. Gathering up the slack in the hose and standing two feet back, he threw it into the pool. Henry reacted as though he was having a tooth extracted. He yelled and ran with malice toward Frank.

"No! No! You can't touch it!"

"Hey, hey, hey, take it easy, man! I ain't gonna hurt it. As I said, I been stocking this pool every month for sixteen years. I know what I'm doing."

"It's all right, Mr. Childs." Darcy's voice screeched. "There's a trust fund that pays for the maintenance of the pool. Frank comes once a month."

Henry paced back and forth, punching the air and muttering under his breath. He swung a pudgy fist that started from his knees and smashed into the imaginary jaw of some perpetrator. He looked to the pool and stared as though looking for guidance. Then, just as quickly as he had become enraged, his face calmed.

"I'm sorry, I don't know what came over me. It's the first house I've ever bought, and I overreacted. Please forgive me."

"Don't worry about it, it's not the weirdest thing that ever happened here," said the stoic pool man. "Why there's been a few very strange—"

Darcy couldn't believe that this man was about to start telling ghost stories. Confused as she was, the possibility of losing this sale slammed her back to her senses. Grabbing Frank by the arm, she walked him to the far side of the pool.

"Tell me, exactly what do you do to the pool each month?"

Frank raised his eyebrows and quickly shook his head.

"Well, once a month, I load up the truck wit' about two hunnered pounds of fish, mostly white fish, and I bring 'em up. Sometimes my boys help out. They're eighteen and sixteen and got a real curiosity 'bout things. When I get here, I like to check the filtration system and make sure there ain't no clogs. If there are, I run a snake. Ain't been bad lately cause it's all new. Then I dump the fish and get the hell out. 'Course I don't get too close when I dump the fish. There been rumors of a shark or sea monster in this pool. I watch Deadliest Catch all time, and I ain't takin' no chances."

"That's ridiculous! A shark? How would a shark get up here?" Darcy checked on Mr. Childs, who was again muttering to himself on the other side of the pool. She doubted he could hear them.

"Well, you see, the intake pipe for the filtration system has a two-and-a-half-foot diameter." He held up his hands in a circle to illustrate the exact size, his fingernails black with pool gunk. "That's big enough for a man to crawl through. A small tiger or blue would have no trouble at all swimming right up into it and landing in the pool. Then, with all the fish I dump into it, he has plenty of food. Could be fifteen, sixteen feet by now." Frank seemed to have this pretty well thought out.

"That's pretty far-fetched, don't you think?"

"Not really. Last sixteen years I dumped enough fish in here to fill the damn thing. Take a look. Do you see any kind of population explosion? You see any fish at all?"

Darcy looked into the pool for a very brief second. She didn't see any fish and didn't care if there were any fish. She only wanted this pool man to go and leave her to her sale. But just as she was turning away from the pool, she thought she saw... what, a flash of color? Darcy backed a few feet away from the edge just in case.

Frank started to check the filter and go about his duties. Darcy walked back to Henry, who was now sitting with his shoes and socks off and his feet dangling in the water. She saw the socks, green wool. She stopped ten feet from both Henry and the edge of the pool.

"Mr. Childs, isn't that water freezing?"

Henry didn't respond. She pulled her phone out of her pocket and checked her notes again. "Well, anyway, Frank comes once a month and maintains the pool. It's part of a trust fund that the original owner set up. The trust owns the house. If the house is ever vacant, the trust buys it back. If you were to buy it and change your mind or whatever, you could sell it back to the trust at any point in time. It's how it was set up. The trust also pays for all pool maintenance costs no matter who owns the house. That's some perk, don't you think? No pool maintenance costs. Forever!"

A smile sparkled in Henry's eye and rolled down his cheek in the form of a tear.

She was becoming certain that Henry Childs was a nut case and penniless. She hadn't checked him out before she'd come up here, repeating a rookie mistake, one that Tim Lewis would be sure to point out. This whole charade could be this whacko's way of getting his kicks. He might even be a criminal of some sort. She started to babble.

"Well, there are many other admirable qualities about this house. Look at that view. Why you could put a patio right outside the kitchen and entertain guests overlooking the pool and the ocean, it would be—"

"No!" Henry leaped up and moved toward Darcy with a menacing gait. His booming voice had a new authority and power. "No! Under no circumstances do I want you to suggest that to anyone."

Darcy jumped and backed away. Not since she was thirteen and a drunk approached her with a broken beer bottle had she been so scared or felt so defenseless.

"Okay, okay. I was just suggesting it. You don't have to do anything you don't want to do." Her eyes started to gloss over with tears, and the fear she had felt in the master bedroom returned.

Henry Childs' face changed instantaneously - again.

"I am sorry, my child. Here, come with me." He held out his big, thick hand with the fingernails bitten back to the quick.

She didn't move. Her impulse was to kick this freak in the balls and get the hell out. But she had to get the sale, so she reached out, and he took her trembling hand. He guided her to the edge of the pool. With her hand in his and his other tentacle hand suction-cupped at the small of her back, she had little choice. As they got to the edge, he pointed to the water. She looked down and saw their reflection. It was grotesque, a real-life Beauty and the Beast but with no possibility of a happy ending. He stood beside her, huge and menacing in a posture that dwarfed her.

She looked at the reflection and saw it change like a special effect in a movie. His face changed to that of an extremely handsome man while her face became old and withered. So withered that small pieces of flesh began to drop from it and make little rings in the water wherever they hit. She blinked her eyes hard to clear the image, but it only caused her left eyeball to drop from its socket and splash into the pool. She screamed, and her jaw left its socket and fell next to her eye. The jaw and the eye floated side by side and slid into position to form a face. Then the jaw began to move, and Darcy heard a terrifying voice. "Welcome, Darcy. I've been waiting for you. You'll be taught the truth, and then you're mine."

Darcy twisted her body like she was being attacked by a swarm of bees, her hand tearing out of Henry's claw-like grasp and her arms flailing around her body. She had taken several steps away from Henry, and her hands went to her face hoping to feel her jaw and nose. Assuring that her face was intact, she turned and bolted for the stairs. She grabbed the bottom of the handrail and attempted to pull herself up the stairs. The handrail broke free of its support, and she fell backward, landing on her backside. Crying hard now, she scrambled to her feet and, looking back, saw Henry Child standing a few feet away.

"This is too weird. You stay away from me, you freak!" She screamed.

Henry held out his hands innocently and said, "Ms. Wainwright, I am not sure what is bothering you, but I would like to discuss a sale. Would that be possible?"

She looked at Henry and then the stairs, desperately wanting to run up them. She took a deep breath, her snotty nose running, and said a little too loudly, "Look, Mr. Childs, why don't we go back into the house? I'd like to go over a few other things. I'm sure once you see them ..." The words came out stilted and uneven between gasps.

Henry looked at her with the softest eyes, "I want it now."

The sob caught in her throat, "I'm sorry, what was that?"

Henry smiled again and said, "I want it now."

Confused, a babble of words came out of her mouth in a very rapid succession.

"It's not that easy. I have several background checks and financial statements that need to be retrieved. We should go back to my office right now and start working on these things." She darted toward the stairs.

"Miss Wainwright," Henry called out. "Darcy, there is no need to worry. I'll pay cash, whatever the price is, I'm fine with it. I really don't want to get too caught up in the legalities. I just want to enjoy my new home."

A cash sale! The magic words!

Darcy had learned one thing from hanging with the boys for beers after work: the salesperson's cardinal rule: when the customer says he wants it, stop selling it. *Shut up!* She was not about to make a mistake like that. Taking full advantage of the opportunity to get the hell away from what was turning into a "Saw" parody, she said, "Well then, why don't I just get back to the office and start things off? You could drop by tomorrow afternoon, I can start the escrow process if you like, and we'll review the terms and paperwork."

Henry took a card from his pocket and held it out to her. "Here is all of my pertinent information. If you need anything else, just give me a call." Realizing that she had to cross over to Henry to get the card, she took a deep breath and ran to him. She plucked the card from Henry's steady hand, careful not to get too close, and ran up the stairs, grabbing her shoes on the way by.

Darcy's tiny car disappeared down the overgrown driveway. As it passed the rusted gate, she could feel the tension in her body release. She was a bit winded and realized that she had run back to her car. As she drove, she simultaneously cried and laughed. She was terrifyingly happy. She was gleefully petrified. As the house disappeared behind her, she wailed and chuckled until she had to pull to the side of the road and vomit.

Back at the house, Henry stood still in the backyard. Frank was starting to coil up his hoses and head out. Henry looked to the water and said under his breath, "I hate that man."

Henry woke in the early morning hours the next day, unable to sleep. His encounter with the pool had changed him in as drastic a way as a cocoon changes a caterpillar. Being free from the travesty that was his body had allowed his true self to be released. He was no longer shackled mentally with the coarse, pathetic shell of his physical being. Henry had seen himself for who he really was. And he liked it! He loved it!

He rose with the courage to do something that he would never have done before. With darkness about to turn to light,

Henry pulled out of his driveway and headed down the coast to his newfound fortress of delight. He would have hell to pay from his mother, but he never gave it a serious thought. She was inconsequential now.

He arrived at the house just as dawn was breaking. He knew that he wasn't supposed to be on the premises without the agent until escrow closed, but he didn't care. That was something the old Henry would have been concerned about. The old Henry wouldn't have been able to cross that line. The old Henry was dead.

He had an awesome feeling of need, a desire to get wet. He was at a crossroads: turn right for eternal bliss, turn left for everlasting damnation.

He turned left into the dark yard. The house cast the entire backyard into shadow, masking it from the rising sun and keeping its warmth from falling onto the pool. The cold was just another obstacle that he would have to overcome to pursue his dream. He stripped off his clothing and slowly walked into the water. It was warm and welcoming as though it had been heated just for him. He had never been skinny-dipping before, and that single sensation alone thrilled him. But the water did more than tickle his fancy. It soothed his soul. He felt the water rise up the back of his calves and boost his spirit. It licked the back of his knees, and he forgot the childhood traumas. It caressed the inside of his thighs, and he stopped missing the friends he never had.

Henry looked down as he walked deeper into the pool and saw a pulsating erection poking out from beneath his massive belly. The water-cooled and contracted his scrotum and all at once engulfed his entire penis. It swirled around his erection in a gentle pulsing motion. The velvety touch of the water was accentuated by a spurt of cold water followed by a current of warmer water. He shivered as he realized what was happening. This wasn't a fantasy. This wasn't an illusion caressing his genitals. This would not turn inevitably turn out to be his hand. This was love and salvation.

Henry's bulbous figure dispersed the water around him as he moved forward, and it lapped at his chest. He felt a giant, luscious tongue lick his body from bottom to top, his toes tingled, his calves prickled, and the few strands of hair on his bloated chest waved.

Once again, he was taken on a journey through time, dimension and reality. A waterspout rose from the pool and encircled him. As he entered the swirling tunnel, he left behind a world that had been cruel and hateful and entered a new world, one that welcomed him and loved him. As he rose into the depths of the funnel, the light around him changed. It was cleaner, newer almost. The funnel became transparent, and he looked out upon the house and the yard. Things had changed. He saw the house as it had been before the pool, newly built, inviting, and spectacular. The house, his house, glowed with a near blinding luster. It was new, strong, and solid. No cracking paint or dead foliage. It was young and vibrant.

A beautiful young woman sat in the yard. She had dark, raven hair piled up high on her head. She wore a long, purple-striped skirt with a ruffled, white blouse buttoned to her neck. Her legs were stretched out in front of her, and her head was tilted back, exposing her face to the sun's warmth. Her arms stretched out behind her for support. It wasn't until she lifted her head and looked in his direction that he could see she had been crying.

His heart ached for her as the tears ran down her striking face reflecting the churning colors of the funnel. She was a mystic illusion, and she turned her head toward him and spoke.

"Henry—" she called out to him. "Henry, my love!"

Her voice overcame him. He ejaculated into the pool, blacking out immediately from the explosive orgasm.

When Henry woke a few hours later, he could barely move. He had been lying on the far side of the pool, on his stomach, thank God. The sun had long ago topped the house, and he was fully exposed. His butt and back were a bright, boiled, lobster red, and he shivered as the cold wind blew over him. He packed himself into his clothes and limped to his car.

But his course was set. His destiny had been determined. Despite the discomfort of the burn, he felt loved and protected for the first time in his life, and deep inside his corrupted heart, he felt at peace with himself.

Chapter 10

The next morning Darcy stepped out of the shower listless and unfocused. She had not slept well and had the remanence of a nightmare rolling around in her head. As she was drying herself, she tried to make a mental list of what the day held for her but she couldn't seem to complete the thought. Her mind kept returning to the reflection in the pool and the foreboding voice she had heard in her head. Looking haggard and not yet awake, she arrived at her office and walked in a daze toward her desk, red splotches on her neck and chest.

"Well, how are you this morning? You look like you got some 'splaining to do." Shelly said with a mischievous grin.

She passed by Shelly without a word.

She dropped her briefcase on the floor next to her chair and sat down at her desk. She stared vacantly at the desktop, clueless as to why she was there or what she was supposed to do. Her mind was replaying the events of the day before and she kept trying to eject the memory chip of those events from her head. She looked up and Shelly was standing over her with a steamy cup of coffee.

"Here you go, sweetie, you must have had one hell of a night. You're going to have to tell me about him. I haven't seen you this blitzed since that lawyer from San Jose."

Darcy took the cup and sipped it quickly. The hot liquid scalded the roof of her mouth and jolted her awake.

"Hmmm, Ouch!" She said, spitting the scalding coffee back into her cup. "That's hotter than hell." The analogy wasn't funny to her anymore.

"Well, we got to do something. You come in here all dumpy and frazzled. Are those hickeys and stuff on your neck? Hell, you even got your blouse buttoned wrong. What the 'F' happened to you?"

Darcy looked down, and sure enough, her blouse was buttoned wrong by two holes. It left a gap right at her bra line, so essentially, she was giving the entire office a shot at her underwire.

"Oh, Christ. Will you look at me?" Her mouth still burned, and she could feel the blister rising on her soft palate. "I'm a damn wreck. Didn't sleep much last night. And guess what?" she said as a matter of fact, "I sold the Thornton Place."

"You flippin' kiddin' me!" Shelly screamed.

"Shhhh. I don't want anyone to know until we close. He could change his mind. I just have to verify his finances, and I can finish this off."

She was re-buttoning her blouse as Stan walked by. He stopped to admire the view.

"I see you're ready for me. I knew you'd come around," Stan said with a greasy smile.

A flash of light zipped in her head, and she had had enough. She stood up and walked over to him, opening the top of her blouse, exposing a portion of the already visible bra. "Is this what you want, Stan? Is this really what you want?

"Well, yeah, sure. Why not?" Stan said, caught off guard.

"Why not? How romantic. I offer you this incredible body, and you sweep me off my feet with "Why not?" Is it because at this particular moment you have nothing better to do that you're ready to do me, or is there something I'm missing?"

"Well, no. It's just, well, yeah, I'd be honored to ...."

"If ever! Too late. Ya snooze, ya lose, buddy boy. Now, do us all a favor and get the hell out of here. I'm not in the mood, in case you haven't noticed." She turned away and sat down.

Stan tried to talk, but Shelly held up a finger to his lips and shooed him off. Stan walked away, calling himself names under his breath.

"Well, that should keep his weenie limp for a few hours. But watch yourself, girl. He's gonna come back strong now that you showed him the goods." Shelly laughed and went back to reception.

No sooner had Shelly walked away than the phone on Darcy's desk rang. She answered it on the second ring.

"Lewis Realty, Darcy Wainwright, can I help you?"

"Ms. Wainwright, this is Henry Childs." She quelled the scream that wanted to burst from her throat. Darcy held the receiver to her leg and took three very deep breaths. *You want the sale, you want the sale, you want the sale.* It calmed her. Lifting the receiver to her ear, she said in a steady, professional tone, "How are you today, Mr. Childs?"

"I wondered how things are progressing with securing the sale of my house."

"Well, I have started the escrow process. It shouldn't take too long. I'll have papers for you to review by tomorrow."

"I would appreciate that. I'm very anxious." Henry's voice slid through the earpiece.

"I'll call you the second the papers are ready. Goodbye, Mr. Childs." She hung up.

Darcy took several more deep breaths, closed her eyes, and re-energized herself. She said under her breath, "It's just urban legend. Stop being such a dork. You want this sale." Her skin began to cool.

With a renewed resolve, she grabbed her phone and checked herself in the selfie camera. Her eyes were clearing up, and her complexion was back to normal. The pasty skin color had gone, and the splotches on her neck had disappeared. "I might just live through this after all."

She opened the escrow forms on her computer and as simple as that, the process started. Darcy thought, *the sooner we start, the sooner we finish.*

Chapter 11

A few days later, Darcy was again at her desk. The images of her encounter were beginning to fade, and she was starting to regain her equilibrium. The details of the sale were straightforward, and Henry wanted little to do with them. She should be able to close by the week's end. Not wanting to jinx it, Darcy kept it quiet around the office. Until she had a check and signed papers, no one would know.

"Darce?" As she walked toward her desk, Shelly said, "Someone to see you." Shelly stepped aside, and Darcy saw Hannah Brower, a Santa Cruz police department sergeant, wearing full patrol garb.

"Hey, Darcy. I understand congratulations are in order."

"Hannah? What a surprise. How are you?" She stood coolly and extended her hand. "Have a seat. Can I get you anything?"

"No, I'm good. I hear you sold the Thornton place. Congrats." She adjusted her gun belt and sat in the wooden chair next to Darcy's desk.

"Well, it's not closed yet or anything. I'm trying to keep it quiet until it's official. How'd you hear that?"

"You think it will?" The sergeant scanned Darcy's desk as she talked.

"Looks like it. The guy has tons of cash, more than enough. No reason to think it won't."

A commotion behind her made Darcy swing around

"What the hell? What did I just hear?"

Darcy turned to see Stan Grossman hanging over her cubicle wall. His nostrils were flared, and his eyes narrow. She stood up and faced him, "None of your damn business now get lost, Stan."

"No, really? Did you just say you sold the Thornton House? Are you shitting me?"

"That's quite a feather in her cap, isn't it? I mean, how long has that place been on the market? Thirty years?" Hannah chimed in.

"Closer to forty. It needs a lot of work." Darcy stood up and backed Stan away from her cubicle. "This is not your business."

"No rookie comes in here and steals my thunder, I'll tell you that right now. The Thornton house! You watch your ass, little lady."

"Was that a threat?" Hannah stood up as well and stepped toward Stan.

"No need to get all official, officer. This is just a little inter-office discussion. We'll finish it later… I promise."

Stan slapped the cubicle wall and stormed off. Hannah returned to her chair.

"A lot of fuss over a dilapidated old house. Remember, in school, we always dared each other to go up there and make-out. Who were you dating then, I forget?"

Darcy bit her lip and inhaled as she sat on the edge of her desk.

"Hannah, that was a long time ago. Can't you move on?"

"Oh, I have. He chose you, no need to carry a grudge, and there you have it."

"It was high school, Hannah, really."

"When was the last time you were up there?"

"At the high school?"

"The Thornton place."

"A few days ago."

"Mr. Childs? Is that the guy who bought it?" Hannah asked.

"Yeah. Is there a problem? Why are you here?"

"What do you know about Mr. Childs? What's his first name?"

"Henry. Henry Childs. He lives in Sausalito with his mother. That's about all I know other than he's as creepy as they come, and he's filthy rich."

"What do you mean, creepy?"

"Well, he's huge for one thing, really fat, in a zeppelin kind of way. And he acted all whacked out while we were at the house. It was really strange."

"You think he could be dangerous?" Hannah had dug a small white pad out of her shirt pocket and began taking notes.

"Don't know. Why are you asking all these questions?" Darcy could feel the red blotches coming back to her neck and chest.

"You hear what happened?" Hannah asked.

"What do ya mean?"

"Well, we found old Frank Jenkins last night, he runs a pool cleaning company. He was down on the beach, right below the Thornton place… he was dead. He'd had his stomach ripped open."

"No way," Darcy said almost in a whisper. "I just saw him a few days ago. That's horrible."

"Yeah, of course, everyone around here blames the house for it. But, I'm not a big proponent of the killer house theory. Did Henry Childs know Frank?

"He met him when we were up there. Frank came by to service the pool. I am so totally shocked." Darcy's now pale and pasty skin highlighted the returning red blotches to the point they looked like bullet wounds.

"We found his truck behind the Thornton property. Looked like he had just finished up. Can you tell me what happened? Did they interact much?"

The entire episode in the backyard flashed through Darcy's memory. How could she explain it to this particular police officer and not sound like a lunatic?

"Well, Mr. Childs was confused about what was happening and thought Frank was hurting the pool."

"Hurting the pool?"

"He got a little upset, but I explained that it wasn't a big deal. He was okay after that."

"Interesting. Anything else that you can remember?"

"Nah. Nothing I can think of."

Hannah took a deep breath and slowly exhaled.

"Okay, then. Do you have a number for Henry Childs? I just want to give him a call and see if he knows anything."

Darcy said, "Sure, I have it right here." She wrote it down for the sergeant.

Hannah took the purple post-it note and shook Darcy's hand. "Thanks for your time, and congratulations again. Don't be a stranger, let's grab a beer sometime."

"Yeah, sure."

Hannah walked off, leaving Darcy stunned.

Poor Frank. She shuddered, thinking he might have fallen victim to the urban legend that she had just sold to Henry Childs. And even more frightening, was that supposed to have happened to her?

Chapter 12

Henry Childs stood in the front yard of the old mansion next to Coley Ford, a private contractor.

"It's hard for me to convey how excited I am at the prospect of this renovation Mr. Ford. I need you to share that enthusiasm with me."

Coley was a thin man with very nervous hands that were always shaking. His skin was splotchy and unevenly colored. His long thin hair hung down over his eyes.

"I totally understand Mr. Childs. As you requested, the service I offer is complete and comes with a hundred percent guarantee. If you ain't satisfied, we keep working till ya are."

"Are you engaged in any other work at this time?"

"I have a small job that I'm finishing this week, but that would be it. I wouldn't take another job until this one was done. By the time you close, I'll be ready to go. I believe in giving each job my undivided attention."

"Your references are a bit old. Looks like nothing from the past two years or so. Why is that?" Henry asked.

"Well, I been working out of state, Montana, on a big lodge. I figured that wouldn't apply to this job, so I just left it off. I can get it if you want?" Coley's voice rose in timber a half step.

"And you agree that I can be present and observe all phases of the remodel?"

"Not a problem for me, sir."

"Even if I ask questions and attempt to learn some of these skills? You will not have a problem?"

Coley raised his eyebrows and shrugged. "Whatever."

"You understand that I intend to restore this house to its original beauty?"

"Yes, sir. I did some research, and there's quite a bit of information and pictures on this place. It's got quite a history, but I'm sure you know all about that." Coley chuckled and pulled out a folder filled with historic photos of the old house during construction and just after it was completed.

"These photos were taken in 1912. This is the original structure."

"That's very impressive research, Mr. Ford. What would be the next step if I hire you?"

"Well, you know what? Before I answer that…

Coley looked left and saw a Santa Cruz patrol car pull into the driveway. A tall, busty woman in full uniform stepped out. As she did, he could see her surveying the grounds and the house, and finally, with intense scrutiny, she gave them both the once over.

Closing the door of her cruiser, Hannah walked over.

"Are you Henry Childs?"

"Yes, I am. And who are you?" He challenged.

"I'm Sergeant Hannah Brower with the Santa Cruz Police department. I understand that you've made an offer on this house?"

"Yes, I have. I believe that it's been accepted as well, so essentially, this is my house now."

"Well, technically, it isn't yours 'til escrow closes, but who's gonna argue with you? It's not like anyone is living here, right?"

"And can you understand that? It is such a beautiful piece of property." Henry gazed at the house.

Looking at Coley, "Do I know you?" Hannah asked.

"Uh, not really. I see you around is all," Coley stuttered, "You know what, Mr. Childs, let me get back to my office, and I'll get you a list of what I think needs to be done. How would that work for you?"

"Well, that would be fine Mr. Ford. Once I see that list, I can make a decision."

"Okay then, I'll get back to you in a few hours. Bye." Coley left walking quicker than he needed to.

Turning her attention back to Henry, Hannah said, "I'd like to talk to you about Frank Jenkins."

"Who?"

"Frank Jenkins, from Frank's Pool Service. He was found dead on the beach below this property." She watched closely for his reaction.

"Dead! Oh my, that's awful. How did he die?"

"He had his stomach ripped open."

"That's horrible." Henry paused and asked, "What does it have to do with me?"

"I'm wondering the same thing. I understand that you argued with Frank a few days ago. Is that right?"

"No. Of course not. Who told you that?"

"I got a report that when you were here looking at the house for the first time, you were uncomfortable with Mr. Jenkin's services."

"Oh, that. Oh no, you misunderstand. I wasn't aware of the trust that supplies pool maintenance. I was just looking out for my new house. It was nothing. We talked it through, and that was that."

Hannah waited for a few seconds before she asked her next question. "Did you see him again?"

"No. I was going to call him to see exactly what his responsibilities were, but ... I guess I need a new pool service now, isn't that right?

"Really? I'll pass along your condolences." She walked back to her cruiser. She picked up her radio mic and said, "SA 202 10/20 at Thornton Mansion. On my way back in."

"Roger that SA 202, see you in a few."

Hannah started the car and pulled out of the driveway. Henry watched as she drove away, and no sooner than her taillights disappeared around the bend, a silver Audi pulled into the driveway. A short, muscular man got out and walked toward him.

"Mr. Childs? Hi, I'm Stan Grossman with Lewis Realty. I just wanted to stop by and ensure that you were being taken care of."

"I'm not sure what you mean, Mr. Grossman? Darcy Wainwright is my broker, and she is doing an excellent job."

"Sure she is... it's just that she's not the most experienced broker we have, if you know what I mean, and I just wanted to reach out and extend an offer of help to be sure nothing falls between the cracks."

"I'm still confused. You work with Darcy, is that right?"

"Exactly."

"Are you friends?"

"Well, sure, we've been hanging out together for a while now, I'm like a mentor to her."

"I see."

Henry's head swiveled toward the house. An expression of surprise came over him, and he simply nodded his head.

"Mr. Grossman, would you like me to show you around?"

"Why, sure thing, Mr. Childs, let's see if I can help you out here."

Henry gestured for Stan to walk around the side of the house. Stan feigned looking at the structure as though he held some special skill in determining trouble before it began.

"A lot of beginners will miss the simple things, you know, mold, infestation, that sort of thing. We can use that to negotiate a better price. What price point are you at right now?"

"I believe it's all in the documentation. Have you not read through that?"

"Well, I skimmed it, of course. I was planning on going through it with a fine-tooth comb when I got back. In the meantime, I think I am seeing a few things that'll work in your favor."

They had made it to the back of the house, and Stan was focused on the structure, so he didn't see the small fog bank developing over the pool.

"You know, Mr. Childs, I think we have a pretty solid case here to present to the owners. We can easily get them to come down on their asking price if we can just...."

Stan had turned to Henry as he was speaking, and once he had fully faced him, Henry drove his knee into Stan's crotch.

Stan dropped to the ground holding his nuts. His eyes were bulging as he gasped for air. After a few very tense seconds, he managed to roll onto his back. He couldn't see anything. He thought his vision had blurred from the pain. He looked down, and seeing his legs pulled up to his chest, he realized that he could see fine. Looking up his surroundings blurred into nothing. He looked left and right and realized he couldn't see because he was enveloped in a dense fog, a fog that surrounded him like smoke in a barroom. He couldn't see outside this ominous shroud, no matter which way he turned.

The fog had a presence. He could feel it touching him. He felt like he was laying on a waterbed, gently rolling right and then left. This fog terrified and intrigued him, a juxtaposition of emotion he had never experienced. He felt wanted and dominated all at once. It made its way into his ears and eyes, up to his nose. It worked its way inside his shirt and up his pant legs. In a second he was inundated by the fog, and the following second was totally at its mercy.

An hour later, Stan found himself sitting at his desk. He was uncertain how he had gotten there. He had no memory of driving to the office or even visiting the Thornton place. Dazed and confused, he attempted to stand and was struck with severe pain between his legs. Grabbing his crotch, he could feel his swollen balls.

"What the hell? Damn, that hurts."

In addition, he had a longing, a desire to serve. He felt obligated but was unsure to what exactly. He saw Darcy walk through the office, and he stared at her. In his gut, just above his swollen balls, he knew that he must watch her, follow her and keep her within reach until she was summoned.

"Hey, little girl, I've got my eye on you."

And then he would deliver her.

Chapter 13

Four days later, Darcy sat in the VIP conference room, jittery and continually shifting in her chair. Her mouth was dry, and she had to keep pulling her lip off her front teeth. Darcy had on a white cotton blouse with an open neckline and was wearing a violet skirt that fell just above her knees. Her light purple three-quarter pumps accented the color of the skirt. Next to her was Tim Lewis, dressed in his best suit and tie, wearing his most professional air. Across from her sat Henry Childs, who more than adequately filled the oak office chair. She had positioned herself to be out of his reach.

"Now, Mr. Childs, if you'll just sign in the places where we've put the little yellow arrows, we'll be done." Tim Lewis said to an anxious Henry Childs. Henry picked up the pen, and Darcy could see the sweat on his palms.

"I know it seems like a lot, but this is the process. So, if I can ask Mr. Childs, a cash sale, what business are you in?"

Henry turned another page and signed on the appropriate line, "My late father had arranged for me to take a job with a start-up dot-com. It went from barely paying its bills to the stock splitting four times in eighteen months. I was very fortunate to hold a rather large amount of the stock." Henry signed another page and turned it with a flourish.

Darcy jumped at the sudden movement. "Oh, I'm sorry. Just a bit anxious."

"There you go," said Henry as he completed the final signature, "Anything else?"

"Just one more small thing. If you would be so kind as to sign the check, the house will be all yours."

"Of course."

Darcy and Tim held their collective breath, fully expecting Henry to change his mind. Henry reached for the check and, without hesitation, signed his name.

"Here you are, Ms. Wainwright. I believe this goes to you."

Darcy reached out and took the check, not getting any closer to Henry than was necessary. She had counted the zeros a dozen times before Henry had arrived and did so again, just to make sure she wasn't reading anything wrong. Once again, there were four zeros after the one, five, two. "Thank you so very much, Mr. Childs. I know you will be so very happy in your new home."

"Now, if you don't mind, I would like to swing by and take another look at the house."

"Mr. Childs, here are the keys. You can do whatever you want. It's your house now." Tim said with a smile.

Henry stood and held out his hand, "Ms. Wainwright, I owe so much of this to you. Believe me. I will never forget all that you have done for me."

"Don't mention it. I was just doing my job." Having no other choice, she reached out and waited for his doughy hand to engulf hers.

"Thank you, again, thanks to all of you."

Henry rolled out of the office.

Tim Lewis beamed at Darcy and said, "Don't you have an announcement to make?"

She took the closing docs and went to the front of the office. As she got closer and closer to the front desk, the anxiety of dealing with the house and Henry Childs began to drop away. By the time she got to the front, she was giddy with excitement.

Sitting at the reception desk was a brass bell. A Lewis Realty tradition: when you close on a property over a million dollars, you ring the bell and make the announcement.

Shelley asked her, "You have some news, darling?"

"If you'll excuse me." Not content to stand next to it, Darcy pulled Shelley from her chair and climbed onto the reception desk. She gave a bell a swift kick and it chimed out. When the bell sounded, everyone moved with excitement toward the front of the office.

"Ladies and gentlemen—and I use that phrase lightly in most instances—may I have your attention, please!" Darcy twirled, exposing a bit of her upper thigh.

She looked over at Stan Grossman and saw him glaring at her. It was payback time.

"Come here, stud! I've got something to show you." She held the closing docs against her crotch like a fig leaf as she gyrated her hips.

"Read 'em and weep." She reached out to give Stan the papers, but he stepped back with a smirk.

"Okay, be a sore loser." Darcy began to read. "287 Willow Hill Lane, Santa Cruz...What? Nobody recognizes this address? ...More commonly known as...The Thornton Mansion." Darcy struck a runway model pose.

The second audible gasp came when she said, "The sale price is..." she paused. The room's oxygen supply lessened as everyone inhaled, waiting. "The sale price is one point five two million!"

A mystified broker yelled out, "Holy shit, she got the asking price."

Darcy struck a sex kitten pose, sticking her index finger into the side of her cheek and sticking her butt out further than would be recommended without the intent of flashing everyone.

Jealousy oozed out of every pore, nearly flooding the office in envy. Faces were flush, and jaws bounced off chests. A moment of silence, and then a huge cheer! Darcy jumped up and down, clapping her hands like a second-grader.

Tim Lewis appeared from his office, holding a bottle of thirty-two-year-old scotch. "I got this from my grandfather. He said don't drink it until the Thornton place closes. Everyone, get a cup!"

When the scotch was gone, Tim took everyone down to D-Breeze. It was the local watering hole and offered an environment of laid-back respectability, good cheeseburgers, and a loose-fitting ocean theme.

The atmosphere at D-Breeze was jubilant. It was an evening where everyone was everyone's best friend, where no one had ever said a bad word about anyone, and where anything could happen.

Tonight, it was all because of Darcy.

Finally, the SOLD sign had been hung beneath the faded, weather-beaten Lewis Brokerage and Realty sign that had tilted in front of the Thornton mansion for years. This sign had served as a source of ridicule and laughter from all the other realtors in town. The sign that dangled beneath didn't matter nearly as much to Darcy as the sign that sat on top. That one, a newer one that had not yet yielded to the extreme variants of the Santa Cruz coast, had her name spelled out in bright red letters. Those letters announced to all who passed that, in only three months, she had accomplished what no seasoned veteran had been able to do in thirty-five years. She had sold the Thornton place.

Tim Lewis went to the stage area, got a microphone, and held up his hands.

"Hey everyone, ladies and gentlemen, please, can I have your attention?"

The bar settled down as the excited crowd turned toward the stage.

"Where's Darcy? Get her up here." He said.

The crowd parted, and Darcy was pushed up front next to Tim. She was smiling from ear to ear, and a giggle escaped her throat every time she opened her mouth.

"This woman, what can I say about her. For thirty-five years, the Lewis Agency has been strapped with the albatross of the Thornton Mansion. My grandfather listed it on a dare, and we have had it ever since. Well, no more. Thanks to Darcy!"

A huge cheer went up, and everyone laughed and hugged.

"Okay, okay. Not only did she make the sale, but she also did all the paperwork, and I do mean 'all' Stan." The crowd laughed at the inside joke as Stan forced a smile, "and a cash sale is a different animal, and she did it all…without a hitch. A great job for her first time at the plate. So, I suggest everyone here, show her their gratitude and buy her at least one drink tonight." He leaned over to Darcy and said in a low voice, "Don't worry about tomorrow. Take the day."

Darcy took the mic and said, "Thank you all. I'm scared now because I don't know how to follow this. Thanks a lot to all of you."

The crowd laughed and clapped, and as she walked away from Tim, people hugged her and kissed her.

Stan sulked in the corner with a warm beer in his hand. He leered at Darcy as she was paraded around the bar receiving congratulations and hugs. His knuckles whitened as he squeezed the glass in his hand. Under his breath, he said, "Just keep your eye on her. That's your job." He set down the beer and walked out of the bar.

An hour later, Darcy sat on a barstool sipping her Lemon Drop. She called it her 'go anywhere-do anything' drink because after two of them she would go anywhere and do anything. She sat at the bar with a smile plastered on her face but emptiness in her eyes. Several guys standing behind her broke out into a coarse simultaneous laugh, and she jumped. There was wretchedness to the sound that brought back the memory of Henry Child's voice and her face falling into the pool in chunks. She turned away from the group and tried to push the memory away.

A handsome man stepped up to the bar next to her. "I take it congratulations are in order."

She looked at him half expecting to see an ogre or demon and instead grabbed him by the back of the neck and kissed him. "Thank you."

Drew, the owner, delivered another Lemon Drop. "From the girls over in the back booth." Darcy turned around and waved at the four girls who lifted their glasses to her. "Thanks," She yelled.

The door opened, and Hannah Brower walked in. She was dressed in her civvies, a light blue cotton blouse with blue jeans and boots under a black leather jacket. She looked over and saw Darcy at the end of the bar and moved down toward her.

"Hey Darce, how you doing?" Hannah said.

"Well, if it isn't Sergeant Brower of the mighty Mounties. What up, sistah?" Darcy slurred at her.

"You celebrating?" Hannah chuckled.

"Oh yeah!" She stood on the rungs of her barstool like a jockey crossing the finish line and yelled, "Hey! Are we celebrating or what?"

A rowdy response came slamming back at her, "Hell yeah!" and she laughed, collapsing back onto the barstool.

"Hell, we closed today on the Thornton place. Done deal. To the bank. Over and out."

"Well, good for you. You must feel great." Hannah said.

Darcy leaned into the police officer, all false bravado gone. "To tell you the truth, I feel like crap. I can't get Frank out of my head."

"Yeah, it's a tough deal."

"You ever find out what happened?" Darcy said, looking for some solace.

"No. I talked with Childs, a dead end. Coroner's report came back, and cause of death was exsanguination due to a rupture of the aortic artery. Something large and serrated ripped him open. I don't see how Childs could have done it. Probably hit a jagged rock on the way down."

"Shit," Darcy said and downed her drink.

Just at that moment, a handsome attorney from a local firm walked up to her. She gave him the once over and said, "You'll do. Hi, I'm Darcy."

The blonde-haired lawyer smiled and said, "I'm Devin. I understand we owe all of this frivolity to you?"

"You bet your sweet ass." She spun him around to look at his behind. "And a very sweet ass it is. Do you think you might be able to give a party girl a ride home?"

When she woke up the next afternoon, her head was pounding, her sour stomach turned, Devin was long gone, and she had the feeling of disaster embedded in her brain.

Darcy lay in bed for three days after the party at D-Breeze. This was, without a doubt, the worst hangover she had ever had. Her head still ached, she hadn't been able to eat anything but soup. She had nightmares centered around her involvement with the Thornton Mansion and the fear that she would never accomplish anything like it again. Fear of failure, fear of the Thornton house, and fear of Henry Childs kept her immobile. She wondered what the scientific name for all that was, Thornton-Childs-a-failure-phobia? Whatever it was, she had it.

The phone rang at one o'clock, and Darcy heard her boss, Tim Lewis, on the other end.

"So Darcy, you ever coming back?"

"Yeah, of course, I am. I just can't seem to shake this cold. I should be better tomorrow." Her limp voice replied.

"Well, when you come back, you'll see a shiny plaque sitting on your desk telling you that you are salesperson of the month," he chuckled.

"No way!" She tried to scream out, but her voice caught in her throat. "That is so cool! Thank you so much, Mr. Lewis. I can't tell you what that means."

"Yeah, well, come in tomorrow and try to explain. By the way, have you done anything nice for Mr. Childs yet?"

Darcy felt like an eighth grader who is called upon in class to comment on an assignment they have not read. "What do you mean?"

"Well, anyone who is responsible for you getting $61,000 in commission deserves something, don't you think?"

She gasped. She had done the math a thousand times but hearing that he was really going to give her the money was incredible.

She smiled, "Yeah, I guess you're right."

"So here is what you do. Go to the Rigid Brothers Awards Company on 4th and there's a gift ready for you to take up to Childs. I ordered it yesterday for you. It's a doorknocker. He'll love it."

"Okay. Thanks Mr. Lewis. If I feel better, I'll do it in the morning."

"No. In the morning, you're coming back to work. Do it this afternoon."

"Uh, sure thing. Thanks again." Even with the good news, she was suddenly sorry that she had ever answered the damn phone.

"And Wainwright, the door knocker costs one hundred and thirty-five bucks, it's engraved, so bring your debit card."

Chapter 14

Three hours later, Darcy sat in her car on the street outside the mansion. She had been staring at the house, with the motor running, for almost twenty minutes. She attempted to have the Rigid Brothers deliver the doorknocker for her, but they informed her it was not their policy. She couldn't ask someone from the office. How would it look if anyone thought she was afraid of her greatest triumph? She had managed to find a clean blouse, blue with a scooped neckline, and a white wool skirt that had still been in the dry cleaning bag. She wore a navy-blue blazer on top of it. It was a simple outfit, but it was about all that she had the energy to assemble. Her brown slip-on shoes weren't the perfect choice, but she just didn't care.

She hadn't been back to the property since her encounter with Henry by the pool. That voice, that sound telling her that her time was coming, rolled through her dreams, turning them into nasty nightmares.

It's just urban legend. But the thought rang hollow in her mind.

With every ounce of courage she could muster, she maneuvered her little car through the dumpsters, pickups, and workers. She parked, locked her car, and fiddled with the key. It always stuck in the lock. Everyone else had a keyless remote, but not her, not in this old pile of crap, another reason to hate the day. Her arms and spine were crawling, and she felt itchy all over. Her brain felt as though it were about to leak out of her ears.

Darcy felt her stomach turn.

God! I'm not gonna chuck again?

She swallowed the urge, but it was unsettling that after three days, she was still hungover. And to top off this perfect day, she had started her period, which always made things worse.

***

In the backyard, a flash of color streaked under the glossy surface of the pool and sensed her presence. It swam around the perimeter at an increasing speed, excitement building with each revolution, preparing to welcome her back. The surface of the pool began to swirl, and a cold breeze rose off the water that arched over the house, the frosty wind sweeping forcefully towards the front, searching for its welcomed foe.

***

As Darcy moved towards the front porch, the breeze, sent from the backyard, swooped down from the rooftop to the ground, ran along the dirt, kicking up a small cloud of dust, and accosted Darcy. With moderate force, it blew up her skirt. She tried to grab the skirt and pull it down as she danced in a little circle, but it was too late.

A voice in her head screamed, *Ladies and gentlemen, if you would turn your attention to the center ring, we present our main attraction. Darcy Wainwright's white lace panties!*

Eight sweaty construction workers showed their appreciation for those white lace panties with enthusiastic applause and whistles.

Shit, she thought as she scooted to the front door holding down her skirt. *I hate this place.*

She didn't bother to knock as the door was ajar. She entered the front hallway, still smoothing her wind-blown hair, and saw Henry and Coley Ford talking. She had never met Coley but had heard a few things. What Henry Childs didn't know was that Coley Ford had been dealing with a rather severe methamphetamine problem. He had spent most of his money and all of the last eighteen months attempting to recover.

"Of course, all of these moldings will want to be replaced. The originals were more elegant, I think." Henry tossed the comment to Coley.

"Sure thing. We can create anything. I got this guy coming in, and he's a miracle worker with wood." Coley spoke with a studied assurance that sounded to Darcy like he was overcompensating.

"You can do that? Make your own moldings?"

"Absolutely. Whatever you want."

"I would like that very much," an impressed Henry replied.

Darcy, tired of waiting and ready to barf again, interrupted. "Hi. Well, you sure didn't waste any time, Mr. Childs. The place looks better already," Darcy said with forced enthusiasm.

Henry turned, annoyed at the interruption, but his mood changed instantly when he saw Darcy.

"Miss Wainwright? What a nice surprise. I thought you were done with me. Are you alright? You look a little flushed," Henry said.

"Oh, fine, just a little breezy out there. And no, I'm not done with you. You won't get rid of me so easily. I want to be sure that my number one customer is taken care of. After all, I owe that 'Salesperson of the Month' plaque to you."

"Salesperson of the Month! Well, congratulations. Good for you. And since you're here, let me show you what we're doing. You took the trouble to drive all the way out here. It's the least I can do," Henry said.

"Actually, I have a little present for you." Darcy dug into her shoulder bag and pulled out the hastily wrapped gift with the pre-tied bow stuck indelicately on top.

"Do you really?" Henry asked, genuinely touched.

With the eyes of a kid who just saw his birthday pony, he opened the gift. He welled up when he saw the gold doorknocker. It glimmered in the late afternoon light and reflected onto his face. The metallic color made Henry's eyes turn from dark brown to sunset gold, and a sparkle bounced off of them.

"I am truly touched. I never expected—" he finally muttered. "Mr. Ford, would you please have this mounted immediately?" He handed Coley the doorknocker.

Henry walked toward her, and she was filled with panic, thinking he wanted to hug her. Her whole body clenched at the thought, but she couldn't back away. She would have to endure the embrace. She would be engulfed in the flab like a fastball hitting a catcher's mitt. She just hoped she wouldn't throw up.

At the last minute, he held out his hand and waited for her to return the gesture. It took a moment for her to unfreeze, but she covered her awkwardness and accepted the handshake instead of a kiss with great relief. Seeing her hand disappear into the puff pastry rolls of Henry's hand brought back the poolside incident and she quickly pulled away.

"It's the least I could do," Darcy finally managed to say.

"Oh, where are my manners, Ms. Wainwright? This is Mr. Ford. I have hired him to complete the renovations for me. Do you know each other?"

Darcy twisted her torso a bit and said, "Not officially, but we've seen each other around town. Nice to meet you."

"Yeah, good to make it official," Coley replied.

"Let me show you what we are doing," he said with reenergized enthusiasm, "I think it's going to be really something."

"I'd love to, but I really have to get back ..." she protested while in her mind she was already running to her car.

"Nonsense. It'll just take a minute." Grabbing her hand again and refusing to let go, he began the tour.

Henry guided Darcy through each room on the main floor and relished each and every detail of the renovation. Darcy was drowning in wallpaper and drywall and woodwork and Italian tile. Not only that, but she was pretty sure that Henry was going out of his way to touch her. He would take her arm and guide her as she moved from room to room and even rest his hand on the small of her back as he spoke.

She was moved to the kitchen, and Henry showed her samples of the tile that was to be laid, paint chips for the colors of the walls, and fixtures for the sink.

"Let me show you what we're going to do outback," Henry said.

Darcy froze. "No, really, I have to get back …."

"Nonsense," he said. He pressed his hand a bit more firmly onto the small of her back, or maybe even the top of her ass. If she ever had the chance to say no, that chance was gone.

As she stepped onto the freshly installed stairs leading down into the backyard, a cold wind hit Darcy. There was a touch of ocean spray in the wind causing goosebumps to pop up all over her arms. It felt a good fifteen to twenty degrees colder in the backyard than it did in the front.

A gust hit her square in the chest and knocked her backward against the house. Henry grabbed for her and helped steady her.

"Whoa, easy there, Ms. Wainwright. These steps are tricky. We just replaced the entire staircase, but they are still slick."

He wasn't particularly alarmed. She had just been blown over by a gust of wind, and he was acting like it was a little stumble, a tripping-over-her-own-feet incident. She stood up and held one hand against the house for support.

"Wow, that wind is pretty strong; we should just go back inside?"

"That's funny, Ms. Wainwright. You have a wonderful sense of humor." He moved her down the stairs.

Darcy looked to the yard and saw the trees and dead, dried shrubs all sitting calm and unruffled; they, too, were unaffected by this cold current of air. And yet, she was still being accosted by this gale, her hair was blown back from her forehead, her blouse was whipping back and forth, and her cheeks were turning red.

With each step, Darcy felt besieged by malice. She tried to separate from Henry, and he held her arm even tighter.

She was shivering from the cold, shaking like a worm on a hook, and Henry was totally oblivious.

How could he be holding me so tight and not notice?

And all the time, he was moving her forward to the pool.

They were off the staircase and moving across the dirt, the pool looming closer and closer. The wind continued to churn around her. Darcy could hear voices in the wind, distant voices that terrified her. She heard indistinct words at first, and then she heard it plain as could be, "Welcome, Darcy, it's almost your time." She let out a scream.

With a formidable effort, Darcy broke Henry's grip and started to run. In six determined strides, she was at the stairs, not stopping to look behind her.

Darcy clutched the unfinished handrail as she pulled herself, hand over hand, up the staircase. The wind blew stronger, it pulled at her, invaded her as she struggled to climb the stairs.

She could sense what the wind was feeling. She could sense hatred as it beat at her from both sides like a boxer going in for the knockout, roundhouse blow after roundhouse blow. It was hate so strong she could smell it. She could smell the rot, the decay, and the putrid aroma of seared emotion as it roasted slowly over the fires of hell.

She was within a few steps of the door when the wind blew her down onto the wooden landing. She quickly rolled onto her back, ready to kick at whatever might be about to attack. But before she could react, icy fingers reached down and grabbed her. The fingers, long and sinewy with ruptured knuckles and open sores, engulfed her chest and lifted her from the floor. The fingers encased her rib cage, thumbs looping over her shoulders, forming a restraining harness like the kind used on inverted roller coasters. But this harness wasn't designed to keep her safe, this harness was meant to keep her from getting away. She screamed a scream that had to have been heard all the way into town. She wiggled and writhed, twisted and turned, trying to break the icy grip.

She was lifted a foot off the landing and was brought face to face with a demon. Where its eyes should have been, there were two tiny slits, oval in shape that came to a point on the outside edges. They started to glow red.

She was shaking, screaming, and mortified. Then she realized she was looking into the lizard like eyes of Henry Childs. His metal voice said, "You'll be back when it's time. She'll summon you, and you'll be back."

Darcy heard a voice in the back of her head. It was calm yet forceful, determined but not panicked. *"You can fight this. She cannot win. You can fight this.*" A golden aura formed around her, bringing with it a strength she was unaware she possessed.

"NOOOO!" A scream exploded from her with a force she had never felt before, her arms flew up over her head, and she broke the grip of the creature. Landing on her feet, she charged and hit it square in its scaly chest. She hit with force so strong that lizard-like Henry was propelled into the air. He flew through the air and landed on his back at the base of the stairs. A snarl crossed her lips as her eyes challenged him to get up and try to hurt her again. He rolled onto his stomach, dazed and barely conscious. She turned and ran.

Chapter 15

The light was muted and fuzzy, brighter on the edges and dark towards the middle. She tried to move but felt as though she had become a candidate for the boneless chicken ranch. Slowly, she forced her eyes to open. The light brightened, but the focus was still out of kilter. As she fought for consciousness, objects slowly materialized before her. The dark spot in the center became the front door, the bright area around the outside of her vision was the sunlight shining through the windows that framed the door. A dark shadow passed over her, and she jumped, started to struggle, and lashed out with her right arm hitting whatever it was that was coming for her. Then the shadow came into focus. It was Coley Ford holding a wet towel and rubbing his forehead.

Grasping reality one tiny bit at a time, Darcy realized she was lying in the front hallway of the Thornton house. She looked slowly around, ready to defend herself if need be. Her skirt was, once again, riding high, and she was quite certain that the group of workers at her feet were, once again, checking out her white lace. She instinctively moved her arm to lower the hem. She had a fleeting image of raising her hands above her head and screaming as the roller-coaster car inverted and looped-de-looped. She looked to Coley, who was still rubbing a red mark on his forehead.

"What happened? Did I do that?" she asked, dazed.

"It's okay. Look, I don't know what happened, but you came running in here like you were on fire, punched me, and fell right on your face. We've called an ambulance for you. How do you feel?" Coley asked.

"I think I'm all right, and I am so sorry about hitting you. I don't know...." She looked up and saw the workers suddenly turn away in an embarrassed, uncomfortable fashion. No one had ever responded to her panties like that before. She looked down and saw a small pool of blood forming on the floor in front of her, being absorbed into her white skirt.

"Oh shit!"

She wanted nothing but to get the hell out. She jumped up and took off running. As she stumbled toward the car, she held her stomach with one hand as she continued to cramp. She could feel the wetness between her thighs, and only the adrenaline rush of sheer terror allowed her legs to keep moving.

Her keys were in the pocket of her skirt, her skirt that now looked like the Japanese flag. In one swift motion, she had them out and inserted them into the lock. Of course, it stuck. She hated this car. She was glad that she was about to stain it irreparably.

"Come on, goddammit!" she screamed, pounding on the driver's side window, kicking at the door. "Open up, you asshole car!"

Finally, the lock clicked, and the door was open. She jumped in and started the old engine on the first try. Not four seconds had transpired from the time she hit the gas until she was headed out the gate.

Forty-five minutes later, Darcy was in the shower at her apartment. She tried time and again to turn on the water but couldn't find the courage. The thought of water pouring into her home, pouring over her body, terrified her. She stood there, naked, covered in dried blood, shivering.

Unable to stop sobbing, she sat cross-legged on the little throw run in front of the shower door. The dried blood on her thighs was beginning to smell.

What the hell? I have to do something.

Retrieving a yellow plastic bucket from under the bathroom sink, she padded to the kitchen. Placing the bucket under the faucet, she turned it on, jumping out of the way as she did, like she was popping a rattlesnake on the head. She darted in to turn the water off and, after two quick jabs at the faucet, managed to stop the stream.

Back in the shower stall, Darcy placed the bucket directly over the basin drain, making sure nothing could make its way up the drainpipe, and using a face cloth, Darcy washed off her soiled body in a series of slow, cautious strokes. She continued to sob throughout the entire process, and even as the water turned cool, she continued to wipe. She could remember nothing from the time she hit the top of the stairs until she woke up in the hallway, nothing except a feeling of explosiveness, tremendous power, and total fear.

The next morning, after a sleepless night, Darcy called in sick again. She stayed wrapped in an old blanket, sitting on the couch, staring at the television. Every once in a while, she would make an attempt to use the bathroom but sitting over a toilet full of water scared her. She knew it was irrational, but it didn't matter. Instead, she squatted over the yellow bucket.

Having to get out of the apartment, Darcy went for a walk. She avoided sprinklers and hoses as she roamed. She wore her favorite jeans, a t-shirt she'd bought at a Remi Wolf concert, and her ratty, grayed tennis shoes. In an attempt to calm down, she talked to herself as she walked.

"Okay, it's a creepy house; everyone knows that. People have died there, and everyone knows that too. But what's up with that pool? I never even knew it existed, and now it wants me dead!"

A young woman and her child strolled by, and Darcy hoped that she had stopped her monologue before they had heard her.

It's not just Henry Childs, it's something more, something malevolent. Every time I go near that place, something awful happens.

"Well, duh! That's the answer!"

If I stay away, it can't hurt me. Whatever was in that pool could swim around in circles till Elvis comes back, and I don't care?

"It can't get me if I stay away."

It was the demonic version of tag, *Olly Olly Oxen Free. If I'm on base, you can't kill me.*

"If I stay away from the pool, the creature's harmless. After all, I've lived here most of my life, and it's never been an issue before."

It was insane to think that this thing could reach outside of its environment. If it could, why did it need Henry? Why didn't it just rise up, chase her down and crush her? The answer was obvious - it couldn't reach beyond its perimeter.

"I'm safe as long as I stay away."

She had no idea how wide that perimeter was, but she did know that at that very minute, there were thousands of great white sharks swimming in the oceans all over the world, and none were a danger to her because she wasn't in the ocean.

"Stay away and stay safe."

With that resolve, she marched back home, searched the apartment for sharks, and, finding none, bravely sat on her toilet.

"Stay away and stay safe." It sounded so easy to do, so why did it sound so impossible at the same time?

Chapter 16

She was running across the grass in her backyard. She knew that if she could just go fast enough, she could jump into the air and fly. If she could just get one extra bit of speed, she could land on that gravitational shelf and suspend herself above the ground. She had to fly. If she could fly, she could save her dad. With one final kick, she launched herself into the air, and she did it. She landed on her stomach, floating five feet above the ground, and didn't fall. She'd defied gravity, and now she could save her dad! And then, even though she was in the air, she couldn't propel herself. She had managed to land on that place between sky and Earth, the place where you could float as long as you remained totally perpendicular to the Earth's surface, but she couldn't propel herself forward.

She tried to fly like Superman. She tried to swing like Spiderman. She tried to swim. She tried to breaststroke forward, butterfly forward, she tried to backstroke her way to help her father. If she could only move forward, then she could find him and save him. But she couldn't move. Maybe if she were in water, she would have better luck. Maybe she could propel herself forward then. And, in an instant, there she was. She was no longer flying in her backyard. She was swimming underwater, looking for her dad ~~Dad.~~ Here she had motion. She was moving like a denizen of the deep, cutting through the depths at incredible speed. She was an Aquawoman, and she would save her father.

Up ahead, it loomed, dark, sinister, and foreboding. A monster that had risen from the seaweed like a wraith from a séance, a monster that was part blob, part jellyfish, and mostly terrifying. In its mouth, it held a woman. A pretty, stylish woman who, despite being gripped in the jaws of a monster, had a very tranquil expression on her face. The monster moved closer to her, and she wanted to swim away, but she couldn't just leave the poor woman to what was surely a terrible fate.

The woman looked at her unruffled and said, "It's your turn next." Her expression didn't change from the beginning of the sentence to the end. And even though they were underwater, she raised her right hand and held a gun to her temple and pulled the trigger blowing out the left side of her face.

In the distance, a phone started to ring. Someone was calling her. Someone was calling the phone…

Darcy jammed her hand into the nightstand, stubbing her thumb as she reached for the phone that had woken her from a nasty nightmare. She dropped the cell, and it bounced off the bed frame and onto the floor. She swept the carpet with her hand until she finally grabbed it.

"Hello." She mumbled into the phone, trying to get her bearings.

"Hey Wainwright, you ever coming back to work?" It was Stan.

"Hi, Stan. Yeah, I'll be in later today. I'm feeling a lot better," she lied.

"I miss that ass of yours swinging around the office."

"Whatever." She hung up.

"Oh man, this has got to stop." She realized she had had that same dream for four nights in a row. Trying to help her father but not being able to fly, the woman blowing her brains out again. How trite. Psychology 101. She should be able to come up with something better than that. As she tried to stand up to shower, her knees buckled, and she fell to the floor in tears.

She had been trying to save her father; from what? He's not dead, at least to her knowledge; he just took off, abandoned them when she was six. Went off to work one day and took the first left right out of their lives.

After a few minutes, she managed the several feet to the bathroom. She showered with the door open, got dressed, and for the first time in almost five days, made the drive to the office.

Her desk felt safe. Her computer monitor worked as it should. The coffee was hot and awful, and the phones all sounded the same. Maybe things weren't as bad as she was making them out to be? She just had to stay away, stay away from the Thornton place, and she'd be okay. *Stay away and stay safe.*

Without thinking, she reached up and rubbed her cheek, expecting to wipe off a few drops of blood splatter.

***

The friction of the water rippled down its body as it moved through its world with a predatory bent. It reacted viscerally to its world, with no words, no conscious thought, just stimulation: pain, anger, revenge, lust, and survival. For years it had been lying in wait, luring, capturing, and killing its foes with an animal determination driven solely by instinct until finally, the time was near. Desperate to fulfill its destiny, it had reached out to the human girl, the last one, and sent her the images, thoughts, and fears. Soon she would come back, as they all had, for the time to terminate was near. Soon the human girl would return to try to stop the terror in her mind, and she would die just like all the others. When she died, the circle would be complete.

Chapter 17

Coley Ford was three weeks into the job, and they were already falling behind. While a dozen men worked on the exterior of the house, he discussed the problem with Fred, the labor contractor.

Fred was a Hispanic man in his fifties who handled the scheduling for all the day-workers. He had gray, scraggly hair that poked out from under a dirty foam ball cap. He sported a grey mustache, and his face was dark and rutted from years of working outdoors in the sun. His ample belly hung low and heavy over his belt, barely contained by a brown Johnson & Wrigley Grain Wholesalers t-shirt.

"Look, man, I know there's some shit that's happening with the supplies, but that ain't no big deal. It really comes down to not being able to do things when we're supposed to." Fred said to Coley.

"I hear ya. Childs is getting in everyone's way, right?"

"Tell me. It's like the guy's in woodshop or somethun'. He's always asking questions, distracting everyone. Yesterday, we were trying to hang the kitchen backdoor. He's all in their face about how it's done. Now, doorways are tricky, to begin with, as you know, but when you have to teach someone how to do it at the same time, it takes forever. It's lame, man."

"Okay, okay, I'll talk to him. But you know, it is his house," Coley said.

"Yeah, but it's your ass. The dude is costing you time, man, and you ain't never gonna finish on schedule. But hey, it's up to you, it ain't my money." He walked away.

Coley fidgeted in place and rubbed his nose. He could feel the sweat starting to form on his palms. Meth had made him brave, and that was why he liked it. The feeling of supreme confidence and invincibility he got from a snort was astounding. But it had also taken everything that he had ever loved away from him. His wife had come and gone several times throughout his addiction until she eventually left. After he had passed his one-year sobriety anniversary, he tracked her down, and they started dating again. She had moved back in with him once he had secured this contract with Childs, another reason that he had to do this job right. He was on day 543 of total sobriety, and he felt for the first time that in his life, he was on the road to recovery. If he could handle that, he could handle Henry Childs.

Sure enough, no sooner had Coley made up his mind than Henry walked around the corner. He was moving with a very purposeful stride and looked as though something was on his mind.

"Mr. Ford, we need to speak."

"Yes, sir, I need to talk to you, too."

"It seems that we are already falling behind schedule. How can that be?"

"Well, that's what I wanted to talk about too. I appreciate the fact that you're so involved in the work process, but I don't think that you really understand the cause for our lack of progress in certain areas. When I started this job, you told me to do what I needed to do to get it done, and that's what I'm gonna do right now." He took a deep breath, "I can't slow things down just so you can watch. I appreciate your involvement, but I got guys sitting around waiting to work until you can get over to watch them start. Now, if you wanna do things that way, we need to redo our deal cause you're going to cause me to be late, and I don't wanna be late."

Henry stared at Coley, blood rushed to his face, and he went flush. Coley thought that maybe the fat guy was going to cry. He could swear that a tear was building up in his right eye. He was trying to come up with something to say to soften the reality, and then, with a moderate amount of force and in the old silent movie style, Henry slapped him dramatically across the face.

"Mr. Ford. You do not tell me how to do this job. I tell you. Now, I will excuse this impertinence this time, but if you intend to be here when this project is finished, do not let it happen again."

With that, Henry turned and shuffled to his car. He drove away, leaving Coley stunned on the front porch.

Coley mentally had to pinch himself to be certain that asshole had done what he had just done. The sting on his cheek and the trickle of blood that was running from his lip to his chin confirmed the assault. He saw that the entire crew had stopped working and was staring at him.

He felt his face flush, burning hot, and yelled, "Get back to work! Now!"

Coley stomped to his truck and drove away.

A half hour later, he found himself sitting on a barstool at a local dive, forcing himself to order a diet Pepsi instead of a shot of Johnnie Walker Red. The drink arrived in a tall, this-is-not-an-alcoholic-beverage glass with the little red straw that yelled out 'soft drink.' The guy next to him didn't fail to notice.

"Hey, what's up with that? You come in here and can't even drink like a man?" The man let out a loud belly laugh.

Coley pushed the barstool away and stood up in one move. As the guy turned to face him, it was already too late. One swing with his framing arm, and the laughing guy was out cold, bleeding from the mouth and blowing snot bubbles.

Chapter 18

Coley opened his eyes and looked at the walls that surrounded him; yep, he was still in jail, and the memory of his wife, telling him to go to hell, was still fresh in his memory. He had spent the night in jail, but that was preferable to buying an eight ball and getting fucked up. He had come out ahead on this one.

The guard appeared outside, "You think of anyone to call and come get you?"

"Well, seeing as I was almost beat up, pissed on, and slept about two seconds because of the damn snoring, I'm ready to eat some humble pie. Yeah, I got someone to call."

An hour later, Henry Childs waited in the lobby of the jail as Coley was released. They walked in silence to Henry's Dodge Ram 3500 and climbed in. Once inside, Henry turned to Coley.

"I was very happy you called. I was worried that you might have misunderstood what happened yesterday. I was out of line, and I apologize," Henry clumsily handed Coley a one-hundred-dollar bill.

Looking at the money, Coley said, "I don't know what the hell you think this solves. I ought to shove this up your ass."

Henry bristled and then nodded, "Can we put this behind us and move forward on the project?"

"I don't know. The night in jail gave me a lot of time to think about what happened. You need to get your head handed to you if you think you can get away with that. I don't care how much I need this job. That shit is wrong."

"I was out of line, and again I apologize. Can you come back and keep working?" Coley could sense an underlying anger in Henry like he had to force himself to apologize.

"And what is this shit?" he said, holding up the $100 bill. "You can't disrespect me and then expect to buy me back. Who does that?"

"I was just trying to make it right."

Coley steamed. He slowly shook his head and slid the bill into his shirt pocket.

"There's got to be some changes. First off, no more meddling. I run the job the way I see best. You stay out of the way. You wanna watch, you do it from a distance, but you don't slow me down."

"Well, let's not forget…"

"And I get two more days for the two days you lost me."

Coley looked into Henry's eyes, daring him to piss him off again. If this fat tub of goo wanted a piece of him, he could have all he wanted.

"Okay, you get two extra days, but no more excuses. I don't tell you how to do your job, but I stay around and remain informed on a daily basis."

Coley's shoulders tensed, and he could feel his right arm pulling back, ready to swing. The thought of punching him right in the kisser seemed like a great idea. But more than he wanted to clock Childs, he wanted to grab his pipe and cook up some meth. Because neither was a realistic alternative, he relaxed his arm and said, "Okay."

"I really only need to learn one more thing. I have to know how to seal a window frame. If I can learn that, I will stay out of your way."

"Fine, I'll show you myself as soon as we get back. Why do you want to know that?"

"It's for another project I'm working on."

"Whatever."

They drove in silence back to the house.

He made it through the day in an almost robotic trance. He pushed the crew, planned out a schedule for the week, and no one challenged him. They could all see the dark mood he was in and mostly avoided any interaction.

At the end of the day, after the crew had left. Coley wandered through the house, trying to control the rage that had been building inside him since his ride with Henry. He kicked open the front door and burst onto the front porch. Stomping left and right across the porch, he felt as though his head would explode. He kicked a rock that had fallen onto the porch, and he heard it strike an object in the bushes. A quick glance into the bush found a cooler hidden beneath. Looking inside, he found three beers floating in mostly melted ice. Without a second thought, Coley popped the top of the tall boy and guzzled it down. The second one went down easier, and the third totally took him away. He roamed the empty house, and his anger began to slip out. He took the crumbled $100 bill out of his shirt pocket.

"Staying sober is one thing, but if you can't do it without losing respect for yourself, it ain't worth it." He balled up the money and threw it into the wind.

"What's the fucking point? Why am I bowing down to this fat asshole? Why do I give a shit?" He kicked over a sawhorse.

"I could so screw you over, Fatboy. A few less dry wall screws and a couple of loose joists. A few years from now, this place will be creaking like a motherfucker."

Coley moved through the downstairs and stopped at the wall leading into the dining room, "Well, I wonder what the dipshit would like to have here? Maybe a giant hole in the wall?" He slammed his left fist into the wall, leaving an indentation in the plaster and breaking his knuckle at the same time. "Shit! That figures! What an asshole. Shit-shit-shit-shit-shit!" He hopped around, shaking his hand, trying to throw away the pain of the cracked digit.

"Goddammit!" He screamed, and he kicked the same wall with his steel-toed work boot. A chunk of plaster fell off, leaving a nice size indentation.

Coley could feel the tickle in his nose and taste the drip on the back of his throat. He hadn't been jonesing this bad since the first week. His hand hurt like hell, and it was swelling up so fast he was becoming unable to make a fist.

"Goddammit, son of a bitch! I gotta find another beer."

He walked through the back porch, outside onto the landing, and looked out over the backyard.

There were weeds, overgrown brush, cracked concrete, and the pool. A pool that Coley had been warned to stay away from on numerous occasions.

What was the deal with that, anyway? Like I give a crap.

It was with a sudden determination that he walked down the unpainted, wooden stairs to the sun-baked ground.

Screw him.

***

In the pool, it swam deep, shielding itself from view among the seaweed that grew plentiful from the bottom. It could sense his presence, his malevolence, his inevitable violation of its world. It responded instinctively, defensively, and called for its minion.

***

Looking at the crystal-clear water, Coley felt the anger sizzle, and he suddenly had a different motivation. As much as his hand hurt, more than anything right then, Coley just wanted to touch it, the way he did with his older brother's things when he was a kid. He would sneak into his brother's room and touch all their stuff just because he wasn't supposed to.

"Yeah, touch it, sure. I'll touch the bitch. Hell, I'll piss in it."

The pool shimmered. He reached for his fly with his good hand and attempted to undo it. He felt dizzy and swayed a bit. "Man, I am losing it? I used to be able to handle my beer."

Finally, he held his belt in position with the wrist attached to his broken left hand and used his good hand to open his zipper. At that moment, a rainbow arc of color shot up from out of the depths. "What the fuck!" Coley stumbled.

He felt mist from the sea breeze as it kicked water into his face. A tingle swept over him, and in an instant, he was pleasantly stoned. The welcomed sensation engrossed him, and he flashed back to the good old days of sitting in his workshop, scarfing a few beers, doing a few lines. A chill licked his ankles, and he looked down. He was standing in the shallow end of the pool. "Shit," he giggled.

He could see the sun reflecting off the swell from the waves. Waves! Why are there waves?

In the middle and seemingly a long way away, Coley could see the island. On the far side, one large rock protruded upward, creating a hiding place. Something was behind the rock.

"Hey, who's out there? How'd you get on that island?"

Coley stared for a few seconds, amused before he could distinguish a giant tail, a giant fishtail. The tail was covered with rows of large green scales that were mixed with rows of blue and purple scales and smaller red and orange ones. All the colors seemed to run together, and there was a shimmer that flashed whenever the tail moved that left contrails of color in the air.

He saw the tail flap against the island. There was a loud "slap" as it struck flat against the rock, leaving arches of color in its wake. To make that motion and produce that sound, the tail had to rise up and slap down flat onto the rock. "Is that a fuckin' fish?"

He had seen the scales. He had seen how they had been so symmetrically lined up and changed color as they rose up the spine... "The spine?"

It was then he realized that the spine was on top. If the spine was on top, the fish could not be on its side. It moved like the tail of a whale or a dolphin. But that wasn't right. Whales and dolphins don't have scales... "What the fuck is that?"

And then, sobriety crashed in on his fantasy, and it dawned on him. "The tail is moving! Holy shit, the tail is moving!"

He didn't care whether it was on its side, its belly, or standing on its head. He didn't care how beautiful it was or why there were beacons of light that followed it as it waved. The damn thing was moving, which meant it was alive, which meant it was dangerous.

Coley went from affably stoned to terrified in the time it took his heart to skip a beat. He didn't want to piss into the pool any longer, but as a matter of fact, he already had. He could feel the warmth of his own piss as it ran down his leg and into the top of his boot.

He looked again, and as he did, a rainbow emerged from the tail, shot into the air, and glided towards Coley in the form of a grotesque and evil face.

The face moved towards him with amazing speed. No longer distorted by the glittery rainbow, the flashback of his fabled buzz, or the feeling of euphoria, he turned to run.

As he turned, Coley was slammed like a racecar hitting the wall at two hundred miles an hour. He started to fall backwards into the water.

As he fell, unable to stop himself, his arms flapping at his side, Coley saw that it was Henry who had snuck up behind him.

Henry was standing at the edge; his chest was puffed out, his shoulder lowered as though he was a middle linebacker stopping a ball carrier. Somehow the milquetoast blob had knocked him into the pool.

As Coley was falling, he knew he was in big trouble. An image flashed into Coley's mind, a cartoon he had seen every day for eight months that had been posted on the bulletin board in the rehab hospital. Bugs Bunny is falling and stops in mid-air, inches from the ground. He pulls out a sign that reads, "Good thing I have air brakes!" It had been meant as a metaphor for controlling your life. Now, it meant something much more literal. Before he was even wet, Coley was putting on his air brakes. He had started to climb out of the pool practically before he had entered it. Had this been a cartoon he would have never gotten wet, but this was not a cartoon. This was a nightmare. The laws of physics and gravity were his enemy and could not be defied. His hand reached for a stronghold, and even before he was totally submerged, he grabbed the side and started to climb out.

***

It had slipped into the water at the same moment Henry had hit Coley, its instinct for vengeance driving it forward. This prey was not part of its destiny, but it had become a danger to its survival, and nothing would stop it from attaining its revenge. It had dealt with such dangers with the others. It could sense the vibrations from the splashing and thrashing as the prey struggled, and its evil heart beat faster. With two swishes of the powerful tail, the enemy-who-would-harm-it was within reach.

***

Henry was breathing hard and glaring at Coley with hatred as he stood at the edge of the tide pool. With a Herculean tug, Coley pulled himself out of the pool pulling his feet up like a high jumper clearing the bar.

"I'm gonna fucking kill you!" He screamed at Henry.

But, just as his foot was about to clear the edge of the pool, it was grabbed. A large claw, with two giant pincers, had clamped down on his right foot and was digging into the flesh of his lower leg.

"Holy shit! Let go of me, you motherfucker!"

The claw had a rough exterior that was accented by nodules and sharp spikes. It was a dirty blue-green color that looked like oil floating on water. Seaweed, which had caught on the spikes, was whipping around like tassels on the sleeves of a biker's leather jacket. There were two long tentacles growing out of where the wrist joint should have been, and they were exploring his leg, looking for a vulnerable point to invade.

"Oh no! No, no, no!" he screamed as he felt the tentacles slide up the inside of his leg. With his good hand, Coley grabbed a crack in the rock to keep from being dragged back into the pool. The giant claw squeezed tighter, strengthening its hold. He saw the claw bite into his flesh, but he felt no pain. The two tentacles were burrowed deep into the muscle. The creature must have been injecting an anesthetic into him as it squeezed.

"Let go of me! I'll kill you, motherfucker." He kicked the claw with his free foot, and he twisted and turned on the deck, holding on to the fragmented rock, hoping it would not give way and allow him to be pulled into the deep. He smashed the heel of his boot into the claw, trying to crack it like a Maine lobster.

With one final kick, a kick that included every ounce of his strength, Coley smashed the heel of his steel-toed boot onto the claw. He heard a very loud crack and a ripping sound and pulled himself free. The recoil of the release tossed him several feet from the edge of the water. He rolled another ten. Jumping up, intending to run to his truck and not stop until he was in the sheriff's office, Coley stepped forward with his right leg in the direction of the house. When his right foot should have hit the ground, it didn't. It kept going. The jolt made him stumble, and he fell face first onto the dirt, twisting his broken hand and sending bolts of pain through his body. "Jesus Christ! Shit." Pushing off with his good hand, he quickly stood again and took another step. Again, his foot didn't hit the ground when it should have, and he stumbled.

There must be a ton of gopher holes in this yard. What a weird place, sea creatures, and gophers.

But Coley didn't see any gopher holes, rabbit holes, or any holes at all. When he looked down, all he saw was a bloody stump where his right foot used to be. He saw the top of his steel-toed work boot still tied and wrapped around his leg, but as he followed the black leather to where his instep should have been, there was nothing. A scream catapulted out of his mouth, and he writhed on the ground. Henry marched towards him with a sadistic grin on his face. He reached for him, and Coley got a good look at Henry's teeth. They were round and pointed as though they had been sharpened like a big, blubbery cannibal.

Chapter 19

The next morning Henry was on his phone calling Darcy Wainwright. The call went to voice mail. "Hi, Ms. Wainwright, it's Henry Childs. I was just calling to thank you again for everything you've done and was wondering if you would like to come to dinner sometime. I'd love for you to meet Mother. She's anxious to meet you, that's for certain. Well, anyway, call me back when you have the time." Henry terminated the call and knew that she would not call back. He had left several similar messages over the past few weeks and was having no success in contacting her. They may have to resort to a backup plan.

In the meantime, he walked out onto the front porch. The workers were all sitting in the shade under a large tree, talking to each other. He looked at his watch, and it was nearly 10:00 am.

A small, red Nissan pick-up truck pulled into the driveway of the Thornton Mansion. A young, handsome man got out and looked up at the house. He wore old jeans, a small rip in the left knee, a t-shirt that flopped freely around his tight stomach, and an air of confidence. He reached into the back of the truck, pulled out a tool belt, and strapped it on, slinging the rainbow suspenders over each shoulder.

He looked over the construction site with a professional eye assessing the progress and anticipating the next course of action. He couldn't help but notice a group of workers lounging in the shade of a giant oak tree. A very fat man was pacing back and forth on the front porch. He knew from the way Coley Ford had described him that this was the homeowner, Henry Childs.

He approached the house with a certain hesitancy. When Coley had called him to come here and work, a tiny voice in the back of his head said, *Stay away,* and as he walked toward the house, he felt the same resistance to this property. He moved forward anyway, not listening to his gut.

"Hey. I'm Kerry Devine. I'm looking for Coley Ford. He around?"

"Well, actually not. I'm waiting for him myself." Henry replied. "Why are you here?"

"I'm the finish guy." Kerry held out this hand. Henry gave him his doughboy handshake.

Kerry Devine had a head of thick, closely cropped, black hair. His eyes sparkled azure blue, which revealed a gentle and understanding soul. People were attracted to Kerry like he was a free pizza on a Saturday night.

"I'm the finish guy, you know moldings and cabinets?" Kerry said. "Coley brought me on."

"Very well. But until Coley arrives, I don't know what you can do." Henry said.

"You know where he is?" Kerry said, already thinking the worst about old Coley.

"No, I don't. This is not like him at all. Forgive me, I'm Henry Childs. I'm the owner."

"Well, okay then, let's see if we can get things rolling till he gets here."

Kerry walked over to the crew and talked for a few minutes. When he finished, he came back over to Henry.

"All set. These guys are here to paint. I'm going to have them start the masking. That should keep them busy until Coley gets here. I bet he's just at a supply house ordering materials or something. Why don't we take a look inside?"

Henry took the lead, and Kerry followed the large man into the house.

"We have all the moldings both upstairs and down that need to be replaced. Coley talked about recreating the original form. Is that possible?"

"No problem." Kerry said, looking around, "We can make anything you want. You have a picture or something of the original baseboards?"

Suddenly, from outside, an argument started. Kerry ran out to see what was happening, and Henry followed.

As Henry reached the porch, he saw one of the workers, a young, well-built, Mexican kid, strangling an older man. He had the man's neck firmly between his hands and was running the poor guy in a circle as though he were trying to separate his head from his body.

There was a circle of men around the two fighters, and they were all yelling and screaming, some with encouragement to the attacker and others yelling to stop them. None of the men were trying to break it up.

Without hesitation, Kerry burst through the circle and grabbed the younger man by the back of the shirt, pulling him off the older man. The younger one threw an awkward roundhouse aimed at Kerry's head. Kerry easily sidestepped it and landed his own punch right on the man's nose. They all heard the crack as the punch landed, and the boy fell to the ground. Kerry then turned to the older man, who was down on his hands and knees, trying to catch his breath. Kerry knelt next to him.

"Are you okay?"

"That little shit was trying to rip my head off," Fred said.

"Fred, you gotta be more careful. You're not twenty anymore." Kerry said with a smile.

Fred looked up and smiled back. "I should have known you'd be showing up here. How ya doin', Kerry?" Fred said, still rubbing his neck. He looked over at that bleeding kid and yelled at him. "I oughta have you arrested, you little puke."

"Whoa, now, let's not get this all started again. What happened anyway?" Kerry asked.

"That little shit over there started in on Coley. He said he was probably off snorting away the rest of the remodeling money and that we were all gonna get stiffed. I told him to shut up before Child's heard him, and that's how it started." Fred sat on the ground, his arms over his knees, slowly relaxing as he talked. "Last thing we need is for Childs to know about Coley and meth..." Fred suddenly stopped talking. A shadow had fallen over him, and without having to look, he knew it belonged to Henry Childs.

Henry had slowly moved closer to the men and was astounded when he had heard this last statement.

"What's this?"

Everyone was silent.

"Kerry. Do you know anything about this?"

Kerry looked trapped. Henry intensified his glare.

Kerry relented. "Yeah, but he's been clean for almost two years. Unless something weird happened, I can't see him going back. He was working at it real hard."

Fred looked up at Kerry, and they exchanged a look. Kerry asked. "What? What happened?" Everyone started inspecting their shoes or the ground beneath them. It was Henry who spoke up. "There was a small incident the other day, but that was dealt with and finished. I have to assume that Coley not being here has only one explanation. He fell off the wagon."

"I don't think you should jump to conclusions just yet," Kerry said. "There could be a very innocent explanation."

Henry's face was turning red, and the veins on his forehead were throbbing.

"No, I have a feeling that Mr. Ford is not the answer here. I have to protect my home. It's time to make a change."

"How about Kerry?" Fred said as he stood up, brushing the dirt from his pants. "He has a great rep all over town. He could finish this for you." The rest of the crew all voiced their approval.

"Hang on here. I'm a carpenter, not a contractor. I don't do that kinda work." Kerry said.

"But could you? Could you supervise this job?" Henry asked.

"Yeah, sure, I suppose, but it's not my gig. I work with wood, not people. You need someone else."

"Mr. Devine, this job is very important to me, and I need to be certain that I have the right man in charge. He has to have certain qualities."

"I'm not sure what you mean," Kerry was already behind the eight ball with this conversation.

"I obviously need someone to head up the renovation crew charged with the remodeling of my home. From all you have demonstrated, you have excellent leadership abilities, and you have the necessary skills to do the job. I want someone who will care about the house as much as I do and who will do everything in their power to improve the overall aura." Henry was using his hands to accent the important parts of his speech, which, judging from the way his hands were flopping around, seemed to be all of it.

Kerry stepped toward Henry and held out his arms to protest when Henry reached out and touched him. There was a simple forcefulness in the contact that made Kerry feel very much at ease.

Chapter 20

The door opened, and a confused Kerry walked into his bungalow.

"Clem, I'm home." He yelled, hoping his girlfriend wasn't there. No answer and a reprieve. He crossed to the fridge, popped open a bottle of water, and sat on the sofa staring at the dark TV, seeing himself in the reflection of the flat screen.

He could still feel the squishy dead-fish handshake Henry offered to close the deal. And the way he carried on about the house like it was a child about to enter a gifted education program. *Improve the aura?*

"Why do I always get the whackos?"

Twenty minutes later, Kerry was still sitting in front of the dead TV. "How the hell did I go from spec'ing a job to a contractor in ten minutes?"

An image appeared in the back of his mind and surged slightly. Kerry had a good feeling all of a sudden. This image settled his misgivings, and his attitude improved.

On the bright side, this could be a very impressive job by the time it's done. I might be able to do some of my best work ever. And the money would be incredible.

With that, the image became a distant shadow.

He had promised himself a little jog around the woods. If he changed now, he could be gone before Clementine got home. She had made plans with some girlfriends to head up the coast for a few days. If she returned before he left, she would monopolize his time with the boring stories of their tanning expedition, and he'd never make it out of the house. He quickly changed into his running clothes and headed out to the trail that ran through the wood.

He was gone about forty minutes, and when he returned, Clementine was still not home.

All for the best, he said to himself. Checking his phone, he had a text from Clem saying that they were staying an extra night. Relieved, he jumped in the shower.

He dried off and threw on a pair of shorts and a sleeveless t-shirt. He went to the kitchen and popped a beer just as there was a knock on the door.

Kerry opened the door to find his buddies, Ken, Mike, and Dave.

Before Kerry knew it, he was missing a case of beer from the garage fridge.

"So, guess what?" Kerry said, sitting up a bit straighter, "I got a little gig up at the Thornton place this morning."

Ken, a convenience store manager whom Kerry had known since high school, broke out in hysterics on hearing the news. "No way. I hope you live to tell about it?"

"Wait. It gets better. Remember Coley Ford, the meth head? He was this guy's contractor. Well, I get there, and Coley's gone vanished. I try to cover for him, but he never shows, and I get the contracting gig."

Mike let out a guffaw. "No fuckin' way. You're gonna be there forever fixing that place up. Man, you are as good as dead."

"It's not that bad. Besides, those stories are just that, stories! We don't know anyone that has really seen anything going on up there." Kerry said, defending his decision.

Mike continued to laugh. "Yeah, right. I know this girl who is a good friend of the person this happened to. This guy was going by there one night and saw three naked women dancing in the window."

Dave said, "No way!"

Ken said, "Get out!"

Kerry said, "I doubt it. If you saw three naked women, what would you do?"

Almost in unison, they all said, "Go in." The four of them laughed.

As the laughter died down, Gary said, "I was up there one day, just at dusk. I was supposed to check out the fencing for that company that maintains the pool, and I swear I saw a shadow of a huge guy with this enormous hard-on."

Dave said, "So you went in."

They laughed again as Ken chimed in, "I understand that the heating ducts in the master bedroom... lead to hell!"

Kerry laughed with all of them, but in the back of his mind, the image returned, and pulsing low assured him none of the stories were true.

Chapter 21

Sergeant Hannah Brower was at her desk when a woman walked into her office. This woman was an over-weight white gal with mousy brown hair, unkempt, and wearing a green mumu-type housecoat with a brown sweater over it.

"Excuse me. Are you Sergeant Brower?" The woman asked.

"Yes, ma'am. How can I help you?"

"I want to report a missing person. My husband. He's been gone for three days, and I'm real worried." The fear could be heard in her tinny voice.

"Have a seat, ma'am." The woman plopped into the bubble gum pink, preformed, plastic chair that sat next to the desk and took a deep breath in an attempt to collect herself.

"What's your name?" Hannah asked.

"Betty Ford," the nervous woman said.

"Really? Is that a fact?" Hannah smiled.

"Oh yeah, I get all the jokes. It's even funnier when you know my husband." Betty replied without a hint of humor in her voice.

"What's your husband's name?" Hannah asked.

The woman, clutching the collar of her housecoat as though to keep Hannah from peeking down her dress, looked at the floor and said, "Coley Ford. He's a contractor."

Hannah perked up immediately.

"I know, Coley," she chuckled, "Oh, I get it. Betty Ford, sorry. When was the last time you saw him?"

"Three days ago, when he went to work. He was in jail that night because he punched this guy out in a bar. I was so mad at him for being in a bar I let him stay there. When I went to get him the next day, they said that he already left. I haven't seen him since."

"Do you think that his disappearance is related to his problem?"

"I don't know. He was in that bar. But he'd been doing so good. Almost two years with no trouble at all. Then he took that job, and all hell started to break loose." Betty was getting upset.

"Is that the job at the Thornton place?" Hannah asked, knowing the answer.

"Yeah, he was doing the remodel for that guy who bought it."

Hannah looked sharply at Betty Ford. First Frank Jenkins, now a missing contractor, and both associated with the Thornton house.

"Mrs. Ford, I'll go up to the house and ask around, see what I can find out. I'll call you as soon as I hear anything. But I have to say since he has a drug issue, more than likely that's gonna be the problem."

"You don't have to tell me, but honestly, inside, I don't think that's what we're looking at. He was doing good, real well, and with all his faults, he loves me. He was almost two years clean. I know the history, but I gotta say, I don't believe that he fell off the wagon. I think something is really wrong."

An hour later, the Santa Cruz PD patrol car pulled into the driveway of the Thornton Mansion for the second time in a month. Activity around the exterior of the house was more hectic than it had been on her first visit, and it was obvious that work was progressing at a swift pace. Hannah turned off the powerful patrol car engine and got out. She surveyed the yard again, as she had on her first visit, and found quite a few changes. The entire area had been cleaned up, and all the garbage that had been accumulated over the years had been hauled away. There were several workers on the three-story scaffolding that had been erected around the front of the house, and they were masking the trim around the many windows in preparation for a new coat of paint. Henry Childs was nowhere to be seen, so she approached the house to see if he was inside.

The front door was open. She poked her head inside and said, "Hello. Anyone here? Santa Cruz police."

A voice from somewhere off in the house responded.

"Hang on. Be right there!"

A few seconds later, Kerry came around the corner and saw Hannah. He stopped suddenly, recognizing the officer. Then, forcing a smile, he greeted her.

"Well, look who it is. Officer Brower. How've you been?" Kerry said.

"Kerry. What are you doing here?" Hannah bristled; Kerry Devine had always been her Kryptonite.

"Well, I work here. What are you doing here?" Kerry continued with his work, avoiding looking directly at her.

"I'm looking for Henry Childs. Is he around?" Kerry bent over to pick up four - 10' x 1"x 3" oak pieces of lumber, and Hannah could not help but stare at his backside.

"No. He took off about half an hour ago. He disappears every day about this time. No idea where he goes. Probably home to his mother, make sure she's okay." Kerry took the lumber into the dining room and started making notes on his yellow legal pad. Hannah followed.

"You expect him back?"

"Don't know. Sometimes he comes back, and sometimes he doesn't. Anything I can help you with?"

"Coley Ford is missing."

"I know. He had this job. The day I started, he didn't show, and Childs hired me to replace him. I haven't seen him at all." She watched Kerry move past her and walk into the kitchen. She couldn't help but take a deep breath as he passed. She followed him into the kitchen.

"Would you stop roaming around, please? I'm trying to ask you some questions."

Kerry stopped in the middle of the curled kitchen linoleum and turned to her.

"What can I do for you, officer?"

"Have you seen Coley Ford? His wife reported him missing," she repeated as though talking to a belligerent child.

"No, he'll show up eventually," Kerry said with annoyance.

"The report says that Henry Childs posted his bail. Do you think he fell off the wagon? Any idea where he might have gone?" Hannah unconsciously adjusted her collar, making sure that it was straight.

"Nah. I don't have a clue. You might try at his AA meeting. Some of his support group might have an idea." Kerry moved to the far side of the kitchen. Hannah stood still. He always had a way of diffusing her common sense.

She saw the door leading to the back porch and asked about that instead.

"Where does that lead?"

Kerry turned and looked at the door. "The backyard."

Hannah thought of Frank Jenkins and moved in that direction. "I think I'll take a look. You mind?"

"I don't, but Childs sure as hell will. He doesn't like anyone out by his pool."

"Are you saying I can't go out there?" Hannah challenged him.

"No, you go right ahead. Nothing out there but dirt and the pool. Knock yourself out." Kerry said.

Hannah moved away from Kerry and walked through the newly installed door. She crossed the back porch and out onto the stairs.

From the landing, she surveyed the yard as an ocean breeze lightly grazed her cheeks. She saw the back gate and remembered it from her investigation of Frank Jenkins's death. She walked down the newly rebuilt staircase.

The plants on the island ruffled in the wind, and small dust devils moved across the empty backyard. Walking past the pool, she gave it a cursory glance as her attention was focused on the gate. When she arrived at the fence, she put her hands on the gate and shook it to test its strength and durability. It had recently been replaced and withstood her test. She tried to open it but discovered that it was locked from the outside by a padlock. Standing on one of the crossbeams at the bottom of the gate, she poked her head over and saw the road and the cliffs beyond.

Everything was as it had been on her investigation into Frank's death. The road was wide enough for a single vehicle, and there was an indentation just outside the gate that could be used as a turnaround. She made a mental note to check the beach below, just to be sure.

Stepping back to the ground, she shook the gate once again and turned back to the pool. She took a few steps toward the house and heard a rushing noise, like a fast-running river.

Rising from the pool just a few feet from her was a giant water funnel. It swirled like a tornado and had bursts of color shooting through it. The funnel danced in front of her like a stripper on a stage, gyrating and contorting. She was terrified and yet unable to look away, like the rubberneckers that always messed up the flow of traffic at an accident.

The funnel skipped over the surface of the pool and touched her face, gently warming it with its glow. Hannah stared into the chasm of the funnel, mesmerized. She saw a woman, or the outline of a woman, reaching for her, beckoning to her. A sudden serenity enveloped her, and she gave in to this spirit. She was pushed onto her back, her arms and legs spread eagle on the ground as the funnel turned to fog and invaded her body.

Chapter 22

Kerry was still in the kitchen when Hannah returned. Her boots were soaking wet, and she tracked water and mud into the house when she entered.

"What happened to you?" Kerry smirked at her. "Decide to investigate the shallow end?"

Hannah looked at him with no idea what he was talking about. Kerry indicated with a glance, and she looked down. She saw her pantlegs were wet up to the knees and that her boots were oozing water.

"What the hell? I must have stepped into a puddle or something."

Kerry shook his head in an amused fashion. "Only puddle out there is the pool itself." He chuckled, looking at Hannah's quizzical look.

"Are you okay?"

She paused for a moment, trying to remember why she had even come up to this old place.

"Yeah, yeah, I'm fine... I have to get going. I'll see you later." She and her wet boots moved towards the kitchen door.

"You be careful, Hannah. Drive safe."

"Sure, thanks, I'll do that." As she moved away from the back door, she regained more of herself. She remembered why she had come. Her eyes seemed too cool, and yet she sensed she had a purpose. "Do you know where Childs lives?"

"No, but you might try the real estate agency."

"You know who brokered the real estate deal?" she asked.

"No, who?"

"Just goes to show how small a town this is. Darcy Wainwright. How about that?" Hannah now had a smirk on her face. Kerry just shook his head.

"If you see Childs, tell him I want to talk with him." Hannah walked out of the house, leaving a trail of wet footprints in her wake.

She climbed into her police cruiser and pulled away. She had no recollection of going near the pool. The last thing she remembered was looking over the fence at the road. But she felt determined and driven, and yet she had no direction. The further she got from the house, the clearer her direction became. Darcy Wainwright! She had to find Darcy and wait for instruction. She didn't ask the most obvious question, direction from whom?

The next day Hannah walked into Lewis Realty for the second time in a month. She passed the receptionist Shelley and walked straight back to Darcy's little cubicle, only to find it empty. Stan Grossman happened to be walking by and, not being one to pass up an opportunity to turn every encounter into a misdemeanor, approached Hannah.

"Well, now, I have a confession to make, officer."

"And what might that be?" Hannah said, not really paying attention to Stan.

"I'm thinking that as fine as you look in that uniform, how great it would look on the floor at the foot of my bed."

Hannah turned to Stan, ready to take him down, but then their eyes met. Instantly they knew. They shared a calling, a directive, a desire that needed no explanation. They were tied together by forces neither of them could explain. She stepped closer to Stan, her breasts brushing lightly against his chest.

"You're watching her here," Hannah said.

"I've got her, but I'm having trouble outside of the office."

Stan dropped his thick, knuckled hand onto her hip.

"I can fix that. If we work together, we can handle her."

Stan slowly reached out with his hand and grazed Hannah's fingers. "I think we can work well together, don't you?"

Hannah opened her fingers and squeezed them around Stan's hand. "Yes. As a matter of fact, I do."

As Hannah stepped away from Stan, she forcefully rubbed her breasts against his shoulder. "I'll be in touch." She left Stan watching her as she walked away, knowing he was looking at her ass.

Three days later, Sergeant Hannah Brower had questioned all of Coley's friends, all the workers at the house and learned about the slapping encounter between him and Childs. She had been to the beach below the house and found nothing. She had finally tracked down Henry Childs, but he offered her little other than he bailed him out, apologized, and drove him back to the house. No question, he had fallen off the wagon and would be back when he felt like it.

As the final form fell into the missing person folder, she decided to call it a day and head home early. She was tired and had not been sleeping all that well the last few nights. Odd dreams had her tossing and turning. Each morning she would wake with thoughts of Stan Grossman in her head, and that was continually distracting her.

Chapter 23

As Darcy woke this very cheery spring morning, the sun was shining through the front window of her apartment. The gloom of March had been left behind. Spring had made its annual appearance, and temperatures were rising. As she enjoyed the spectacular color that the light produced when it hit the honey carpet, she realized that she didn't feel anxious or apprehensive. Maybe she was getting over the whole Thornton/Child's experience after all, and what did they say, 'Get over it or die with it?'

She strolled into the bathroom, walking barefoot through the sunlight, enjoying the warmth on her toes. She stood in front of the bathroom mirror and looked at herself. Her skin was vibrant and full of color. Her eyes shone bright with confidence. She liked what she saw. Not just physically but spiritually. It used to be that she would stand in front of this mirror and see an outrageous life-of-the-party girl. Now, she saw someone who was accomplished and responsible. She liked this mature version of herself. It was as though she woke up one morning and realized that she had a brain and had been tricked into using it. It had also helped that the nightmares were toning down. She had them less frequently and, with the help of a sleeping pill or two, hadn't had one in several nights. Her theory seemed to be panning out.

She picked up her phone and saw that she had another voice message from Childs. With practiced ease, she erased the message without listening to it. *Stay away and stay safe*: easy words to live by

An hour later, with a cup of coffee in a cardboard, sixteen-ounce cup with a white plastic sippy top cooling on her desk, she talked with a client on the phone.

"Mr. Williams, escrow has started. They're not going to back away now, they'd have to forfeit the down, and they won't do that. That's great. I'll call if there are any developments but rest assured, we have made the sale.... Goodbye."

As soon she hung up, her phone buzzed again. She was at her desk for five minutes, and it had started already. She smiled sweetly to herself and took pride in the fact that she was getting used to that occurrence. Since the sale of the Thornton place, she had been on fire. She currently held 14 listings and had made five sales, all in the last month.

"Yeah," Darcy said, hitting the speakerphone function button.

It was Shelly. "Guess what? Mr. Childs on line three."

Darcy dropped her head into her hands. "What does that creep what with me? We closed the deal three months ago. I gave him a gift. I'm done with him. Take a message."

"You got it." Shelley hung up.

Darcy couldn't figure out why he was calling, but no way she was going to answer. Stay away and stay safe. That was her mantra.

Tim Lewis walked up to Darcy's desk and asked, "Have you seen Stan? I haven't seen him in two days."

Darcy looked up, "Hi Tim, no, I haven't. He's probably embarrassed that I've been kicking his ass for the last few months." She chuckled.

"No doubt about that. You are on fire, girl! Keep it up, and if you see Stan, tell him to come find me."

Tim walked away toward Stan's office up front. An office that would soon belong to Darcy, she was certain.

The shadows were laying low, and the sky was growing dark when Darcy said out loud, "Enough. I am done for the day." The phone rang again. She reached for it and suddenly pulled back her hand. "This is Darcy. Leave your name and number after you hear the tone because I am too damn tired to do any more work today." She let the call go to voice mail.

Thinking that she was leaving early, she was surprised to discover that she was once again the last person in the office. She checked her new iPhone for the time. 7:02. Well, it was early for her anyway. She went back down the aisle and did the now habitual close-down as she shut off lights, coffee pots, etc. She had become very proficient at this and, within a matter of minutes, was walking out to that soon-to-be-replaced piece of crap car and heading over to D-Breeze.

The atmosphere in the bar was not that of a typical weekday night. There was a vibe in the air, and Darcy felt it the second she walked in. She had arrived just as the main after-work crowd was thinning down. It was that time in the evening when the married folks head home to their spouses, and the single folks decide if they're going to eat at D-Breeze or not.

Minutes after she had entered the bar and placed her first drink order, Darcy saw Kerry Devine sitting by himself at one of the booths. The vibe she had felt when she entered struck a chord, and she recognized the tune. She grabbed her drink, a Tequila Mojito, and strolled over, saying *hi* to a handsome accountant on the way but not feeling any real urge to investigate his backside.

Kerry was sipping a beer straight from the long-neck bottle, lost in thought. A dirt-smudged manila folder with an inch of paper in it sat open on the table in front of him.

"Stuck in a private moment, fella, or aren't you glad to see me?"

Kerry looked up and took a second to recognize Darcy. When he did, his eyes brightened, and a smile spread across his face. He stood up and gave her a hug. She held on to him and could feel her breasts press against his chest. Darcy inhaled a hint of mint soap, cheap shampoo, and sawdust, an oddly alluring combination. He invited her to sit down.

"So, what were you thinking about?" Darcy asked teasingly. "Looked like your brain was running full tilt."

"I've been working at the Thornton place."

Darcy gasped out loud and recoiled a bit as she did.

"Is that guy creepy or what?" Kerry asked.

"You don't know the half of it. I guess you heard that I sold him the house?"

"Yeah, Hannah told me." The two shared a slow head shake as they shared a past experience. "She is relentless. I'll give her that."

"What are you doing up there?"

"Coley Ford had the gig. He fell off the wagon, and no one's seen him since. I'm heading up the whole shebang."

Darcy made a face. "You have to be kidding."

Kerry saw the face and asked, "Why do you say that? Do you know something I don't?"

"Let's just say that between selling him the house and being out there a few times after, I don't care if I never see the place again. There is some weird stuff happening with that freakazoid, and I don't want any part of it."

"Did something happen to you out there?" Kerry asked.

Darcy paused and tried to figure out how she could tell him about the wind and the backyard and the bleeding, but she came up empty. "It just gives me the creeps. Especially the backyard."

"Yeah, but he doesn't like me going out there. It's really weird."

"Be careful. She's very jealous."

"Who's jealous, Hannah?"

Darcy couldn't answer that question. Who was she?

"You know, I don't know why I said 'she.' I suppose I meant 'it.' The pool."

"Isn't that the weirdest looking thing?" Kerry asked. "It gets pretty hot sometimes, a little dip would be just the ticket, but he won't let us near it."

"It'd be the last ticket you'd cash in, buddy. Childs would run you outta there in a second if he found you in his precious pool. The whacko is whacko about it. He so freaked out when the pool guy put his hose in it."

"Well," said Kerry with a smirk. "He wouldn't have been the first guy getting dissed for putting his hose where it doesn't belong."

Darcy laughed hard for the first time in a long time and immediately felt guilty about it.

"Actually, the guy died. They found him on the beach a few days later. And then Coley disappears? Do you know what happened to him?"

"No. It's strange."

"The whole place is strange." Without realizing it, she reached over and took Kerry's hand. His skin was rough, and his palms calloused from his work as she touched him, the chord that had been humming inside her since she walked in vibrated stronger.

"Are you doing anything tonight?" she asked.

"Matter of fact, I'm baching it. Martha Stewart is out with the girls."

"Doesn't sound like everything is happy in paradise. Anyone, I know?"

"Nah, I met her at the festival in Berkley last summer, and she followed me home."

"And yet things don't sound good?"

"No, not really. I don't want to get married, and she's keeping me awake with her biological clock. I keep trying to tell her that twenty-two-year-olds don't have a working biological clock, but she insists. Do twenty-two-year-olds have a biological clock?"

"They have one, but the batteries aren't usually attached yet. Is she really that bad? It's Brigid, right?"

"Nah, she was last year. This one is Clementine."

"Oh, m' darlin'. Lost and gone forever?"

"I'm beginning to wish she was. She's nice enough and everything, but I'm not looking to get married, and that's all she talks about. I'll tell you, to be honest, if I could walk away right now and not hurt her, I'd be gone."

"Well, that pretty much says it all, doesn't it? You should think about being honest with her." Darcy offered.

Changing the subject, Kerry looked at her and said, "Look at you. You know, I hardly recognized you at first. I mean the clothes and all look great but the way you move and the way you talk, you're so different. And I mean different in a good way."

"Well, you can't stay the party girl forever. There's been a lot going on in the last few months. I started a career. I'm pretty happy, too, despite having to thank the Thornton place for most of it. And you. You're looking real good. I bet it won't take ten minutes before you have someone else dangling on the hook. Just choose with your heart this time and not your eyes." Darcy laughed.

"I think I'm taking a break here for a while. I just want time to be myself. You're the only woman that's ever really let me be that. The rest... they all see me as the father of their children, the guy they can take home to their dad, or who knows what else. I'm gonna wait for someone like you to come along."

Darcy stirred in her seat as her temperature started to rise. "You know, I can't have too many of these tonight," pointing to her drink. "You want to take a walk?" She asked.

Kerry didn't need to be asked twice. He tossed a ten-dollar bill on the table, and they left.

"Wanna go down to the beach and walk there?" Kerry asked when they got outside.

"No," Darcy said a bit too fast. "I know a great trail through the redwoods. It's a full moon, so we'll be able to find our way with no problem. It kinda overlooks the beach, so that'll be cool."

"I'm easy. Let's go."

Kerry followed Darcy to the top of a ridge, and they parked their cars. They walked for about an hour and then went back to Darcy's apartment for coffee. Kerry fell asleep on the couch, curled up around Darcy as a movie played to the silence of their slumber.

When Kerry finally made it home, Clementine was waiting.

"Do you know what time it is?" She screeched at him.

"Look, Clem, I ran into an old friend and lost track of time. No big deal."

"Who is this old friend? One of the bimbo's of the past?"

"Bimbos? Are you saying that's all I dated?"

"If the shoe fits..."

"Okay then, what does that say about you?"

"Oh fuck you, Kerry. You are such an ass. The girls were telling me to look out for you, and I guess they were right."

"The girls? Well, if 'The Girls' say it, it must be true."

Clementine paused for a brief moment. "You don't even care, do you? You don't care about what I think or feel! You know what? Screw you. Go stay with your stupid bimbos. I'm out of here. I'm gonna find someone who gives a shit!"

She stormed into the bedroom and slammed the door.

Kerry walked back to his car and climbed into the back seat. "Hmm, that went better than I thought."

Chapter 24

Henry stood at the altar of his new home. This time, however, he stood beside his mother, Edith Childs.

Cold, demanding, and insensitive were his thoughts when he was angry with her. Indomitable, unnerving, and aloof were the good things he could say about her. Begrudgingly generous was the best he had ever considered her.

But now, Henry no longer was intimidated by the presence of this woman. Yet, even though he had changed so drastically, he had the presence of mind to realize that Edith had not. It would be easier all the way around if he could convince her that this was a good idea. If he could get Edith to willingly move into the house, things would be better for everyone.

Henry looked at the frail old woman and said, "Well, what do you think?"

She looked at the newly painted relic before her.

"Henry, why on earth are we here? Tell me what the devil is going on!"

"You'll see, you'll see," Henry said as he slowly ushered her up the ramp leading to the front porch. Edith was walking with her cane, so the going was slow.

Once he had her on the porch, Henry fished in his pocket and handed Edith a key tied up with a red bow.

"Here, Mother. Surprise!"

Edith looked confused.

"You tell me what the hell is going on here, and you tell me now!" she demanded.

"Mother, it's the surprise. I bought the house... for you." He lied.

Edith looked at her son, her face expressionless.

"You bought me a house? What am I going to do with this monstrosity?"

"We're going to live here. This is our new home."

"Our new home?" snapped Edith, "This isn't my home. I live in the city. I have no intention of moving anywhere. Not at my age, I don't."

Edith turned, using her cane like you'd use the oar in a canoe, and started back toward the car. Henry reached out, grabbed her arm, and swung her around to face him.

"Mother," Henry said with arsenic in his voice.

Not one to be intimidated, she glared straight at him with her look, the one that said, *I am not to be questioned.* For the first time in his life, Henry glared back. His eyes radiated as though the dingy brown orbs had been covered with red-hot contacts. The edges of his pupils pulsed with emotion. He was starting to shake, the rolls of flab undulating under his not-quite-so-transparent skin.

A bolt of pain shot through his brain, rocketing across his eyebrows from right to left. The pain caused his head to twist violently over his left shoulder as though he had been slapped. His hand convulsed, and his mother cried out in pain.

"Henry, you're hurting me!" Edith twisted her arm to extricate it from his grasp. She stared at him as if he were a total stranger, backing away, unsure of who she was talking to.

"You must realize what a shock this is. You didn't ask me if I wanted to move. I'm sorry, I'm just surprised. Please give me a moment to adjust."

At her words, Henry's mood shifted, and he calmed down.

"You'll see, Mother. This is the best thing to do. You'll see." The pain in his head disappeared.

"When you saw this house before, you said it could really be something. You just don't remember. I bought it for you as a present and am fixing it up. A present for everything you've done for me all these years. It's almost done. This is our new home."

Edith looked at her son, not recognizing this forceful man, and her knees went weak.

Chapter 25

It had been a liberating day for Kerry. Clementine had managed to vacate his place with a minimum of fuss. He was feeling light and breezy and had a smile of relief plastered to his face.

The job at the Thornton mansion was going as it had a hundred times before. The client shows the impossible things they want, and Kerry gets it done. He always finished a job within a half-day of when he said he would, and he never left a mess. It was common to be asked for dinner or taken out when he had completed a particularly taxing remodel.

He had arrived at the site half an hour early and was taking some measurements with the twenty-five-foot Stanley that hung incessantly from his belt. Alone in the dining room, he had an uneasy feeling nestled deep in the pit of his stomach.

The look on Darcy's face when he told her he was working here intruded onto his imagination. He forced himself to think of something else, and truly, there was only one other thing on his mind—Darcy. He still didn't understand how those old feelings for her had been dredged up after all these years.

Kerry found that thoughts of Darcy snuggling against him all night distracted him further, so he shook off those thoughts for the moment and turned to the baseboards that lay along the bottom of the wall. Just as he was finishing with the downstairs hallway, Mr. Childs returned.

"Good morning, Kerry. What do we have to see today?" Henry said as he entered.

"Morning. I'm about ready to start on the baseboard moldings. I have some samples for you to see."

Kerry laid out the six different choices of molding for Henry to view. Each piece had a different shape, and each was a different wood. He also showed Henry the portfolio that contained a dozen or so choices that Kerry thought would be appropriate. He explained that it was a Chinese menu. "Pick and choose what you want."

Henry looked perplexed.

Kerry explained, "The three-curve design displayed in oak can also be cut into the maple. Or the two-curve design in cherry could be cut into oak, and so on."

"I'm just not sure how I can choose. These are all so beautiful. Do you have any thoughts?"

"That's so true, but if I had to choose, I love the Asian maple."

Henry's face squinched up, and he slowly shook his head. "I just don't know. This is a very important decision for me."

Kerry offered a suggestion. "If you like, you can take these samples and talk with someone you trust, someone who can help you decide."

"That is an excellent suggestion. I shall return shortly."

Henry took three samples, his three favorites, and excused himself. Kerry figured he was going home to check with his mother, but to his surprise, Henry headed out back. Kerry was left waiting by himself in the foyer.

Henry took the three samples into the backyard and stood by the edge of the pool. It used to be that he went to his mother for these decisions, now he came here.

As he stood by the pool, a fine spray kicked up that lightly brushed his face. The caress of the water reassured him, and he began to lose the feeling of indecisiveness almost as quickly as it had formed.

As it had many times since the first day Henry stood here with Darcy, the pool reached out to him. The spiraling funnel engulfed him and soothed his soul, easing his doubts with the gentle hand of a mother powdering a baby's bottom.

When Henry opened his eyes, he was floating above the world,

Looking down on creation and the only explanation he could find was the love that he had found ever since he bought the house. It had taken him right out of his mind.

It may have been that Henry was singing in his newly acquired voice. It was hard to know. In any event, he saw himself once again, standing at the edge of the pool, looking at himself objectively from the outside. Only it was a bit different this time. He was not quite as revolting. He had lost weight, and his complexion was darkening, being that he was outside so much. Of course, his voice was downright seductive. He thought that the figure he was looking down on was not a total loss after all. With some work, this body could become something better. Wow! That thought had never crossed his mind before. The world was full of firsts. First, he never had a chance, and now he does.

Will wonders never cease?

How wonderful she is to show me this. She felt my pain, my apprehension, and she allowed me to see who I really was, Henry thought.

As Henry floated in his haven of ecstasy, he was brought around to the realization that it is not who you are that is important, it is who you are *perceived* to be. And so it is with

Henry, a blob with no personality who is his own worst enemy. He had lived a life spent in terror of the world and the pain it can inflict. He was a man perceived to be weak and spineless, so that is what he had become. But that is not reality. It is a perception, and he can change perception.

Henry knew that he had already started to make the change. He had lost weight, he had darkened his complexion, and he had begun to take control. He could talk to people now and not have them wince as he tried to explain himself. He could be whoever or whatever he wanted to be. He could become someone that was respected and revered. He could become a leader.

But a leader of what? He asked himself next.

He could organize a volunteer group to help the homeless and those less fortunate: a waste of time. They would only go back to being lazy once he left them, and he really didn't give a shit about the poor and the homeless.

He could join a local club, like the Lions or the Elks, and become involved in their work. What was their work? They seem like a bunch of guys who sit around and drink for eleven months and then throw a charity car wash.

Or he could become mayor. Mayor of Santa Cruz? Mayor of San Francisco? Mayor of the world!

Why not? He could enter local politics and gain power in the community. He had money, what he needed next was power. He could do that! The pitfalls of public life didn't scare him. He had an advantage! He had an impeccable background. Hell, he was a virgin! How much purer can you get? He was obviously someone of great moral prowess, and he could answer all the moral questions of this decadent world. He had no skeletons in any closet in the world. (Except, of course, for this one, but who would ever find out?) With a future of power and politics in front of him and all the wisdom that he possessed, ready to share with an unenlightened world, why shouldn't he be able to pick out a baseboard pattern? Well, he can, dammit! He can and he will.

And with that, Henry was swept from the bosom of the rainbow funnel and back into the mortal coil to which he had been cursed and chose the Asian maple with the three-curve design.

Chapter 26

Kerry's work at the mansion was done for the day. He headed out to his truck to run a few errands before heading home to his now quiet house. Just as the engine turned over, his phone rang. It was Darcy.

"Hey stud, whatcha doin'?" her voice caught him off-guard.

He turned off the engine to hear her better. "I'm up at Mr. Creepy's. I was just leaving."

The phone went silent. For a second, Kerry thought he had lost reception.

"You still there? Darcy, can you hear me?"

"Yeah, I'm here." The excitement had left her voice.

"I have to run some errands, and then I'm done for today. What are you doing?

"Well, I thought I might buy you a drink a little later. If you're not scared off by my forward nature."

"If you haven't scared me by now, then I guess I'm going to be okay." Kerry paused, "You know, I did a pretty poor job of explaining where I was the other night."

"Yeah, I guess that must have been uncomfortable. Look, I'm not trying to mess up your life. I was just thinking of a drink... as friends, you know, no big deal. I know you have a girlfriend; I probably shouldn't be calling."

"She left me… to find someone who "gives a shit," was her exact phrase."

"I'm sorry. I didn't mean for that to happen." Darcy said.

"Not your fault. I'm a big boy. If I wanted to maintain that relationship, I wouldn't have fallen asleep wrapped around you."

Simultaneously, goose bumps popped out on their arms as though there was an electrical charge flowing through the phone.

"So consequently, I am free for a drink, and if you promise to leave your biological clock at home, I'll meet you at D-Breeze in an hour."

Darcy laughed. It was an honest laugh, and it made him feel good.

"So, D-Breeze. In about an hour."

"I'll be there. See ya." They hung up.

It started over the pool but rose over the house in an instant. A chill wind whipped through the open windows of the truck, shaking it from side to side. Kerry felt the truck rise as though it was about to take off. He grabbed onto the steering wheel and held on for dear life. He felt the truck move to the left and had visions of being picked up and dropped onto a wicked witch. As quickly as the wind had come, it disappeared. He shivered.

What the hell was that?

Having had enough weirdness for one day, Kerry reached over and turned the key, anxious now to get off this property and get to D-Breeze. The truck moaned like a dying hippo, and then there was nothing but the click-click-click of a dead battery. "Shit!" he yelled, slamming his hand on the steering wheel. "You lousy piece of shit!"

Kerry got out and popped the hood. Droplets of water hung under the hood and ran toward the hinges as he raised it. The battery, which was only six months old, was covered in corrosion. "What the hell?"

Kerry could see the shiny, black casing in some areas while other parts of the surface were melted and flaking with corrosion.

He poked at the terminals, and the positive cable disintegrated in his hand. "It was just working!" The hair on the back of his neck tingled. It made no sense to him at all.

Kerry considered his options. If he could get someone to take him to the auto shop over on Highway 9, he could get a replacement cable and a new battery. That would solve the problem but not the mystery.

He needed to get rolling. He didn't want to miss his date with Darcy. Kerry went off looking for help. "You can bet that Mr. Die Hard'll be getting a visit very soon," he said as he literally kicked the truck.

As Kerry walked around the house, he found a few of the guys sweeping. He asked if any of them had a car, and they all shook their heads.

"No, senor. We will get a ride with Fred when he comes back. Maybe one hour."

"An hour. Right. Thanks, anyway."

Kerry's next thought was of Darcy. Maybe she wouldn't mind. He hated to impose so soon on their new relationship, or whatever this was, but he had little choice. He grabbed his phone.

"Hey there. You aren't bailing on me, are you?" She said, answering on the first ring.

"No way, but I do have a bit of a problem."

"You don't want to wait an hour to see me." She chuckled.

"Well, that too. My battery died. Damn thing corroded right through. Sea air, I guess. Can you swing by and pick me up?"

Darcy fell silent.

She was safe as long as she stayed away.

"Hey, you okay?" Kerry asked.

"Yeah, it's just that place gives me the creeps like I can't tell you." Darcy's voice was weak and shallow.

"Well, you don't have to get out of the car. I can meet you at the end of the driveway. Would that work?"

Darcy's breath caught in her throat.

"If I don't have to get out of the car... I guess that would be okay."

"Thanks. I owe you one. I promise. You're really spooked by this place, aren't you?"

There was a pause, and Darcy said, "I'm not getting out of the car."

He got to his truck and pulled out his paperwork and schedule for the next day. He locked the truck and started to walk down the driveway when he heard his name call from the house. It was Henry.

"Kerry. Oh, Kerry. Before you go, can I talk to you for a minute?"

Chapter 27

Darcy had been stalling, hoping to come up with a means of getting Kerry from the house without going up there herself. But she was the one that he'd called. This was the type of thing that you do for your friend, or whatever this was, and she knew that she had to do it.

What the hell am I doing? Darcy approached the left turn that would take her up to the house.

Stay away and stay safe.

Shaking her head, amazed at her own stupidity, she took the left turn, a mindless heroine going back for the cat.

She pulled up to the end of the driveway, the roof of the house barely visible above the arborvitae that lined the drive. Kerry wasn't there. She honked and waited. He didn't show up. She backed up a bit to see further up the drive, but he was still nowhere to be found.

"Great. Just what I didn't want to happen." She put the car into drive.

She pulled through the gate and began to feel the beads of sweat accumulating under her arms. A large drop dribbled down her side, absorbing into the fabric of her blouse just above her waistline. She saw Kerry's truck, the hood popped open, looking like a cadaver. She eyed it and felt like a largemouth bass about to grab a worm. Like the bass, she knew better but couldn't stop herself. She pulled behind the truck.

There was no sign of Kerry. She texted his cell and waited. No reply.

Honk! Honk! The last one was laid on for about three seconds.

If you want a ride, you better get your ass out here now!

The final blast faded into the cliffside, and still no Kerry.

Damn him!

She sat there, with the windows closed, sweat oppressively forming on the back of her neck and behind her knees, trying to get up the courage to open the door and go look for him.

The circular driveway was silent. There was no rustling of leaves, no birds cawing overhead, no sound of the distant waves crashing against the shore. She was about ready to get the hell out.

Probably inside talking with Creepazoid Childs. Great!

Why hadn't she already turned around?

I must really like this guy.

She stared helplessly at the house. Should she go to the door, wait, or leave? Before she could decide, she saw a shadow move in one of the downstairs windows. It was a quick movement at first that immediately disappeared. She looked closer, and the shape reappeared in the window directly to her right. It was the silhouette of a woman, her hair piled high on her head, ruffles around the collar of her shirt, and what looked like a waistcoat. Her arms were waving wildly as though she was in an argument.

In the window to the left, a second silhouette appeared. This one was obviously a man, taller and broader than the woman. His arms were also waving about, and he had something in his hand. The woman stepped out of her window frame and entered the frame of the man. She grabbed at his hands, and a struggle ensued. They were wrestling for the object that they held between them. It became apparent that this object was a pistol. Darcy yelled, but it was too late, the gun went off. The man clutched his chest and then crumbled to the ground, out of sight, below the sill. The woman stared down at the man's body and dropped her head. She knelt, and Darcy could only see the top of her head as it shook over the fallen man. She stood shaking and reached for the curtain that covered the window. The curtain slowly parted, and for the first time, she saw an actual person, not just a silhouette. She raised the gun to her own head and pulled the trigger.

"NO!" The car door blew open, and she ran to the house. With her first step came a breeze that rode up her pant leg.

Darcy grabbed the handle to the front door and twisted it with all her might. It was locked. She began banging on the door with her fists screaming, "No, no, no!" In the doorknocker that she had given Henry, she saw her reflection. Her face pinched with outrage. She half-expected the damn thing to come to life and talk to her like something out of A Christmas Carol.

She kicked at the door and pounded it with her fists screaming, "Let me in! Let me in!"

The door opened, and there was Henry. His eyes were calm, his demeanor subtle and controlled, not a hair out of place. He seemed unaware of what had just transpired.

"Well, hello, Miss Wainwright. It is nice to see you again. I've been trying to reach..."

Darcy pushed past him and ran to the living room. She expected to see blood and the body of two corpses. Instead, she ran right into Kerry's chest, nearly knocking him over.

"Whoa, what's up, Darcy? Are you okay?" Kerry asked.

"Kerry, oh my God," Darcy said, panting, and she threw her arms around his neck.

"Ok then... what's up?"

She ran into the living room. There were no shadows haunting the walls, no blood dripping down the windowpanes. There was nothing in the room but a sawhorse, no signs of mayhem at all. She then realized that despite everything that she had done to stay away, she was standing in the living room of the Thornton Mansion. Her knees started to tremble.

"I'm sorry I wasn't waiting outside, Darcy. I had some last minutes things to discuss with Mr. Childs."

"You're here for Kerry? I didn't realize you knew each other." Henry's voice betrayed his surprise.

"We've been friends for years." She said, sounding very much like a lost little girl.

"Of course, I should have realized..."

Darcy was shivering, and her bladder began to squeeze. She had to pee.

Not a chance of that in this house. She thought.

Her skin tingled, and ripples of fear began to run up her arms. There was a powerful force in the room. It was a force that was dangerous, a force that was surely deadly, and a force that, oddly enough, was not unfamiliar. She was afraid of Kerry, for Kerry. She turned her head to yell for him to get out but was shocked when their eyes met.

She didn't see the same guy she had seen a few moments before.

Instead of seeing the face she expected, the face with the day-old growth of beard, the jet-black hair lying disheveled on the perfectly shaped scalp, the strong neck that she had been thinking about since they fell asleep on her couch, she saw something more. Kerry had an aura of bright, white light surrounding him. The aura was so bright, it obscured his features, like an overexposed video shot.

In that single moment, she realized something that she had always known and yet never acknowledged. She loved this man. He was her first love, and it appeared that he was her true love. Something in this room brought out the true goodness in him and allowed Darcy to see him for who he really was. This room...

She realized this place was reaching out for her, trying to control her, fool her. The awareness that she was being duped crushed her. Her love for Kerry had to be a fabrication. It came from the room that was controlled by the house, that was controlled by the tide pool. This place wanted to harm her, and they had obviously recruited Kerry to be the bait. The one lure it knew she couldn't resist.

Shaking all over and tears running down her face, she turned and ran to the doorway. Pushing Henry out of the way, she ran to her car without looking back.

Henry was astonished. "What in the world...?"

"I'll see you tomorrow, Mr. Childs. We can finish this discussion then." Kerry ran after Darcy, leaving Henry standing alone, frustrated.

As Kerry got to the porch, Darcy was pulling out of the driveway, the driver's side door swinging wildly, unable to latch. She sped off. Having no choice, he grabbed his stuff from the front porch and started walking into town.

Chapter 28

A while later, Darcy was sitting at the bar in D-Breeze. Her beer sat in front of her, untouched. The door opens, and Kerry enters. He walks over and sits next to her. He looks at Drew and silently orders a beer.

"So. You have me pretty much confused. Wanna tell me what's going on?"

Darcy looked at him, not at all surprised that he would be here, and shook her head.

"I don't even know where to start. I'm sorry I left you. I just couldn't be there."

Darcy avoided direct eye contact. An awkward silence sat between them.

Kerry finally asked. "What is it that bugs you so much about that house?"

Darcy tried to find the right words.

"It's like the best and the worst thing that ever happened to me."

"It's just a house. You don't believe all the BS about it, do you?"

Darcy took a swig of beer and winced at the flat taste.

"Yeah, I think I do. Every time I go in there, I get a feeling that I've been there before. I get the feeling that whatever happened to me was not good. I even get the feeling that someone doesn't like me and wants to get even."

"I feel like… there's something or someone there that hates me. And something else, I sense… something—desire, whatever."

"Desire? For what?"

"For me... sometimes I feel that Childs might have the hots for me. I feel like he tries to get me there, to the house, and… I don't know. It's creepy.

"I can see why he might have a few thoughts about you. You're a gorgeous woman," Kerry said, taking her hand. "Childs might be creepy and weird, but he's not dangerous. Besides, if he was, he'd have to deal with me."

Once again, despite the dire circumstances, Kerry had managed to make her smile.

"Well, if anything would make me feel better, that would be it."

"Glad to be of service, ma'am. Anything I can do to help." He said in an old western, quasi John Wayne accent. "And just for the record, I thought that living room was pretty creepy myself. For a minute, while you were standing there, I could hardly see you. I felt like I was about to black out or something. It wasn't until you took off that I snapped out of it."

"You see? It's not just me. There is definitely something going on."

"I think it's more likely some gas floating up from the cellar through the fireplace or something like that. I don't think it's a ghost."

"It's not a ghost. I know that for a fact. It's not a ghost." Darcy looked into his eyes and saw the love she felt for him. It overwhelmed her, and yet she knew it was a trick. She knew that it was the house that had made her feel this way. What a cruel twist of fate. She grabbed her purse and keys and stood up, "I have to go. I'll call you tomorrow."

Without any further explanation, Darcy left Kerry sitting alone at the bar.

Chapter 29

Henry watched Darcy run to her car and drive off. He had that all-too-familiar sense of failure in the pit of his stomach. It had been so long since he had felt total inadequacy, he had almost forgotten the emptiness that it brings. No sooner did the panic start to rise, but he felt her reach out for him. She was calling him. He turned away from the front door and headed out to the pool.

In the coolness of the water, Henry now floated naked, with a sparkle of color swirling around him. As he bobbed in the silky luxury of the pool, the water began to swirl. The euphoric feeling of weightlessness consumed him as the funnel grew. He looked to the flue expecting to be lifted out of his horrific shell of mortality, but today it was different. The monolith of water stopped just short of engulfing him and instead opened itself up to Henry.

And for the first time, he saw her.

From out of the rainbow of color that made up the funnel, she stood in all her glory. Her creamy skin reflected the colors bounding around her. Her hair was flaxen with tiny flecks of mica and gold that sparkled brightly. Her eyes were kind and gentle. Her lips were full and red and ready. She rose up from the funnel, naked and unashamed, her breasts standing firm and supple, and he desired her more than any woman he had ever fantasized about.

She looked down at Henry and smiled.

"I am not deserving of your love," he said to her, "I have failed you." He bowed his head and cried.

She reached out and stroked his cheek. She pulled him to her and kissed him, soft at first but building in intensity. She slid her tongue into his mouth, and his body quivered.

She enveloped Henry in a vise-like embrace and spun him with her into the depths of the pool to consummate their collaboration. When it was time, together, they would end it all.

Henry woke next to the pool, naked in the moonlight, spent. He would wait for her to give him the sign. When it was time, he would succeed and fulfil all her desires.

Chapter 30

Kerry had been on the job now for almost four months. It was a rocky start, but once he got the schedule in place and the routine down, things began to happen. Fred had remained in charge of the labor force, and between them, the checklist had started to shrivel. There were still weeks of work to be done, but he could finally see the end of this project. While Fred managed the workers, Kerry had spent his time focusing on the finished work. The kitchen cabinets were installed and looked fantastic. Vivid Italian tile had been laid in the kitchen. The crown moldings and baseboards around the entire house were coming along well. Another week and he would be done. The second and third floors were essentially complete, with some minor touch up still to be done. This morning, Kerry arrived at the Thornton House ready to take on the final stages of the job and was surprised by the moving van in the driveway. He saw Henry in the middle of a flurry of activity and walked over to see what was going on.

"Morning, Mr. Childs. What's all this?"

"Well, I decided I couldn't wait any longer. Mother and I are moving in today. The upstairs is in fine shape, and she won't be in the way. I'll be able to spend more time here and help out in any way I can." Something caught his eye. "Put that sofa in the upstairs bedroom. The one marked as 'Mother.'" He yelled at one of the movers.

Kerry was taken aback. The house wasn't ready for anyone to move in, but...

"Well, in that case, I think we should make your mother's room a priority, and we should be able to have it totally done by the end of the day." Kerry offered.

"That would be wonderful." In an instant, he was off directing the movers again. Kerry went to find his crew. They would have to be very careful since furniture and personal items were now on the premises, not to mention the dialogue between the men would have to become more restrained.

At the end of the day, just as the movers were heading out and the crew was breaking, Henry's new Dodge Ram 3500 pulled into the drive. He got out and ran to the passenger's door. The door opened, and with great effort, out slid Henry's mother, the indomitable Edith Childs.

Kerry saw this tiny, frail woman, yet he could tell that she had once been formidable.

"Why the hell are we moving so fast, Henry? For God's sake, the place isn't even finished. Why can't we wait at least until it's finished before you make me live here?" she screeched at Henry.

"I told you, mother, it's best if we're here to help the carpenters. This way, we can supervise the construction that much better."

"Oh, for chrissake's, Henry, how the hell are you going to help? Climb up on the roof and lay shingles? You'd be dead in a day. Don't be absurd." She pulled her arm away from Henry and hobbled toward the house. As she passed Kerry, she looked at him and barked, "Who are you?"

"Kerry Devine, ma'am. I'm the contractor and finish carpenter."

"Well, don't stand around talking to me. Get back to work so you can finish this godforsaken rat hole." She ambled on by. When she got to the porch steps, she let out another holler.

"HENRY!"

Henry came running. He assisted her up the front steps and into the house.

Kerry shook his head and said under his breath, "Well, this just got a hell of a lot tougher."

Henry assisted his mother to her room. He returned to Kerry. "So, Kerry. How did we do today?"

"We did very well. Lots of progress, as I'm sure that you can tell. Your mother's room is done. We should have the stairlift installed by end of day. Everything else is coming along well."

"You know, Kerry. I've been thinking. It would be so nice if you and that lovely Miss Wainwright would join mother and I for dinner some night. What do you think?"

Kerry looked at Henry like he was from Mars.

"Dinner? Well, I have to say I haven't really seen Darcy lately."

"Oh really. That's too bad. You seemed like such a nice couple."

"Yeah, I thought so too," Kerry said with legitimate sadness.

"You should call her. Lord knows that these things blow over. Maybe she's calmed down by now," Henry said, not knowing where that advice had come from. He'd never had a girlfriend in his life, much less one that he had fought with.

"You know, you're right. I should do that."

Chapter 31

The gearshift lever slid down into the reverse position, and the brand-new, bright red Infiniti G37 AWD pulled out of parking spot twenty-six. Darcy sat tall and proud behind the wheel. She wished that she could attach a chain to this amazing machine and wear it around her neck like a pendant.

She considered how different the things in her life had become. Here she was on her way to her office, driving her new car, with only twenty-three miles on it, open-air sound system with noise cancellation, sixty gig MP4, real time navigation, user interface climate control and intermittent windshield wipers. Upon arrival at her destination, she will work on closing one of the many listings that she had on the market. In the past week alone, she had listed and sold two different pieces of real estate, one of them an apartment complex on Sumner Ave that actually sold for more than the Thornton place. With the current stack of commission checks that were pouring in, Darcy had been able to pay cash for her new car. That was a true thrill.

Her life had become something from a fairy tale, hometown girl becomes a princess and rules the land. And there was the cutest little house over by Soquel Ave near Live Oak that she had her eye on.

Darcy had changed her route to work immediately after she had closed on the Thornton Mansion. Her original route had taken her past the base of the hill on which the house sat, much too close for her mantra of staying away and staying safe. The new house she was looking at was on the other side of town, and she would never have any reason to drive in the direction of the Thornton house again.

Along the most direct route, there was a stoplight at the street that would take you up to the house. When she got caught at that light, she could feel the house reaching out for her. Not coincidently, she was sure, she would have a nightmare that same night. The images were morbid and violent, with suicides and murders that became more complete with each dream. The woman with the ruffled collar and her hair piled high on her head along with the man with the gun, went at it each night. Each time she got anywhere near the house, she felt a shadow surrounding her, reaching out for her. She felt there were eyes, somewhere, constantly on her. She tried to shut out the thoughts of gunshot wounds and dead bodies, but it was something she could not deny. There was a psychic stalker in her head.

Consequently, she would now drive east about a mile and then cut back across town to get to her office. It added ten minutes to her drive but compensated with peace of mind.

She coasted to a stoplight. This was where she had to turn right and begin her daily detour.

As she executed the turn, a smile as wide as the horizon on her face, she did not see the silver Audi merge into her lane two cars back. Behind the wheel was Stan Grossman. He had been following her since she left her apartment. He continued to follow her all the way to the office.

Darcy pulled into the parking lot and headed straight for her "Employee of the Month" EP-M reserved spot, the spot she had now held for three consecutive months. The spot was still stained with the oil that had dripped from her Escort, but she knew that would fade. She used her new keyless remote to lock the doors on the incredible Infiniti and trigger the alarm. She loved the twirping sound it made when she locked and unlocked it.

Twirp! Click!

It was locked.

Twirp, click, thunk!

It was unlocked, and the dome light popped on. Oh, what a wonderful world. Locking it again, she laughed out loud and headed into the office.

Stan pulled into the lot as soon as she was inside. He parked, and got out, knowing no one would ever be able to explain the key scratch on the side of the Infiniti.

Sometimes life's a bitch!

Stan came over to Darcy's desk a while later. "Tim wants you to come with me to check out a property. You free?"

Darcy looked at Stan and wondered why Tim would do that. But she also knew that he was in San Jose for the day, and she didn't want to bother him over something as stupid as her disgust for Stan.

"Does Tim want you to work with someone to help boost your confidence? You haven't exactly been hitting it out of the park lately."

Stan blenched. "There's a beachfront that is going to hit the market. He wants us to go over and convince the owner that we are the people to list with. A friend of his gave him the lead."

Darcy inhaled and exhaled loudly. She wanted to just tell Stan to fuck off, but a beachfront would be a huge commission, and she was not going to give it to this slime bucket.

"Okay, but I drive."

Stan smiled as she grabbed her purse and reached for her keys.

In the parking lot, Darcy was admiring her new car. She walked towards it and then screamed.

"What the hell?" She raced to the car to see a vicious scratch running down the entire driver's side.

"Who would do this? Oh, come on, you've got to be kidding? The damn thing has thirty miles on it."

Stan walked over and shook his head. "That is awful. I can't believe someone would do that. You have insurance, right?"

Darcy looked at him as though he were the biggest moron on the planet, which he may very well have been, "Of course I have insurance, that's not the point. It's my brand new car, and someone keyed it? What the hell?"

They were now heading north on the PCH. She hit the steering wheel with the palm of her hand, and tears were forming in her eyes.

"I know, it sucks. But it can be fixed, it's not the end of the world." Stan offered.

"But who would do that? Why would anyone do that?"

Stan smirked a fake sympathetic smile and said, "Well, you haven't been making many friends around here. You know, you could share the wealth, I'm just saying."

"You think it was someone in the office?"

"It was in our private lot. Hard to think it would be anyone else."

"I can't believe that. Who would be so cruel? Brandon? Do you think Brandon would do something like this?"

Stan put his hand on her arm. "Well, I don't know, but he was pretty upset about you closing on Sumner Ave. That put you up at the top again, and he lost out on the EP-M spot."

"So, what? It's just a parking spot. He made a ton on the deal he closed. You think he could be so petty?"

"I don't know. Okay, turn left up here at the light."

Stan gave her directions that took them to the beach. She parked the car, and as she got out, she stepped back to look at the damage one more time.

"God, this makes me mad. I am going to kick Brandon's ass when I get back."

Stan moved away from the car and looked south along the beach. "It's down this way about a block."

The beachfront was fairly unpopulated. There was a small row of businesses that had been there for decades. Had they ever tried to open at this location today, it would have cost them millions. There was a convenience store, a Laundromat, and a bar/restaurant called, Inkydan's. The bar had opened in 1928 and still served the same menu, beer, hard drinks, and seafood, *Best Octopus in Town,* the sign said.

Darcy began to get an uneasy feeling, as though she was somewhere she shouldn't be. Looking down the street, she saw the cottage that they were going to visit. Wanting to get this over with, she moved Stan along.

"Let's go. It's right over there."

They heard thunder roll in from over the ocean.

"Great, if it starts to rain, we are going to be stuck. Let's get a move on." Darcy hurried down the street. As she did, she looked up at the cliff, and her heart skipped a beat. About three hundred yards down the beach and sitting atop the cliffs was the Thornton Mansion. She was suddenly in the exact place she didn't want to be.

Thunder cracked again, and this time closer and louder. Darcy looked to the skies and saw a formation of clouds over the mansion. It looked like rain. As she looked at the clouds, clouds that were oddly moving in opposite directions like they were being shuffled in a three-card Monty game. Sitting in the middle of the shuffle was a larger, dark cloud, ominous and foreboding. The smaller clouds moved with purpose around the larger ones like soldiers on the marching field. When they settled, she saw it.

A face...

A face in the clouds. She wasn't talking about that children's imagination game, "I see a zebra! I see an elephant!" This was a real, honest to God, evil, sadistic, steal-your-children's-innocence face.

There was a giant, grey puffy eyebrow guarding the area over the right eye, acting as a roadblock to any portion of the forehead that might want to invade the cheeks or chin. Several long, stringy wisps defined an area on the brow that looked very much like worry lines. A darker, oval thunderhead was positioned where the mouth should be; long wisps of thin, vaporous clouds streamed from the skull like white hair blowing in the wind of a torrential storm. But what truly terrified Darcy was that the face was missing its entire left side.

The wind shifted, and the face moved. The eye was now visible, or at least it would have been had there been an eye. Where the pupil should be, there was nothing, yet, she couldn't see the sky behind it. The eye must be blind, but she knew as soon as the thought crossed her mind that it wasn't true. This thing could see her. With its one empty eye, it could see her.

The face turned ominously to the right and then to the left, scanning and probing with its vacant, dark gray socket. Wisps of cloud spilled from the missing left side of her head like steam coming off a hot cup of coffee. As it turned, Darcy could see the full dimension of the thing; it wasn't a flat image. It had depth and fullness. As it looked to the left, she could see the right ear and the hair flowing down the back of its head, wild and unruly. As it turned right, Darcy could see straight into her skull.

She raced to the nearest building, the old bar, and plastered herself against the wall so she could not be seen from above. She wanted to scream out for help. She wanted to run for her life. She wanted someone to come and save her, but she was on her own.

Stan had been lagging behind her. He had an odd grin on his face and was mumbling to himself. He seemed to reach a conclusion in his inner dialogue, and shaking his head in affirmation, he trotted over to Darcy.

"Uh, just what are you doing?"

"Shhh, just stay still, don't draw attention to me."

Over Stan's shoulder, the cloud hovered. It had targeted Darcy; she could see it moving into position over her like the Death Star.

"No!" She started to move to escape the deadly stare of the oncoming demon. She was totally exposed on this boardwalk with no cover or hiding place to be found.

As the cloud drew closer, she felt a change come over her. A bolt of brilliant white light radiated down on her. Confused as to where this light was coming from, she looked up. Without a doubt it was emanating from the Thornton Mansion. At first, she thought it was another assault, but as it bathed her in its illumination, she felt a power welling up inside of her. A voice repeated, *"You can fight this. She cannot win. You can fight this."* And then, she wasn't afraid. She was angry. She was filled with a sense of empowerment.

Darcy stepped out from the shadows and looked up to the sky

"Time to introduce myself."

The dark, horrific face stared down at her. Darcy looked the menace in the eye and channeled a power that generated from somewhere deep inside of her. The closer the cloud got, the stronger she felt. She pointed to the sky, right at the face in the cloud.

"You want a piece of me!"

The face reacted with amusement.

Just then, the wind picked up, the cloud began to move, and in a matter of moments, the cloud dissipated, and the face was gone.

Darcy took a deep breath and walked to her car. As she opened the door, she threw her fist in the air and yelled, "Come back anytime! I'll be ready for you!"

She drove off, leaving Stan standing on the boardwalk.

Darcy burst through the back door of the realty office and marched directly over to Brandon Walker's desk. She grabbed him by the collar and placed her face very close to his. "If you keyed my new car, so help me, you will pay like hell for doing it."

Brandon went white, and his eyes bulged. "Darcy... I have no idea what you're talking about. You got a new car?"

Darcy could see in his eyes that he was telling the truth. He had no idea what she was talking about. She loosened her grip and then let go. He slid back into his chair.

"Yeah, I just picked it up yesterday. It has 43 miles on it now, and someone keyed it in the parking lot right after I got here this morning."

"Uh, I was in Aptos for a breakfast meeting and just got back about 10 minutes ago. It wasn't me."

Darcy had not seen Brandon that morning, and he often took business breakfast meetings.

"Yeah, that makes sense. Sorry, I'm just in love with that car, and I sort of lost control."

"No problem. I would have felt the same way, to be honest."

"Yeah, sorry." She helped straighten out Brandon's shirt and walked back to her desk.

Sherry walked over and said, "Now, that was intriguing even though I have no idea what the hell it was."

Darcy shook her head. "I don't know. All of a sudden, I'm not going to be intimidated. I'm just not. I don't know what it is either, but I'm not going to live in fear anymore."

"Well, if that's the way you react, I think the rest of us'll be the one's living in fear." Sherry chuckled and went off to answer a phone leaving Darcy to take deep and purposeful breaths.

"Yeah, you know what? I am not going to be living in fear. What do I have to be afraid of anyway?... I know what I want."

She took out her cell phone and called Kerry.

Chapter 32

At the end of the day, Darcy was in her apartment, pacing back and forth. "Stay away and stay safe. Stay away and stay safe. As long as I can stay away, I will have nothing to fear." She had pulled the drapes closed tight, and the late afternoon sun shone through in golden streams, leaving patterns on the carpet.

She poured herself a glass of wine. Before she had the chance to sit, the doorbell rang. She opened the door, and there stood Kerry. Without saying a word, she stepped toward him and hugged him tightly.

Kerry responded and then pulled back. "Hi. So, what's going on? Your call was a bit confusing."

She gestured for him to come into the apartment. The kitchen sat to the immediate right as you walked through the door. There was a tiny breakfast nook between the kitchen and living room that held a new dinette set with four matching chairs. The front room had a new leather sofa and love seat along with a new 60" flat screen that sat atop a bookcase that sported a few pictures of Darcy, her mother, and some friends.

"Want a beer or something?" She asked.

"Yeah, sure, whatever you got."

She handed Kerry a Pliny the Elder from the Russian River Valley and then sat on the sofa.

Kerry recognized the brand and whistled low in appreciation. He sat next to her.

She had calmed down a great deal since this morning, and she spoke in objective and precise terms.

"It was so weird, Kerry. It came for me right out of the sky. We went to the beach, and I didn't realize where I was. I thought that if I just stayed away that I would be safe."

"Stayed away?"

Her body language became more animated and her head shook from side to side.

"It was her. I don't know who "she" is, but she sure as hell hates me."

"Darcy, can you hear yourself? Do you know how crazy that sounds?"

"Of course, I do. I'm being stalked by an evil spirit, but I'm not out of my mind."

Kerry sat back on the sofa and dropped his hand on Darcy's knee. She reached down and put her hand over his.

"Thanks for coming. I don't know why but I really need to talk with you."

"Hey, who ya gonna call?" Kerry said with a wry smile.

"You don't believe me, do you?" She asked.

"I just don't understand."

Darcy paused to gather her thoughts. She took Kerry's hand and looked into his eyes.

"Since the first time I went up there, that first time with Childs, to show him the house, strange things have happened to me. He tried to kill me, Childs did. He tried to push me into the pool and feed me to whatever the hell is in there."

"Whatever is in where?" Kerry said.

"The pool, the tide pool. But I managed to get away from him. I figured that if I just stayed away, I'd be okay. Then you called about the dead battery. I didn't want to go up there, but I wanted to help you out. Something happened to me that day. You were there, you felt it as well. I know you did. But today, she reached out for me. Came for me at the beach. I didn't stay away, I got too close."

Kerry squeezed her hand.

"And today... I don't know what the hell happened, but I suddenly felt like I could confront her. I could take her, you know? I felt invincible. She laughed at me and blew away."

Kerry took a pause. "You know how this sounds?"

"Tell me! I barely believe it myself, and I was there."

"What happened when you came to pick me up?"

Darcy took a second before she looked at him.

"It's hard to explain. I was like, invaded. Something came into me and started to manipulate my emotions. The living room seemed to really set it off. I looked at you for help, and suddenly, you were like this entity, this entity that consumed my entire life. I looked at you and felt..."

"Love."

Darcy was astonished.

"Why do you say that?" She asked.

"Because I felt it too. But then again, I've always felt it."

Her eyes started to fill with tears. "No, it's just the house. The house is playing with our minds, making us feel things that aren't true." She got up off the couch and crossed to the other side of the room, afraid to look at him.

"I've loved you for years. I was just never ready to see it." Kerry said simply. "In the living room... that afternoon, you were glowing! You were so radiant, and I wanted to hold you so close. I realized it right on the spot. I just knew that I loved you."

"No, don't you see? It's the thing in the pool. It's making you think that you love me." She started to cry.

Kerry rose and crossed behind her. He gently put his hands on her shoulders.

"Darcy, you are the woman I have compared every other woman to for my whole life. You've broken up every relationship I have ever had, and you weren't even there. Make me love you? I have always loved you. I just never realized it for real till now."

He gently turned her to him and kissed her, not hard, not overly passionate, just the pure and simple first kiss of two people in love. They held it, absorbed in the purity. As they parted, they looked into each other's eyes.

"How can I be sure I can trust this? What if we are both being deluded by some kind of power outside our control?" She said.

"What do you feel in your heart?"

"Love."

"I feel it too. No power on earth could make us both feel like this if it wasn't true."

Kerry leaned over and kissed her again. She kissed him back. She reached down for the edges of his t-shirt and, in one fluid gesture, pulled it over his head. Her hands ran up his stomach and over his chest. He cupped her face with his hands and kissed her, this time with more passion. Guiding her to the floor, he laid her down on the golden carpet, and in her living room, with the curtains pulled tight and the light seeping through from under the sill, Darcy and Kerry made love for the first time since high school. It was a unique experience for them both because the first go around was about sex and discovery; this time, it was about love.

Chapter 33

A few exhausting hours later, they lay naked in her bed, cuddled in each other's arms. Kerry had a layer of dried sweat stuck to him that formed an adhesive bond with Darcy's cheek, nestled on his chest. Darcy had her eyes closed but wasn't sleeping. Kerry was awake and gently stroking Darcy's hair.

"So, where do we go from here?" he asked.

Darcy opened her eyes and slowly peeled her cheek away from his chest. She found a cool spot against his rippled stomach and plopped her head.

"I guess we just take it a day at a time. What else can we do?"

"I meant about the house. What are we going to do about this entity that has you so terrified?"

Darcy lay still. "I was hoping that we were talking about us. I don't want to ruin this moment."

"Okay, then how about I start. Logically, I'm going to have to choose between you and the job, right?"

"I can't ask you to do that. We haven't even been back together for four hours. Kinda early to be making demands, don't you think?"

"You aren't making any demands. I understand the deal. Eventually, that's going to be the issue, and you know what? It's just a gig. I can get another one tomorrow. You mean more to me than any job."

Darcy raised her head and looked at Kerry. "No. Really, you can't do that. Nothing has happened to you up there, and this is an important job for you. I'm not going to be that girl that starts taking things away from my guy just to prove that I can."

"If my being there is going to interfere with being with you, then screw it. I don't need the damn job," he said with conviction. "Childs will just have to get along without me. He's gonna go ballistic, but too damn bad. I don't give a crap about him. All of a sudden, you're my whole world. I have to be a good environmentalist and take care of that world. What kind of tree hugger would I be if I didn't?"

Darcy pulled herself close to Kerry and kissed his chest. She held on to him with all her might as tears of joy ran down her face. "I really don't want you up there, but not because I'm testing you, I don't want you to get hurt."

"Now, we have to be realistic. I don't know if I can just walk away. It wouldn't be very fair, not only to him but also to the guys on site."

"I can see that. I'm not going to pick you up from work, but I can understand," she said with a smile. "Just be careful and stay away from the pool. There is something very nasty out there, and if you are involved with me, it might put you on the radar."

"I can take care of myself. You don't need to worry." He leaned over and kissed her again. Suddenly, he couldn't seem to kiss her enough, which made sense. After all, they'd wasted the last ten years or so.

Chapter 34

Stan stood on the boardwalk with a smashing headache. She had beckoned him to get her here and he had, yet somehow he felt as though he had failed. The last thing he remembered was Darcy... doing something and then leaving him behind. He ordered a Lyft who dropped him at a hole in the wall bar where he drank. An hour later, the door to the dive opened and in walked Hannah Brower. She made her way directly over to Stan.

"How about this," Hannah said bluntly, "I get a drink, you finish yours, and we head to your place. Maybe we can find a way to ease our troubled minds."

Stan waved for his check.

"Fuck that! I have stuff to drink at my place. Let's go."

Two hours later, they lay naked on top of the covers, satisfied in a way that was new to them both. Hannah rolled over, her back to him, and asked, "So what are we supposed to be doing? I feel unprepared all the time like I'm not doing what I'm supposed to be doing."

"Who the fuck knows. I find myself watching Wainwright all day long like she's gonna turn into a goblin or something." He placed his hand on her ass and rubbed it because he could.

"I drive by her place four or five times a day like something is going to happen. Waste of time, but it seems I have no choice."

"I just wish I knew what the fuck was going on..."

As he said that, the room developed a weird reddish glow. Hannah sat up and looked around.

"What the hell? I thought you were lighting candles or something. What is..." She stopped mid-sentence. Stan watched as her eyes rolled around in their sockets, and she moved in front of him. Her hands came up, and she cupped his face firmly, fingers poking into his cheeks. Her head moved back and forth, up and down, until she spoke. It was not her voice that he heard, but he recognized it as the voice he had heard in his head.

"Darcy's a whore! She's fucking everyone, everyone but you. She hates you. That's why she won't fuck you." The voice creaked out of her like a car crash. "She's fucking that carpenter for chrissake, and she won't fuck you."

"I can make her want you." She tightened her grip on Stan's face as though to squeeze the sanity out of it. "The time is coming. Bring her to me, and I can make her want you, fuck you, and only you."

"Yes, yes, I want that. I want to fuck her. I want her naked and crying and to make her my slave." He screamed out.

"When the time comes, bring her to me, and she will want you above all others."

Her grip tightened, and Stan groaned. He struggled against her strength and finally broke her grasp. She immediately came back at him, and he slapped her hard across the face. She fell to the bed in a heap. Hannah moaned with pleasure and looked up at Stan. She had lust burning in her eyes.

"You motherfucker… fuck me now!"

She threw Stan on his back and ravished him repeatedly.

Chapter 35

The next afternoon, Kerry went looking for Henry Childs and found him in the living room staring at the west wall.

"Mr. Childs," Kerry started, trying to get his attention, "Do you have a minute?"

Henry did not respond. He was staring, in a yoga-like trance, at a newly wallpapered wall.

"Mr. Childs? You okay?"

Henry started to bob his head. With a slight shake, he blinked his eyes and became aware of his surroundings.

"I'm sorry."

"Are you alright?"

"Yes. Fine. Never better. I was just appreciating how beautiful the house is becoming. What can I do for you?" He turned to face Kerry.

"This is hard to explain, but I'm going to have to leave." Kerry said.

"I'm sorry? What do you mean?" Henry asked, confused.

"I have to quit. I can't work for you anymore. I'll find someone to replace me." Kerry said in rapid-fire succession.

Henry paused, still not clear on what Kerry was saying.

"But we're not finished."

"I know, but I have to give the job to someone else. It's hard to explain, but I really need to do this."

"I don't understand. Are you saying that you are not going to finish this job?" Henry was starting to bluster.

"Well, something's come up, and I have to go. I'm really sorry."

"What came up? What could have possibly come up that you would leave? Things are going so well. Surely, we can talk about this. There must be some arrangement we can come to. Can I offer you more money, anything?"

"There's nothing to say. I have to quit."

The two veins that ran across Henry's forehead were about to burst.

"You can't leave me. You must stay on until it's finished?"

"I'll stick around until we can find someone else. I already have a few guys in mind. I'll call them today, and we'll get them up here so you can meet them."

Henry's face was strawberry red, and his eyes were boring a hole through Kerry's forehead. He forced a deep breath and some color seemed to seep down his neck.

"I was just going to make some coffee. Why don't we have a cup, and we'll talk about this some more." Henry insisted with a chill in his voice that frosted the air in front of him. Without turning back, he softly spoke. "If you betray me Mr. Devine, you will be very sorry. I am not the one to screw with."

Kerry had never heard this tone come from Henry Childs.

"You threatening me, Mr. Childs?"

Walking into the kitchen Henry's head slowly bowed and from behind it suddenly looked like he was headless, his blob-like shoulders creating a valley where his head should have been. Kerry heard a snicker, and then a snort came from Henry.

He turned toward Kerry. There was drool running from the corner of his mouth and a river of snot ran from his right nostril. "Maybe you had better follow me. When you see this, you'll have second thoughts about betraying me."

He entered the kitchen and crossed immediately to the door that led out to the backyard. Kerry could see Henry's reflection in the upper portion of the glass. It was a new door, solid, three-pane upper with cut glass in the corners. The optical effect allowed Kerry to see several Henry's, each looking more displeased than the first.

As Henry's hand reached for the knob, a scrawny, nearly fleshless hand burst through, shattering the glass from the outside, spilling shards over the front of Henry Childs. It grabbed Henry's wrist and pulled him toward the door, breaking several other panes as it did.

Blood appeared around Henry's wrist as it scraped across the remnants of the glass.

Kerry was instantly on the move. He grabbed Henry and pulled him away from the door. As a soldier would throw a wounded comrade into a foxhole, Kerry threw Henry to the floor and hovered over him protectively.

"Someone call 911. I need some help in here."

He left Henry lying on the Italian tiled floor, and without words, he ran onto the porch, searching for the source of the danger. Kerry's mind went back to Darcy, naked and sweaty, begging him to stay away from the pool.

In an instant, however, Kerry threw those thoughts aside and dashed down the stairs. He came to a stop directly in front of the pool.

He saw nothing.

There was only the pool.

The water was shimmering in a Caribbean way, too blue for the northern California coast, crystal clear in parts, hazy in others.

It was then that he saw her.

On the island in the middle of the pool, a young woman dressed in nineteenth-century clothing appeared to be stranded. Her hair piled high on her head, and a ruffled collar encircled her neck. She hung her head and cried softly to herself.

"Hey... are you okay?"

He barely recognized his own voice, shaky and horse as though he had rust on his vocal cords.

She responded by slowly raising her head. She had a tortured look in her eye. He thought eye, singular because, for some reason, he could only see one of them. As the woman completed her turn and faced him head-on, he saw that the entire left side of her face was missing.

She let out a cry of anguish that shook him.

As her mouth opened, he saw rows of small, pointed teeth. Her tongue raked back and forth as she licked her lips, and strips of ripped flesh fell from her mouth. She reached for him from across the pool. Instead of being safely out of reach, she was suddenly right in front of him, and he was in her grasp.

Kerry pushed out his arms to protect himself and screamed.

He fought and twisted and turned trying to get away from this monster. A flash of color blinded him. He fought as only a terrified man can fight. He felt the warm water dripping off her as he struggled to pull away. The more he struggled, the wetter he got. He was being held down as though she suddenly had four arms. He kicked his feet and twisted and turned before he realized it was Henry standing over him with a towel. Fred and a couple of the workers were holding him down. The warm water was actually blood gushing from a gouge in his forearm and onto his chest as he struggled with them to escape.

He was lying on the freshly installed Italian tiled kitchen floor. It was his arm that was bleeding. It was his arm that had gone through the glass door. It was his arm that needed to be stitched. This couldn't be... it was Henry... it was.

Chapter 36

At the weekly sales meeting, the office had been informed that Stan Grossman would no longer be working at Lewis Realty. He was leaving 'to pursue other opportunities,' which everyone recognized as code for being fired. His performance had dropped off so drastically in the last few months that no one was surprised. Just after that announcement, he also announced that Stan's old office, the larger one in the front of the building, now belonged to Darcy. There was a small spattering of applause, and everyone headed off to 'sell some properties.'

Darcy had just completed the move into the new space, unsure of exactly what she wanted to do with the walls and the color, when Shelly came racing back to Darcy's desk, "Darce, there's been an accident." Her tone brought back a childhood memory of her mother phoning everyone she knew in a panic, trying to find her father. The young Darcy, not more than six years old, could remember the desperation and anguish in her mother's voice. She heard those same qualities in Shelly's.

"What is it?"

"There was an accident. Kerry's been hurt. He's at County."

Darcy went white. Immediately, she knew that it was her fault. She let him go back to that hell hole of a house, and now he was hurt. She reached for her purse and keys, her hands shaking visibly.

"Oh no! You aren't driving, not like this," Shelly said.

"I'll take you to the hospital," Brandon said, reaching for her hand.

Numbed by his words, Darcy lifted her hand to his and allowed him to pull her to the front door of the office.

"What happened?" She looked at Shelly.

"I'm not sure. They just said to get there as soon as you can." Shelly said.

"I'll take you. It'll be all right." Brandon reassured her.

"It doesn't matter. Let's just get there." The only thing that mattered to her at that moment was Kerry.

It took them eight minutes to get to the hospital and another four to find the emergency room. Brandon dropped her off. "Would you like me to stay?"

She didn't answer and ran to the desk.

"I'm looking for Kerry Devine. He was just brought here?"

The woman behind the counter, a heavy, African American woman wearing a green sweater over a blue t-shirt, looked up from her crossword puzzle and asked, "You related?"

Darcy stumbled a bit, wanting to say that she was his fiancé but meekly stated, "No. I'm his girlfriend."

"Well, girlfriend," the woman said, "We don't give no info to no girlfriends. Most times, they the ones that sent these guys here."

"Look," Darcy said with growing anger, "My…friend was hurt in a work accident. I didn't send him here. I just want to know how he is. Could you please let me know if he's alive? We just got back together, and..."

Just then, she heard his weak, beleaguered voice.

"Hey. How'd you get here?" Kerry said from the confines of his wheelchair.

She spun around and saw him sitting there, his right hand in a cast, and a young nurse pushing him toward the front desk.

"Oh my God, Kerry! What happened? I was so scared. I thought she got you. I thought you were dead!" She threw her arms around his neck and kissed him hard.

When she finally pulled away, Kerry said, "If this is your reaction, I'm going to get hurt more often."

"Shut up. You scared me to death. What is this?" she gestured to the cast that encompassed his entire right forearm.

"Long story. Look, I really just want to go home."

"Yeah, sure, of course," Darcy said.

At that moment, the doctor walked up. He was a shorter, stout man with graying temples and a bushy salt and pepper beard.

"Hello, I'm Doctor Chandler. Are you with Mr. Devine?"

"Yes, I'm... his friend. What happened?"

"Kerry apparently put his hand through a plate glass door. He hit it at a slight upward angle and sliced a jagged tear through the anterior surface of the wrist in his right hand, right about here," he said, indicating the spot on his own wrist. "When we went to stitch it up, we discovered he had severed a nerve, and I had to go in to repair the damage. He's going to be out of commission for two months, minimum."

"Why is the cast like that?" She asked, referring to the bent wrist and the severe right angle of the setting.

"The position of the wrist is important in the healing process. We have to stabilize it at a forty-five-degree angle to allow the nerve to heal properly. There will be some loss of sensation along his index finger and thumb. Over time much of it will come back, and I don't see it being disabling in any significant fashion."

"Thank you, doctor. What do I need to do to take care of him?"

"Just take him home and let him sleep. He'll be in some discomfort for the next day or so, but that will pass. If you have any other questions, just give us a call."

Doctor Chandler walked away. Darcy turned to Kerry and, with forced cheerfulness, said, "How ya doing there, stud?"

"I'm ready to get out of here."

"Okay then, let's go." She walked behind the wheelchair and started to push him toward the door. "Oh my God. I just realized; Brandon drove me. I don't have my car."

From out of the waiting room walked Stan Grossman, "No prob, I'll take you wherever you need to go."

"Stan? What are you doing here?" Darcy said with surprised suspicion.

"I heard about Kerry and wanted to be sure you guys were okay. I wasn't far away, so I just popped over."

"You 'popped' over?" Darcy asked.

"It's not a big deal. Do you need a lift somewhere?"

"I'd appreciate it," Kerry said.

"Sure. I'll bring the car around."

He turned and sprinted to get the car.

"Are you crazy? What the hell?" Darcy asked Kerry.

Kerry looked at his cast and said, "It'll be fine."

Darcy nodded, and she leaned close to Kerry and asked, "Was it the pool?"

"I'm not really sure what it was. I remember standing in the backyard, and there was a woman on the island dressed in antique clothing."

"In the backyard? What happened?" Darcy asked.

"You know, I don't really remember. I was talking to Henry, and he was pissed. Then, there was a woman with no face on an island? It's all a blur. I don't know. Honestly, I don't know."

Just then, Stan blew the horn. Darcy pushed the chair out to the loading area and helped get Kerry into the front. She ran around and climbed in behind Stan, and they were off.

"Where to? I'm sorry, but I don't know where you live, Kerry." Stan said innocently enough.

"We're going to my place, turn left at the light," Darcy said, leaving no room for negotiation. Stan grimaced.

Twenty minutes later, Stan was helping Darcy deposit Kerry onto the sofa in the front room. Kerry had actually not needed much help, but Darcy was over him like he was a wounded fawn.

"Okay. I've got the prescription the doctors gave you. I'll go pick it up. Will you be okay for a few minutes?"

"I'm fine," Kerry said, about to fall back asleep.

"I'll stay with him if you want," Stan said.

"Oh, that's not necessary, really. I'll only be gone a few minutes."

"It's no trouble. I'll just keep my eye on him while you're out."

Kerry waved to Darcy, "Just go. It'll be fine."

Darcy kissed Kerry on the cheek and grabbed her purse as she ran out.

After she was gone, Kerry said, "You know, Stan, I really appreciate all the help. You don't even know me but I appreciate it just the same." Kerry settled himself on the sofa.

"No problem. Darcy's told me all about you." Stan moved to the armchair facing the sofa and sat. "Don't feel you have to stay awake on my account. If you need to sleep, go right ahead."

But he was talking to himself. Kerry had already dropped off.

Watching him on the couch Stan's expressive smile turned into an acidic sneer. He looked at the sleeping carpenter as his mind filled with hatred. This was the man that stood between him and Darcy's luscious lips. He picked up one of the throw pillows from the sofa, thinking that he could take care of this problem right away, cover his face, and apply pressure. But it wasn't his choice to make. It would be up to her if he lived or if he died.

The front door opened. There was Darcy, breathing heavily as she had just run back up the stairs.

"What are you doing back so soon?" he asked, feigning surprise.

"I don't have a car. I left it at the office. You're going to have to drop me off to get it. Would you mind?"

"What about Kerry? Will he be okay?"

She looked over at the sleeping Kerry.

"He's already asleep. If I hurry, I bet I can be back before he wakes up."

"Okay. If that's what you want." Stan said, happy to be alone with Darcy yet again.

In the car, Darcy said, "I'm really sorry about what happened with Tim. But you've been so irresponsible lately."

"No worries. I was pretty tired of that old grind anyway." Stan muttered. "I'll land on my feet."

He dropped her in the employee lot at the office, and Stan watched her run to her car. She opened her door and jumped in. Darcy's car sped out of the lot, her brake lights illuminating his face in a malevolent, red glow as she turned the corner and disappeared.

It's almost my time, you bitch.

Chapter 37

"Mother, I'll be going out to run some errands, so you're on your own for a few hours. Can I get you anything before I go?" Henry said, bustling into his mother's room.

Edith Childs was standing at the window looking out over the front yard.

"Why are they all just sitting around? You have all of those Mexicans sitting on the lawn smoking. Why aren't they working?"

Henry crossed next to her and glanced out the window.

"Mother, don't concern yourself with that. There is a method to the madness that you simply would not understand."

"Well, where's that tall, good-looking man, the one in charge? Shouldn't he be putting those men to work, telling them what to do? Doing his job?"

"Yes, he should, and I will talk to him about that. Please, sit down and watch your programs. I'll be back in a bit. Do you need anything else before I go?

Edith looked sideways at Henry, scoffed, and sat down.

"I'm fine. Just go off and run your very important errands. I'll stay here alone and watch the damn television."

Henry took a deep breath and, with great restraint, said, "Very well, mother. I'm off, see you later. Be certain not to use the stairs."

Henry made his way down the front staircase and walked out onto the porch.

On the grass, under a tree, sat the three-day workers who had actually shown up. They were leaning against a pallet load of bricks, smoking. Since Kerry's accident, the number of men who would report to work had decreased exponentially. Fred, the foreman, wasn't returning his calls. Not knowing what else to do, he walked over to the group. Fortunately, one of the workers spoke decent English.

"What is the plan for today? Where is everyone?" he demanded.

"Dunno."

"Where's Fred?"

"Dunno. I think he is not coming. He's afraid of the boogeyman that lives here." He said with a smirk.

"Boogeyman? What on earth?"

"When Senor Kerry is hurt, many men don't come back. They afraid of this place, 'La Casa de la Diablo' they all say."

The man scrunched up his face and used his hands to give himself devil horns. The other two men covered their mouths as they stifled hearty laughs.

"Oh, they do. Do they? And what about you? Aren't you afraid?".

"No, senor, we not afraid of you." The man looked at his amigos, causing them to laugh even harder.

The years of ridicule came rushing back to him.

"Get out of here. All of you. I don't want any of you ever to set foot on this property again. Get out!"

Henry picked up a shovel that had been lying in front of the trio and started swinging it over his head in a helicopter motion.

His face was pinched in rage, and veins popped out of his fleshy throat as it whipped back and forth under his chin. His stomach quaked with each gyration. The shovel rotated over his head as he yelled, "Get. Out. Of. My. Yard!"

The three men rolled away from Henry in different directions and made their way quickly to their feet. They fanned out instinctively to surround Henry in an attempt to keep him at bay.

"I want you out," Henry screamed as mounds of fat roiled with fury under his cardigan. "I want you out, now!"

"You, a goddamn loco motherfucker," the man with the red bandana said. "I outta fuck you up." He started laughing and dancing in front of Henry, inciting him, making devil horns on his head and then jabbing at Henry with quick stabbing motions as if he was going to knife-fight him.

Henry spun around several times and launched the shovel in the direction of the man with the red bandana, bouncing it off the pavement. The shovel threw up a wave of sparks as it hit the asphalt and then, bouncing up, raked the man across the shins. He fell to the ground screaming and clutching his leg, his dirty jeans were ripped open by the shovel. Blood was beginning to absorb into the faded blue fabric.

"You crazy motherfucker. I'm gonna rip your ass," he growled, clenching his teeth together in pain.

Henry reached down into the pile of red bricks and picked up one in each hand. He threw one at the downed man, who rolled out of the way just as the red brick shattered on the driveway.

"Get out of here now, you assholes. I want you out of my yard!" He heaved the second brick toward them.

Carrying their wounded friend, the men scurried down the driveway and around the corner, yelling over their shoulders as they ran. "We'll be back, you crazy fuck. You gonna pay for this, shithead."

Henry was wild with frustration and anger, and without a thought, he picked up another brick and heaved it at the house. The brick sailed much further than a sane Henry would ever have thrown it, ripping the skin off of his palm as it was released and shattered the window of the front door.

Henry slumped to the ground. He was at a loss. He stared at the house for the first time with contempt. So what if the house was never finished? The remodel was merely a means to an end, a pretense of disguising his actual objective. He had obtained the necessary knowledge to accomplish his true mission. He began to see the silver lining.

Henry stood and headed to his car, filled with thoughts of freedom. No more interruptions, no more furtive glances as he left or came back from his afternoon sojourn. Henry climbed into his Dodge Ram and turned the key. Slamming it into gear, he headed out of the driveway humming to himself.

Henry turned right at the base of the driveway, beginning the routine that he had developed over the last few months. In five short minutes, he arrived at the florist at the bottom of the hill, the one in the little strip mall on the corner of the Pacific Coast Highway, where he had a running account.

Each and every day, he would pull into the sweet-smelling shop and pick up the same order, a dozen white water lilies.

"Good afternoon, Mr. Childs. I have your order ready to go, as usual." The man said, cha-chinging the cash register in his head.

Henry thanked the man and climbed back into his car, turned left onto the Pacific Coast Highway, and drove exactly one and four-tenths miles until he came to a small turnout. He signaled and turned left again, completing the giant circle that would bring him to her.

Beyond the inconspicuous turnout, there was a dirt road that led up the hillside to the back of Henry's property, the same road used by Frank's Pool Service to stock the pool.

This sunny afternoon Henry drove the big truck up the hill and parked under a large cluster of brush that hid it from view. He stole up the sandy cliffside unseen, carrying the dozen water lilies.

Hidden on the ocean side of the cliff was a cave that led to an observation room beneath the surface of the pool. She had shown it to him on their first date. Henry soon learned that the room had two entrances. One was in the backyard, inside a dilapidated shed, and the other was accessible from the cliffs below the house. The cliffside entrance was out of view of the house, and he could access this sanctuary without prying eyes questioning him.

He ducked under the branches of the ivy brush that covered the opening and stepped into the cooler shade of the cave. A few feet inside the mouth of the cave was a door. It was a new, heavy, wooden door that had been weather treated and hung on twelve-inch gate hinges attached to a substantial doorframe. The whole assembly was inset into the cliff. Around the frame was an airtight rubber seal. Henry punched in the eight-digit code on the keypad, and the big door swung towards him without a sound. He had never hung a door before, and the fact that it had worked so perfectly thrilled him to no end. He had Coley Ford to thank for that. He was the one who had given him the secret of hanging doors. Of course, no one ever hangs a door perfectly the first time, and Henry was no exception. He had hung it in such a fashion that it opened out. Exterior doors were generally meant to open in so that they could be barred against intruders.

Once inside the exterior door, he reached to his right and picked up a yellow flashlight that lived on a small shelf against the wall. With a flick of the switch, Henry filled the little chamber with light. He pulled the first door silently closed behind him.

When the outside door had been closed and sealed by the rubber gasket that outlined it, Henry turned to the interior of the space. The little tunnel he was standing in was only eight feet wide. It was reminiscent of the kind of mineshaft seen in the old westerns that he had watched as a kid.

Holding the flashlight under his arm and the flowers in one hand, Henry stepped to the second door, punched in a different eight-digit code, and the deadbolt opened.

Henry pulled the door open and was careful to close it tight to maintain the airtight seal. This door also opened out. He turned to the room and let out a sigh of intense satisfaction.

This was his underground sanctuary.

The room that Henry basked in at that moment was quite a bit different from the dirty, insect infested, spider habitat that he had entered several months ago. When he first saw this space, stagnant pockets of water dotted the floor and had been the drowning pool for more than a fair share of rodents. The beams that supported the rock ceiling were rotted, and it would not have been too long before they had failed. Henry had replaced them just in time.

The walls had been covered with thick, green moss and algae, and Henry had rubbed his knuckles raw, removing the stubborn vegetation. Underneath, he found beautiful red rock walls that cast a subtle copper reflection over the room when the light from the pool bounced off it.

On the back wall, he discovered a work of art scratched into the soft rock. It was a rock fresco depicting the masthead of a ship, an ancient drawing of a woman, naked from the waist up, head pointed straight ahead, her hair blowing behind her as she boldly led her crew out into the vast undiscovered ocean. Beneath it were the words, 'My Life Is Yours.' Like scrimshaw, each chisel mark had been intricately executed. The image was almost the full height of the wall and nearly as wide. Henry had meticulously cleaned the etching and had managed to restore a good deal of its beauty. He clicked on the three battery-powered key lights he had hung. They illuminated it with a soft glow. Yet, as beautiful as it was, the etching was not the centerpiece of the room.

That honor was reserved for the observation window.

The window was spectacular. Thirty feet wide and ten feet high, there were three vertical supports that dissected it from top to bottom, making each window panel ten feet by ten feet. The observation window was concave, so it wrapped around the observer, creating the illusion of being in the pool rather than watching it. He had replaced the rotted wooden frame around the window with a new one, simpler but just as elegant. He stained it crimson red to match the rock. The glass had remained intact and secure, holding back the water and allowing him to become part of her world.

Against the side wall, there was a king size bed with a large wrought iron headboard. The mattress was encased in a plastic sheath to protect it in this humid environment. There were cotton sheets on the bed and a black bedspread. The bed stood on a small, concrete pedestal that raised it a foot above the cavern floor.

As he admired his handiwork, the light from the sun emanated through the depths and into the room, the water casting aqua-blue, rippling shadows across the floor. Beams of sunlight streaked through the water, illuminating a sandy sea floor thick with vegetation.

The room was exactly as she had demanded it to be, completely returned to its original glory.

He walked to the window and placed his cheek against the glass. He followed with his entire body, arms spread wide, and started to hum. The sunlight outlined his pudgy face as he pressed it against the glass, his warm breath clouding in front of his mouth. The heat from his body contrasted with the coolness of the glass and caused a thin layer of condensation to form an outline of his mass.

Momentarily the light began to change. A flash zipped by the window teasing him with a glimpse.

Henry smiled.

The sunlight streaking through the pool began to revolve on its axis and change in hue like an underwater disco ball. The streaks became different colors. There was a vivacious blood red, a brilliant pine green, a yellow so bright it hurt to look at it. A deep blue streak set itself off against the blue of the water and made the water look muted and lifeless by comparison.

There was another flash, and the room was suddenly filled with colors bouncing around the cavern like pool balls after the break. Henry reveled in it.

He pulled his face away from the glass, leaving an almost perfect outline of his profile where the condensation had accumulated. He moved to the far end of the window. There, a steel cover, much like the hatch found on the top of a submarine, securely covered a quiet little pool of water, only three feet across. This hatch was an entrance, a passageway in and out of the pool from the chamber. The chamber itself was an airlock that allowed direct access into the deepest portions of the pool, hence the double-door entryway. With no escape for the air, the room maintained a positive pressure that kept the water from flowing into the chamber, creating, in essence, an erotic air pocket. Henry grabbed the two levers that secured the hatch in place and opened them. Lifting the gun metal hatch, color began to shoot out from this smaller pool. Henry giggled like a schoolboy caught peeking into the girl's bathroom.

The water started to twirl. It became a whirlpool running counterclockwise. It twirled faster and faster, opening a funnel in the center. From the center of this funnel, a head appeared, and she rose slowly out of the water.

She was here: Henry's vision of holiness. Roxanne to his Cyrano, this lovely creature rose full out of the water and beckoned for him. She floated in front of him, a testament to absolute beauty. She was naked from the waist up, and her long, flowing hair hung down well past her waist. Her breasts were full and firm, and rivulets of water ran between them. Henry caught his breath as she stood before him, and he fell into her as if she were his grave.

Chapter 38

Kerry bolted upright, covered in sweat, and thrust out his hands.

"*Run*! Darcy, run!"

Darcy popped out of a dead sleep and jumped out of bed, disoriented and confused. She broke through the fog and began to grab reality from the jaws of sleep. She saw Kerry, all the color drained from his face, his hair plastered to his soaked forehead.

She rushed back into bed and held him tightly in her arms. The sheets around him were soaking wet.

"Hey, it's okay, it's a dream. I'm right here. Nothing to worry about. It was just a dream."

Kerry exhaled deeply.

"Are you sure?" he whispered.

"What do you mean? Of course, it was. What else could it be?"

A veil of confusion settled on his face. He said, "A memory."

"Of what?" Darcy asked.

"I had a dream, but it felt like a memory. We were in the Thornton house—" Kerry told Darcy his dream.

Darcy and Kerry had been dating for two years, since they were thirteen. Kerry had previously been seeing Hannah Brower, the future police sergeant, but he left her once he met Darcy. On this hot summer day, they were looking for somewhere to be alone and make out. They had a routine. They would kiss and hug, and whenever he started going too far, she would emulate the 'time-out' gesture of a football referee and Kerry would stop before things got out of control. He had countered with the argument that there are three time-outs per half, so he should get at least that many, but Darcy had never fallen for that lame argument and kept vigilant control of their sexual activities. She had a strict set of guidelines, and being a red-blooded adolescent male, Kerry challenged those lines every chance he could. The farthest he ever got was one hand on one breast outside of her clothes. But he held out hope for more. It had been two years, after all.

On this brisk fall day, on a dare from several of their friends, they rode their bikes up to the old Thornton Mansion. They were supposed to break into the old house and make out for ten minutes. If they could do that and get out alive, they would gain some serious schoolyard cred.

As their bikes passed the 'For Sale' sign that stood by the old, rusted gate, they giggled. Dropping their bikes on the porch and taking each other's hands, they walked to the front door. The front door was not only locked but nailed shut with large, galvanized spikes.

"Guess they really don't want anyone in here." Kerry chuckled. "But I'm not giving up so easy." Darcy smiled, impressed by his determination.

Looking to his left, he saw that there was a broken window, and after kicking out the last few shards, he managed to climb through.

"See, nothing to it. Come on."

Darcy giggled as he helped her through. Once inside, he took her hand and, in that instant, realized that they were alone in the abandoned house. The combination of fear, mixed with anticipation created quite a palpable vibe around the two of them.

They crossed through the front hallway and into the living room. The old fireplace, the mantle splintered and rotting, and the stone faded and chipped, dominated the far wall. There were two decaying bookcases on either side of the fireplace, several shelves missing. It was dusty, chilly, and dark, but the two found it very romantic.

"What do you say? This looks cozy." Kerry said.

Darcy spread out the old blanket they had brought, sat down, and let out a nervous giggle. The idea that this was a haunted house was creating an additional level of sensuality to the moment. Kerry sat next to her and took her hands.

"Well, we've made it this far. Time to do our duty and make out!"

Kerry leaned over and kissed her softly. She scooted closer to him and wrapped her arms around his neck. Kerry slowly moved his hands over Darcy's back. She responded to him in a way that he had never felt her do before. He pulled her closer, and they fell to their sides on the blanket. She shivered and moaned, getting him very excited. Her hands caressed his face, stroking his cheeks and neck.

His hands began to roam. In a heartbeat, his hand was cupping her breast over the sweatshirt she was wearing.

"Aren't you a bit hot in that sweatshirt?"

"Yeah," said Darcy, and with that, she sat up and grabbed the lower corners of the sweatshirt and ripped it off over her head. Underneath, she was wearing a T-shirt with the inscription, "My parents went to Alcatraz, and all I got was this stupid shirt." The word 'Alcatraz' was stretched almost perfectly over her breasts.

In no time at all, he had made it to 'Alca,' and he alternated soon to 'Traz.' Her body shivered under his touch and settled as she leaned into him.

Getting bolder, he made his move. He slid his right hand under her shirt and rested it high on her hip.

Darcy had no response.

He slid his hand a little higher over her peach-fuzz stomach and touched the base of her bra, still no stop sign. It was his lucky day! The erotic nature of the house and being alone together had altered her aversion to skin-to-skin contact, and he had no intention of questioning her choice.

He proceeded north.

This was the first time Kerry had ever had skin-to-bra contact. He felt the stiff ridges of the elastic and the amazing, soft fabric of the cup. He was drawing a mental picture of what the bra looked like by exploring it with his fingers. He felt some type of embroidered image on the bra, probably little flowers. He had seen them on his sister's bra as it had come out of the washer.

Kerry's face was buried, alternately kissing her ear and the nape of her irresistible neck. His hand was roaming like a blind man reading a Braille Penthouse Forum, alternating from left to right to be sure he didn't miss anything.

There is no way she realizes what I'm doing because she'd have called time-out by now.

He wanted to look at Darcy's bra but was afraid that if he raised his head to see it, she would be alerted to what was going on, and she would stop him.

His hand maneuvered to the top of the bra cup, and he felt the lacy edge pass under his fingers. He was skin to skin with the top of her breast. Not waiting to see if there was a stop sign coming, Kerry slid his fingers under the lace and along the silken flesh of Darcy's left breast. He moved in for a better grasp. He could feel the nipple with his fingertip and pushed his whole hand into the bra cup from the top to get a better hold.

Still no stop sign.

This was amazing. He could feel the knobby texture around the nipple and the hard, jutting point that was being thoroughly explored by his enthusiastic forefinger. The bra crushed the nipple, so it was a bit harder to stroke, but he seemed up to the challenge.

No stop sign.

If she was letting him get this far, then he had to take the next step.

The bra must come undone! With his right hand occupied, in the inverted position necessary to slide under her bra in the front, his left hand cruised around her waist to the middle of her back and snaked up to the bra hook. Houdini himself would be stumped at the physicality of this maneuver. However, Kerry was gifted. With a quick pinch, slide, and pop, he unhooked his first bra. Recognizing the freedom, switched positions and attacked from beneath.

Even with this advancement, there was no stop sign.

She should have stopped me by now.

If she didn't stop him, not only might he pop the buttons of his 501 jeans, but he might have to go all the way.

What if I actually have to make love to her?

There were too many variables in that scenario, and he had no idea how to sort them all out. Even though he knew pulling back his head to talk to her might alert her to the fact he was fondling her naked breasts with a certain amount of gusto.

I gotta say something!

He pulled his head out from the sweet folds of her neck and looked at Darcy. Expecting to see an expression of ecstasy or joy or relief or even panic, he was stunned by what he saw. Darcy was staring blankly at the wall on the opposite side of the room.

"Darcy?" Kerry said, puzzled but unwilling to release her breasts just yet. "Darcy? What's wrong?"

She stared straight ahead. There was no ecstasy in her eyes. There was no exhilaration on her face. There was nothing. She hadn't given him the stop sign because she really hadn't realized what he was doing. Kerry learned in that instance that the worst thing a woman could do was not to scorn you or berate you or torture you but to be completely indifferent to you. She was staring blankly into space, not only unmoved by his fondling but unaware of it. He felt immediately guilty.

A movement reflected off the glassy pupils of Darcy's stare. Panic raced through him as he turned to see what was behind him.

What if it was her mother?

But he wasn't that lucky.

On the wall across the room, there was a fading, yellowish shadow. It could have been the shadow from a tree or a large bush… but it wasn't. It could have been a faded area of the wallpaper that was catching the dusky light, but it wasn't. This thing was more than a shadow, it had more substance, more texture. It floated languidly on the surface of the wall, undulating with a slow, steady rhythm making him wonder if it was real or just in his imagination. Kerry knew that there was no source for this figure. The shape was a source in and of itself.

Then it began to move.

The shadow moved with deliberation from left to right, circling the room. It was first shaped like a tree, then an animal, then a man and a woman. It shifted between figures as though it was deciding which best suited its purpose. On its second rotation of the room, it settled into the shape of a woman. A charcoal caricature of a woman, like the kind you'd get down on the boardwalk, the head out of proportion, and the body all shapely or muscular. This shadow was like a hologram of one of those caricatures. The head was larger than it should have been. The hair was Medusa-like and unruly. The torso was thick at the shoulders and slender at the waist. It was a cross between a bodybuilder and a model, disproportionate and incongruous.

The figure started to move with more purpose. It clung to the walls as it swam across the wallpaper, arms waving up and down like a warning. Kerry watched it shape-shift to fit the contours of the wall. As it slid toward the corner of the room, it made the ninety-degree turn and continued moving around them.

He was mesmerized by the motion until he felt Darcy's young heart pounding under his right hand. He had not yet removed his hand from her left breast, and the pounding of her heart vibrated beneath it.

Coming back to his senses, he quickly released her breast and grabbed her arms. He shook her in rapid short bursts.

"Darcy! Wake up! Wake up!"

She didn't respond. Darcy's eyes followed the slithery gray object's every move. When her eyes had reached their limit of movement, they swung back to the opposite side of her face and waited.

Kerry had to turn his head to look for the shape. It was circling the room and picking up speed as it did, arms waving in a histrionic manner. The centrifugal force of its own movement was propelling it faster around the walls of the room. It shape-shifted over the fireplace and the doorframes, adapting to whatever contour it encountered. It circled them with increasing speed. Something inside him said that if they were still in this room when that thing was moving fast enough to cover all corners simultaneously, they were done for. The shadow continued to pick up speed and was beginning to blur. Kerry yelled out, "Run, Darcy, run!

Chapter 39

As Darcy listened to Kerry explain his dream, she remembered the bike ride, she remembered climbing through the window, and she remembered the room exactly as he had described it.

"But it feels like I saw the movie as a kid and only remember bits and pieces."

"It makes a kind of bizarre sense. In the dream, we're in the living room at the Thornton house, and a woman's shadow is haunting us. We were in the same living room when you saw the aura around me." Kerry turned on his side to face her.

"The cloud that attacked me was a woman. I'm sure of that."

"And there's a woman on the island in the pool. Tell me this is all coincidence. We have to do some research on this house. Do you have any paperwork or historical data at the office?" Rubbing his eyes, Kerry crossed to the desk and opened his laptop.

She thought of the old manilla folder. "Well, yeah, but I never really read it all."

"Maybe what we've got is a ghost or something that's looking for closure and is asking us for help. You know, Ghost Whisperer-er."

"You don't really believe that do you?" Darcy asked.

"Now come on, you've been having your fair share of dreams too. I can tell by the way you're tossing and turning. What are they about?"

Darcy's face looked as though she'd forgotten to feed the cat for the last month.

"I don't remember. But I know you're right," she shuddered and dropped her head on Kerry's shoulder.

"There's a lot of urban legends attached to this place, but who do we know that has really died there? I mean, name one person."

"I can't," Darcy said. "Is it all just legend?"

He searched the web for the next hour. He found a number of newspaper articles, each chronicling a death or bizarre event that had been connected with the Thornton House. He had found names and dates, and further digging only produced more trivial information. There was a surprising amount of pictures of the original structure and that offered a different perspective on the house itself but nothing that was really relevant to their cause.

He turned to share what he had learned with Darcy, but she was asleep. Her head was moving up and down, and her face was contorted. He knew in an instant that she was having another nightmare

Chapter 40

In the nightmare, Darcy saw herself lift the gun, hold it to her head and pull the trigger. She felt the bullet enter her skull and almost at the same time felt the back of her head explode outward.

Reset!

She was walking down the street. A car pulled up, and a man leaned out the window holding a gun. He placed it against the front of her head and pulled the trigger. She felt the back of her skull explode.

Reset!

She was dancing with Kerry. He swept her off her feet and twirled her around. She spun away from him and then was pulled back into his chest. He had a gun and placed it against her forehead. He smiles, says that he loves her, and pulls the trigger. She feels the back of her skull explode.

Reset!

Darcy woke the next day tired and scared. Kerry was sound asleep next to her, a printed stack of everything that he'd learned about the history of the Thornton Mansion by the computer. She slipped out of bed, dressed as quietly as she could and headed to the office.

The dog-eared file had been put back in the general office file in the back room. She pulled it out with two fingers, afraid that the pages would come to life and devour her. Sliding it into her bag, she went back to her car and drove home. Her phone buzzed, and she looked at the incoming text.

Woke up & u were gone. Where r u?

office. file. BRB.

By the time she arrived, Kerry was making breakfast. She dropped the file on the table, threw her arms around him and held him tight.

As she devoured her scrambled eggs and bacon Kerry said, "Okay, this is what I found out last night from my search. It only went back to 1928, but here we go. Sandra and Harry Bellows were both schoolteachers. They inherited a modest amount of money from Sandra's father. Using it as a down payment, they moved into the house in the spring of 1928. They moved out in October of '28 and sold the house back to the trust for the original purchase price. No explanation that I could find."

"Over the next... thirty-two years, the house sold four times, and each time it was sold back to the trust within a year."

"Wow, it's like the house didn't want anyone living there."

"The next time it's bought, and this is when the real trouble starts, is by Harry and Colleen Van De Lin. They bought it in 1960. They'd relocated from Sacramento to open Harry's law office. He was involved in water rights, which is a big business in California. Colleen stayed home and took care of their daughter, Theresa. Harry and Colleen were found a month later- drowned in the pool."

"They were both naked. It was assumed that during a romantic tryst in the pool, the lovers became tangled in the sea vegetation and drowned. It was later determined that Colleen was pregnant. There's nothing here on what happened to the little girl."

"Okay, I am now freaked. We just named dead people in the house," Darcy said as she held the printout of the Van De Lin's story, the paper shaking in her hands. "So much for maintaining urban legend status."

"And here we go again, from 1961 until 1987, the house was sold twice, and both times the owners resold it back to the trust. Then, in '87 Mrs. Theresa McFadden, a wealthy widow, bought it. She lived in the house from 1987 - 1991."

"Mrs. Theresa McFadden, widowed wife of Thomas McFadden of McFadden Industries, moved into the house in the fall of '87 and lived there until the summer of '91 when the widow was discovered in the laundry room, eviscerated with a knife used to shell clams. Her male secretary had killed himself by jumping from the cliffs in the back corner of the yard. He was found dead in the surf below, an apparent murder/suicide."

"That's how Frank the pool guy died."

Kerry reached for the next printout that would tell them about Phil and Mary Hale.

"We're coming into the electronic age, so there's a bit more information available." Kerry said, "Phil Hale, adopted son of a millionaire and heir to the Gerald Hale fortune."

"Hale, as in Hale Hill?"

Darcy was already certain of their inevitable deaths.

"That would be the one. He bought the house on a bet in 1993."

"A bet? How did you find that out?"

"It was in a Gambler's Anonymous magazine. It was referenced in one of the articles, and I was able to track it down. Kind of a 'Don't Let This Happen to You' story. The terms of the bet stated that if Phil could live in the house for a year, he would win $50,000 plus be reimbursed for the price of the house. The stipulation was that he had to spend every night of the year in the house and had to be around at the end of the year to collect."

"This is like watching a B-grade horror flick. 'Let's hide in the cemetery!'"

"Phil had a best friend, a guy named Blackie Jordon, and they took a statement from him. Blackie says, "Phil didn't believe in ghosts. He didn't believe in all the hocus pocus of curses and spells. Plus, Phil wasn't the kind of man who would back down from a challenge. So, against Mary's wishes, he accepted the bet, and they moved into the Thornton house."

"He told me that after the first night, he looked at his wife and said, "Three hundred and sixty-four more to go, sugar. That'll be the easiest money we have ever made." To which she replied, "This will be the only money we've ever made.""

"The year passed. The celebration was planned, and all Phil had to do was collect his money at midnight."

"We all arrived around seven. Mary welcomed us at the door, so very grateful that she never had to sleep in that house again. I had the check all set to hand over to him and asked where the golden boy was, but no one knew. After a thorough search, we found his shoes lying next to the pool, kicked off as though he were going for a swim. At the far end of the pool, floating like a drowned ghost, was his starched tuxedo shirt. His body was never found."

"Oh my God."

Darcy walked away from Kerry.

"Mary moved away and remarried. Looks like she started a family, and that was the end of it. What does that file say?" Kerry pointed to the yellowed folder she had brought back from her office.

The folder sitting on her kitchen table didn't look dangerous. It didn't look like it could change her life. It looked like an old folder with some ancient papers tucked inside. She picked it up as though it would snap at her.

The file listed all of the owners in chronological order. In addition, there was a separate biography of each owner giving a brief personal history along with some insight offered by each agent that was associated with them.

Darcy read the list of owners out loud.

"Okay, here are the original owners, Mr. and Mrs. John and Sheila Taft. They built the house in 1907. Owned 1907-1910."

Kerry turned to his laptop and searched the names.

"I've got nothing. No record of either of them. Is there anything else there?"

"Yeah, listen to this." Darcy sat gingerly on the edge of the sofa. "Mr. John Taft and his wife, Sheila, built the house in 1907. Mr. Taft had the house constructed shortly after he found it necessary to leave San Francisco due to a series of business failures."

"I wonder what that could have been?"

Darcy continued, "Taft lived in the house with his wife… until he shot her and then turned the gun on himself."

Kerry stared at her in disbelief. "Holy crap!"

Memories of her dreams flashed through her mind, the gun pressed against her head, the bullet exploding through her skull. She swallowed hard, trying to bring moisture to her parched throat.

"The very first thing that happens in that house is a murder/suicide. Shit. What else does it say?"

Her face tingling, Darcy went back to the file. She scanned the documents looking for the next clue of this unfolding horror show.

"Okay, here it is, this makes sense. The next owner was George Thornton. He was a cattle baron and took ownership of the house in 1910, after the deaths of John and Sheila. He remodeled it significantly. That must be why it's called the Thornton Mansion and not the Taft Mansion. George turned the house almost completely around. The back porch was moved to the north side of the house and totally enclosed. Any windows that faced the ocean or backyard were closed up and covered over."

"Thornton did that?" Kerry thought that by shutting off the view of the backyard, it was like George wanted to keep it modestly tucked away.

As Darcy read further, her anxiety level rose. Her face flushed, and then she went pale.

"What is it? Darcy?"

Darcy closed the file and dropped it on the coffee table.

"George Thornton put in the pool."

"Holy crap, does it say why?"

Kerry picked up the file. Leafing through the pages, he said, "There's a handwritten note here. Check this out."

Kerry read the notation aloud, "Mr. Thornton commissioned the installation of a swimming pool. It is more of a giant tide pool than a customary swim pool. When asked why he answered that he loved the ocean and wanted to pay homage to the sea."

"That is just creepy, especially since he lives on a damn cliff overlooking the ocean." Kerry scanned forward. "I take that back. That's not near as creepy as this. Five years later, George drowned."

Darcy fell back on the sofa, shaking her head. "I'm telling you, it's that damn pool. It sits up there, on top of that hill, like a giant mound of flypaper, enticing whoever it can into its clutches."

As Kerry turned to his laptop and inputted George's name, he said, "But it's more selective than that. Look at the people who bought it and then sold it back. It was like they didn't meet the specifications to be murdered there." While he waited for a glitch in the internet connection to correct itself and bring back the information, Darcy picked up the file and read on.

Here's another note, 'Mr. T. created a trust fund to maintain the house and the pool in the event of his death.' It's dated a week before he died."

"Found something," Kerry said as he moved his mouse around the screen and opened a document. "I have a police autopsy report. They say cause of death was drowning. Apparently, he had suffered a heart attack and fell into the pool. They did not suspect foul play. They ruled it an accidental drowning and closed the case."

Darcy looked back at the paper file in her hand. In the margin was another handwritten note, the author unknown, which asked a simple question, "Why a trust fund?"

Kerry scanned through his research and then the real estate file, counting, "I have twelve dead that we know about since the house was built" Mrs. Taft, she was really the first, right? She was murdered in the house by her husband."

Darcy dropped her hand on Kerry's shoulder. He reached up and gently squeezed it. "Yes, let's start looking there."

Chapter 41

An hour later, they had the documents from the Thornton file spread out across the right side of the kitchen table and Kerry's internet research spread out on the left. Kerry had his head resting in his left hand while he tapped the table with the cast on his right.

Darcy let out a sigh and shook her head. "I don't think Sheila Taft's part of this deal. She was killed before the pool by her husband. No one knows who killed the others, and all of those deaths were water related. I think she was just an unlucky coincidence,"

"But she's still another dead body. Dead is dead." He paused to consider things. "Okay, let's just say that she's out of the picture – then victim number one would be old man Thornton. He builds the pool, and it killed him."

"But what killed him?" asked Darcy.

Kerry didn't have an answer. "What else does it say about the pool?"

She picked up the folder and looked through it again.

"It's five hundred thousand gallons of natural seawater, there's a filtration system that feeds directly into the Pacific, and there was an observation room built for underwater viewing. I didn't know that. I wonder if Childs knows about it. I wonder if it's still there."

"Don't go getting any ideas. We have enough trouble without you looking for more. Like you told me, stay away and stay safe!" Kerry shuffled through some of the documents, unsure what he was looking for.

"Yeah. You're right. That place must be a holy terror, can you even imagine?"

Darcy stopped as a realization hit her.

"Every time I go to the Thornton house, you know what I feel. Hatred. Like I did something really bad up there and have a payback coming."

Kerry took the final swig from a water bottle and shook his head. "I don't have a clue what we should do. But if there is something up there, and it's after us, we better do something."

Darcy crossed to the sofa and threw herself, face down, onto the cushions. She buried her face in a pillow and screamed!

"This sucks! It's not fair. We didn't do anything."

Kerry crossed over to her and sat on the edge of the sofa. He rubbed her back with his good hand and tried to comfort her.

"We can only do what we can do. We just have to stay calm and figure this thing out."

"Figure it out! How the hell do we do that? All we know about the house is a sketchy history of murder and mayhem, we know even less about Childs. He could be an escaped mental patient for all we know."

"See, another lead. Duh! Let's just see what Mr. Henry Childs was up to before we met him"

Kerry crossed to his laptop and typed in Henry's name.

"Anything?"

"There are a couple of articles about an electronics company in which Henry was a shareholder. When the company went public, Henry had become very wealthy. Otherwise, there's nothing anywhere since his birth."

"If Hannah wasn't such a bitch, we could ask her to run a check, but I think that's a dead end," Darcy said.

She dropped her head back into the pillow and screamed again.

Kerry's eyes lit up, "You know, we may not know much about him, but we know someone who does. His mother."

Darcy's head popped up from the pillow.

"His mother's living there now. She's pretty whacked out most of the time, but she might talk to us if we ask really nicely. All we would have to do is go up there in the afternoon when Childs normally disappears, and we could talk with her, no problem."

Darcy rolled over to face him. "The problem is that she's in the house, and I'm never going up there again."

"Yeah, I know. That's why I should go. I can pretend it's a work thing and get in to see her. I could be there and gone before anyone ever knows."

Darcy sat up, worried. "But..." she tapped his cast, "You aren't immune either. What happens if you get in trouble? There'll be no one to watch your back."

"Well, maybe I could get someone else to go with me, you know, someone who..."

"I don't want you to go."

Kerry took her hands in his, "We really don't have a choice. We have to find out everything we can. I'll be fine, don't worry."

He kissed her and grabbed his keys.

A few minutes later, Kerry's truck was pulling out of the apartment's parking lot, and Darcy stepped directly in front of him.

Darcy said in a loud voice. "Who am I trying to fool. I can't let you go alone, and we can't get anyone else involved.

I'll go. I'll go up with you, but we are in and out in a heartbeat, got it!"

"Are you sure? I can do this alone." Kerry said intently.

"No, I'll go. It started with me, and I have to be there to end it."

He then looked at his watch. "Childs normally takes off for a few hours every afternoon. He should be heading out anytime now."

"Fine, but we are taking my car. If he sees us, he won't recognize it."

Chapter 42

Up at the Thornton house, the door to Edith Childs' room opened, and Henry strode in. She noticed again how he was changing. Her pudgy little boy was growing up. He was no longer so pudgy, for one thing. He had lost some weight in the last few months, and he was developing muscle tone in his upper body as well. He claimed that working around the house was getting him in shape. He handed her a cup of coffee. She set the cup on the tiny table that sat, like a longtime friend, to the right of her chair.

"I'm going into town this afternoon, Mother. I have to check on the new fish supplier. I don't think he's sending a full load every month. You know these people. If you don't stay on top of them, they'll start to cheat you."

Edith wasn't sure what to make of the new Henry. Six months ago, he would have never said a phrase such as, "they'll start to cheat you." He had regarded her differently as well. He looked at her sideways as though she were old, no longer a pillar of strength.

"When will you be back?" Edith said, seeking a glimmer of the intimidation she used to so easily command.

"When I'm done," he replied, not even trying to hide the irritation in his voice. "While I'm gone, you'll have to fend for yourself. But please be careful if you go downstairs. I wouldn't want to come home and find you a motionless heap at the bottom of the stairs."

"And don't forget, stay out of the backyard. The ground is treacherous out there. You'll kill yourself." With that last admonition, Henry was gone.

Edith heard the Dodge Ram pull out of the driveway and head off down the road. "Stay out of the backyard! The ground is very treacherous." Edith mocked him to herself. "What the hell does he think I'm going to do? Bring up a bunch of surfers and go skinny dipping?"

Edith was annoyed at the way Henry had been treating her. The times were more and more frequent when she could sense Henry's irritation.

"Stay out of the backyard! Why do I have to stay out of the goddamn backyard? It's my house too. If I want to go into the backyard, then let's see someone try to stop me."

Edith decided that as soon as 'The Young and The Restless' was over, she was going out back and sit for a while. In the meantime, she reached under her knit afghan and pulled out a small flask of bourbon. She splashed a generous pour into her coffee and licked the rim before she replaced the top.

Chapter 43

Darcy and Kerry sat in her new car a quarter mile from Henry's driveway. Sweat coated the back of her neck, and her breathing was shallow. She opened her mouth and, in a weak, thin voice, said, "Isn't there a better way, really? I mean, why don't we just move to Oklahoma."

Kerry squeezed her hand and said again, "You don't have to do this. I can go alone."

"The only thing that scares me more than that house is losing you to it. If you go, I go, but I am asking you not to go."

"Sweetheart, something in there wants to hurt us, and we can't stop until we know that we're safe. If it reached out to get you at the beach, it could reach out anywhere. We have to get to the bottom of it."

Just then, Henry's Dodge Ram 3500 exited the driveway and turned toward town. As soon as it was out of sight, Darcy looked at Kerry one last time, hoping for a reprieve. It didn't come. She hit the ignition button, and they pulled into the driveway.

Darcy was on the alert for a sudden wind, an ominous cloud. She had worn jeans and a sweatshirt anticipating an assault. Kerry stood next to her as he knocked on the front door. There was no answer, as expected, and he tested the knob. It was locked, but Kerry still had one of the spare keys. The key turned without issue, and the door swung open.

They held hands as they made their way up the grand staircase. Of course, as soon as Darcy took her first step inside the house, she needed to pee. "Damn it. Entering this house for me is just like dipping a sleeping girl's hand in a bowl of warm water."

Kerry squeezed her hand. "You'll be okay."

By the time they got to the top of the stairs, she had managed to control her bladder but not her imagination. Every shadow seemed to move around her. Every step she took sounded like a Chinese gong ringing in her ears. She had hugged the wall as she climbed each torturous step remembering the back porch stairs and how the wind had tried to push her away from the building. "What the hell are we doing? Let's forget this."

Kerry held her hand tighter. "Wait, listen."

She heard the faint sounds of a television.

They moved down the hall toward the buzz of soap opera music. Her head was on a swivel, turning in every direction it could. She wasn't going to let anyone, or anything sneak up behind her. Two doors down Edith was sitting in her chair, watching her stories. Kerry quietly knocked, which she thought was odd since they were, in fact, trying to attract Edith's attention.

Edith didn't respond. Maybe she was asleep. Kerry knocked again.

"Hello?"

Edith turned and looked at them.

"Who the hell are you?"

Kerry and Darcy were caught off guard by her brusqueness. Darcy stepped forward.

"Hi, Mrs. Childs. It's me, Darcy Wainwright. I'm the realtor who sold you the house."

"You didn't sell me anything, Missy. I wouldn't have bought this death trap for all the tea in China." Edith turned back to the TV.

Darcy walked closer.

"Oh, you don't mean that, Mrs. Childs. Henry tells me you love this place." She moved in front of Edith.

"Bullshit! He dragged me out of my nice condo and has imprisoned me here on the second floor. I don't know who he thinks he is, but I'm not someone who's going to take that from anyone. 'Stay out of the backyard!' Like I was a damn five-year-old."

Kerry stepped in.

"So, you didn't want Henry to buy this house?"

"I just said I hate it here, didn't I? He hardly lets me downstairs anymore. Why, just a few minutes ago, he told me to stay out of the attic. Like I have any reason to go into the attic."

"I thought you said the backyard?" Darcy was trying to follow her.

"What? Shhh!" Edith's stare was fixed on the TV. "You see that guy there, the blond with the hard butt. He's cheating on the redhead with her sister, and now she's pregnant." The end music chimed as the camera went close up for Mr. Hard Butt's reaction.

Darcy tried again. "What were you saying about the backyard?"

"Oh, that damn Henry. He wants me to stay out of the attic. Well, you know what? To hell with him. I'm going to go up there right now."

"Mrs. Childs! Is that really a good idea?"

Edith stood and grabbed her walker. Fueled by her anger, the bourbon, and a demented comprehension of the world around her, she stood up and headed out into the hall. "Out of my way, Missy, or I'll run you down" She took a right out of her bedroom door, her aluminum walker clanging along the baseboards as she shuffled and stopped three doors down. With a frail right hand, she twisted the knob and swung open a closet door. "Damn it, this isn't it."

She slammed the door and moved to the next one, the attic door. Kerry and Darcy followed a few feet behind.

She peered up the steep, narrow staircase with contempt. She attempted to maneuver her walker into the narrow stairway that led to the attic with the subtly of a snowplow. She made it up the first step before she was stuck.

"Hey, you!" Edith called out. "Aren't you gonna help me?"

They rushed to the door and almost laughed when they looked in. There was Edith, sitting on the stairs with her walker stuck between the walls of the staircase. It was suspended above the stairs like a piece of modern art lodged at a peculiar angle as though it had been intended to elicit an emotional response. And it did. It made them want to laugh.

"Whoa, let me give you a hand there," Darcy said as she helped Edith stand up. "Maybe this isn't such a good idea."

"You're either with me or get the hell out," She turned to mount the stairs again.

Kerry whispered to Darcy, "If we help her, we may soften her up and get some info on Henry."

Darcy nodded, and Kerry moved to Edith.

"You know what? If you're set on doing this, let me get the walker out of the way first." Kerry banged the walker free with a good punch to the underside of the handle and, nearly bonking Edith on the side of the head, took it to the top of the stairs.

"What's up there?" Darcy yelled.

"Mostly an empty attic, a solid floor, a few old pieces of furniture, and a couple of boxes."

Edith took the steps one at a time. Literally. She would take one step and rest. Kerry was in front, helping her reach the next step, while Darcy was behind, making sure she didn't fall backward. The exertion caused Edith to break wind a number of times, adding to the absurdity of the endeavor. With the combined smell of the farting and the bourbon, this jaunt was proving to be more taxing than anticipated.

When they finally reached the summit, Edith had to sit on an old chair for a few minutes before she could continue.

While she recouped, she examined the attic. "Well, much to do about nothing, if you ask me. Why would Henry give a damn if I came up here?"

Edith looked around again.

"What's that?"

Darcy went over and pulled back a tarp covering what looked like a large box. To their mutual surprise, they found an old hope chest made out of wood, varnished to a silky sheen with brass buckles on the straps holding it together. The buckles were tarnished and stained. There was even an old lock sitting open in the brass hasp.

"Wow, that's beautiful. Great craftsmanship," Kerry said as he examined the exterior.

"Well, open it. Don't just stand there gawking," Edith coughed out.

Darcy helped Edith over to the chest and brought the chair along for her. Kerry stared at the lock, hesitant to reach out and remove it.

"I feel like I'm about to open Pandora's Box."

Her bladder started to scream again. To make the moment perfect, Edith let out another of those sissy farts that she'd been producing ever since step three.

As Kerry reached for the lock, a draft ran through the attic. Darcy's sweatshirt ruffled, and the lingering cloud of Edith's fart flew right into her face. When combined with the musty smell of attic and dust, it produced a smell similar to that of dead fish. Darcy's nose wrinkled, and a scowl covered her face.

"Well, open it for Chrissake. What are you waiting for?" Edith snapped Darcy back to reality.

"Okay, keep your bloomers on. He's opening it."

Kerry slid the lock out of the hasp and opened the top of the chest. Darcy pulled her head back just in case something leapt out at her.

Carefully peering over the edge of the trunk, she stole a glance inside. Inside there were things that you would expect to find in an old chest, linens and candlesticks, some silver, and other household items, probably old, forgotten wedding gifts.

"Are these yours?" Darcy asked Edith. "They're beautiful."

"Mine? Why the hell would they be mine? I don't know who the hell they belong to."

Darcy looked deeper into the chest. "With all of the different occupants over the years, it's weird that this chest is still here."

"Maybe it belonged to the last owner," Kerry said.

"No way, that would be the mid 90's. This stuff is much older than that."

Darcy reached in and held up a hand-embroidered wedding veil made of delicate lace detailed with exquisite handiwork. She had never seen anything so distinctive. Edith looked at it in awe.

"Oh my, isn't that beautiful? I had one just like it, you know when I married Henry's father. It was just like this. It was a beautiful wedding. Everyone said so. I worked with the dressmaker for three months until they got it just right. They were a real challenge, but I got my way in the end. Oh, the wedding night was something, too, I'll tell you. I ended up wearing nothing but the veil."

Darcy blushed a bit and smiled, placing her hand on Edith's knee, and Edith patted it ever so gently. It was the first sign of compassion that Darcy had seen in the old woman.

While Edith was lost in the lustful memories of her wedding night, Kerry turned back to the chest. There were some more clothes and a few other personal items, including a ceramic chamber pot.

"Look at this. Maybe it was a planter?"

Edith laughed.

"Have you ever heard the expression, 'He doesn't have a pot to piss in?'"

"Sure," Kerry said.

"Well, where do you think it came from?" Edith laughed again. "This is a chamber pot. You kept it in your room at night in case you had to pee."

"I may have to put that to use any second now," Darcy said.

Instead, she looked back into the chest and pulled out a photo album.

Edith perked up at the sight of the album. Darcy rose and sat on the edge of the chest while Edith leaned over so she could see the photos. Darcy opened the album and thumbed through it.

Inside there were dozens of photographs from the turn of the century, men and women, families, all staring expressionless at the lens.

"Why do they always look so stern in these old pictures?" Darcy asked.

"You had to stand very still, or the image blurred. So instead of trying to maintain a smile or some sort of frivolous emotion on your face, it was easier just to hold still. Does it say who these people are?"

Darcy looked, but there were no captions attached to any of the photos. There were no notes written along the edges or on the backs, no dates.

Darcy looked through fifteen pages of photos when one, in particular, caught her eye. She had a vague feeling of recognition when she saw it, from one of her dreams, perhaps? She studied it closer. There was a woman and two men. Both men were older than the woman, and one was old enough to be her father. The woman was wearing a print dress. The younger of the two men was standing next to her, and the older man was seated.

She looked closer at the woman's face. It was strong and willful. Even though she was staring into the lens, she could not hide that fact.

The old man, however, was the typical stern ogre seen in so many old photos. He lacked any personality or hint of life. If he had been more regal, Darcy supposed he could have been called stoic.

The younger man looked to be in his mid-forties, but it was so hard to tell in those days. Everyone looked older than they were.

"The guy standing looks like the husband. He sure isn't happy, though, is he?" Kerry snickered.

Edith was equally fascinated. She stared at the picture as though it was bringing back a memory. Edith started to mumble.

"He's so cold to me, Father. This has changed him so much."

They both stared at Edith. Darcy was certain that these were not Edith's thoughts, and she was sure as shit it was not Edith's voice. The voice coming out of the old woman was much younger and filled with legitimate concern. A shiver ran up Darcy's spine.

"I'm getting very angry with him. I am not a piece of property that he can control as he will."

"Now, you just stop it! You can't start talking in tongues or whatever it is you're doing! I have to go."

Edith looked at Darcy with bewilderment in her eyes. Her lips moved, and she said, "What the hell are you talking about? You can't leave me up here alone. For Chrissake, if you want to go, then take me with you."

This voice was definitely Edith's. A wave of relief flowed over her.

"We wouldn't leave you here Mrs. Childs. Let me help you." Kerry said as he moved to the old lady.

As Kerry helped Edith stand, Darcy tottered a bit and knocked the album off the chest onto the floor. It fell open to a page they had not yet seen. Darcy looked down, and she stared at the picture in the center right part of the page. It was the same old man but a different woman who was a bit younger and yet held a resemblance to the other. There was no more uncertainty, no more wondering, no déjà vu. She knew what she was seeing, and it terrified her.

With absolutely no control, Darcy left Edith and ran from the attic. Her bladder let loose somewhere in the upstairs hall, and she did not stop running until she was at the car. Sobbing and hysterical, she slid down the driver's side front door and plopped onto the ground. Pulling her knees close to her chest, she sat there and sobbed.

A few minutes later, Kerry came running out of the house and headed straight to her. She looked away, embarrassed by the dark stain around her crotch. She buried her face in her knees, almost overwhelmed by the smell of urine. He knelt next to her and stroked her hair. It helped to calm her just a tiny bit.

"What happened up there? What spooked you so badly?"

"That album? Did you see it?

"Yeah, a bunch of pictures of old folks. I brought it with me."

Her head pulled back, and she looked him in the eye.

"Really? Good. Let's get the hell out of here."

Kerry climbed into the car. Darcy threw her sweatshirt onto the front seat and opened all the windows. She drove off the lot... again. It was a disturbing pattern that was developing. Every time she left, she swore she would never come back, and she swore it again now, the difference being that this time she knew she would have to return.

Chapter 44

As the Infiniti pulled out of the Thornton house driveway, neither saw the silver Audi sitting across the way. Slumped down behind the wheel was Stan Grossman.

Stan had been watching Darcy's apartment all day. He had followed Kerry and Darcy to the house.

Why would they come here?

Once they had turned the corner at the bottom of the hill, he started up his Audi and pulled into the driveway. Fearless, he got out of the car and walked to the side gate. As he approached, the gate opened as though it had an automatic electronic eye.

He walked to the backyard and saw the pool immediately. Without hesitation, Stan stripped off his clothes and jumped in, relishing the tingling drop in temperature and the refreshing coolness of the water.

Color started to swirl around him, but he had been prepared for this in his many dreams. He tossed his head back and welcomed the rush.

"You're trespassing."

The woman's voice came from behind him, and he spun around.

Standing at the edge of the pool, in full uniform, was Sergeant Hannah Brower.

"What?" Stan said.

"You're trespassing. I could arrest you for that."

Stan saw the look in her eye, and it told him that of all the possibilities that were before him, being arrested didn't make the list.

"I'm also naked, and you're not. I should arrest you for that. It's a crime covering up that incredible body," he said, wading over to stand just beneath her.

Her eyes glowed cat-like as gold flecks ran across her corneas.

"Well, I don't want to be breaking any laws. How would it look for the police sergeant to be cuffed and dragged downtown?" She loosened her tie.

"I don't know about dragging you downtown, but the cuffed part I think might just work out." He reached up and stroked her calf.

Her tie fell to the ground, followed by her gun belt, shirt, and pants. In a second, Hannah stood naked at the edge of the pool. Stan rose out of the water and crossed to her, his trusty divining rod pointing the way, and he grabbed her

295

sadistically by the hair on the back of her head. She let out a surprised moan of pleasure.

They kissed, biting each other's tongues, and together fell into the pool, baptizing themselves into her service.

Chapter 45

Kerry and Darcy rode back to her apartment in silence. Kerry was afraid to speak, and Darcy was just afraid. Once she had showered, changed, and thrown her soiled clothing in the washer, she took the photo album to the kitchen table. With great courage, she opened it and thumbed through the pages until she found the one that had scared her.

She looked closely at the picture again, hoping that she had been mistaken. She had not been. She saw the picture exactly the same way she had seen it before and the time before that. Kerry came up behind and looked over her shoulder.

"Is this what freaked you out?" he asked.

"Yeah. I've seen this picture before."

"When? Were you in that attic before today?"

"No, I didn't see it there. I saw it at my house. My mother's house that is. It's in a family photo album."

Kerry asked, "Why would that picture be in your mom's album?"

Darcy turned to him. "We have to go to my mom's house."

"Didn't she move to Sacramento a few years ago?

Darcy got up. "Yep, and if we leave now, we can get there before dark." She grabbed her coat and her cell phone and headed out to the car. Kerry shook his head in bewilderment and followed her.

It took almost three hours to make the trip to Sacramento. There was more traffic than usual, and Darcy got lost, as she always did when she got off the freeway. But she finally found the giant mall and the little side street that led to a Spielbergesque residential community that housed Darcy's mom.

As Darcy drove slowly down the street, three boys zoomed by on silver and blue dirt bikes while a small group of preschoolers played in a front yard under the watchful eyes of two moms who talked on a front porch. This scene always made her chuckle because this was so unlike her own mother.

Gail Wainwright lived in a four-year-old, two-bedroom house. It was a white, single-story rancher with blue trim. Darcy pulled her Infiniti into the short driveway and turned off the motor.

"Okay, let me do the talking. You just be your normal charming self with my mom, okay?"

"Sure, it's what I do best," Kerry said and got out of the car.

Darcy knocked and walked into the house, calling out for her mom as she always did. From the back of the house, she heard Gail scream. At the sound of Darcy's voice, she came running from the back of the house.

"You gotta be shittin' me! What a surprise! Hello, baby! How are you?" She grabbed Darcy and gave her a huge hug and a sloppy kiss.

"My God, look at you. You look terrible. Is something wrong?"

She saw Kerry.

"Well, Jesus H. Christ! Kerry Devine! What the hell are you doing here? Darcy? You been holding out on me?" She wrapped him up in her arms and squeezed him as though he were a play-doh figurine that needed to be reshaped.

"Well, yes, Mom, I have," with a knowing smile, she whispered. "I'll tell you about it later."

Gail laughed and hugged Kerry again, glad to see them both.

"Come on back. We can sit on the patio. It's getting a bit warm these days, and there's a nice breeze out there."

Gail grabbed a bottle of wine and three glasses, and they headed out to the backyard.

The yard fit the residence the way the vineyards fit the nearby Napa Valley—perfectly. The enclosed space with nice landscaping and a pool, neighbors within breathing distance, and the illusion of privacy all combined to give Gail the place she called home.

Darcy stopped and stared at the pool as soon as she walked through the sliding doors. Kerry walked up behind her and placed his good hand on her shoulder. He whispered, "Your mother's pool. No monsters allowed." Darcy chuckled and walked on by.

The three sat and chatted. Gail was trying to catch up on Kerry's life and asked all about his hand. He told a limited version of the story. Darcy talked about her job and her recent success omitting the part about the Thornton mansion; that would come later. After a bit, Kerry excused himself, on Darcy's signal, to use the bathroom.

"So, what's going on? Is there some trouble? You look like crap. Aren't you sleeping?" Gail burst out in a steady stream.

Darcy looked at her mother.

"Do you still have that old green photo album? The one that belonged to Nana?"

"Oh, somewhere. I think it's in a box in the garage. Why?"

Darcy bit her lip nervously.

"Come on," Gail said, "I can always tell something is up when you start biting your lip. What gives?"

"I need your help with something." Darcy reached into her bag and retrieved the album. She showed it to her mother.

"Take a look through this and tell me if you recognize anything."

"Whose album is this? It's really old."

Gail began to turn page after page. The deeper she got into it, the more nervous she became. Darcy could see the trepidation in her mother's mannerisms.

Gail stopped at a page that held four pictures. One of the pictures was of the young woman and her father. She stared at it in amazement.

"Honey, this is your father's great-grandmother. Where in the hell did you get this?" she said in absolute amazement.

Darcy nodded, "That's what I thought. I wasn't sure, but I thought that's who that was. What do you know about her?"

"Well, not a lot. She was on your father's side of the family. She died around the time of the First World War. I don't know how? Your Dad's family was kinda strange.

Even your grandmother, Hazel, never talked too much about them. I don't even know this woman's name. I always assumed they weren't very close for some reason. To be honest, I think Hazel was embarrassed by the family." Gail laughed.

Darcy moved in a bit closer. "Do you know where Nana Hazel grew up? Was it in Santa Cruz?"

"No, she never lived there. Your Dad grew up in Phoenix. We moved up north from Scottsdale when your father got that job with the tire company. After he left, it just seemed silly to move. Where did you find these pictures?"

"In the attic of the old Thornton mansion."

Gail gasped out loud.

Darcy told her mother the story of selling the Thornton mansion. She told her about Henry and Edith and finding the album. She omitted the parts where she was attacked, stalked, or humiliated.

Gail sat stunned as her daughter told her the story.

"And you found this album in the attic of the Thornton mansion? How did it get there?"

"I was hoping there might be a clue in the green album. Let's go see if we can find it." Darcy said.

"Well, I haven't seen that old thing in years. I don't even know if it made the move." Gail said.

Darcy headed into the garage to search for the old album. Gail lagged behind.

"Are you coming?" Darcy asked her mom.

"I'll be right there. You go ahead. Just be careful. There's a lot of crap piled up in there." Gail sat back down and took a gulp of wine as her face grew pale with worry.

Kerry saw Darcy pass down the hall and followed. She filled him in with the details as they moved boxes from an overhead shelf looking for the right one.

Gail walked into the garage with a new bottle of wine and watched as Darcy and Kerry searched through the boxes that contained the past lives and experiences of the Wainwrights.

After an hour of going through box after box, stopping to reminisce about certain items from Darcy's childhood, her first bra, her first-grade report card, and her senior class picture, which of course, also contained Kerry, they hadn't found what they were looking for.

"I threw out everything I hadn't used in a year. I figured if I could go a year without using something, then I really don't need it," she said. "I collect too much junk as it is to keep a lot of crap laying around that I don't use." Gail was fidgety and quietly anxious.

"I really don't know if it's even here."

Kerry saw another box up high on the rafters of the garage. "What's that one way in the back?" He said.

"Oh, just more stuff I haven't thrown out yet," Gail said.

"Well, maybe it's what we're looking for." Darcy was up a ladder and into the box with little effort.

She brought the dusty cardboard box down from its lonely perch as Kerry steadied the ladder with his good hand. Clumsily dropping it on the floor of the garage, she knelt next to the old box and tried not to get too excited. The box was old and faded and held the logo of a grocery chain that had gone out of business thirty years ago. Ripping off the tape that held the box closed, Darcy opened the flaps.

On top was a sweater that held a school logo. On the lower right pocket was a number that indicated the year the owner graduated. On the left sleeve were three red stripes, indicating the number of years the owner had lettered. On the right sleeve were three different patches, a football, a basketball, and a set of crossed baseball bats. On the left side of the sweater was a giant red C, which stood for Coronado High. She held it up and looked at her mother.

"It was your father's," Gail said. "He was quite the stud."

"Oh wow!" Darcy's eyes began to tear, thinking that she was holding something that had belonged to her father, something that he had worn, something that was undoubtedly one of his most valued possessions. "I never knew you had any of his things." She unwittingly hugged the sweater to her chest.

The next item that she held up was a photo album, not the green one but an album covered in white lace and beading, some of which separated from the cover and fell back into the box as she picked it up.

"You gotta be kidding me! This isn't yours, is it?" Darcy could not believe her eyes. "Is this your wedding album?"

"We weren't so unconventional that we didn't take pictures of our wedding," Gail said. "We were in love once."

Darcy giggled like a kid. She quickly opened the album and saw a much younger version of her mother with the man who was her father, Bill Wainwright.

"Your Dad was smart and confident and looked like someone you could put your trust in. And maybe if he had ever stuck around long enough, we could have found out if that was true." Gail said as she lowered herself carefully onto a small, empty wooden case of wine.

"You know, I never really knew what happened to him," Kerry said, hoping to get more information from her.

"Join the club," Darcy slowly nodded her approval, and Gail spoke.

"Turns out he was a me-first guy and was the first one out the door. But he did have charm. Look at that chin," Gail said, giving in a bit to the memory.

Darcy smiled, "I can see what you saw in him. He must have been irresistible."

He had a self-confident air about him, an attitude that said, *Don't underestimate me*. Gail took the album and remembered it all as she saw the pictures that she hadn't looked at in so many years.

Darcy stood and moved behind her so that she could see. Gail slowly turned pages. She let out a small laugh as she remembered the circumstances of the photo in front of her. "This was just as we were leaving for our honeymoon if you could call it that. He had his hand on my ass just out of the frame and was pinching me in an indelicate manner, if you get my drift."

Darcy laughed. "No wonder you look like that."

They turned another page and then another.

Gail was mesmerized by the image of herself standing next to the stranger that had fathered Darcy.

"He had his moments."

There was a picture of the two of them at the beach with a little girl. It was a family outing with their little daughter.

"Why is this in here? Where was it taken?" Darcy asked, looking down at Gail.

Gail smiled and took a closer look. "That was a hell of a long time ago, I can tell you that. You were so little and cute. What the hell happened to you?"

It was the first attempt at humor Gail had made since they walked into the garage. Tears started to well up in her eyes. Gail had been so strong for so long that Darcy had never considered the fears and the loneliness she must have gone through when her father left. At the time, she had been about the same age as Darcy was now, and she'd had a kid to look after. Darcy reached down and covered Gail's hand with her own. Gail grabbed back at Darcy's hand and squeezed.

"That was in Arizona. Canyon Lake, I think. We took a long weekend and camped out." She handed the album back to Darcy.

"Why haven't I ever seen this stuff before?" Darcy asked as she moved back toward the box.

"I don't know," Gail responded. "I guess I was waiting 'til you got older, and then when you did, it really didn't matter. We were doing so good that I just forgot about it."

"Check this out," she showed a picture to Kerry. In this one, Bill had on a leather jacket and a fedora that was pulled down over his eyes. He was a cross between a gangster and a Hell's Angel.

"He looks like a Matrix biker who's gone to the dark side," she chuckled. "Mind if I take this album with me? I'd really like to spend some time going through it."

Gail paused for a second. Darcy thought she was going to say no. "Go ahead. Just be careful and bring it back."

"You know, your father had a real fascination for the Thornton Place. He and his buddies used to talk about it all the time. They used to laugh at some of the rumors that were told about it. He always said that he could stay there without any problem. Took me there once."

"Really? How ironic." She glanced at Kerry with a sly grin, "One of his favorite pastimes turns out to be my biggest success. I guess he would have been proud," Darcy said with an edge to her voice. "Glad I could have made him happy."

She set the album aside, careful not to lay it in an oil slick, and looked back in the box.

Darcy then held up a wedding veil, simple and short with a single headband that held it to the bride's head.

"This was yours?" Darcy asked her mom.

"Yeah, it was my mother's. You know the routine. I always thought I looked goofy wearing it. Funny that I've kept it all this time."

"I just saw one like this. Weird!" Darcy put it on her head and posed quickly for Kerry. Kerry laughed and took it off her head and put it on his own. Both women laughed as he did the wedding walk across the concrete garage floor, holding his right arm up in a girlish motion. The sea monster cast only added to the ridiculousness of the charade.

Gail was still laughing at Kerry as Darcy turned back to the box and dug down to the bottom of it. There, under the remaining memories that Gail had secreted away, was the old green album.

Darcy let out a yelp and pulled it from the box, spilling the remaining contents on the floor around the box.

"All things come to those who wait!"

Chapter 46

They were in the car and on the way home. Darcy had expected Gail to put up a fight about them not staying the night, but she didn't. Of course, she couldn't have stayed. If she were to stay with her mother, it might put her in harm's way. Darcy had no way of knowing the range of the power in the pool and didn't want to test it.

Kerry was looking through the green album as Darcy drove. He propped it up against his cast and turned the pages with his left hand.

"This kid must be your mother. She's a hottie!" Kerry teased.

"From what she says, which I assume is about half of the truth, she was a wild child herself."

"And this little boy is your dad? Why are there kid pictures of both your parents in the same album?"

"My grandmother did it. She wanted to put both family's history together."

"And is this your grandmother?" Kerry pointed out a woman who was heavy-set, wearing a pillbox hat tilted to the right.

"Yeah, Hazel, my dad's mom. We called her the wicked witch of the west," Darcy laughed. He loved it when she did that. Of all her incredible qualities, her laugh rendered him the most helpless.

"Why'd you call her that?"

"She was a terror. This woman once told me that if I let a boy touch me under my clothes, I would get warts on my face, and everyone would know. I finally figured out that boys had been touching girls for a long time, and no one had warts on their faces."

"She sounds like a sweetie. Were you close?"

"Like oil and water. We never really hit it off. I was too much like Mom. Apparently, she was never in favor of her son marrying my mom. They say that you're supposed to get along with your grandparents more than your parents … well, not in my case."

"She still around?"

"Oh no. She died about years ago. Alcohol poisoning."

"Wow, a big drinker, eh?"

"Yeah, ever since my dad disappeared. She never once came to visit us. We always had to go there. She would never come into Santa Cruz. Hated the place."

"Weird." Kerry turned a page. "Who's this?"

"That would be my grandfather, Stuart Peterson. I barely remember him. My mom's dad. He died when I was, like, four. It was Christmas night, I think. I remember my father telling me that Papa had passed away. Funny, it's like one of my first memories, and it's the last memory I have of my dad."

"What happened with your dad, really?"

"I always hoped he was captured by aliens. My mother used to say he died, but really, he just never came home. He went out one morning and then just never came home. No one ever saw him again."

"Wow. That sucks."

Kerry turned the page. There it was, the picture that had freaked everyone out. It was a shot of a man in his early sixties and a younger woman. It wasn't quite identical to the photo Darcy had seen with Edith, but it was obvious from the same sitting. The difference here was that there was a caption. Kerry lifted it with his good hand and held it to the light. The ink was faded, but the handwriting was very even and steady. Kerry read it. "Holy shit," he muttered. He read it again to be sure.

Kerry looked over at Darcy, who was waiting for him to say something.

"You find something?" she asked.

"You know what, I gotta pee. Why don't you pull off up ahead here?"

"Hey, a man's gotta do what a man's gotta do, right? You want the service station, or will any old bush do?"

"Let's go first-class. The service station, please." Darcy pulled off at the next exit.

When she had pulled into a parking slot, Kerry turned to face her. He reached out with his good hand and held her forearm firmly.

"You're sure that picture from the attic is your dad's great-great-grandmother? Right?"

"Yeah. That's what my mom said. Why?"

Darcy was getting that feeling. Sometimes, right before something significant happened, she would get a funny feeling that ran from the pit of her stomach to the nape of her neck. She cautiously looked into Kerry's eyes. It was right there, dead center of his pupils. The look that says, "I am going to shatter your life with my next words."

"What? What are you saying?"

Kerry slowly took out the picture. He held it up to show Darcy. "Look familiar?"

Darcy saw the photo and instantly recognized that it was a similar photo to the one she found in the attic.

"I knew it. That's where I saw it before. But that's not the same picture, is it?" she asked, waiting for the other shoe to drop.

"No, but it's the same people. And there's a caption." Kerry turned the photo over and showed her the deliberate handwriting on the back. Darcy took the picture and held it in the light. There, in faded ink that had absorbed into the fibers around it, were the words that shocked her to her core.

Rosemary and father, George Thornton, on the porch of their house, 1912.

Darcy's mouth dried up so quickly that she was sure dust would fly out if she sneezed. She reread the caption several times just to be sure that she had read it correctly, and each time it came out the same. She was the great-great-granddaughter of Rosemary Thornton and the great-great-great-granddaughter of George. She ran her tongue over her teeth in a futile attempt to separate her upper lip from the bond it had formed with the enamel of her molars. She reached out for Kerry's hand and squeezed it tight as reality set in. She was a direct blood descendant of George Thornton.

Chapter 47

Henry Childs was in his underground haven, and he was nesting. His meticulous planning was beginning to pay off. The house was mostly done and livable, so he had lost interest. His criteria had relaxed now that his underground hideaway was nearing completion. His intention to restore the house to its original glory was merely a means of acquiring the skill needed to complete the observatory. Whether or not the house was ever finished didn't matter to him in the least.

Henry's current project was the remaining hallway. This hallway was on the side of the pool closest to the house. It actually ran under the backyard and connected with the stairs from an old shed on the far north side. Once he was finished and his mother had moved on to greener pastures, or under them, as it were, he would be able to access the room without driving around to the cliffside and climbing up. It would save a lot of time that would be better spent with his love.

He had started to replace the rotten timber, and with any luck, it would be done by the end of the week. He glanced at his watch and saw that it was nearly five-thirty. He would have to stop and return to the house. Henry surveyed his progress with satisfaction. He was making some decent strides toward finishing.

But now came the moment that made all the sweat and hard work worthwhile. Checking to be certain the air-tight doors were both secure, Henry went to the wading pool and opened the lid. He waited with great anticipation as the water started to swirl and the colors began to fly. Without prompting, he quickly stripped off his work clothes and crawled into the whirlpool.

Cleansing himself in the soothing water, he first felt her gentle touch on his ankle. Slowly her velvet hand slid up the inside of his leg, over his thigh, and right to the throttle of his passion. She slithered up his lower extremities and engulfed him in her mouth. He could feel her breasts pushing against his thighs as she apparently was attempting to swallow him whole. His head fell back, and he was once again the most powerful man in the world.

Her head came up to his, and she stared into his eyes. He was going on a journey.

Henry felt himself fly through the funnel. He rode the glitter highway to the top and floated above the pool, looking down on the backyard. No matter how many times he had taken this trip, he was always exhilarated and excited. His stomach had that lighter-than-air feeling, as though he were perpetually falling, and yet, he was actually floating in mid-air.

As she took him on these journeys, she was telling him a story at the same time. The story of the pool, the house, and the people who lived there. Each time he had been witness to an event, all surrounding an old man and his family. He had not yet identified everyone, but he was fairly certain the old man was George Thornton, the man who built the pool. Oddly, whatever these scenes represented, they were being shown to him backward, like reading a novel from back to front. They had started with George, dangling a foot in the pool and realizing that he needed to create a trust fund to protect it, and moved backward in time. As this vision came into focus, he saw George sitting in a garden chair, staring into the backyard. The pool was not in yet, and the house had not been remodeled. George sat alone. Henry could feel his sorrow, a sorrow so great that it nearly stopped his heart from beating.

A face appeared in the kitchen window above, and, seeing George, it disappeared. Immediately after, the door on the landing opened, and a young, pretty woman walked down the stairs and approached George. She was wearing a loosely fitted dress, and her crimson hair was coifed neatly in place. For the first time, Henry could hear the buzz of voices. It came to him like a distant radio station, muted and full of static and white noise. He thought he could make out snippets of the conversation but couldn't catch any of the major nouns or verbs that might give him a clue as to what was happening. The woman was crying, trying to explain something to George, and George was upset with the woman. That was as much as Henry could glean until one word popped out of the static.

Daughter!

George was fighting with his daughter. At one point, he turned and pointed to the woman's stomach. Looking closer, Henry could see that she was pregnant, five or six months along. The woman was failing in convincing George of whatever it was she was trying to convey and giving up. The woman left George and climbed the stairs toward the house. When she arrived on the landing, she turned to her father, who kept his back to them, and she cried harder.

He looked back at George, but before he could glean his mood, Henry felt himself being pulled back from the vision in a way that was unusual. Instead of drifting back to reality, he was yanked back, hard and jarred awake. As his earthly senses returned, he felt danger all around him. She rose from the pool and looked into him.

Protect me!

Henry quickly dressed and raced out the hillside entrance looking for imminent danger. He saw nothing but the trees, the road, and his car. He thought he heard something up on top of the hill. He listened closely, and he heard voices, slurred, vehement voices. Without hesitation, he started to climb the hill to protect his love from violation.

Chapter 48

His left leg was in a cast, and his arm yielded twelve stitches from his encounter with Henry Childs a few days earlier. His name was Julio, and he was madder than hell. With him was Alejandro, one of the other men who had been working at the Thornton place. They were both bitter, drunk, and working on a liquid-courage helping of revenge.

"That puta!" Julio said, then gulping down another half bottle of cheap beer. "He wanna mess with Julio. He pays the price, right?"

"That son of a bitch still owes us money too, ain't that right?" Alejandro slurred at his friend.

"So, what are we gonna do?"

"We gotta kick ass. We gotta fuck him up real good." The beer was doing most of the talking.

Alejandro jumped over the fence to get into the backyard and promptly fell from the top, landing squarely on his back. The fall knocked the wind out of him, but he found it funny at the same time, and he started to laugh.

"Hey, Mijo?" Julio yelled, "You wanna stop laughing and help me? I can't climb this bitch. This cast sucks."

"I tell you. I'm gonna go through the house and open the goddam front door. You gonna walk in this fuckin' place like a man, Esai. Go meet me there." Alejandro left for the back door.

He walked to the back corner of the house and looked around the yard to see if he was alone. He saw the yard, all torn up and in the middle of re-landscaping, but he saw nothing moving. Thinking it was safe, he started to stagger to the stairway that led up to the back porch, weaving badly as he moved.

He was halfway across the yard when his stomach turned. In an instant, a six pack and a half of cheap beer was shooting out of his mouth and nose. The projectile vomiting was so severe that it knocked him over. Even laying on the ground, he did not stop vomiting. Laying on his back, he looked like a geyser, the force of the vomit holding his head flat to the ground. The vomit flew high into the air and fell right back onto his face fighting for space in his mouth and nose which were already occupied with spewing beer.

Vomit clung to his face and upper body like a cast, coating him in stomach acid and stale, partially digested beer and pretzels. When he finally was able to open his eyes, he was at the lip of the pool, kneeling on the jagged flagstone. He could feel the stone cutting into his knees, and he knew without looking that there were tiny pools of blood surrounding each one.

Unsure of how he had gotten to the pool, he lay flat on the flagstone and splashed water on his face, clearing his eyes just enough to see his reflection in the water. As the water settled, he saw himself clearly. Dead, rotting skin hung from his face, and small chunks dripped into the pool, disrupting the disturbing reflection. Behind him, there was a shadow, and it made him roll over and look up. He had just enough time to register the fact that Henry Childs was behind him, holding the shovel above his head, before Henry slammed it down, splitting Alejandro's skull.

Julio had limped around to the front and was waiting for Alejandro to open the door. Unzipping his fly, he took a long piss onto the front steps knowing that in a few hours, it would seep into the unprotected wood and, after sitting in the sun for a few hours, would wreak for a very long time.

He then turned to the door and jumped. Standing behind him had been Henry Childs. Julio had not even heard him open the door.

"Well, won't you come in? I see that you won't be needing the facilities. Your friend is out back. Perhaps you should visit him." Henry smiled.

"What you do to him, you sonofabitch? You hurt him. I'll kill you." Julio pushed Henry aside and limped through the house, finding his way to the backyard. He burst through the back door and hobbled down the steps as fast as he could. When he got to the bottom, he stopped and looked frantically around the yard. He saw nothing but the pool at first.

Then he saw a shoe.

An old, white, ripped tennis shoe, like the one Alejandro had been wearing, sitting near the edge of the pool.

Julio slowly approached the shoe, and when he was within a few feet, he stopped. He was close enough to see a few drops of blood around the top. He felt his face flush and his breath came in short, quick bursts. He called out. "Alejandro. Al. Hey man, let's blow this place. This sucks."

There was no answer. He took another step forward and saw a bit more blood on the shoe. He leaned over to get a closer look, the way someone would lean over the edge of a bottomless abyss and saw that the shoe was bloody because Alejandro's foot was still in it.

Chapter 49

Henry pulled the Dodge pick-up into the front drive. He walked up the front stairs and peeked in on his mother. She was snoring quietly in front of the TV. He would take this chance to grab a shower.

Henry stripped off his clothing, which always ended up smelling like seawater, and dumped them in a pile. He turned on the water in the shower and waited for it to heat up. As he stood there naked, he caught a glimpse of himself in the mirror. At first, he didn't recognize his own body. Mirrors had never been his friend, but the body reflecting back looked nothing like the body in his memory. He looked cut. For crying out loud, he looked buff!

Weeks of working underground had sweated quite a bit of fat off him. Lifting and carrying heavy lumber beams had done the rest. He wondered why no one had been commenting on the change.

When Henry stepped out of the shower, he checked the mirror once again. Amazed, he stepped on the scale for the first time in a year. Two hundred and eighty pounds. He was down to two hundred and eighty pounds!

My God, I've lost almost seventy pounds! No wonder I look so good.

Once he had dressed, Henry headed back down the hall to see if his mother was still snoring or, better yet, no longer alive.

As he walked in, Edith was trying to stand up. He went to her immediately and offered a helping hand.

"Where are you going?"

"I'm going back upstairs and see what all the commotion was about," Edith said as she moved toward the door.

"Upstairs? What are you talking about?" he asked.

"Well, Mr. Smarty-pants! You said that I couldn't go upstairs, well I did! What are you going to do about it?" She turned away from him and chuckled.

"I never said not to go upstairs, although it's an excellent suggestion. How in the world did you get up there? You certainly didn't climb those stairs all alone." He was humoring her.

Edith entered the hall and headed for the attic door. "I had a little help," she admitted. "That nice real estate girl took me. She's very nice but skittish, can't seem to sit still."

Henry followed her into the hall. "You mean Darcy? That real estate girl?" He could hardly believe what she was saying. Then it occurred to him: she was obviously delusional. If Darcy had been here, he would have known.

"Now, Mother, why would Darcy take you into the attic?"

"Because I told her to. I can go wherever I want to go. It's my house, too, you know," she said as she pulled the attic door open.

Henry saw the steep attic steps and laughed. "Mother, be serious. There is no way you made it up those steps."

"I most certainly did. That nice young woman helped me up. Of course, she stranded me there, and that handsome man with the cast had to help me down," Edith told Henry.

"The man with the cast?" Henry was beginning to think that maybe she was telling the truth.

"Stay here."

He charged up the stair and into the attic as though he expected to find a prowler or vandal defacing his house. He saw the same things they had all seen, the old furniture, the collection of dust balls, and the trunk. Next to the trunk lay an old sheet, balled up and discarded. He looked to the floor and saw a path of dusty footprints that led between the stairs and the trunk.

Someone had been up here.

He crossed to the trunk. It seemed undisturbed, but how could he know? He bent over, removed the lock, and opened it. He expected to find some old clothing or the like inside. Instead, it was dark and cold, an empty void that seemed to extend down forever.

A light began to glow from within the darkness. It was a multicolored light like the one that would summon Henry at the pool. It began to swirl around the interior of the trunk and cast a combination of light, color, and shadow onto Henry's face. The undulating light accentuated his nostrils, eyebrows, and massive chin.

He reached his hand into the trunk, hoping she would take it, but instead, it disappeared beneath the whirlpool of color. A jolt of energy ran up his arm, charging his body. His hair stood straight up on end, and his eyes rolled back. The color began to crawl up his arm and envelope him. He was pulled into the trunk and into the darkness.

The first thing Henry saw was himself kneeling next to the old steamer trunk. He saw this just as he had seen himself standing next to the pool on his very first journey with his love. He was confused and scared, he had never taken a journey away from the pool. He slid down into the depths of the swirling light, melting away into the abyss.

In an instant, he hovered over a young girl sitting at a desk in her bedroom. She was in her early twenties and quite fetching. Her long raven-black hair was tied up in a pile on her head, her freshly scrubbed cheeks glowed pink, and happiness emanated from her eyes. He knew that this had been a good night. She opened a drawer and took out a leather-bound journal with a simple brass lock on the front binding. There was an inlay of gold thread that ran around the front cover. In the middle of the front cover was a framed square that held a title, *Sheila's Diary.*

The young woman opened the lock with a key she kept on a gold chain that hung around her neck, and she wrote into the diary. As she did, Henry could hear her thoughts as though she were speaking.

March 15, 1903

I am starting this journal to help me remember the significant moments of my life. I have never been one to record such events, and consequently, I have realized that these events dim in my memory faster than they should. With the help of this diary, I will be able to create an accurate record of my life for posterity, should anyone ever be interested. My first entry will probably be one of the most significant. John proposed today. After these many months of courting, I am finally to become Mrs. John Taft. I know that we will be happy. John's construction company is doing very well. He was just offered a very large contract to construct housing down by Fisherman's Wharf. This will be a gigantic boon for his business, and it will put us in a very comfortable financial position. More important, of course, is the fact that I love him dearly. He is the most gentle of men, and I know that he loves me deeply. We will move into a new home directly after the wedding. It sits up on the hill on Market Street. It is not large, but we don't need a lot of space at the moment. I suppose when children come along, we will have to move, but that is something for then, not now."

Henry hovered over the woman and the image blurred. He could sense specific events as they flashed frame by frame in front of him, and he could tell that he was moving forward in time. When the focus returned, he saw the same woman, Sheila. A bit older and more mature, she wrote again, this time in front of a fireplace.

January 23, 1905

"I had a visit from Rosemary today. She is the most infuriating person one could possibly imagine. She is continually coming to visit unannounced, and she takes up a tremendous amount of time that I would prefer to spend with John. John is dear about it, of course. He seems to enjoy her company, and if he finds her annoying, I have not been able to tell. I know that I am an evil person for thinking bad thoughts toward her, but sometimes she is

simply too big a pill to swallow. I hope that she finds herself a husband soon. That will occupy her time in a much more constructive fashion."

Another cosmic hiccup, and the image in front of him blurred. As it refocused, Sheila was found in a kitchen, sitting at a table with a linoleum top.

April 6, 1907

John came home tonight in a foul mood. Ever since the earthquake, things have literally and figuratively fallen apart. There is talk of criminal charges being brought against him for the deaths of the six people, as though it was his fault we had an earthquake. They say that he did not build the houses properly, that he cut corners in order to increase profits, but I know that is not true. John would not do a thing like that. He grows more distant and he is forever irritable. He has become a man different from the one I married. Father is doing what he can to help, but it will be a long road, I am afraid, before things are settled. I know that John is innocent of any wrongdoing and I hope that he knows that I believe and support him at every turn.

It is time for bed, and I will try to take John's mind off his problems. It seems that no matter his mood, he is always in the right frame of mind for some loving attention.

After all, it is my duty as a wife, and if I happen to enjoy it, who's to know?"

Henry's dimensional cocoon shifted yet again as he leapt forward in time.

This time the woman sat on a porch overlooking the city.

August 19, 1909

The house in Santa Cruz is almost finished. We move at the end of the month. Since John managed to avoid any significant repercussions from the collapse, Father assures us that it is the most judicious thing to do, and he was very adamant that we leave the area in the event someone has a change of heart. Out of sight, out of mind is his thinking. I do like the new house, though. It is very beautiful and offers us much room to grow. I long for children and am becoming afraid that I might be barren. John says not to worry, but I feel that is more his lack of desire than a word of encouragement. I also hope that John will return to his normal self once he is out from under the pressures of the earthquake and the situation that was brought with it. He must, for I do not know what I shall do otherwise."

Henry transported once again. This time, as he refocused, he found himself at home, yet he wasn't hovering over the scene. He was standing in it, in the original front hall of the Thornton Mansion.

This house was decorated in a Victorian style with striped wallpaper, ornate throw rugs, and lace curtains. The entire color scheme was green and earth tones. To his left was the living room, as it had been originally designed. A sofa and two chairs sat against the far wall with a small table and lamp between them. The fireplace was brand new and in it burned a small fire. To the left, there were double doors that led to a veranda.

As he was adjusting to the grandeur of this version of his home, he heard voices. Not the muted buzzing from his last trip, but the clear actual voices of two women arguing. They appeared to be coming from the kitchen, and as Henry visualized the kitchen, he was transported, materializing through walls and doors, arriving in the very spot he had seen in his mind.

The kitchen was drastically different. There were three huge windows that looked out over the back yard allowing sunlight to shoot through in three strong golden beams.

In the kitchen, looking splendid in the tremendous light, were two young women. These two women were dressed in long skirts with ruffled blouses. They were facing each other and embroiled in a heated conflict. Unlike before, however, he wasn't hearing their thoughts, he was hearing their words.

Sheila wore a silk blouse with many buttons running up the back. Each button was made of pearl and hooked through an eyelet. The younger one, equally attractive but with shallow eyes, wore a boa made of ostrich feathers over a blue waistcoat, ruffled cuffs extending over gloved hands. They did not acknowledge Henry.

"You have *no* idea what you are talking about. John is having trouble at the moment, that's all. He'll work through it," Sheila said strongly.

"I know in your heart, you believe that is true, but look in his eyes and tell me he hasn't changed over these past months. Father is worried."

Father? They must be sisters.

"Well, he's my husband, and I should know if there were something wrong. I would appreciate it if you would all just mind your own business.

"I don't know why you insist that there are problems between us. It's as though you want us to be unhappy. Why do you do this to me? Why can't you just leave us alone?" Sheila could no longer contain the tears. She fled from the room.

The younger sister shivered as the older one left. Having nothing left to say and no one to say it to, she left the kitchen with a determined stride. As she did, she passed through the space Henry was standing, passing through him as well. He could feel her thoughts, and they were not at all the same as her words. There was a secret that this sister hid within her. He visualized the front door and was there in an instant.

The younger woman was standing on the front porch. Henry tried to go out to her, but he could not. It seemed that he could not travel beyond the boundaries of the house.

He saw a taxi pull up. A middle-aged gentleman stepped out and, seeing the woman asked the driver to wait. As the man walked toward the house, his eyes brightened. She waited on the porch, under the portico, for the man to come to her. When he approached her, he scanned all the windows facing him. Satisfied that they were empty, he embraced the woman. Henry had learned the difference between the embrace of a friend and the embrace of lovers. There was no question that these two were lovers. She pushed him away and began to bay at him.

"John, what are we going to do? She's not budging. How are we going to explain?"

"Well, we'll think of something. Is she home?" the man asked.

"Yes, we just had an awful fight. She hates me already, and she doesn't even know."

"I have to go inside. Have you told your father?" he asked as he moved to the front door and approached Henry's position.

"I haven't had the nerve."

"Yes, well… I'm sorry, but I must go. Will you be all right?"

"I'll be fine," the woman said. "I'll go home. We can talk tomorrow."

She turned with great sorrow and entered the taxi. The man watched her drive away. She did not look back.

As he entered the house, he passed through Henry's space, just as the young woman had, and Henry felt his soul. It had anger and violence in it. He felt a protective rage build up inside of him, a rage built of jealousy and vengeance, and he began to transport once again.

He opened his eyes and found himself standing next to the steamer trunk, soaked in sweat, his hand holding a wedding veil made of exquisite lace. He was back in his body and back in his house. He was weak, exhausted, sweat running down his face and his shirt stuck to his moistened skin.

Chapter 50

Darcy and Kerry were searching through the old records at the library, looking for information about Rosemary Thornton.

"We know she had a child, but I can't find anything that resembles a marriage certificate," Darcy said.

"What if she didn't get married? Imagine what a scandal that would have caused back in the day?"

"Are you saying my great-great-grandmother was a ho?"

Kerry smiled. "Well, I don't imagine she would have been the first woman who dropped her bloomers before marriage. Okay, let's be logical about this. Let's go over what we know and see if we can find something that connects."

"Right, we know that Rosemary Thornton had a child who was my great-grandmother or father. They, in turn, had my grandmother, Hazel, who had my father, who met my mother and had me. We can find no record of a marriage license being given to Rosemary, so it might be that she was never married. If she was never married, then who is my great-great-grandfather?"

"Let's change directions for a minute. Let's forget about the husband, and let's see what we can find out about the house. What do we know?"

"Well, going back to the original owners," Darcy said, reading from the monitor. "John Taft was a real estate developer. He had constructed private homes and apartment buildings in downtown San Francisco. But he cut corners when he built them and got caught."

"Who caught him?" Kerry asked.

"Mother Nature. The 1906 earthquake. Brought everything he had built crashing down. He was nearly indicted and charged with the deaths of six people.

"After that, Taft packed up his wife, along with his rather substantial savings, and relocated to Santa Cruz."

"Man, that doesn't tell us anything. This is about as successful as a diet in December." Kerry's arm was hurting. "What good does it do us to know that Taft moved here and built the house?"

Inspiration hits at odd moments, and it chose this moment to slap Darcy across the face. "Duh!" she said out loud.

"What?" Kerry asked, hoping for a break.

"Okay, we know Taft built it, but how did George Thornton get the house?"

"What do you mean?"

"It's called the Thornton Mansion, not the Taft Mansion. How did George Thornton get the house? Did he buy it? If he did, then there has to be a record of that transaction."

Darcy pulled out her cell phone and called City Hall. Because she had to research the history of particular properties around town, she had often used this number to get her answers. The phone was answered after one ring.

"City Hall records," the male voice said.

"Junior? Is that you?"

"Darcy, baby, when you gonna come get me out from here and give me a shot at sweeping you off your feet?"

"Junior, I got some bad news for you on that front. It looks like I'm off the market. I got me a regular fella now." Darcy and Junior had never met face to face, but they had developed a phone banter that both enjoyed.

"Say it ain't so! How's a guy supposed to make it through a shift without the sexy tones of the lovely Miss Darcy?"

"Well, we can still talk, I guess. No harm in that, is there?" Darcy giggled.

"Yeah, we'll always have extension 204. What can I do for you today?"

"Do me a quick favor. Look up the Thornton mansion history and tell me how it comes into the possession of George Thornton."

"I thought you already sold that monstrosity. To the fat, geeky guy."

"I did, but something's come up, and I need to know as soon as possible," Darcy tried to sound important without being desperate.

"Hang on." She heard a click and the dulcet tones of Muzak filled the airwaves.

Darcy looked at Kerry. "I have this relationship with this guy in records. Never met him, but he's in love with me. I'm lucky he'll still do me these favors now that you've annexed my body." She smiled and reached out for Kerry's hand.

"Yeah, well, I better not catch him calling you at home," he smiled.

Junior came back on the line.

"Okay, sweetness. I got it right here. It says that George Thornton inherited the property upon the death of his daughter. Her name was Sheila Taft, and she died in 1910. Does that do anything for you?"

Darcy subtly pulled the imaginary victory handle.

"Junior, I'll think of you every time I google. You're the best. Thanks."

"Don't stay away so long. It gets lonely down here. See ya!"

"Well, I guess this makes sense. Not sure why we didn't think of it. Sheila Taft is George Thornton's daughter and Rosemary's sister. She was also my great-great-aunt."

As Kerry and Darcy celebrated their breakthrough outside, sitting in the silver Audi, Stan and Hannah alternated groping each other and keeping an eye on the front entrance of the library. They were waiting for Darcy and Kerry to come out. They had followed them to the library a few hours earlier and were passing the time as best they could. The time was drawing near, and it was their job to keep track of the demon girl.

Chapter 51

It took Darcy and Kerry an hour to find the gruesome details of Sheila Taft's death. It was in the old editions of the *Santa Cruz Courier*. On September 22, 1910, despondent over failed business dealings, John shot his wife and then took his own life with a single bullet to the brain.

There were a number of follow-up stories attached to the Taft deaths. A number of articles focused on John's failed construction business and how he had lost it.

They discovered several articles dealing with the family of Sheila Taft, and Darcy found these the most informative. They already had a good deal of information about the father, but when she found an article about Rosemary, she got very excited. With a slight quiver in her voice, she read the article aloud to Kerry.

```
Rosemary's Sister

By Harlan Quinlan

December 14, 1910

Rosemary Thornton Wallace went to church this
morning. Not a newsworthy event for many of us,
but in Rosemary's case, her situation rises above
the rest. She went to pray for a sister, a sister
taken from her too early and too gruesomely.
Rosemary's sister's name is Sheila. Sheila's
```

husband is John Taft. They both died in a brutal murder/suicide just two months ago.

Life started out well for the two Thornton girls, and as they grew older, they took different paths. Rosemary went off to Stanford while her older sister Sheila chose to marry. Rosemary was the maid of honor, of course, yet she objected to the tradition of the ceremony. She felt her sister had to cast off the veil and the vows and stand toe to toe with her new husband as his equal. Yes, Rosemary was a suffragette. She spoke her mind. She definitely had opinions. But her sister Sheila longed for the white veil, the walk down the aisle, the white picket fence, and she found all of it right here in our sleepy little community of Santa Cruz. Even though Rosemary would often chastise her sister's submissive ways, Sheila was content, kept a wonderful home, and made a wonderful wife for her husband… until he turned a gun on her.

Rosemary Thornton Wallace went to church this morning. She went to pray for a husband. A husband that was there one minute and gone the next, a husband that did not live to see his unborn child. Last week, Ronald Wallace was killed when he fell from a trolley, an impossibly cruel twist of fate.

Rosemary had married Ronald in a small, private service shortly after they met at

Stanford. She soon discovered that she was expecting.

So, Rosemary Thornton Wallace went to church this morning, exactly as she did the morning before and the morning before that.

She will go to church tomorrow morning as well and pray for her husband. She will pray for her unborn child. She will pray for the strength to forgive her dead brother-in-law. Most of all, she will pray for forgiveness … for herself. Why? It may be the biggest tragedy to come from this awful episode is the guilt felt by Rosemary Thornton Wallace. The guilt of losing a sister. The guilt of surviving such a heinous event. The guilt of knowing something was wrong and being unable to act. The guilt of now being alone.

Maybe next time you are in church, you can say a prayer for Rosemary Thornton Wallace. I think she could use the help.

"Well, not the best prose, but it looks like she did get married!" said Kerry. "That's some story, though. God, I feel awful."

"Yeah, I hear ya," said Darcy. "But a least now we have a last name. Rosemary Wallace, wife of Ronald Wallace."

"She probably got married over in Palo Alto. It says it was a private ceremony. Maybe George and Sheila weren't even there."

"Now we have a date. This article was written in December 1910. That means she was probably married sometime that summer. That should help us a lot."

"I'm going to find a genealogy site and see what they can tell us about Rosemary Wallace."

Hunger finally drove them from the library an hour later, laden with research material that all dealt with the Thorntons, the Tafts, and the house. They packed all of their material into the back seat and headed out, looking for a little refreshment and quiet time. Naturally, they headed to D-Breeze.

Neither of them noticed when the silver Audi pulled out behind them and followed at a discreet distance.

A half-hour later, Darcy and Kerry sat at their booth in D-Breeze with the stack of research material in front of them. Kerry had his laptop open and continued to work.

"So, where to from here?" Darcy asked.

"Let's keep following Rosemary. She seems to be the key. We have to figure that Ronald is your great-great-grandfather, but maybe not her husband. I've been searching the records for the entire Bay area from 1905 to 1911 and am finding nothing about a marriage between Rosemary and Ronald."

"Well, we know he existed. We have the article that tells us about his death in the trolley accident." Darcy was exasperated.

"Maybe he did exist but his death was just a convenience that she created to cover up the fact she was knocked up," Kerry said off the top of his head. "I mean, he supposedly died a month after they were married. The way they did things then is it weird that no one would have had the chance to meet him?"

"Would she do that?" asked Darcy. "Would she make up a husband just to cover up a pregnancy?"

"Hey, back in those days, that was a huge no-no. Gals just didn't lift their skirts unless they were already walked down the aisle. If she'd been messing around and got caught, she might do anything to avoid the stigma of being an unwed mother,"

"Including making up a husband? Okay then, what if Ronald wasn't the father? What if she never even knew him? What if you're right, and she made the whole thing up?" The excitement in her voice was building. "If Rosemary wasn't married, who was the father of her child?"

"Let's recap. John and Sheila were married on April 26, 1903. The earthquake hit, toppling John's buildings in '06. The house started construction in '07, and Sheila and John moved to Santa Cruz in '09. Which means they'd been married for six years at the time. They lived in the house for about a year when on September 22, 1910, John murdered Sheila and then killed himself. Sometime in 1911, George Thornton inherited and remodeled. George died in the pool in 1915. Well, there you go," said Kerry. "What does this tell us?"

"I don't have a clue. Let's look at what we can verify. We know Sheila and Rosemary were sisters, that John and Sheila were married."

"What we don't know is the father of Rosemary's baby. God, just that phrase freaks me out. We don't know when she had the baby, and we don't know when or how Rosemary died."

Kerry thought about it for a few seconds. "I suppose I should try obituaries and see if we can find anything about her death. There's a whole category on this program that searches obits all over the country. I'll run her through."

Rosemary Thornton netted nothing. He then tried *Rosemary Wallace,* and he got sixteen returns. Two of them were listed in 1914.

"Okay, check it out ... Rosemary Wallace died on March 15, 1914. Mrs. Wallace was born Rosemary Thornton on March 15, 1883. Rosemary Thornton married Ronald

346

Wallace of Palo Alto. The couple had one child, a boy, George John Wallace. She was preceded in death by her husband Ronald, who perished in a trolley accident. Services for Mrs. Wallace were held at the Holy Trinity Episcopal Church. Her son was placed in the care of her father, George Thornton."

Kerry looked at Darcy, who had been holding her breath as he read.

"So that's it. The boy was my great-grandfather, George John Wallace." Darcy said breathlessly. "We can trace the line from there."

"Yeah, we sure can. How about that, though? She died on her birthday. I always think that's weird." Kerry said. "Shakespeare died on his birthday too."

That tidbit of information warranted a quick sneer from Darcy.

"Yeah, whatever. Find out what happened to little Georgie."

"George initially had custody, but he died a short time later. I can drop him into the genealogy program, and we can probably find out right away. Let's give it a try."

"I'll get us another couple of beers. Be right back." Darcy grabbed the empties and headed over to the bar. She set the bottles down and asked Drew for two more.

"Sure thing. You guys look plenty busy over there. What's up? House hunting?" He gave a little chuckle as he pried.

"No, Drew, more like ghost hunting."

"Really? What kind?" He set two cold ones in front of her.

"Just some research into the Thornton place. We've been having some issues," she said as she turned to go.

"Wow. I don't doubt it, what with your dad and everything." Drew wiped off the countertop with a wet white dishrag removing the condensation rings the cold bottles had left.

Darcy stopped in her tracks and turned back to Drew.

"My father? Why would you say that?"

"Well, last time anyone saw him, he was pulling into the driveway up at that old place. I thought you knew that."

Darcy looked at Drew as though he had just given her winning lotto numbers. She set the bottles on the bar and shook her head.

"How do you know that?"

Drew leaned over to her and talked in a low voice. "I'm really sorry. I thought you knew all about it. That's why I figured you always hung out here."

"What the hell are you talking about?"

"I was the one that saw your dad drive up to the house. I really thought you knew. That made me the last person to see him."

She stared at Drew as though he was a winning lotto ticket. "You knew my father?"

"I worked with him at the tire store. We hung out all the time. I even had dinner with your mom and you when you were little. We used to have barbecues at your mom and dad's place all the time ... before he got weird."

"Weird?"

"Yeah, just before he took off. He was talking to himself and mumbling about nightmares and stuff. He looked like hell. I just figured that him and your mom weren't getting along, and he was upset about it. It wasn't my business."

Darcy finally said, "Drew, how long have I been coming in here?"

"I don't know, before you were supposed to, I know that."

"And in all that time, you never once mentioned that you knew my father?"

Drew shuffled a bit behind the bar. "I figured if you wanted to talk about him, you'd ask. I figured your mom would've told you. It's not a secret."

Darcy slowly swiveled back and forth on the stool. She had been totally unprepared for this bit of information, and it had left her dazed and confused.

Drew went to the other end of the bar to fill a drink order. He came back as soon as he was done.

"You saw him drive up to the Thornton place the morning he disappeared? Any idea what he was doing up there?"

"Nah, he used to always talk about the place, say how he wasn't afraid of it and stuff. I figured he was going there on a dare or something. I never got the chance to ask him."

"It was in the morning, you're sure?"

"Hell, yeah. I was out running." He patted his swollen stomach. "I used to be in pretty good shape. I saw his car pull into the driveway. I was going to follow him but had to get back in time for work. I figured I'd ask him about it later."

"Shit."

"Yeah. Well, listen, you have any more questions or if you ever just want to talk about it, you call me anytime, okay?"

He reached over the bar and patted her hand. A waitress was calling him from the other end of the bar, and he walked away.

Darcy picked up the two bottles of beer and walked back to the booth, where Kerry sat furiously working on his laptop. She slid in beside him.

"I think I have something here. I may have found your great-grandfather." Kerry said as he reached over and grabbed one of the bottles. After a long swig, he said, "It looks like George John Wallace was placed with a family when he was 3. Their name was Colombe, and they changed his to match. He married a woman named Mildred Fleming in 1930. They had two kids, Colleen and Hazel. Hazel is your grandmother."

He raised his hands in the touchdown gesture and laughed. He looked at Darcy for the first time since she had sat down and was taken aback.

"Whoa, what's up? You look like you've seen a ghost. Well, okay, you kinda have, but … what's up?"

"I'm at the bar, and Drew tells me that he knew my father. He tells me that he saw my dad the day he disappeared. He told me that my dad went up to the Thornton house that morning, and no one ever saw him again."

Kerry did an actual double-take. Not a perfectly timed, comedic double-take, but an actual two turns of his head, like he was trying to shake the information deeper into his skull so that he could get it to his brain and comprehend it. "You gotta be shitting me?"

"No, I'm not. Drew knew my dad. He was the last person to see him … and he never said anything till now."

She took out her cell phone and face-timed her mother.

Gail answered it after the second ring.

"Hey Mom, I just had a conversation with Drew over at D-Breeze. He told me what happened the day daddy disappeared. Do you know more than you told me?"

"I don't know anything. He saw him go to the house, and no one ever saw him again." Her mother's voice was starting to crack.

"Did anyone ever find his car?" Darcy asked.

"It was at the house. The police think that he hitchhiked because the car was about to be repossessed."

"What else do you know about his family? I know there's something else you aren't telling me."

Gail paused again. "I'm not sure, but I think Rosemary, the woman in the picture, killed herself in that house."

Darcy sat back in the booth and looked at Kerry. She rolled her eyes back and slowly shook her head.

"You have any idea why you think that?"

"Just from things your grandmother would say from time to time. Rosemary was her grandmother, and I got the impression that's what happened. As you know, we weren't the closest of friends. Honey, what's going on?"

"What happened that day? When Dad left."

"I was home baking. You were in kindergarten, and he was supposed to pick you up on his lunch break. The school called and said that no one had shown up. I went to get you and forgot about the cake. When we got back, the apartment was filled with smoke, and the cake was ruined. It's funny. I started to cry because I had ruined his birthday cake. I had no idea I'd never see him again."

Darcy swallowed hard. "You were making a birthday cake for Dad?"

"Yeah, he disappeared on his birthday. I thought you knew that?"

"No, Mom. No, I didn't know."

There was a moment of silence between them.

"Honey, whatever is going on, you have to be careful. That house is bad news."

"We are learning that the hard way," Darcy said. "Love you."

Darcy closed her phone and looked at Kerry. "My Dad disappeared on his birthday."

Kerry took Darcy's hand. "This isn't a pattern yet. Let's not jump to conclusions."

"I'm not sure I believe in coincidence where this house is concerned. Rosemary died on her birthday. My Dad disappears on his birthday … maybe he didn't leave us after all."

Chapter 52

As they walked to the car, Kerry said, "You know what? I gotta ask Drew another question. Why don't you pull the car around, and I'll be right out?"

"Okay," Darcy said without much enthusiasm.

Kerry strode back into the bar and called for Drew.

"Yeah, what's up?" Drew said, wiping his hands dry on a towel.

"You know, it's pretty strange that you knew Darcy's dad and never said anything about it." Kerry started.

"Well, like I said, I just figured that she'd ask if she wanted to know."

"I get that. What I don't get is why you suddenly told her tonight? Did she ask?"

Drew started to play with the booze bottles sitting in his well. He finally looked at Kerry straight in the eye.

"Well, you know Hannah Brower, the cop?" Drew said.

"What about Hannah?"

"She was in earlier, and we got to talking about Darcy and the house and stuff. I told her about Darcy's Dad. It just got me to thinking that we'd never talked about it.

I was wondering how I should go about telling Darcy when she walked up and mentioned the Thornton place. It was the perfect opening. I'm really sorry for not mentioning it before. I hope she understands."

"Yeah, okay. Take it easy." Drew turned away and walked out of the bar.

Out front, he looked for Darcy's car and didn't see it. He moved in the direction of the parked car, and he saw the commotion well before he arrived. A short, stocky man with a ski mask was dragging Darcy across the lot toward a green car. Behind the wheel of the car was another person in a ski mask gesturing wildly for him to get her inside. Kerry ran towards them. He body slammed the smaller man from the back, right between the shoulder blades. The masked man's head snapped back, and he released Darcy instantaneously. She fell to the ground holding her throat. Kerry rolled off the man before he had even stopped moving and was back in a standing position before the masked man could lift his head.

"Who the hell are you?" Kerry screamed.

Suddenly he heard the squeal of tires spinning on the asphalt, and the car moved forward in a fast, jerky motion. The movement of the car pulled Kerry's attention away from the masked man for just a moment, but it was a moment too long. The masked man reached out and grabbed Kerry's ankle and jerked. Kerry went flying into the air and landed hard on his back. He raised his head only to catch the masked man's foot with his chin. Kerry's head snapped back, and he rolled over, trying to protect himself from a follow-up attack. Kerry continued to roll until he was able to generate enough energy to pop to his feet, anticipating an attack. Instead, he saw the man running across the parking lot and jumping into a pale green sedan. The door slammed, and the car took off.

Darcy was lying on the ground, her notes and books scattered all around her like bystanders unable to help. Kerry kneeled next to her and helped her to a sitting position.

"You okay?"

Darcy gasped. She took heavy breaths as though she had been drowning and had just broken the surface.

"It's okay?" Kerry now had her in his arms, and they sat on the asphalt. Kerry held her and rocked her slowly until she was breathing normally.

"What the hell was that?"

"I have no idea."

Darcy looked at Kerry, and tears started to well up. She dropped her head on his shoulder and shook it side to side.

"Who were they?"

Kerry held her tight for a moment and then helped her to her feet.

"Come on. Let's get out of here before they come back. We'll call the police from your place."

He helped her stand, and they collected their research and notebooks as quickly as they could and headed for Darcy's car.

Darcy screamed. Her car, the brand-new, bright red symbol of her financial independence, was full of water. Not just water, but seawater, complete with kelp and seaweed. Kerry couldn't believe his eyes. The sunroof was open, and there were tiny waves lapping the rubber seal that circled the opening, tiny tsunamis destroying the fabric of their minds. As he moved closer, he saw movement inside. There was a moray eel circling the gear shift.

Chapter 53

An hour later, Kerry and Darcy lay in her bed. She was wearing an old D-Breeze T-shirt. It was tattered and faded, but she loved it because it was the first thing she had ever won.

The competition was simple; a hermit crab, picked from dozens of others by chance, was set in the middle of a circle with other contestants of the same species. She had taken to calling it Lefty since it always canted to the left and used her fingernail polish to put an 'L' on its shell. All the contestants were placed under a bowl in the center of a big circle. At the word 'go,' the bowl was raised, and the crabs ran for the outer circle. The first crab to cross the outer circle won. She won the prelims and moved all the way to the final round. One more win, and it would have been a 4-day trip to Maui. Lefty let her down. So, instead of Hawaii, she got the t-shirt along with a certificate for $100 worth of beer. The certificate was gone a week later. She still had the t-shirt, and it was in that t-shirt that Kerry held her close. She had finally fallen off to sleep, and not too long after, Kerry had done the same.

And then his dream continued.

The shadow picked up speed as it circled the room. One revolution every two or three seconds.

Kerry grabbed Darcy and stood her up. She was dazed and barely responsive.

"Darcy, you gotta wake up. We gotta leave, now!"

He could see a flicker in her eye and knew that she could hear him. Probably like you hear your mom when she comes in to wake you up, a disconnected voice in your subconscious. He had to get Darcy to pay attention to him now. He had to wake her up.

"Darcy! Wake up!" He screamed and slapped her face.

Darcy screamed. She slapped Kerry back as hard as she could.

And with that, she started to fight. Darcy kicked and screamed and scratched and punched poor Kerry until he almost let go of her. Then she saw the shadow.

Her screams turned from outrage to terror. Kerry wasted no time. He grabbed her hand and ran toward the door. Suddenly he realized they couldn't just leave. He slammed on the brakes and grabbed Darcy just before they ran through the door. He knew instinctively that they couldn't let the shadow touch them.

He was watching the shadow as it circled the room and saw it had picked up a good deal of speed. It was barely two seconds now for it to make a rotation of the room.

"Are you crazy? Let's go!"

"We can't let it touch us. We gotta time it and then jump through the door without it touching us."

"Yeah, I get it."

"As soon as it passes, we go. We'll let it take three turns and then go after the third. Got it?"

"Right. Here we go." She squeezed Kerry's hand.

Just at that moment, the shadow shifted. Instead of circling the room, it now moved from the left side of the archway back to the right, making a full rotation around the room. It was leaving an opening for them to escape. And just to be certain that there was no confusion about what they were to do, a high-pitched scream came from within the living room and nearly forced them out.

The scream added that extra bit of motivation for them to move, and he pulled Darcy through the archway and toward the broken window.

"Run, Darcy, run!"

They were up and through the window in a nanosecond and on their bikes pedaling for home. Window glass was breaking from the high-pitched squeal, and they heard it shattering as it hit the concrete paths that surrounded the house. They didn't look back, terrified that eye contact would invite the thing to follow.

After about a mile, along a wooded path that was a shortcut to their homes, Kerry and Darcy stopped to catch their breath. They looked at each other, dropped their bikes, and hugged, holding on for dear life.

As they pulled apart, Darcy became aware of the fact that her bra was unsnapped and hanging quite loose.

"What the ...?"

"I'm so sorry. You never gave the stop sign, so I just kept going. "

"You just kept going? I was mostly unconscious."

"I didn't know... and as soon as I did, I stopped. That's why I slapped you to ..."

Darcy grabbed Kerry's face in her hands and kissed him passionately. The groping, the frightening experience, and the clean get-away provided all the adrenaline she needed. They dropped to the grass along the side of the path and made love. It was spontaneous, impassioned, and pure. It was the perfect first time. So intense, intimate, and unique that neither of them had ever again experienced lovemaking like that … until recently.

Chapter 54

Kerry awoke the next morning sore and exhausted.

"I had the dream again, only this time I finished it."

"I know," Darcy said, wiping the sleep from her eyes.

"How do you know?" Kerry asked. "Or don't I want to know?"

"I had it, too. It was our first time, and I remember it perfectly now. I'd always considered that time on the football field after the Harbor High game our first time. I never even remembered the real first time." Darcy said.

"You think that's what started it? Us going up there that day." Kerry asked.

"I don't know. It's always felt weird to me, even thinking about it."

"Yeah. I took a lot of shit from the guys cause I'd never go near it after that. Now, look at us. You sell it, and I remodel it. What the hell were we thinking?"

"Talk about repressed memories. I wonder what else we don't know?"

They lay silently next to each other, holding hands, for several minutes. Then Darcy spoke.

"The thing that scares me most is that it'll hurt you."

"I don't think it's after me. I think it wants you. For whatever reason, there is a connection that you have with this thing and your family."

"Any ideas?"

"Aside from moving to Oklahoma, no, I don't."

Darcy sat up suddenly. She looked at Kerry and jumped out of bed.

"What! What is it?"

"Oklahoma! You just made me realize something." She ran into the kitchen, where all of her notes and their research had been dumped on the kitchen table.

"Didn't one of the couples that owned the house sell it quickly and move to Oklahoma?" She frantically dug through the material.

Kerry was standing in the kitchen, naked, staring at her. "Yeah, it's why I said it. So what?"

"Well, as we've been learning more about this stuff, my relatives and all, the names have always sounded familiar." She was rifling through the papers looking for some specific information.

"Find that genealogy stuff on the laptop," she said as she continued flipping through the pages.

Kerry sat down and fired up the laptop.

"Go to the beginning. Rosemary Thornton."

"Okay. Rosemary Thornton."

"And her son was George John Wallace, my great-grandfather, right?"

"Yeah, adopted by a family named Colombe when he was 3. They changed his name."

Darcy flipped through the file from Lewis Realty. "Who were his kids?"

Kerry scrolled through some more of the information and finally said, "Two kids, both girls. Colleen and Hazel, your grandmother."

"Colleen. There was a woman killed at the house named Colleen Van De Lin. Any chance that she's the same one?"

Kerry looked up at Darcy.

"Holy shit. If that's true ..."

He quickly found information about Colleen Van De Lin and read aloud, "Colleen's maiden name was Colombe. She was the daughter of George and Mildred Colombe of Atascadero, California. Born July 23, 1936. Married Harry S. Van De Lin on June 14, 1958."

Kerry blanched, "Died July 23, 1960."

A chill ran up both their spines. "Colleen died on her birthday." Kerry's eyes rose to meet hers over the computer monitor.

"This is getting freaky. Does she have any kids?"

"There was a daughter, Theresa. Let's see what we can find out about her."

Kerry went back to his file and inserted the name, Theresa Van De Lin.

"Okay, there's a couple of them. The first one was born on August 5, 1948. That would make her too old. Let's see the next one. This might work, November 26, 1953. She was born in …"

"Never mind." Darcy cut him off. She had been scanning their notes and remembered the widow who had moved into the house with her male secretary. "Look for the one whose married name is McFadden."

Kerry turned back quickly, hoping not to find what he was certain that he would find.

"Theresa Van De Lin, born December 7, 1959. Married Thomas McFadden, age 46, on August 14, 1985. One child... given up for adoption? Harsh. Thomas died March 12, 1987."

Darcy read, ...*the widow was discovered in the laundry room, eviscerated with a knife used to shell clams.*

"Theresa died ..." Kerry stopped and looked at Darcy.

"Don't tell me, on her birthday."

"Your relatives have a funny family tradition. Who's next?"

She glanced at the papers and said, "That rich couple, Mary and Phil, but they don't seem to fit in here. There's no one in the family with those names."

Kerry said. "True, but we now have an adopted child floating around... pardon the pun."

Kerry entered their names and got back the information. "Okay, Phil Hale was the oldest son of Francis Hale, the railroad magnate. His wife Mary was his father's partner's daughter. These guys hung out with the Rockefellers. There's no way I can prove it, but I'll bet ya that Phil was adopted."

"If this is all true, all of my relatives died at the house with the exception of Rosemary, George John, and Hazel. Hazel would never come to Santa Cruz and died an alcoholic in Sacramento."

Kerry searched again.

"Well, George John died in World War II in 1941. He won a Silver Star posthumously."

"So, his death is not connected to the house? What date did he die?"

"August 14, 1941. Doesn't match. He was born in February. But does it really matter? People die in ways other than murder. Maybe fate just stepped in."

"And Rosemary? What can you find?" Darcy stood up and walked behind Kerry and wrapped her arms around his shoulders. Kerry patted her forearm and continued typing.

"Here it is. Rosemary died in 1914." He spoke slowly. "She died on her birthday from a self-inflicted gunshot wound in the backyard of her father's house."

Darcy's knees gave way, and she slumped down. Kerry caught her and, sliding out of his chair, guided her into it in one swift motion. He turned to the kitchen sink and got her a glass of water.

"So, Rosemary died at the house too. And was the first one to die on her birthday." Kerry said.

As she drank the water, Kerry leaned against the wall next to her and slowly slid to the ground, sitting with his knees to his chest. His left foot softly dropped onto Darcy's, and he slowly rubbed the arch of her foot with the bottom of his own.

"I have to ask this, sweetie, because I can't remember. When's your birthday?"

Darcy had no color on her face, her lips were white, and he hands were shaking. With tears rolling down her cheeks, she looked at Kerry with the sweetest expression she could muster and said, "Tomorrow."

Chapter 55

Edith was experiencing a rare afternoon of lucidity. She was more like her old self than she had been in quite a while. Her hip felt glorious and pain-free, and her spirits were high.

Henry had left for the afternoon, again, leaving her alone in the house. Edith thought about her trip to the attic, and she embarrassed herself with the memory.

I can't even tell someone to go to hell anymore.

"Stay out of the *backyard!*" She could hear Henry tell her that for the thousandth time. Not the attic. ... *but just because I can't do it all the time doesn't mean I can't do it now. I think a trip out back is just what the doctor ordered."*

With a resolve she hadn't felt in a long time, she put on a pink striped sweater over her beige patterned housecoat, and with welcomed ease, Edith grabbed her walker and headed to the stairs. A stairlift had been installed on the front stairway before that tall, handsome man had left.

The chair glided softly down the twin aluminum rails and coasted to a stop at the bottom. Gathering her walker, she headed toward the kitchen. She pushed the walker in front of her but was not relying on it to stand. How glorious a feeling was that? She entered the kitchen and went straight to the back door. She saw that it had a broken pane of glass, and it looked to Edith as though there was blood on the glass.

"What in the world is that all about?"

Edith and her walker moved through the mud room and the screen door and onto the landing. It was the first time she had ever been out here. It was quite pleasant.

Yes, I am going to like spending afternoons here.

She moved to the steps that led from the landing to the ground.

More stairs! Why are there so many stairs in this damn house?

This time she did not have the advantage of a stairlift, but she was not to be deterred so easily. Approaching the top of the stairs, she grabbed the handrail and turned around. With her back to the stairs, she carefully lowered her right foot from the top of the landing onto the first step. The handrail in one hand, she dropped her left foot onto the top step and there she was, one step closer to the bottom. She repeated this process, bringing the walker along after her, and in a matter of minutes, she was standing on the ground in the backyard.

She saw the pool and moved in that direction, and there was not a whisper of a breeze. Odd. It was almost as though the wind had died, not died down but actually died. She longed for a cool breeze to tickle her neck and dry the perspiration that had formed on her upper lip.

Edith was ten feet from the lip of the pool when she stopped to catch her breath. She was growing tired, and her hip was beginning to throb. She hadn't walked this much in a long time. She then realized that she had accomplished her objective. She was in Henry's precious backyard. She dropped the plastic seat that was stowed in the center of her walker and sat down, looking out over the blue Pacific. She would sit here, in the sunshine, and wait for Henry to come home.

As she sat enjoying the warmth, Edith became troubled. Something seemed out of sync. She turned to look back at the house. Tracks in the dirt exposed the route she had taken, and yet something about the yard was bothering her.

The ground! The ground was as solid as a rock. Henry had lied to her. He had told her a hundred times how treacherous the backyard could be, yet this ground had better footing than the front path, and she managed that several times a week.

"Who the hell do you think you are, young man? We are going to have a little chat about this, yes, siree."

She stood up, about to march back into the house, when she heard a strange sound coming from behind her. She would have expected to hear the mechanical sounds of a pool filter, but this sound was nothing like that. It wasn't mechanical. It sounded almost like an animal wailing.

Off to the side of the yard, the side furthest from the stairs, she saw a structure that seemed to be the origin of the sounds. Momentarily taken back, her anger calmed, and she moved a bit closer, using the walker to aid her. The sounds grew louder.

"Hello? Is anyone there?"

There was no response. She reached out and tested the door to see if it was locked. One easy pull on the knob answered with a resounding 'no.' The door swung open. As it did, the sounds grew louder.

Although she knew she should walk away and wait for Henry, she couldn't help herself. With much trepidation, she moved inside the ramshackle hut and waited for her eyes to adjust to the darkness.

She felt spider webs cross her face and quickly wiped them away. Her eyes were used to the bright sunlight of the outside, and she couldn't see a thing in front of her. She dropped the seat on her walker once again to sit and recoup while she waited for her eyes to adjust to the darkness. While she sat in the doorway, the very strange sounds continued to come from deep below her.

The sound reminded Edith of a dog tearing at a bone. Then it changed and became a purr with a very sweet quality, like a lullaby. It raised the hair on the back of her neck and arms. As her eyes made the adjustment, the sounds continued, and this time it contained elements of both—growling delight?

As her eyes grew accustomed to the light, Edith realized she was on a landing. There was a circular staircase in front of her that led down. She was very grateful that she had stopped where she had. If not, she would have surely fallen down these stairs. The noises from below shifted and became more of a moan. Unable to deny her curiosity, she grabbed hold of the handrail, turned cautiously, and began to descend her second stairway in the last half hour.

As she took the first step down into the darkness, she wished there was a safety light. The stairs were very steep and very narrow. Each step was shaped like the blade of a fan, narrow on the inside and wider at the outside edge. It made it very difficult for her walker to fit securely enough that she could trust it would hold her as she reached for the next step below. The walker was banging and scraping the sides of the iron railing on both sides, and she knew that she was marking the old nemesis irreparably with each movement.

Maybe this isn't such a great idea.

Looking back to the landing, she attempted to move her walker up one step and discovered that it would not go. The walker had become an impassable roadblock to the top of the stairs. The only direction she could move was down. She was five steps down a flight of rusted wrought-iron stairs, with the top and safety so plainly in sight and yet impossibly out of reach.

Oh hell, what choice do I have now?

It appeared that the staircase itself was getting narrower as it went down. Edith took another step down and moved the walker with her. It wedged itself between the two railings and was not touching the steps. She knocked it from underneath with the palm of her hand, hoping to knock it free. It moved slightly. She hit it again in a good swift upward motion, and she felt her hand bruise. It moved a bit more.

One more good hit should knock it right out of there.

She took a deep breath and swung her hand again. The walker popped out of the stair and fell towards her.

She could feel her bruised hand swelling as she grabbed the walker and moved it away from her, careful not to let it fall back into a wedged position on the stairs.

"What the hell do I do now?"

She knew that she would need it at the bottom, but it obviously wasn't going to fit inside the railings for the rest of the descent.

"Ah hell, just drop it and get it when you get down there."

She maneuvered herself so that she could lower her aluminum burden over the side of the railing and let it go. The walker bounced off of the staircase a few times before it eventually hit the ground, creating a racket. It took longer than she expected to hit, and when it did, it made a very loud clatter that reverberated up the stairwell. It sounded to Edith that she might have a bit more of a journey in front of her than she anticipated.

"If there were any scary critters down here, that should frighten them away for sure."

She grabbed the two handrails, which were very close, considering the narrow staircase, and kept moving backward down the wrought iron torture track. She paused for a moment, realizing that she now had access to the top of the stairs, but even if she were to get back up, with her walker on the floor below her, she would be stuck in the shack, unable to get to the house. She continued down where she knew there was someone who could help.

Providing that these sounds are coming from a person.

The steps were so steep she felt that she was climbing down a ladder. The railings were quite rusted, and they scraped at her palms as she slid them down with each step.

One painful step at a time, and ten minutes later, she finally reached the bottom of the stairs. She was exhausted and sore and wanted nothing more than to be in her room watching TV but instead was at the bottom of a tunnel and lost in her own backyard.

She saw a soft glow of light coming from down the tunnel. There was a small LED light that had been placed indelicately on the wall. She was grateful for otherwise she would be in pitch black. She looked about for her walker. The badly scraped aluminum frame faced her, and she could tell immediately that the walker had landed awkwardly. The two front legs were bent and had caved in on the rest of the framework. Without the front two legs, it was useless for her. It wouldn't be helping her move about anymore.

The noise continued from the chamber ahead. If it was an animal, it could rip her to shreds. If the sound was produced by a human, the prospect was even scarier. Of all the things that it could be, though, the sound represented the one thing that gave Edith hope—that someone was down here.

Using the wall to steady herself, she moved toward the end of the walkway, and the sound became more distinct, like someone in the throngs of sexual ecstasy.

"Oh my," she said aloud as the feeling she was peeking into somebody's window engulfed her. She was reminded of the time she and her sister snuck outside one night to look into her brother's bedroom window. They watched her brother undress and were suitably shocked when he turned full face to the window and reached for something on the bed. It was the first time she had ever seen an adult male naked. She couldn't look her brother square in the face for weeks.

Mercifully, she came to the end of the walkway a few moments later. It was a door. She felt for a knob and with a simple turn, and the door opened. It led to a small chamber that appeared empty expect for a second door on the opposite side, another LED light glowed softly. Edith heard the noises again, louder now that she was inside the chamber. She heard words, a human voice groaning out words.

She froze and listened very intently. She heard it again.

It was Henry's voice.

So that was it! He had lied. He had managed to make an illicit appointment with his concubine, and he had brought her to their house. He didn't think she'd catch on, did he?

Well, time to blow the whistle on Mister Casanova!

Edith charged forward, revitalized. She crossed the chamber as quickly as she could, using the wall as support. The door behind her closed as she moved away. She yanked open the second door with considerable force considering her abilities, the pain in her hands momentarily forgotten. This door led to a large room with a giant window that looked into the pool from below.

The sight of the pool underwater was unnerving. As angry as she was one moment, she was equally apprehensive the next. The light shot through the water and into the chamber, casting multicolored shadows that ricocheted all around her. There were ghosts dancing on the reflective surface of the glass, and they made Edith back away.

As she backed away, she slipped on something on the floor and fell. Her fall was broken by something much softer than the concrete floor, which undoubtedly saved her from a broken hip. She had no idea what she had fallen on but was very much aware of the puddle of a sticky, wet substance she had landed in. Her arms, hands, and the left side of her body were now covered in whatever this was, and the light reflecting through the window made it look red. The smell was awful.

There was a little river leading away from the puddle, and she followed that stream with her eyes. It led to a darker corner of the chamber. Looking closer, she saw the source of the liquid. It was blood that had come from an amputated leg. Next to the leg, in a grotesque pile, were several dead bodies. They were mangled around each other, wrapped in a morbid game of twister.

Edith gasped and recoiled from the sight. The one face she could see was frozen in a scream filled with pain and terror. For the first time in her life, Edith panicked. She turned to where the sounds were originating and called out.

"Help me, please, Henry, help me!" She called out.

Edith saw movement on the other side of the room and reached out a blood covered hand. "Henry, is that you?" She crawled forward to get a closer look leaving a snail trail of blood in her wake. She quickly realized that it was not her son that she saw. In front of her, lit by the sun as it reflected through the window, was a horrifying creature. This thing was flopping on top of her Henry, her naked son!

The creature that Edith saw was not the creature that Henry saw. She was under no spell. Edith could see the scrawny backbone straining for freedom under a thin veil of putrefied flesh. The creature's hair was a matted web of seaweed, covered with loose scales that glittered dully in the reflected sunlight.

The creature's back was naked and had human form, but her lower half was covered with scales that lay dull and infected across her backside. Scales shed as she moved, and a significant pile had accumulated on the bed and the floor surrounding it. At the base of the tail was a giant fin. It flipped vertically as the thing bounced up and down on top of Henry. The ends were ragged, and strips of it flew about as though it was a tattered cat-o'-nine-tails flailing a wayward prisoner.

Henry lay on his back, straining against the creature. He was moving his hips up and down as though he were trying to bounce it off from on top of him. She knew that wasn't the case. Henry didn't want this creature off him. He was screwing it. He was having sex with a monster. The huge fish tail was flopping up and down in a hideous fashion on top of her naked, groaning son.

"HENRY!"

Henry, startled by the sudden scream, spun his head around and saw his mother.

"NOOOO!"

The creature spun toward Edith. Its face was a jumble of skin and bone. Massive wounds adorned the left side of its face, most of which was missing. Edith could see the ripped tissue hanging from its scalp. Its mouth was filled with pointed, tiny teeth laid out in several rows that were twisted and turned. Its lips were still and rigid as that of a tuna. The creature let out a screech of such malevolence and evil that Edith covered her face with her arms in a vain attempt to protect herself.

Henry leaped to his feet, dripping from a combination of seawater, sweat, and the creature's juices, and ran to his prostrate mother.

"Henry ..." the tiny voice whispered.

He released all the rage and hatred that had built up over the years. He kicked her and beat her with all his might. He planted his left foot into the space where Edith's eye ceased to be. His right foot smashed into her shoulder, and the frail bone snapped. He stomped on her upper torso, separating and splintering her rib cage from her spine. He fell to his knees and beat this woman who was now mercifully beyond pain.

Henry was in a fury for which there seemed no end. In a final burst of hatred, he picked up the tiny corpse and flung it into the rock wall, smearing the wall with blood as the skull finally gave way and split open.

He turned back to the creature, who looked more beautiful and more radiant than ever. Henry, the triumphant protector, the jubilant victor, was coming to her to receive his spoils. He took the siren in his arms and pulled it close to him. Leading tongue first, he kissed her hard and deep. They lay beside the mangled corpse of his mother and completed the lovemaking that had been so rudely interrupted.

When Henry was finally spent, the creature's voice sang to him. "It is time," she told him. "It is time to join me. Live with me in the pool, live with me forever."

Chapter 56

While Kerry scrambled late into the night to find a defining pattern between the deaths, Darcy had fallen asleep on the sofa. They had spent the better part of that day researching and charting everything they knew about Darcy's family and hadn't come to any type of conclusion. Kerry was convinced that there was a reason each member of her family that had associated themselves with the house had died on their birthday. It was a fact too consistent to be attributed to coincidence. He used an online form to put together a timeline of her past. Beside each name, he listed the cause of death.

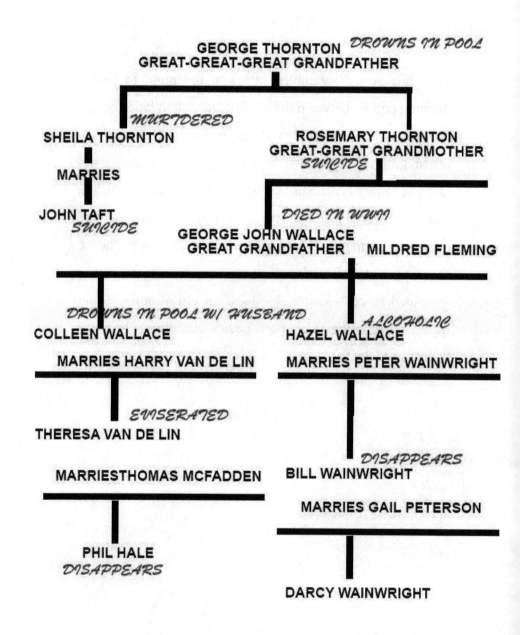

GEORGE THORNTON *DROWNS IN POOL*
GREAT-GREAT-GREAT GRANDFATHER

MURDERED

SHEILA THORNTON

MARRIES

JOHN TAFT
SUICIDE

ROSEMARY THORNTON
GREAT-GREAT GRANDMOTHER
SUICIDE

DIED IN WWII

GEORGE JOHN WALLACE
GREAT GRANDFATHER   MILDRED FLEMING

DROWNS IN POOL W/ HUSBAND
COLLEEN WALLACE

MARRIES HARRY VAN DE LIN

EVISERATED
THERESA VAN DE LIN

MARRIESTHOMAS MCFADDEN

PHIL HALE
DISAPPEARS

ALCOHOLIC
HAZEL WALLACE

MARRIES PETER WAINWRIGHT

DISAPPEARS
BILL WAINWRIGHT

MARRIES GAIL PETERSON

DARCY WAINWRIGHT

Sheila and John had been the first to die at the house, neither of them on their birthdays. Rosemary was next and, it appears, shot herself in the head in the backyard, the first birthday death. George then builds the pool and eventually drowns... Kerry had not checked his date of death, so he quickly looked it up, and, sure enough, he died on his birthday. George was the second family member to die on his birthday.

With two exceptions, all of Darcy's blood ancestor's deaths had a connection to the house and the pool. George John had died in WWII and her grandmother Hazel drank herself to death from a deep-seated fear of Santa Cruz.

He looked at the sleeping form on the sofa and softly walked over. Taking the red afghan from the back of the couch, he laid it gently over her shoulders and torso. Her eyes were moving back and forth under her lids, and he knew she was having another nightmare. He felt helpless, impotent.

His mind worked harder as he sat there looking at her smooth skin squished up in a scowl. Maybe there was something back at the house. Maybe there was another attic with additional information that might explain why all of her relatives were murdered, at the house, on their birthdays. Her birthday was today. He was running out of time, and he had to do something.

Darcy moaned low as she turned onto her side, her eyes moving rapidly right and left.

Kerry leaned over and kissed her wrinkled brow. He grabbed his keys and quietly slipped out of the apartment. He was going to save her one way or the other.

Chapter 57

She was flying and had managed to leap into the air and levitate above the ground. But she was stationary, she had no means to propel herself forward. Just ahead, not terribly out of reach but far enough that she couldn't grab him, stood her father. He was a young man wearing a blue letterman's sweater with a big red 'C.' He was reaching over to her, trying to take her hand.

Darcy strained with all her might to move. If she could only move a mere six inches, she could grab his fingertips and pull herself to him. He was so very close. She could see the pores on his skin, the five o'clock shadow of his beard, and the tiny hair that grew from his left ear. He was her father, and she could save him if she could just reach out six more inches.

Darcy curled up into a ball as tightly as she could. With one explosive effort, she uncoiled, kicking her feet and, reaching out with her arms. She moved forward about an inch. Quickly she did it again, and miraculously she moved forward again, closer to her father now than she had been in years. She reached out for him, but as she did, he slid backward. She curled and kicked again, and as she slid forward, her father slid away. He was still just out of reach.

It was as though there was a magnetic field between them that kept them from actually touching. She curled and kicked and curled and kicked, frantic to make contact, and with each movement, he slid further away. She was out of breath and started screaming for her father to do the same thing, "Curl and kick! Curl and kick! Com'on! I'm doing all the work. You gotta help me."

Still, he slid further and further away, getting smaller as the distance increased between them.

"I gotta get underwater. I can propel myself underwater." In a blink, she was underwater.

She saw her father floating now, off in the distance. With a quick thrust of her upper body, she was Aquawoman, flying through the depth. She moved quickly toward him, and as she did, he moved toward the surface. She accelerated and saw a fishing line in the water. Her father was dangling from the end of this line, a hook in his mouth. He would move away and then drift in place. Each time she approached him, he would be pulled a little further away still, his body flopping as the line yanked him, making him dance in the water.

Darcy swam faster in an attempt to save him. With great effort, she managed to finally reach him, only to have him pulled away. One more giant push, and she grabbed his leg.

Just as she did, she saw a shadow beneath her. She quickly looked down just in time to see the giant jaws open.

"No, Daddy!" Darcy came awake with a scream.

A half-hour later, Darcy sat at the table, on her birthday. Kerry had left and she didn't know where he was and he hadn't answered her texts. In front of her was the pile of research that Kerry had compiled. There were hundreds of pages of family history and sordid deaths, all of them seemingly independent and yet somehow connected. She touched the keyboard, and the screen came to life. He had been running down the descendants of Rosemary Wallace. It started with her son, George John, son of the mythical Ronald Wallace. Darcy fixated on the name. He was obviously named after his grandfather, George John the third or whatever. Darcy touched the keyboard and scrolled to George Thornton's page. She looked over his information, and then suddenly, her mind snapped clear. She read the first line, George Stephan Thornton 1846 – 1915. George STEPHAN Thornton! *Why the different middle name?*

She grabbed her cell phone from the table and hit Kerry's speed dial when the doorbell rang.

She didn't want to open it. She didn't want it to be the police telling her that something had happened to Kerry. She was frozen from fear and anxiety, unable to move.

The bell rang again, followed by a hard knocking. She broke free of the paralysis that had snared her and took three tentative steps to the door, terrified that her life was about to change by the mere act of opening it. Glancing through the peephole, she gasped and dropped her head. Standing outside, in her official uniform, was Hannah Brower.

"Darcy? I know you're in there. I can see your shadow through the peephole. Open up. It's important." Hannah called through the door.

Darcy bowed her head and wished with all her might that the first words out of Hannah's mouth weren't going to be, "Darcy, there's been an accident."

She slowly opened the door.

"What do you want?"

"Mind if I come in?" Hannah walked past her. She turned and looked at Darcy.

"You been crying? You look like shit. What? A lover's spat?" She said with a smile.

"No, it's nothing. What do you want?" Darcy spat back.

"Kerry here?"

"No. I don't know where he is."

Hannah walked over to the table and looked at all of their research. She lifted her head slightly and indicated to Darcy.

"I understand that there's been a crime? Someone vandalized your new car. That's a shame."

"Yeah, we filed a report already. No need for you to get involved." Darcy said, leaving the door open.

"What? If my good friends have a problem, I'm here for them."

"Look, we're fine. Thanks for your help." Darcy tried to move her toward the door.

"You want to back away there, sweetie? I don't like being crowded, you know." One hand fell onto her service revolver.

"Hannah, what's this all about? What do you want?"

"Well, sugar. You know, a long time ago, you stole from me. I'm here to return the favor."

"Hannah, you have to get over that. It <u>was</u> a long time ago. I'm really sorry, if I could change it..."

"But you can't now, can you."

Darcy looked at the front door. It was still open.

"You can't get away, you know. You're thinking right now that you could turn and make a run for it. But you can't. Go on. Try."

She turned and ran to the door.

As she hit the threshold, she was stopped by the squatty bulk of Stan Grossman.

"Wow! Where's the fire?" Stan said with a smile.

Darcy looked into his eyes and wasn't sure what she saw.

Stan saw the police officer and they exchanged a knowing glance.

"Officer, is there a problem here?"

"No. No problem here. I was just following up on a vandalism report. I guess someone filled this poor girl's car with seawater." She moved into the middle of the room.

"Really? Well, that sounds terrible." He turned to Darcy, "Was it your new car?"

Darcy slowly shook her head.

"Man, that sucks. That was a great car." Stan turned back to Hannah. "Did you find the people that did it?"

"No. No luck there. We're still looking." Hannah said.

"Well, then, is there anything else we can do for you here?" Stan asked the officer.

Hannah stared at Stan for a long moment and then shifted her gaze to Darcy.

"No. I guess not. I'll be going. I'll see if I can find any tanker trucks cruising the area." Hannah snickered.

As she walked past Darcy, she placed her hand on the nightstick hanging from her belt, causing it to jut out. It rubbed across Darcy's thighs as she walked by.

"I'll let you know soon as we hear something. You take good care of our boy now, you hear?"

Darcy closed the door immediately as she passed through it.

"I think you might have actually hit her in the ass with the door. Good for you. What was that all about?"

Darcy moved quickly to the window and peeked through the curtains. Hannah was walking down the stairs with a little skip in her walk. She appeared to be whistling.

"I have no idea. She's been out to get me since high school."

Stan walked over to her and put his hands on her shoulders. "Well, she's gone now, and you have me as a witness that she was harassing you in case she comes back. Where's Kerry?"

"I don't know. Why are you here?" Darcy asked as she walked away.

Stan followed and took her hand. He gently turned her around to face him.

"I've got a confession. I'm in love with you." Stan came right out with it.

Darcy blinked fast and said, "What."

"I'm in love with you."

She had heard him right.

"Stan, it's not like that."

"No, wait. You're thinking of the old me, the whore-me that would do anything that moved. I've changed, and you're the biggest reason for that change. I think I'm ready to settle down, and you're the one I want to settle with. I want babies and a house and years of toys all over the place. I want you."

Darcy walked to the middle of the room and turned to face him.

"Stan, I don't know how you got this idea. But, Kerry. You know about him. I'm in love with Kerry. I have been most of my life."

Stan stood and gently crossed to her.

"He'll understand. I'm sure that someone is out there for him. Don't you see, we're meant to be together. It's destiny, fate, kismet, whatever."

Darcy stared at Stan for a long time before she said, "I don't know what the hell is happening here."

"Kerry? What does he do for you? Can he protect you like I can? I don't think so. Do you think that your car would have been trashed if you'd been with me? Do you think you'd have eels swimming around in it if you were with me? You think anyone would dare attack you if you were with me?" His voice became louder and stronger with each sentence. He grew more forceful with each sentence as well.

Darcy stepped back and said, "Stan, it's not going to happen." She moved toward the door.

"You better leave now."

Stan stood perfectly still. He cocked his head and smiled at her impetuousness. "Do you really think I'd leave you today? Today of all days, when it is most important that you are not left alone? I don't think so, Darcy."

Stan walked past her and closed the drapes.

"I think it best if we have some privacy."

Darcy quickly moved to the other side of the room.

"You're scaring me, Stan. Stop, okay?"

"I don't mean to scare you, but this is very important. You do realize that I can keep you safe. I am the only one that can keep you safe."

Darcy stopped short. "How did you know about that? Hannah only talked about the car. She didn't say anything about the eel."

"Oops. My bad. I should have been more careful, huh?" He rubbed his neck, and Darcy saw the bruising that encircled it. A chuckle escaped his slimy lips.

"Yeah, Kerry got in a few good one's last night."

Stan was now in front of her. They were about the same height, but he was easily fifty pounds heavier, with amazing strength for someone his size. He pinned her to the wall in one swift display of agility and strength, his hand on her chin as though he were trying to hang her on a hook.

He leaned in and kissed her neck as she squirmed to escape. "You know, I have always loved the way you smell." He licked her ear.

Darcy wriggled and squirmed to get free, but he held her tight. She brought up her knee to hit his crotch, but he swiftly moved out of the way without releasing her. "Nice try, but that's happened to me before. Not this time, honey."

"Stan, this isn't you. You don't know what you're doing. Please let me go."

Stan leaned against her and pinned her body to the wall. He draped one arm around her and pulled her close to him, pinning her arms between their bodies.

"No. Actually, I don't have to do anything. You belong to me now. Kerry is gone. He won't be coming back. Our loyal police force will see to that." He kissed her neck again and again.

"The police...? You and Hannah?"

"He'll be okay. She's only going to do with him what I'm going to do with you." He picked her up off the ground and started moving toward the bedroom.

"I've waited a long time for this baby. It is gonna be sweet."

Chapter 58

Kerry pulled up the street and parked across from the Thornton house. The sun had fully risen and was streaming from the east, dousing the house in an eerie glow. The radio was playing a Springsteen song. He remembered trying to master the guitar riff in the sixth grade for his band audition. He didn't make the cut.

Tramps like us, baby, we were born to run!

The Boss was pumping up his adrenaline and putting him a little more on edge than he needed to be.

Kerry had no idea if Henry was home or not. Maybe he had taken his mother out to breakfast. The Dodge Ram was not in the driveway, but that wouldn't necessarily mean that he wasn't home.

He'd been sitting across the street for ten minutes when it finally occurred to him that he could call the house on his cell phone. If Henry answered, he could say he was just calling to check up on things. A landline had been installed because his mother was most comfortable with that instrument.

Kerry hit his speed dial; the number was still recorded in its memory.

The phone rang four times, and then the machine picked up. He heard Henry's creepy voice asking for him to leave a message and hung up.

Kerry had a small window of opportunity to explore and see what he could find. If he was caught, the best that could happen would be his arrest for breaking and entering. The worst? He preferred not to consider that.

He turned the ignition off, throwing the car into silence, the Boss's voice dying in his head. His heart was racing. He checked his watch - 8:30. If Henry was out with his mother, he would undoubtedly be back soon, so he had to hurry.

He crossed the street and headed up the driveway.

He went to the front door and used the brass knocker. He rapped loudly, hoping to ensure that the house was indeed empty.

There was no answer. He didn't hear anyone scurrying around inside hurriedly hiding dead bodies, so he executed the next step in his plan. Using the key, he opened the door.

He looked to his left and was surprised by what he saw. The dining room was in the exact same condition it had been the last time he was here, the day of his accident. There had been no work done on it since he left.

He turned to the living room and saw the same situation. He saw the stone fireplace and the empty space on the floor in front of it. For a second, he saw himself and Darcy at 15, groping each other on a blanket. The sense memory of their shared dream spooked him, and he checked for shadows.

He stepped into the room and felt a chill come over him. He walked to the center and tried to keep the entire space within the scope of his vision. He spun three-hundred-sixty degrees as he walked, not wanting to give anything the opportunity to sneak up behind him.

He stopped in front of the old fireplace. It had been built during the remodeling and was over a hundred years old. Grey round river rocks comprised the fireplace façade with wide cement grout holding them in place. The facade rose from floor to ceiling, and the fire pit itself was four feet high and three feet wide. Stepping onto the hearth, Kerry examined the mantel closely. It was oak, about four inches thick and ten inches deep. It was cantilevered from the stone facade and covered in a deep coat of dust and dirt.

Inset into the walls on either side of the fireplace were two bookshelves. They were empty now, but he could imagine at one time that they were a focal point of the room. Their replacements were leaning against the wall to the left. He had not had the chance to install them. Symmetrical in design, each had four shelves with a storage cabinet below. Moving to his left, he walked in front of the bookshelf and felt a breeze coming from the perimeter of the shelf. *Odd,* he thought. Upon further inspection, he noticed that the entire outline of the shelf was not actually sealed.

"Where the hell is a breeze coming from?"

He opened the bottom cabinet and knelt down to take a look. Along the left side of the cabinet was a large knot in the wood. He ran his hand over it and felt it was slightly protruding from the wood. On a hunch, Kerry gave it a push. To his surprise, the knot moved back into the wood, and he heard a click. Immediately following the click, the bookshelf itself swung back into the wall.

Kerry gave the shelf a push, and it swung inward, revealing a passageway behind it.

"Get out of Dodge! Are you kidding me?"

Kerry stood and pulled out his phone to open the light. As he moved to shine the light into the passageway, a voice behind him made him jump.

"Hey there."

Kerry spun around and saw Hannah leaning against the entryway of the living room.

"Jesus! Hannah! You scared the shit out of me." Kerry said, gasping for breath. "What the hell are you doing here?"

"I was about to ask you the same question. We got a call from the alarm company. Something about a break-in."

"Alarm company? I wasn't aware he had one." Kerry said.

"I could arrest you right now, you know." She said as she crossed to him. "On top of that, you're destroying private property."

"This is hardly 'destroyed.'"

Hannah walked over to the bookshelf running her hand across Kerry's butt as she passed.

Kerry jumped away from her. "Hannah. You know I'm with Darcy. What's this all about?"

Hannah stepped in closer to him and touched his cheek with her hand.

"Nothing. I just thought that it might be nice to, you know, relive the old days for a little while. We never did get to go all the way. Maybe it's time to end the wondering."

"That isn't going to happen. I can't go tripping down memory lane with you. I'm sorry."

"Well, it was worth a try. You can't blame me, can you, Kerry? I was in love with you for a long time."

"I'm really sorry. I hope that we can put it behind us and be friends from now on. You think we could do that?" Kerry asked honestly.

"I guess. Can we seal the deal with a kiss?" Hannah leaned in and gently kissed Kerry on the lips. He held it for a moment and then pulled away. He wanted to wipe his mouth, but he didn't want to offend her any more than he already had.

"Okay, then. Friends, right?"

"Right. So, what the hell are you doing in here, anyway? Did you find a secret passageway? How Scooby-Doo of you."

"I don't know what this is. I was going to use my phone to look behind it, but since you're here, my friend, can I borrow your flashlight?"

Hannah smiled as she slowly slid the small black mag light from the leather holder on her belt.

"Here you go. Take a look."

Kerry took the light and twisted the front end. It instantly filled the room with a strong beam of light, the disconcerting glow emulating the shadows from years earlier. He swung the beam to the bookshelf and into the space beyond.

Looking inside, he saw a passageway that was lined with the reverse side of lath and plaster. The wooden lath pieces were set about an inch apart, and the plaster from the walls they supported was squeezing through between each slot.

"A secret passageway behind the stone fireplace; this is something out of Scooby-Doo."

Kerry stepped into the space behind the bookshelf, Hannah close behind, and they started to follow the trail.

Chapter 59

Darcy's head bounced off the mattress as Stan threw her onto the bed. She used the momentum and, by kicking her feet over her head, bounced cleanly off and landed on the opposite side. Stan moved into position to block the door. The room wasn't very large and the bed filled most of it. Darcy found herself trapped between the bed and the far wall, opposite the door, and had no way out.

"Stan, come on. You don't want to do this."

Stan laughed. "Baby, I've wanted to fuck you since the first time you walked into the office. I'm just tired of waiting."

"Come on. We can talk about this. I never thought you were serious. I thought it was all just part of a game."

"A game! Do you think this is a game? You are mine. You were given to me, and it's time to put up!"

"What do you mean I was given to you?"

"Oh, stop being so stupid. You know what I'm talking about. She said I could have you if I brought you to her. Well, not that I don't trust her, but I don't think you're gonna be in any shape to fuck when she's done with you, so I'm taking my piece now before it's too late."

"She? Who's she?" Darcy asked.

"The one with the power. The one with the needs. The one who brought you to me. She told me that first time, if I bring you to her, I could have you."

Darcy heard the voice again, inside her head. *Don't be afraid. You can win. You can do this.* It was a calming, confident voice, and again, she wasn't afraid, she was mad.

Stan slowly walked around the end of the bed, unbuttoning his shirt as he walked.

"It won't be that bad, I promise. I've never had any complaints." A sadistic chuckle slid out of him.

Darcy turned to face Stan. There were no tears in her eyes. There was anger. She felt a power rising up inside of her. A scowl covered her face, and she said. "Stop."

Stan chuckled and said, "This is my reward …"

She stood tall and took a stance like a boxer. She had never had any fight training but had seen enough movies, and this pose felt good.

"So, Stan, you still want a piece of this?"

"Bring it on, baby! I love a woman I have to fight."

He stepped toward her as he pulled his shirt off. Before he could bring his arms back in front of him, Darcy lowered her shoulder and charged. She hit him right under the chin and drove him backwards, her hands under his arms. She drove him into the wall behind him with such force that he indented the drywall. She released him, and he slid to the floor. She took one step away and kicked him square in the temple with her right foot. His eyes rolled back, and he fell sideways to the carpet.

Darcy's eyes glowed, and she took several very deep, very satisfying breaths. She jumped onto and over the bed and put herself in the doorway.

He moaned, unable to talk.

"I'll call for help… if I remember."

Darcy turned from the wounded man, grabbed her purse, and headed out the door. She opened her Lyft app and requested a ride, which should arrive in 3 minutes.

Chapter 60

Kerry led Hannah down the passageway, testing the flooring as they moved. The passageway was about three feet wide and followed the exterior wall of the house. About fifteen feet from the entrance, the passageway diverged; a stairway to the right going up and a stairway to the left going down.

Kerry pointed the flashlight up the stairs, and they saw that the passageway continued at the top. "I'll bet you anything that goes up to the master bedroom."

"How convenient," Hannah said under her breath. Kerry chose to ignore the comment.

Kerry said, "Let's follow the stairs down and see where it goes."

"Are you sure you don't want to try out the master bedroom?" Hannah said with a mischievous grin.

Kerry ignored her.

They walked down fifteen steps, and he saw sunlight shining through the wall. A rotted sideboard had come loose and was allowing the sun to stream in from the outside. The board was a few feet above his head, but Kerry pushed on the board, and it fell away, falling into the backyard. Using the lathe on the exterior wall, he pulled himself up to look out and get his bearings. Looking through the opening, he saw something he would never be able to unsee.

There, in the middle of the pool, on the island, was Henry. He was naked and waltzing as though he was at a cotillion with his date. In his arms, he held a tattered ragdoll that was his partner.

Kerry was terrified at first, thinking that this doll was Darcy. But after a closer look, he could see that it was not, but it was definitely a woman, and she was definitely dead.

"Holy shit. You gotta see this."

"Um, can you give me a hand? I'm not quite as agile as you are." Hannah said.

Kerry squatted down and interlocked his fingers to form a step. Hannah placed her hands on Kerry's shoulders and her left foot into his laced fingers and leaped up. As she did, she moved her body close to Kerry so that she rubbed his face on the way up. Her chest stopped just about at the level of Kerry's mouth.

"Go ahead, take a look," Kerry said, holding her up to the window.

Hannah looked out and laughed. She immediately jumped to the floor and doubled over. "Whoa! I really could have done without that visual thank you. What a tub of lard!"

"What are you laughing about? Aren't you going to do something?"

"About what? If that weirdo wants to dance naked in his backyard with a blow-up doll, then it's nobody's business but his own."

"Doll? That wasn't a doll. It was a dead woman," Kerry almost screamed.

"Yeah, like that doofus would have a dead woman lying around. I think your imagination is running away with you here, sweetheart."

"Come on, maybe this leads to the backyard."

Having seen the backyard through the hole in the wall, Kerry had a solid idea of where they were in relation to the backyard. They were still a floor above the ground, just below the kitchen wall, he thought.

"This has to lead to the backyard. There must be an exit somewhere down here."

Hannah tried to move past Kerry, and in the process, she pinned the two of them together in the tiny hallway.

"Well, for someone who is in love, you seem very friendly." Hannah cooed.

"If you just move to your left, I can get by," Kerry said.

"Maybe I don't want to. Maybe I want you to be pressed against me." Hannah raised her arms and placed them on either side of Kerry's head. "I'm finding this rather cozy."

"Hannah. Come on. Let's not do this."

"I'm having too good a time to stop. Seems that you're enjoying this too, whether you want to or not."

"Hannah, please, move to your left so I can get by."

Hannah moved but not to her left. Instead, she pressed closer to him and dropped her hands to his hips.

"We could knock one off right here, and she'll never know." She rubbed the side of his buttocks and then up to his rib cage.

Kerry squirmed, and using the wall behind Hannah, he pushed back, hoping to create enough space for him to slide out. Instead, the wall behind him gave way, and he fell backward down a narrow staircase into a black abyss.

Chapter 61

The Lyft dropped Darcy off at the end of the driveway, and she ran to the house. Hannah's patrol car was in front of the porch. She didn't bother to knock and went straight for the knob.

It was locked.

She banged her fist against the door and screamed for Kerry.

"Kerry! Can you hear me?"

No response.

She kicked at the base of the wooden door.

Still no response.

Without waiting any longer, she turned away from the door and headed to her left to the south side of the house and toward the backyard. In one smooth, fluid motion, she pulled herself over the top of the wooden gate. She whipped around the back corner of the house, and there was the dirt-dead yard and the shale rock that surrounded the tide pool.

The pool looked innocent, but she knew better. She took a tentative step toward the water, hoping not to find what she was almost certain that she would find, Kerry floating just beneath the surface.

The Siren slipped through the depths of the pool, a murky trail of putrefying scales in her wake. Her body tensed as she intuitively sensed the human girl's approach. Her mighty tail, long ago a vibrant parade of color, now dull and diseased, rippled with anticipation. A low growl rattled in the base of her throat releasing tainted air bubbles in the swirling water as she moved into position. The surrounding sea life scurried to other points in the pool, points far away from her. She had the bastard girl within reach, and she would not be denied. She summoned the elements and dark, roiling clouds began to move toward the cliff. A rumbling began, low and ominous as she pulled with all her power to begin the end. The girl's death will fulfill her destiny.

***

Each time Darcy had been in the yard, her presence had been felt, and the elements had responded. This time, though, there was nothing. She took another tentative step. She expected something to happen, and yet nothing did. No wind, no water in the face, nothing. This lack of action alarmed her.

"She knows I'm here," she whispered to herself. "She doesn't want to scare me away."

She took another step toward the pool when a giant crash erupted behind her. She jumped a foot in the air and spun toward the origin of the noise.

As she did, she saw a portion of the house explode out, and a figure came shooting through it to land on the dirt a few feet away.

It didn't take an instant for her to recognize that the figure that had tumbled through the wall and now lay in a dusty heap was Kerry.

"Kerry!" She ran to him and jumped on top of him, crying from relief and gratitude.

"Oh my God! You're okay! You're okay! I love you." She kissed his face, filling her mouth with dust and dirt.

Kerry's head was spinning, and he tried to push her off as he struggled to get his bearings.

"Okay, okay, let me breathe." Kerry finally managed to get out. "Whoa, that was some ride. I guess I found the tunnel that leads to the backyard."

"What tunnel?" Darcy asked.

"In the house, I found a bunch of secret passageways. They all lead here, to the yard, so whoever, could get out here without anyone knowing it. Hey! You're not supposed to be here!" Kerry said in a stern tone.

"I came to get you, and now that I've found you, let's get the hell out of here." She stood up and helped Kerry to his feet.

As if on cue, a wind ripped down the side of the house and blew them backward. It hit them with such force that she had her breath knocked out of her as she bounced off the hard dirt, scuffing her palms and the right side of her face. Kerry landed a few feet away.

"Darcy, you okay?" Kerry asked in a low moan.

Darcy was on her stomach with her butt in the air. She rolled to a supine position and said, "I'm fine. I scraped my palm and got something stuck in my hand. Pull it out." Darcy's voice was quivering. Kerry looked at her left hand, and it had a three-inch-long splinter sticking out of it. He grabbed it as close to the base as he could and pulled it out in one fast, strong motion.

"Owww, damn it!" The open wound started to bleed.

They were both still on the ground in between the house and the pool.

Above them the clouds were gathering. As they lay on their backs, they watched them move from all directions to congregate over the house. There was movement inside the clouds, and they began to realign into one giant portentous formation.

"Is there any other way out of this yard without going through the house?" Kerry asked with one eye on the clouds.

"We might be able to get out the back onto the cliffs, but we'd have to walk past the pool," Darcy said, knowing that further explanation was unnecessary. "Both sides of the house have ten-foot fences. I climbed over it pretty easily when I thought you were going to die. I imagine that I can do it again, trying to keep you alive. Think you could do it with the cast?"

"Beats the hell out of sitting here."

They both jumped up and sprinted for the north side of the house, the side furthest from the pool. As they approached the side, a bolt of lightning struck about thirty feet in front of them and blew them off their feet. They rolled back to where they started. The fence was badly damaged, and a small fire had started. The dead brush and the newly splintered wood of the fence acted as perfect kindling.

"Okay! Okay!" Kerry yelled. "We're not going anywhere. You can stop!"

The wind died down; the fire continued.

The two of them lay on the ground, side by side as though they were lying in a family crypt, afraid to move. Darcy then whispered to Kerry. "Slowly turn your head to the left."

Kerry did.

"Do you see that shack?"

"Yeah," he replied.

"Watch it for a minute."

He watched. A few seconds later, he saw a flash of light generate from inside.

"What was that?" he asked.

"Ya think it might lead to the observation room under the pool?"

"I suppose it could, so what?"

"That must be where Childs went. If we can find him, maybe we can reason with this thing."

"Reason with this thing? We don't know what the hell it is or what it wants."

"I've been thinking about that, and I have a theory," Darcy said hesitantly. "It's gonna sound crazy, but what isn't anymore?"

"What is it?" Kerry asked

"The woman you saw on the island when you hurt your hand. She was dressed in old clothes, right?"

"Yeah, kinda that early 1900s stuff. Why?"

"And she was missing the side of her head. Just like the cloud was missing the side of its head. Like it had been blown off, right?"

"Yeah, and?"

"In this whole story, where is the only gun?"

Kerry thought for a second, and then it dawned on him. "Well, we sure make crummy detectives. It was right there the whole time. Sheila Taft. She was shot by her husband. She must be …"

They both looked at the pool.

"Right. And Sheila was Rosemary's sister, so that makes Sheila my great-great-aunt. I'm related to her. I think she wants to tell me something. That's why she won't let us leave," Darcy said with a sense of accomplishment.

"There is a certain logic to that … if you believe in ghosts, that is," Kerry said.

"Stand up," Darcy told Kerry. He did and he saw that the fire was still burning by the fence before he was blown right back to the ground.

"Any more doubts?" she asked. He had none.

"Okay, so how do we get her to tell you whatever it is she wants to say if she won't let us stand up?" Kerry wanted to know.

"I don't know."

They both lay there silently, at a loss for what to do.

"Try talking to her. Tell her who you are and that you want to talk with her," Kerry said.

"God, this is stupid. Okay. Let's give it a try." She rolled onto her stomach and faced the pool. "Aunt Sheila? Are you there? Aunt Sheila, it's me, your great-great-niece, Darcy. Can I talk to you?"

There was no answer. Kerry had a thought, "Try sitting up. See if she heard you."

She slowly sat up. Nothing happened. No gale force wind, nothing. Kerry sat up slowly as well.

Kerry looked toward the house and could see that the fire was getting a bit bigger. The fence was attached to the house so if it kept going things might get even worse.

"You better hurry. Keep talking," Kerry whispered.

"Aunt Sheila, it's me, Darcy. Is there something you want to tell me? Is there something I should know?"

Suddenly there was a loud bang that made Darcy and Kerry jump. Darcy screamed. "Holy shit!"

Off to the side of the pool, the door to the shack had blown open and smashed against the side wall. It was an invitation.

"Oh no," Darcy said.

"Darcy, your Aunt Sheila obviously wants to tell you something. We'll never get out of here unless we listen." Darcy rose up to her full height and Kerry stood up beside her. No wind. No earthquake, just a fire moving down the fence line. Without much of a choice they shuffled toward the shed.

As Kerry and Darcy approached the shack, a light appeared faintly from below.

"We're going to just walk in there, right? We're just walking in there of our own free will to talk to a dead woman," Kerry said.

"There's no reason for you to go. She wants to talk to me. Why don't you wait here? It'll be okay," Darcy said.

Kerry glanced at the fire and saw that the dead brush between the fence and the shack would lead it right to where they were standing. And, as almost on cue, a branch of the flame leapt to the dead brush and began to light up.

"First off, you're not going in there alone, and if you ever doubted that I love you, you can rest assured… and probably will."

"Probably will what?"

"Rest assured. Rest eternally assured," he wasn't even half joking. "Besides, I've got nowhere else to go." He jerked his head in the direction of the flames.

Holding each other's hand, they stepped to the door which was swinging freely on its hinges.

"You ready?"

"Here goes nothing." They stepped into the dilapidated shack.

Inside, the light was soft, like a reflection and the source of the light was not visible. With extreme trepidation, they looked down the circular staircase that lay immediately inside. "Oh, for chrissake! You have to be kidding me?" Darcy said as she slowly shook her head. "A flipping circular stairway. All we're missing now is bats.

"Careful what you wish for, missy." With that, the smell of smoke hit them both as it started to enter the chamber. He took her hand, and they started down the stairs.

***

The Siren's spine tingled as her defenses went taut. It was killing time, tearing time, time for satisfaction. With a quick twitch of her tail, she was off, sliding into her hiding place among the rocks where she would wait, chameleon-like, for her chance to strike.

She could sense the human girl as she got closer, moving cautiously through the underground tunnel toward the little room where she would die. She could feel her movements, studied, cautious and timid. The human girl was scared. Of this, she was certain. The realization made her stomach leap with excitement as she excreted a tainted waste into the depths of the water.

When the girl was dead, she would be done. The Siren had no feeling of what would come next. Those thoughts were beyond her comprehension. She knew only of here and now. She swam, practically unaware of her own existence except for the immediate needs that were necessary for survival. And yet, her instincts told her that survival was no longer a concern. She will have fulfilled her destiny, a destiny that started so very long ago.

Chapter 62

Darcy and Kerry started down the circular wrought-iron stairway.

The trip down the old staircase was uneventful other than a few creaks and groans from the stairs bearing weight for the first time in years. (Edith hardly counted, as she was so frail, to begin with.) At the bottom, they stopped to get their bearings, and Darcy saw Edith's walker.

"This can't be a good sign," she said. The walker lay on its side, twisted and broken as a foreshadowing of things to come.

Having only one direction to go, they moved down the dimly lit corridor exactly as Edith had done a short time earlier until they came to the first door. Kerry had noticed that all the timber and the supports were new. That was certainly significant.

Darcy pushed against the door, and it swung open easily. Kerry followed and took in the scene himself. This was like a front hall or an entryway to a different space. It was fifteen feet long and led to another door. It was like an underground mud room. All it needed were coat hooks and a bench to take off your dirty boots, and it would look exactly like the one in the back hall off the kitchen. As they considered what to do next, the door behind them slammed shut.

Darcy screamed at the sound and quickly turned. Kerry rushed to the door and grabbed the handle. He tugged at it to no avail. He noticed that it had a rubber seal all the way around and realized that, for whatever reason, this room needed to be airtight.

As he tugged on the door handle, on the opposite side of the small anteroom Darcy reached for the knob of the door in front of her, and it pushed open with ease. She stepped through without concern and stepped into the observation room.

Kerry saw Darcy enter the main chamber. Being at the opposite end of the anteroom, he was too far away to stop what happened next. The door started to swing close, and before Kerry could cross the fifteen feet of the little room, it slammed shut in front of him. He twisted the knob, but it would not budge.

"Darcy! Darcy! Open the door!" He yelled as he pounded on the wooden door with all his might.

It did not open, and he could not force it.

Kerry threw his shoulder into the door to no avail. His breathing was labored and sweat began to pour down his face. She was inside, and he couldn't get to her. He kicked at the doorknob, and still, the door stood strong. He lowered his shoulder again and, with all his might, lunged at the door. Nothing.

With his shoulders bruising rapidly, he took several deep breaths and tried to calm down so that he could think. He had to get into that room, and he had no time to waste.

"There has to be a way in. Old George went to all that trouble to create secret passageways and everything. There has to be another way in," he said to himself as he paced like a caged tiger. "Think, Kerry, think. If you're George Thornton and you built this place, what would you do? How else would you want to be able to get in?"

Frustrated at his inability to answer that question, Kerry launched himself at the door one more time with similar results. This time, the force he had generated was so great that he bounced off and landed on his butt, his head banging slightly against the floor.

Bruised, scared, and helpless, he sat there, remembering falling through that false wall into the passageway that led to the backyard. Hannah was still running around somewhere. He wondered if she would help him.

Then it hit him. He jumped up and yelled, "Of course!"

As Kerry revisited his fall down the tunnel and crashing through the wall into the backyard, he realized that if he was George Thornton, the only reason to build a secret passageway with so many entrance points would be to get to the underground room. Why else would he bother?

Kerry knew what he had to do. He reached out and opened the door that lead to the circular staircase. Just as he thought, it opened easily. With Darcy inside, there was no need to keep it inaccessible. The smoke had thickened but not so bad that he couldn't deal with it. He raced back to the spiral staircase and started to climb. He had to get back into the house and find the tunnel that led to the underground observatory, and he had to do it fast.

Chapter 63

Inside the chamber, the observation window magnified her fears. She was startled by the size and grandeur of it and was scared by its beauty. Behind her, she heard the door slam and she knew that she would not be able to open it. She heard Kerry banging from the other side, and she took solace in the fact that he was safe. It wasn't right that he should be hurt, and she felt better knowing that he was now unable to get to her. Turning away from the banging, she moved toward the window.

In the reflection, she saw the room behind her and looked into the chamber. The woodwork was all re-done. Not done well, by any stretch of the imagination, but done with care. On the wall was a giant mural, some odd lighting fixtures that had been hung without precision, and a whaling harpoon. The harpoon was old, from the turn of the 20th Century, and hung over the mural as a reminder of a time gone by. She saw the bed and in the bed were two figures wrapped together under the sheets. Having no other real choice, she moved to the bed to wake the sleeping Henry, and whatever was with him.

She approached the bed with extreme caution, the way you would approach an unexploded firecracker. The fuse was lit, and it was thrown, but it never went off. She reached down to shake the shoulder, ready to jump back should it explode. She touched it and pulled her hand back sharply. Slick, sticky moisture clung to her fingertips. She looked at her hand, and it was covered with blood.

Darcy stepped toward the bed and, in one quick motion, pulled the covers off and exposed the mutilated body of Edith Childs lying amidst a mass of body parts arranged like a jigsaw puzzle. There were two heads, three arms, and parts of four legs, all fondling or violating Edith in some perverse manner. One head lay between her legs, another at her putrefied breast. A hand had been placed on her ass, and another had its fingers in her mouth.

Darcy screamed, and panic ran through her body as she backed away from the perverted death scene.

In her panic, Darcy did the exact wrong thing. She ran blindly to the door and tripped over the wading pool's steel cover, ripping open her shin. She fell to the floor, grabbing at her leg.

From within the wading pool, a light began to grow, shining upward to the ceiling. She saw a figure rise.

It was Henry.

He was naked, covered in brine with rotted pieces of sea vegetation stuck to the folds of fat that encased him. His mammoth stomach folded over his crotch, making him look like a eunuch. Water dripped off him, and he shook his head as he wiped the hair from his eyes.

"So, you are finally here. I am so sorry that I couldn't meet you at the door. I was otherwise engaged." He looked over to the bed as he climbed out of the pool. "As you can see, Mother and her dates are a bit under the weather." He laughed aloud.

"What do you want?" Darcy demanded. "What kind of freak show are you running here?"

"Oh, you'll see. You'll see soon enough. Now, go over to the bed and have a seat. Mother loves company." Henry growled. She knew it was better to comply than resist. Darcy limped over to the foot of the bed that contained the mutilated remains of Edith and her boys.

"At first, I didn't understand why she was so angry at me. I mean, I never really touched you. Did I, Miss Wainwright? I never even asked you out. But she was so angry. It was hard for me," Henry explained.

"You mean your mother? She didn't want you to see me?" Darcy said, more to hear her own voice and reassure herself that she was still alive than to strike up a conversation.

"Mother? Oh no. She would have been delighted when she was in her right mind, which was less and less the case. You see, Mother was very old and not very productive anymore. All she was good for was nagging and berating, and belittling. No, not Mother." He whispered with a coy grin, "There is someone else."

Darcy was catching on.

"You mean my Aunt Sheila?" Darcy dropped the bombshell and hoped that it would explode in the right direction. "Look, Mr. Childs. I think I know what's going on here. The thing in the pool it's my great-great Aunt Sheila, Rosemary Thornton's sister and John Taft's wife," she said, her voice noticeably shaking. "She's the thing that wants to hurt me, isn't she?"

He looked through Darcy and appeared to try to melt her with his stare. Henry's eyes narrowed and took on an oval, reptilian shape as they bore into her soul. The corneas were red and started to glow. She had seen that stare once before when she woke up bleeding all over the foyer. If she thought it terrified her then, it absolutely mortified her now.

Chapter 64

Kerry burst through the door of the shack after having run up the iron staircase. He was planning on heading into the house and starting from the beginning, at the fireplace, but as he ran across the yard, he saw that the fire had advanced considerably. The north side of the house was covered in flames. That outside wall was the north side of the living room where the fireplace was, and that wall looked very close to being engulfed. Likely the passageway was already destroyed. Then he remembered the hole he had made when he fell through the wall. He ran as fast as he could to the far side of the house, away from the flames, and like a kid climbing up a covered slide, he crawled through the jagged hole and scaled the tunnel looking for clues and detours along the way.

The tunnel had wood framing that formed a ladder, and the climb was surprisingly easy. There was a slight hint of smoke in the walls but nothing substantial at this point. On the right side were two one-x-twelve boards set side by side, which acted as flooring for the trip down and on the left side was the exposed framing which acted as a ladder for the trip up. On his decent, he had obviously been lucky enough to stay on the right and slid down without bouncing over the studs.

He arrived at the top of the passageway inside a minute and poked his head out into the hallway, looking for Hannah. She was nowhere to be found. Kerry crawled into the space and stood up. He looked both ways and had no idea which way to go. If the tunnel that led to the observatory was covered up like this one had been, it might be impossible to find.

He started thinking like a builder and tried to figure out where the best place to put that access tunnel would be. There were some significant issues in reaching a place that was at least thirty feet underground from a floor that was ten feet above it. Seeing as that was the case, there really couldn't be a tunnel that led there. It would have to be a ladder. That helped narrow the search field.

Kerry turned to his left and headed back toward the fireplace. The density of the smoke was beginning to increase as he moved in that direction. He wasn't sure how far he would be able to go. He found a switch that controlled a series of light bulbs hung on the passageway walls and connected by bare, exposed wires. These dim bulbs illuminated the tunnel just enough that he could maneuver his way through.

Following this string of lights led him into a small junction room where four of these tunnels met. It seemed that all tunnels led to this one spot.

"Why the hell do you do this?" he said to himself. "What's the reason to be able to get to the rest of the house from here?"

Then he realized his mistake. George hadn't wanted to get to those places from here, he had wanted to get to this spot from those places. All tunnels led to the very spot he was now standing. Wherever the door was that led to the observation room, it had to be somewhere in this tiny juncture.

With renewed enthusiasm, he pounded his fist against the outside walls while at the same time he stomped against the floor. It was getting hotter in the room, and he had to move fast. In a matter of seconds, he got what he wanted. He heard a hollow thud return from under his feet. He kicked the spot again and saw dust pop up into the air like it was on a trampoline. The floor was hollow. Dropping to his knees, he started to examine the floor for a handle or some way to pry the floor up and see what was under it. He found a seam, and it took only a moment to find the ring handle that was used to open the trap door.

Determining the outline of the trap, he stood to the side and lifted the ring. The trap door swung up and revealed a wooden ladder descending to the ground.

The trap was rimmed with a rubber seal that had suffered some decay but still seemed formidable.

Another rubber seal?

He opened the trap door, and after testing the rungs with a good kick, he fearlessly climbed down into the tunnel that he was certain would take him to the pool. He closed the trap door above him, protection against the fire, the little good it would do, and that plunged him into darkness.

In the dark, he had only one choice, to climb down the ladder. He had lost the mini-mag light on his fall to the backyard, but he still had his phone in his pocket. The screen was now cracked, but when he hit the light, it came on with no problem. He took one careful step at a time as he began feeling his way down. He had descended about fifteen steps when he realized that the tunnel was growing narrower as it went deeper, and the wooden frame that had encased the first fifteen feet had started to deteriorate as the depth and moisture of the years had rotted the wood away. The musty, wet dirt smell was mixed with a salt brine aroma and was making it more difficult to breathe. There was a faint glow now in the tunnel and as he looked up, he could see the crimson red glow of flames building above him.

He descended another step, hoping that the ladder would not just give way under his weight, and he heard voices, they were distant and muted, but he was certain that they were human voices. And they were coming from beneath him. Encouraged that he was moving in the correct direction, he dropped another few rungs hoping to hear the voices more clearly.

At about twenty-five feet down, the voices were closer but not yet intelligible. That is until a scream rattled through the tunnel and he knew immediately it was Darcy.

Without worrying about the consequences, Kerry stepped off the ladder and fell into the unknown darkness of the shaft.

He theorized that he was only five or six feet above the bottom of the shaft and expected to land quickly. He was prepared for that. What he was not prepared for was that when he hit bottom, it was not a level ground but the beginning of a slide. His feet went out from under him, and he landed on his butt. The force of his jump propelled him forward and he began to slide further down. He gained momentum quickly, and before he knew it, he was crashing through a wall... again.

Dirt and mud and wooden planks went flying into the room, followed immediately by Kerry Devine. He landed roughly and bounced onto the floor.

The sudden explosion startled Henry and Darcy both. Henry pulled Darcy away from the sudden intruder. He threw her against the wall and turned to face this new foe.

As he was bouncing off the floor, he saw Darcy fall. He was covered in mud and dirt and was bleeding from both elbows, and yet as soon as he hit the floor, he was back on his feet and he lunged at Henry. He hit him right in the sternum and drove his head up into Henry's chin, exactly the way he had so many years ago when he was the All-City linebacker. Henry was driven back into the window. His head snapped back and smashed against the glass. A tiny crack appeared. Kerry grabbed Henry and threw him to the ground. He jumped on top of him and started to punch him in the face. He hit him with his left arm and then would slam his cast into the side of Henry's head. He pummeled him mercilessly, breaking his cast in three places.

As he pulled his left arm back for another slam into Henry's face, the room started to change. Suddenly it was filled with a bright light. Kerry rolled off of Henry and looked frantically around the chamber to find the source.

The light was coming from the pool. A light source of some type was floating inside. He slid across the concrete floor to Darcy.

The light changed. It became full of color. Green, blue, and red shafts of light shot throughout the underground chamber. The colors were so radiant that they mesmerized him. Yellow and purple flashes came close to blinding him.

Kerry saw Darcy and her face was filled with terror. He turned back to the window. Suspended in the water directly outside of the window was the most hideous creature he could have possibly imagined.

It was a juxtaposition of fantasy and reality. It was a mermaid but not a mermaid. It was a beautiful woman that had become a hag. It was good that had turned evil. The creature looked to be seven feet tall from top to tail. Her upper body was that of a woman, but the skin seemed to be falling off as though she were decomposing before their eyes. The breasts sagged and even in the buoyancy of the water looked as though they were weighted down with buckshot. Her arms were thin and sinewy, and Kerry could see the veins pulsing beneath her skin. Half of the face was gone, blown away.

The creature had a tattered fish tail that was not more than a muted coat of mud covered with slime. Something that oozed like pus came running out of an open wound and floated away into the depths. Scales were hanging off its body in a diseased fashion. As the scales rose to where the body began, there were open sores and parasites hanging onto what might have once been human skin. This skin had a greenish tone and was covered in slime and filth.

Then she moved like lightning toward the bottom of the window and disappeared.

Kerry saw the steel cover that sat next to the giant window. The rubber seals! He realized that the creature could enter the chamber through that hatchway. He knew why all the doors had rubber seals. They made this chamber airtight. She could enter without flooding the room, which meant that she was coming in here.

He yelled to Darcy, "Quick, help me with this thing." But the cry fell on deaf ears. Darcy was still staring at the spot where the creature had been. Kerry ran to the cover and sat on it, trying to keep it from opening. He looked to the sides and saw that the latches were open. He tried to close the clasps that sat on either side of the round turret, but with his cast, it was a futile gesture at best. Before he could secure either one, the cover exploded open, and he was thrown high into the air, smashing his head against the rock ceiling of the chamber. He fell to the floor, landing on his right leg, mangling it.

The funnel of light formed, and she entered the room, filling it with the fetid stench of death. Henry lay in front of the window, bleeding but functional. He rolled over and crawled to the creature. He started to cry and grovel in front of her.

"My love, I have brought you the bastard girl. I did it, no one else. She is here, and she is yours. Are you happy?" he whimpered to the creature.

The creature ignored him. She hissed softly and slithered over and settled next to Darcy.

Darcy was still staring at the window, in a trance, unable to move. The creature hissed louder and, with one withered arm, pulled back and smacked Darcy across the face. The blow knocked Darcy backward, and she landed flat on her back, jarring the wind out of her. After a few seconds, she raised her head, and the first thing she saw was the creature. She let out a scream that pierced the air and shook the room around them. The creature smiled, exposing her tiny, pointy teeth.

Darcy knew she was going to die.

What had happened? Where was she? Who was this creature?

The world around her seemed to go into slow motion. Each answer came to her in what seemed hours but was actually nanoseconds. She had been looking for Kerry. She was in the underground chamber by the pool. This creature coming at her *was* her great-great-aunt, Sheila. That was it!

"Aunt Sheila?" Darcy said. "Aunt Sheila, it's me, Darcy. I'm your niece. Do you know me?"

The creature stopped. It rose to its full height and hissed loudly. Darcy was lost in the shadow of evil that the creature spread before her. She could tell that the creature was not impressed with their bloodline. She had to try harder.

"I know we've never met, but my father is your sister's grandson. That makes us family. You can't hurt your family, can you?" Darcy was trying whatever it took to calm this thing down. Unfortunately, the use of the term 'family' seemed to incense the thing even more. As Darcy spoke the word, the creature began to writhe and contort in the most grotesque manner. The creature's hand went out, and she made a swirling gesture that circled her head. Color started to emanate from her hand as it spun around, and it filled the room. Darcy felt herself being picked up and taken away from the chamber, the pool, and her very life.

442

In a heartbeat, Darcy was floating above the backyard of the house. As Henry had experienced, it was not the backyard that she was familiar with. It was the house and the yard before the remodel and before the pool was installed.

She was transported inside the house and now was hovering in the living room, the living room as it had been originally. A woman ran into the room and fell into the gold armchair that sat before the windows. She was crying hysterically. Darcy recognized her from the pictures in the photo album she had taken from the attic. This was a very upset, Sheila.

A moment later, a man followed her into the room. Darcy recognized him as Sheila's husband, John Taft. He had been drinking, and he was in a rage.

"Just stop it! Stop crying, you silly bitch. You're going to have to accept the fact that I am leaving, and I am *not* taking you with me," he yelled at the woman. "I have had enough of your self-righteousness. It was not my fault. It was *your* fault. If you had been a better wife and supported me when I needed you, this would never have happened."

John was pacing back and forth like an animal. However, having vented all his anger, he was losing steam. The woman continued to cry as her whole world collapsed in on her. John dropped his head and closed his eyes. He went to her and knelt beside her.

"Sheila. Sheila, please stop. You must understand. I never meant to hurt you. It just happened."

Sheila lifted her head. Her eyes were swollen and red, and tears were streaming down her face. Darcy could see the forearm of her dress had been soaked with tears.

"John, how can you say you never meant to hurt me? How can you look at me and say that after what you have done?"

John shook his head. "I guess I'm not as good a person as you are, Sheila. I make mistakes. I made mistakes in my business, and then I made mistakes with you. But I can't go on this way. I must leave. Once your father finds out the truth, he will blackball me anyway. I'm finished. I have no choice," John was starting to show his fear.

Sheila felt for John. It was apparent by the expression on her face. But the pain he had caused her was too great to forgive.

"I cannot help you. There is nothing I can say or do that will ever make this right. You should leave tonight."

John dropped his head, and the first tear ran down his cheek. "Yes, you're right … I'm so sorry. I never meant—" John stood and turned to leave.

"Not just yet." A voice from the hallway yelled out. It startled both John and Sheila, and they turned to the source of the voice.

"Rosemary!" John said with a start.

From the hallway stepped Rosemary, Sheila's sister. She had a gun.

"You aren't going anywhere. You are *not* leaving me like this." Rosemary shrieked at John. "You are not leaving me after what you've done!"

"What I've done? Don't you mean what we've done?"

"What difference does it make? I'm having your baby, and you are not running away from that." Rosemary pointed the gun at John.

Sheila was crumpled in the chair but straightened up as Rosemary entered the room.

"Rosemary, please. Put the gun down. Haven't you done enough?" Sheila said. Rosemary whipped around to Sheila.

"Just shut up! You have always had everything your way, and it ends now. I am no longer your silly little sister. I am my own woman, and I will do what I want!" John took a step toward Rosemary, who sensed the movement and swung the gun back to him.

"Don't, John. Don't even think about it. I am in charge now, and this is what we are going to do. We are going to kill this bitch and then start our new life together."

"Kill her? You can't be serious!" John said, "How can you kill your own sister?"

"I'm not going to kill her. You are. Right here and right now. You will strangle her, and we will leave here together," Rosemary said without an ounce of regret in her voice.

"John!" Sheila cried. "She can't be serious."

"I think she is, Sheila," John said, staring at Rosemary. "Unfortunately, I think she is." John moved with deliberate intent toward Sheila. Rosemary let down her guard as John moved, and he found his opportunity. In a blink of an eye, he ran toward Rosemary to wrestle the gun away. Rosemary, startled, raised the gun and fired. John had seen the action and turned his head slightly as he rushed toward her. The bullet caught him in the right temple, and he dropped to the ground, dead.

Sheila screamed and raced over to John. Blood gushed from a four-inch wound on the left side of his head. There was no question that he was dead. Sheila held him in her arms and wailed at her loss. Even though John had betrayed her in the worse possible way, she still loved him, flawed as he was.

Rosemary was in shock. She sank to her knees as Sheila cradled the dead body.

"This is all your fault," Rosemary screamed. "This is all your fault. If you had just divorced him like Father and I wanted, this would never have happened."

Through her tears, Sheila looked at Rosemary with hatred. "My fault! You betray me by having an affair with my husband. You undermine our relationship so that you can take him for yourself, and it's my fault? You are an evil woman, Rosemary! You're an evil, nasty woman, and you should burn in hell!"

Rosemary raised the gun once more, and without emotion, she pulled the trigger. The bullet entered the right side of Sheila's chest, and she was dead before she hit the floor.

Rosemary sat very still for a few minutes and formulated a plan. She staged John's body close to Sheila's and put the gun in his hand, making the scene look like a murder suicide. She took off her dress, which was covered in blood, and wrapped it up. Wearing just her petticoats, she turned and walked up the stairs to Sheila's room, where she put on one of Sheila's dresses and left.

Darcy saw what Rosemary did not. Sheila's soul rose from her lifeless body and hovered above the gruesome scene. She looked at her dead husband and slowly shook her head in regret. Then, to Darcy's astonishment, she looked at Darcy and raised her hand as though she were passing on a blessing. Darcy heard the voice in her head one more time. *"You can do this. You can win. Be strong."* She dissolved into the walls of the room.

The funnel began to move, and Darcy was transported back to the chamber and Henry.

The creature was lying under the light from the window, and Henry held her. She was subdued, in some sort of trance. Apparently, transporting someone into the funnel took a lot out of her. She wondered how long it would take this thing to recover.

Darcy stood and wobbled a few steps to get her bearings. That was the most incredible journey she had ever been on, and yet something did not sit right about it. With her mind as foggy as it was, she couldn't grab hold of it, but there was a fact that she was not interpreting correctly.

She heard Kerry moan in the corner and went to him. He sat up as she supported him. His right leg was twisted in an unnatural position under his body and he was bleeding from a cut on his head. She rolled Kerry onto his side and was able to get his leg put from beneath him. His leg was swollen and bleeding.

"I know why," Darcy whispered. "I know why she hates me."

"Who?" Kerry asked, slowed by the bump on his head.

"Aunt Sheila. That creature *is* Sheila. Her husband, John, is my great-great-grandfather. John knocked up Rosemary."

"Did Sheila kill him then?" Kerry asked.

"No, Rosemary killed them both," she said very softly so as not to arouse the creature any further.

The creature was stirring as Henry stoked its matted hair. She woke rapidly and licked his face with her fish tongue and caressed him.

"How do you know that?" Kerry asked as the cobwebs cleared.

"I'll tell you later. Right now, we have to get out of here. I'm a direct descendent of Rosemary and John and not high on her 'favorite relative' list. Can you walk?"

"I think so. But where do we go? If we get out of here alive, she'll just come for us again." Kerry realized.

"You're right, but what else can we do?"

Kerry looked around and saw the wading pool. The steel cover was open, and he could see the water lapping the sides of the shallow pool. He looked across the chamber and saw the door on the opposite side of the room. That should be on the cliff side of the property. An idea began to form.

"I am betting that door over there leads to the outside, probably identical to the doors that we came in, one outside and then the one that enters the room. We need to find something that we can jam under these doors to keep them open. Something to act like a door stop."

Darcy looked around, there was nothing within reach, and she knew that if she started to move around, she would attract the attention of the creature. Knowing that the creature was coming for her soon enough, she chose not to do so. Kerry was also looking and then saw Darcy's shoes.

"Your shoes! Take them off. Give one to me, and you hang on to the other. When I tell you to, run to that door over there, open it, and jam your shoe under it, so it stays open. I'll be right behind you and jam the outside door with the other shoe. Then we have to get the hell out of the way."

"Why, what'll that do?" Darcy asked.

"This whole room is air tight. The air pressure inside here is greater than the pressure of the water in the pool. That's what keeps the water in the little pool from flooding the room. If we open both doors and allow the air pressure to escape, the pool will empty into this room and flood it. It'll then run out those doors and down the cliff, taking the creature from the black lagoon with it."

"What if she closes the lid?"

"Shit, okay. I'll jam it with my shoe before I open my door. It's our only chance."

"Okay, I guess. But let me jam the cover. I can move faster. Are you going to be able to run with your leg like that? You just open the first door; I'll get the lid and then the second door." Darcy said. "Give me your shoe." He took off his shoe from the healthy ankle.

"Okay." Kerry squeezed her hand. "Just start running when you do, and don't stop."

"Oh shit." She said as she got into a four-point stance, ready for action.

The creature was still occupied with Henry, but at any minute, she would turn her attention to them. Darcy looked at Kerry. He was holding her shoe in the fingers that stuck out of his cast, his swollen ankle tucked against his body. She could see the pain he felt with every movement.

"Are you *sure* you can do this?" Darcy asked.

Kerry replied, not being brave, just realistic. "It's the only shot we have."

"Say when." Darcy gripped her shoe a bit harder. Kerry slowly adjusted his position so that he would be ready to move. Looking at the creature and seeing that she was about to rise, he yelled, "Go."

Darcy darted across the chamber and headed for the cover. Kerry struggled to his feet.

Darcy made it to the cover before the creature was aware of her movements. She was able to jam Kerry's shoe under the cover right by the hinges. The shoe slid in and stuck on the first try. She looked back to see what the creature was up to and saw only Henry, sitting up with a dazed look in his swollen, bruised eyes and blood trickling from one nostril.

"Oh shit! Where is it?" Darcy said, and as she started to turn around, she was hit hard from behind and went flying into the wading pool, dropping Kerry's shoe as she did. In an instant, she was underwater, being pulled down by the creature.

Darcy felt herself being dragged out of the chamber and into the depths of the wading pool. The claw-like grip of the creature pulled her through a tunnel and into the pool. In a second, she was looking through the window again, this time from the poolside and thirty feet underwater.

Kerry saw the creature grab Darcy and his heart about left his body.

Kerry needed to get the outside door open to create a draft through the chamber. That would eliminate any air pressure from within and flood the chamber immediately. He looked through the window into the pool as he went by. There was Darcy, struggling with the creature to get to the surface. The creature held her in place effortlessly, toying with her by letting her go and then grabbing her leg and pulling her back down just when Darcy felt she had gotten away. The creature had developed giant claws in place of her arms. They were lobster-like and deadly. With these claws, the creature would pull Darcy back to her and embrace her and fondle her. Kerry could see the gleam in the creature's one eye as she watched Darcy drown. She looked through the glass at Kerry and smirked. She pushed Darcy up against the glass, smearing her face flat so that Kerry could see her die. Kerry screamed, "No!"

He hobbled to the outside door, the pain in his leg intense, and he was presented with a more immediate challenge. After two steps in the direction of the door, a hand grabbed his ankle and tripped him. Kerry had forgotten about Henry.

Henry grabbed Kerry's leg and started to flail at him uncontrollably. Fortunately, Henry had grabbed Kerry's left leg, so he wasn't inflicting more pain onto his mangled right. Unfortunately, Kerry could not stand on his injured leg at all, so he fell to the ground. The delusional Henry kept grabbing and hitting him with blind roundhouse punches that made Kerry winch with each blow. Kerry felt the other man's teeth sink into his leg. The pain almost made him black out again. He fought back nausea, unconsciousness, and Henry Childs all at the same time.

Henry crawled further up the prone body of Kerry Devine, struggling to keep him from destroying the pool. He was biting and hitting as he fought for his survival and the survival of the woman he loved. Anyone that had known Henry would never have believed that he had it in him.

Kerry protected himself as best he could but was losing the battle against the raging Henry. His head turned toward the window, and he saw the creature holding Darcy in the depths of the pool. Darcy had turned toward the window, and their eyes met. She knew she was dying, and her eyes were saying goodbye to Kerry. The rage inside of him burst out. He could not let this happen. Kerry brought his knee up hard and fast and caught Henry right under the jaw. Kerry raised his right hand and brought his now-fractured cast down on

Henry's head, splitting the scalp open and bathing them both in blood. Henry continued to rage, but the tide had turned. Kerry threw Henry off and made it to his feet. With as much effort as he could, Kerry punched Henry in the face, driving the other man's head against the wall and knocking him out cold.

In the struggle, Kerry had lost the shoes. He then reached down, grabbed Henry, and dragged him to the first door. Kerry took a last look at the window. Darcy was still struggling and a crimson red glow backlit her as she did. He saw that the tiny crack that had formed when he smashed Henry's head into the window had grown. It was spreading slowly down the length of the glass.

With no thought other than accomplishing his task with the utmost speed, he pulled the inside door and it would not budge. He tried again and then, out of instinct, he tried pushing the door. It easily swung open. Surprised but not stopping to think about it, Kerry dragged the limp blob of Henry Childs in front of it, creating a human doorstop. Without hesitation, he lunged for the knob of the outer door and pulled with all his might. Again, it refused to budge. He pushed on the door. It opened easily. *How weird,* he thought. Outside doors normally did not do that. He was grateful for small favors.

With the airlock broken, the pool gushed into the chamber and out of the tunnel with tremendous force. Kerry was thrown forward by the rush of air and water that was now flowing freely. He managed to grab the door as it swung out, and the force threw him against the side of the cliff, out of the way of the now surging torrent of water.

The volume of water blowing out of the chamber was incredible. The added pressure fractured the window, and it crashed in on the room, flooding the chamber and emptying the pool at an astonishing rate. Laying on the ground behind the door, Kerry saw Henry Childs fly by and disappear over the edge of the cliff carried by the raging current escaping from the pool as it exploded out of the chamber and formed a geyser spewing out over the cliff.

Kerry didn't stay to admire his handiwork. He scrambled up the top of the hill, his mangled leg delivering relentless pain with each movement and made it to the gate leading into the backyard. It was locked, and he had to climb over it, bumping his leg twice in the process and causing him to vomit. Once on top of the gate, he slowly lowered himself to the ground. He threw up again on the run as he still had to get Darcy out of the pool before she was swept away.

Before he got to the pool, Kerry saw the house, or rather felt the intense heat from the house as it was now nearly engulfed in flames. He moved faster.

When Kerry got to the edge of the water, the pool was down almost ten feet. That was an incredible amount of water pouring out over the cliff at an astounding rate. He had a very short amount of time to find and rescue Darcy.

He moved to the shallow end, or what had been the shallow end because it was now the empty end, sat on the edge, and lowered himself into the pool, landing on his right leg. A few fish had been left behind and were flopping around, trying to knock themselves back into the water. The heat from the fire and the cool mist from the pool created a very weird juxtaposition for Kerry. The irony of the moment was too much to think about just then. He made it to the water's edge and waded out as far as he could without getting caught in the current. He was calling her name with desperation and fear. The cool water brought mild relief to his contorted leg. He knew that the pool dropped off somewhere, and he was careful not to fall in himself.

"Darcy? Darcy!" Kerry yelled. She wasn't answering. He was afraid that she had already been sucked out of the pool and was now rolling down the cliffside, her body ripping open on the rocks as she fell.

"Darcy!" He cried out again with desperation.

"Over here." A voice replied from the side of the island that was now only ten feet away.

Kerry looked up and saw her as she slowly climbed onto the rock formation that was now protruding twelve feet into the air in the middle of the pool. She looked up at the burning inferno that was the house.

"What the hell?" She yelled.

"We gotta move." He yelled back.

"How are you?" she said. She stood tall on the island, breathing hard and dripping wet.

"I hurt like hell, but I am damn happy to see you," Kerry said, and he laughed out loud. "We just have to figure out how to get you out of there."

"No worries. I've got this," Darcy said.

"What happened to your aunt?" Kerry yelled across to her.

"I'm sure she's not far away," Darcy said.

"She probably got sucked through into the chamber and washed out to sea. Now she can sit on the rocks and call ships to their—"

But he didn't get to finish. The creature rose out of the water in front of him to her full height and let out an ear-piercing screech. Kerry fell over from the surprise and was on his butt in a foot of water. The creature dove at him. He had little time to react but managed to roll out of the way before she could strike. She hit the rocks and left behind torn pieces of flesh from what remained of her forehead. Kerry leaped to his feet directly out of his roll and turned to face the creature hopping on one foot. She was back in the water, using her tail to elevate herself, so it appeared that she was walking on water, like the dolphins in a water show. Water splashed up all around her. The fire from the house reflected in her eyes giving her an even more menacing appearance... if that was possible. She was screeching and swinging at Kerry with giant pincers snapping.

Kerry was against the side of the pool, the top edge a good ten feet above him. The water level kept sinking as more water escaped through the chamber and over the cliff. As the current rushed past his calves, the way a receding wave rushes out to sea, the skin on the back of his neck was beginning to burn and blister.

Time was running out on the creature, and she knew it, just as time was running out for Kerry and Darcy and he knew it. With a final death scream, the wraith lunged at Kerry, intent on killing him. But she never made it.

Darcy had fallen back when the creature rose out of the water to attack Kerry. As she stood, she felt the power inside of her begin to rise as though empowered by the flames and engorged by the heat.

You can do this. You can win. You are strong.

Again, she had reached inside to find a seemingly unending strength, from defeating the lizard-like Henry Childs on the back porch to standing on the beach facing down the cloud to dealing with Stan Grossman. Darcy felt that strength, again, build inside of her. She flashed back to the journey, and she saw Sheila as her soul floated out of her body. The smile, the blessing, and realized that she was the source of her strength. Sheila, who had suffered betrayal and hatred and had her heart broken by the people who should have loved her. Sheila was the one who now summoned that inner strength to save Kerry. From the island, Darcy leaped toward the creature and, using her body weight, smashed it to the ground. Darcy had the creature pinned, and it was then Darcy saw it all.

In a rerun of mystical proportions, Darcy saw every victim that had fallen to this amphibious evil thing pass within the black depths of the creature's eye. She saw the face of George Thornton, whom she recognized from the photo album. She saw Sheila Taft falling with a bullet wound in her chest. And somewhere in the back of her mind, Darcy knew that something wasn't right. Sheila was shot in the chest, she had seen that, and this thing was missing the side of her head.

It was then she understood. It wasn't Sheila that had become this twisted, murderous mutant. It was Rosemary who had killed her lover and her sister, who had made up a husband to cover her pregnancy, and who had then killed herself. It was Rosemary trying to cleanse the gene pool of her treachery and deceit. It was Rosemary who had become the murderous hag that had taken so many lives along the way. Darcy saw it all unfold in the eyes of this creature.

Chapter 65

After the deaths of John and Sheila, the house sat empty for almost a year. Once the legalities had been cleared up, George Thornton had found himself as the sole owner. He had wanted to move into the house in memory of his darling daughter but could never find the strength. He soon realized that the only way he could move into the house was as if he had remodeled it from top to bottom. After a year, he had finally accomplished the task, and at his daughter Rosemary's suggestion, he built the pool. Rosemary was of the mind that a hobby, something to occupy his time, would be of invaluable service toward soothing his soul.

On this dreary afternoon, Rosemary came to visit her father. As she stormed into the room, she found him sitting in the living room, alone, with a glass of scotch.

"Father. We need to talk." Rosemary said.

George did not respond.

"Father, you can't ignore me forever. We must deal with the reality of this situation." Rosemary was not asking, she was demanding.

"Father, you don't understand."

"You are absolutely correct in that assumption. I don't know how to look at you, how to look at George John. The poor boy is three years old, and his grandfather can't stand the sight of him. Do you think I don't see the resemblance? Do you think I'm so stupid as to believe you married a man and I would have never met him?"

Rosemary stood silent.

George hesitated and then turned to her. "This situation? Girl, you betrayed your sister's trust, fornicated with her husband, and bore that man a child. As a result of which, John killed your sister and himself. How exactly do we deal with this reality?"

Rosemary stepped toward George and reached out her hand. "Father, the first step toward forgiveness is understanding. I know what John and I did was wrong, and I am so very sorry for my actions. But there is nothing that can be done to change that. It was never my intention for them to die. I cannot fathom what came over John to do such a thing. I only know that we are left behind. You, me, and your grandson. Can we raise this boy in a family filled with hate?"

George stood up and set down his drink.

"Rosemary, I do not have the capacity for forgiveness in this matter. You have no comprehension of the pain that is involved in losing a child. I have known no greater misery than this. I cannot forgive you. Now please leave."

George left the room and climbed the stairs up to his room.

Rosemary was filled with rage. Her father had always preferred Sheila. Even in death, he still preferred her sister. She picked up the glass tumbler and threw it across the room, shattering it on the wall. In a rage, she moved about the room overturning tables and tossing chairs. She started to punish herself, one punch after the other. She bloodied her own nose and split her lip. Kicking over the last standing end table, the drawer flew open, and a pistol shimmied across the floor. Her father had kept it there in the event of a break in and had probably forgotten it was even there. Rosemary stared at the weapon.

You have no comprehension of the pain that is involved in losing a child.

Rosemary took the gun. Kicking walls and slamming doors she moved through the house. She kicked open the swinging door into the kitchen and burst inside. No windows. Who does that? Who blocks up all the windows to the beautiful view of the ocean? With the thought of the ocean, she marched into the backyard. There was the pool, quiet and shimmering in the sun. The cool ocean breeze salved her skin, and the beauty and peace of this place calmed her.

Rosemary took a deep breath and realized, "He loves it out here. This is his little sanctuary where he can sit and pine over Sheila. I bet he cries out here missing her." She screamed, "What about me? Father! What about me? It's my birthday, for god's sake, and you didn't even remember."

She stepped closer to the pool and looked up at the house. She raised the pistol hoping to see a silhouette of her father. Waving the pistol back and forth, she fired randomly into the house. She turned to the pool and screamed a hate filled curse. "You'll be sorry, old man. You'll be so sorry that you did this to me." She raised the gun to her head and pulled the trigger blowing out the entire left side of her face. Her body dropped into the pool, and she floated.

Chapter 66

Darcy finally understood. Staring into the stone-cold fisheye of this creature, she had been shown exactly what had happened to her long gone relatives. She wanted to turn away now, she had seen enough and needed to get back to the matter at hand and end this awful thing forever. But before she could, in the creature's eye, there was still more story to be told. Darcy saw his face as clearly as she saw the creature itself. She saw her father.

She watched the twisted vision as her father walked to the pool and cursed the evil that had brought him there.

"I won't do it." He screamed. "I will never hurt my daughter. You can't make me. If you want a sacrifice, then take me, but you won't take my daughter. You bitch!" From out of the depths of the pool a giant claw rose and in one swift motion ripped him to pieces.

Her own father had been a victim of this wicked thing. He didn't leave them! She killed him! He was a descendant of Rosemary's, her own great-grandson, and she had killed him!

Hatred exploded from Darcy. She screamed, "No!" and jammed her hand into the eye, ripping it out of the creature's head, tendrils of blood and muscle falling across the hag's face as she did.

The creature screeched with pain and jolted violently, flopping like a fish on the deck of a boat. Darcy was thrown off and rolled into the wall of the pool.

The creature flailed about, trying to find Darcy, the remains of her vacant socket dangling the muscles that used to hold her eye. She rose to her full height and cursed the world with an ugly scream filled with hatred and terror, and pain.

Kerry had shaken off the pain and moved to the edge of the pool to hobble around and attack the thing from behind. He moved low by the pool wall to protect himself from the heat as the house surrendered itself to the devouring flames. Interior walls had crumbled, and the exterior supports were about to fail. Its time of death was approaching.

Without warning, he was struck to the ground by a blow from behind. He hit the rocky surface of the pool and brought his hands up to cover his face from further attack, and in between his spread fingers, he saw Hannah Brower coming at him with her flaming baton raised, her uniform was on fire and her hair matted and nearly burned off. She had launched herself from above and landed on Kerry from behind. She writhed in pain and vengeance as she moved in to finally get her revenge on Kerry Devine.

Behind Hannah, the creature seethed in pain and anger, blindly swinging its claws, snapping at any sound or sensation, attempting to kill anything within reach. Hannah focused her attention on the supine Kerry. She sneered down at him and screamed, "Now it's my turn, asshole. You get to pay for what you did to me." She raised her flaming baton to club Kerry to death as her clothes glowered, and her hair melted. She swung hard, but Kerry rolled to his right and away from the falling nightstick. As he did, he swept his legs at Hannah and caught her just above the ankles. She flipped in the air and fell into the pool, hitting the bottom with a thud.

"You son of a bitch! I'm going to kill you!" Hannah screamed, and she pounded her fist on the bottom of the pool and her left sleeve extinguished itself in a puddle.

The creature slashed toward the sound of the woman's voice. Her huge pincers were snapping uselessly in the air until one snap happened to meet with a crazed Hannah. As she was trying to stand a huge red claw swung in and, in a single pinch, cut Hannah in half, just about the gun belt. The top of her body was thrown into the whirling pool, dousing the fire and producing a huge hiss of steam, and the bottom half stood where it was for a moment, smoldering, and then crumpled to the ground.

Darcy moved into a position to get closer to Kerry. She looked at him, and he yelled, "It's time to finish this."

The creature snapped and spit and screeched. Darcy looked into Kerry's eyes, "Time to end this forever."

Kerry moved as nimbly as he could to a launch point behind the creature and signaled to Darcy that he was ready. Darcy ran to the opposite side of the pool and yelled. "Over here, bitch!"

The creature turned toward Darcy, and as she did Kerry launched himself at the creature, once again utilizing his All-City tackling techniques, and drove her to the ground. With Kerry pinning the creature to the floor, Darcy ran to the creature and manipulated the pincers that were still wildly reaching for something to kill. Bending the right pincer upwards and toward the creature's throat, she maneuvered it into exactly the right position. With a small smile on her face, she gave the pincer one final push and the powerful claw opened and closed. A torturous scream filled the backyard as the creature slit open its own throat.

As blood left the creature's body and it lost any ability to fight back, Darcy and Kerry pushed the creature forward and into the current that was draining the pool. She struggled to break free of the current, but the water cascading through the shattered observation window was too strong for her to fight. A death screech flew from her throat as she was pulled under the water and through the chamber. She was gone.

Behind them they heard a giant bellow. There was a twisting and breaking sound, a tortuous and furtive cry as beams and floorboards and years of history of a once glorious house began to collapse.

"We gotta move. Come on, Darcy. Follow me."

Kerry took Darcy into the pool. The level was about halfway down the observation window and while the current was still thundering, it was beginning to slow.

"What the hell, Kerry? I'm not going back down there. Are you crazy?" She screamed.

"I know it's crazy, but we can't go any other way. We can't climb out of the pool now, the walls are too steep. The house is about to collapse. We have to get into the chamber and work our way back toward the staircase. We'll be safe from the heat down there and it's deep enough underground it shouldn't collapse."

A giant piece of the roof fell at that moment and landed in the backyard just feet away from the pool.

"This whole place is coming down and it's going to end up in the pool. We can't stay here!" Kerry yelled.

Darcy screamed, "Just once, can something be simple? Okay, don't let go."

Kerry held her hand as tightly as he could, and they moved toward the busted-out observation window. He was moving slowly, the pain in his leg making every step a nightmare. The house continued to sway, and it was about to come down at any moment.

"We just have to hang on till we can get into the room. Then we swim against the current to get to the first door. The circular staircase is where he have to get. We should be safe there until everything dies down."

Darcy looked at Kerry and kissed him. The kiss was full of love, desperation, and regret that this might be the entirely of their life together. She was about to argue with him when she saw the south balcony of the house fall to the ground.

"Let me go first, you can barely walk." She said.

She guided them to the south side of the pool to get next to the observation window. Once the water was low enough, they could jump through and move away from the cliffside.

The house was lurching front to back now. Flames shot out of the attic windows, and they could hear the spirits, the ghosts and the condemned souls leave this world and traveling on to the next. Some, they felt, were escaping while others were condemned to a painful eternity.

When the water level hit close to the bottom of the window Kerry squeezed Darcy's hand.

"Stay close to the wall and don't let go." Darcy said.

They moved to the edge and in an instant were pulled through into the room. They were pushed across the room in a swirling current and ended up near the bed frame, the mattress had already been sucked out to sea. They had footing and handholds along the wall and floor. As they stood to move to the chamber door a screech arose from the far corner of the room and the Siren rose out of the darkness. She was spewing blood from her neck; the tendrils of her eye were waving as her head shook from side to side. She could sense their presence but couldn't find them.

Kerry looked above the bed and saw the whaling harpoon. He moved in that direction but his leg wouldn't let him stand up to grab it. Without hesitation Darcy jumped past Kerry and reached up to pull it down.

"Now! Now it's time to end this!" She said.

She stumbled toward the creature holding the harpoon in front of her like a jousting lance as though she were Lancelot in a tournament. The current was sweeping toward the cliff, and she could feel the pull from the churning water.

Darcy cried out, "Over here you bitch!"

The siren's head swung around and she moved swiftly in Darcy's direction. Darcy stepped in front of the wraith, dropping the handle of the harpoon against her foot and raised the tip. In her rage, the siren rushed toward Darcy and literally impaled herself onto the harpoon. Darcy screamed and drove her backward toward the open door. "Die you bitch! Die!"

The current did the rest. As Darcy pushed her to the ground, the harpoon impaled in her chest, she was caught up in the current and they watched her get sucked out of the room and over the cliff.

Darcy quickly fought her way over to Kerry and they hugged. She was finally gone. Holding each other as tightly as they could they started to slowly walk the perimeter of the room toward the chamber door, careful not to get pulled into the current. Once they moved away from the broken window the current eased up. Slowly and carefully, they made it to the first door. Kerry pulled it and it slowly moved. Darcy grabbed the handle as well and between the two of them it finally opened. Kerry pushed Darcy through and squeezed past the door himself. The door shut behind them, forced closed by the water in the chamber. They moved quickly to the second door. Kerry grabbed the handle of the second door and it opened much easier as there was no current now in the small chamber.

They closed the door behind them and waded in ankle deep water to the bottom of the stairs. Climbing a few steps up, they sat and waited. They could feel the heat from above but there was nothing to burn down here so they knew the fire would look elsewhere. They huddled on the stairs, alive and grateful to be so.

As they sat on the stair, waiting for someone to find them, Darcy saw a shadow float through the door and move toward them. For just a moment, it hovered over them and formed a face. Darcy could make out the features well enough to know that it was Sheila. They shared that same small smile. Darcy thought back to Kerry and their adolescent escapade in the living room and now understood. Sheila had run them out of the old place all those years ago. She had protected them and brought them something that no one else ever could have. She had brought them together and made them recognize their love. It was why the living room always had a special feeling, a feeling that was scary and yet safe. Sheila had looked out for her great-great niece the way her great-great-grandmother would never have. She did what she could to protect them, and with the siren gone, she was free to move on to the next world.

About an hour later they heard the first bumps and thuds of a rescue crew. They shouted immediately.

Ten minutes later, light shown through a hacked-up door, and they heard the sweetest sound ever, "Anyone down there?"

Chapter 67

The water pouring over the cliff along with a four-alarm fire, had been reported by many people, and fire and rescue, police, and medical emergency vehicles had been called. They had the fire contained but the house was almost in ashes by the time they did. Search and rescue found the two of them in the circular staircase and got them out. Paramedics took Kerry to the hospital. Darcy had multiple cuts and abrasions but was remarkably unscathed otherwise. She called her mom to fill her in, and in a panic, Gail jumped into her car and came to Kerry's bedside. He had been taken straight into surgery for his leg and had his arm recast.

As Kerry lay in his bed, asleep, recovering from his surgery, Darcy and Gail sat vigil. Darcy looked at her mom and said, "Mom, I have something to tell you. It's about Dad."

As Darcy finished telling Gail the story, she held her mother's hand, and together they brought her father back into their hearts. He hadn't deserted them, he was taken. A deep sense of relief flowed over them both.

"So, this thing was trying to end the Thornton bloodline, one generation at a time?" Gail asked?

"Yeah, it seems to be the case. I was the last in the line and had she succeeded, the bloodline would have ended with me."

They both exchanged looks and took a deep breath. "And the house burns down…fire is the devil's only friend, right?" Gail said and let out a chuckle.

With Henry and Edith dead and Darcy the legitimate descendent of George Thornton, it turned out that she controlled the trust fund, and she inherited the estate. It took Darcy about a nanosecond to decide what she wanted to do. A bulldozer took care of the rest.

The debate raged in bars and coffee shops all over town. *Were Kerry and Darcy crazy? Was there really a ghost in the pool? What should she do with all that money?*

But they had survived, and no one else had ever done that. They were now local celebrities. Consequently, most of the town came to their wedding.

The birdseed hit Darcy in the eye and stung for just a moment. *What a stupid tradition*, she thought. How did it ever develop that people would do this? After a long discussion, they had decided that rice was not a good environmental choice, so instead, they had their guests throw birdseed. After all, when a bride and groom set off for their honeymoon, you must do something and left to their own devices, who knows what Kerry and Darcy's friends might find to throw?

They had been married three months after the Thornton place had burned down.

Where the Thornton house once stood, there was now an unobstructed view of the Pacific Ocean. It was a unanimous opinion around town that the view was preferable to the old house any way you looked at it.

Henry's body had been found a week later by some fishermen. It was badly decomposed and missing the left side of its head. Edith and the other bodies were never found. Stan Grossman had received a severe concussion when Darcy smashed him to the wall. It took several operations to relieve the pressure in his skull, and he eventually would come out of it with minimal damage. Darcy did not press charges against him as she knew better than anyone what had possessed him.

As for the creature, well, Darcy and Kerry knew that it perished on the cliffs the same way Henry did. The evil of Rosemary Thornton was dead and gone.

But, they moved to Sacramento anyway and now live a few doors down from her mother. They figured, why take any chances?

Epilogue

Santa Cruz, CA 17 years earlier

Gail's slender fingers intertwined with Bill's as she clutched his calloused hand with lustful anticipation. It was a hot summer afternoon, and even as sweat pooled between their palms, neither of them was willing to let go. In her free hand, she carried the old red blanket from the trunk of their car, and he held a small cooler with a six-pack of beer. He squeezed his love's hand tighter, and with a quick kiss, they walked up the driveway.

They approached the old, deserted house with a mixture of excitement and trepidation.

"I feel like I'm in a scene from Children of the Corn." She felt the cool ocean breeze swirl around them, chilling the sweat that ran down the back of her neck.

They had heard all the ghost stories and the second-hand tales of horror that had surrounded the Thornton Mansion, just like everyone else, and in a normal circumstance, that would have been enough to keep them away. But they had stronger motivation today, it was their seven-year wedding anniversary, and they had no intention of spending it in a one-bedroom apartment with their six-year-old.

Handing the child over to a friend for the afternoon, they made their way to this deserted spot for a few hours of alone time. Even the local roach motel was too expensive for their meager budget, so they had settled on a sex-filled afternoon in this supposedly haunted mansion that sat alone on the cliffs overlooking the Pacific.

They approached the porch giggling.

"Are you sure there's no one here?" she said, expectation evident in her smile.

"Who would be here? The damn place has been empty for thirty years. Besides, who's crazy enough to hang out here except us?" He squeezed her hand tighter, and she responded by grabbing his butt.

"Well, let's not just stand here then, get us inside."

They walked onto the decaying porch stepping over the missing board on the third step. He tried the doorknob, but it was locked tight. Moving to the far end of the front porch, he looked into a window. The grime that had accumulated over the years offered a very limited view. Undeterred, he grabbed the bottom of the frame and pulled with a mighty heave. The window offered no resistance, and the force of his effort popped it off the track as it disintegrated in his hands. The sash snapped in two as an uncharacteristic screech leaped from his mouth. He jumped back just as the glass shattered on the porch floor. His quick reflexes had saved him from the embarrassment of losing his toes along with his dignity.

With the remaining pieces of broken window frame in his hands, pieces of glass covering his shabby tennis shoes, and a foolish look on his face, he turned to his wife. Her hand shot to her mouth as she tried to stifle her laughter. Unsuccessful, she burst into hysteria. He had no choice but to follow suit, and suddenly, the two of them were clutching each other to keep from falling over.

"Nice Buzz Lightyear impression, very manly."

"I try to impress. Well, here we go, to infinity and beyond," Tossing the wooden frame aside, he climbed through the open window, careful of the broken glass.

One foot touched the floor and then the other. He turned back to his wife and said, "I'll meet you at the front." She giggled and ran to the entryway.

Now that he was fully inside, he turned to face the room, and the lightness of the laughter died. A pall descended on him as the ambiance of the house coated his enthusiasm. His eyes darted from wall to wall, from corner to corner. All he saw was an empty, old house; high ceilings, cobwebs in the doorframes, peeling Victorian wallpaper, and the dry, dusty smell that comes from years of abandonment. There were no boogeymen, no spirits flying about, and Casper was nowhere to be seen.

Phantoms of the stories he had heard growing up echoed in his mind, and he could taste the bile rising in the back of his throat. Evil stories of murder, decapitation and vile, wicked acts ran like a movie preview in his head. He had heard the kids, who would ride their bikes close to the house, taunt the ghosts with a rhyme:

The Thornton House is a big ol' shed

Go into the house, and you'll wind up dead.

His sense of adventure and unbridled excitement dissolved like an antacid. He saw movement out of the corner of his eye and plastered himself against the wall. A small sparrow flew past him and up the shabby staircase. He exhaled loudly, and a pathetic chuckle escaped his lips, "Maybe we should find a deserted spot on the beach."

But just then, he heard his wife pounding on the front door, "Unless you're starting without me, you might want to open the door and let me in."

At the sound of her sweet voice and the realization that she would soon be naked, his fears were pushed aside. It had been a long time. With a determined stride, he crossed to the front of the house and opened the door that sealed his fate.

He welcomed his beautiful girl into his arms.

She looked at the grime and dust and decrepit surroundings and said, "I must say, you do know how to woo a girl. How do any of them keep their panties on?"

Within minutes they had spread out their blanket in front of the dead stone fireplace and snuggled up close. The feel of her lustrous skin melted away his apprehension. The musty smell that enveloped the old house and the years of dust that had settled over the interior mingled with their sweat and passion producing a surprisingly erotic effect. It made them feel naughty being naked, in the daylight, in an abandoned house.

She laughed again. Her laugh thrilled his heart. Her dark hair, sweat soaked and plastered to her face, made him love her all the more.

She cupped his face in her hands and went nose to nose with him, "I love you."

"Even though all I can offer you is a dirty old floor, a six-pack, and eternal love?"

"Especially because of the six-pack. The cold one, I mean, not this ticklish hairy one." She began to tickle his stomach unmercifully.

By the time the afternoon had passed, and the amber light of dusk began to fill the house, they had remembered why they were together, why they were in love, and they wiled away the remainder of the day wrapped in each other's devotion.

As they left hand in hand, he stopped in the driveway and looked back at the old mansion. Inside he felt a pull, a desire to return, to learn more about this ramshackle place. She tugged his arm gently and said, "Come on, honey, we've got to get back. We have to pick up Darcy." He pulled her close and framed against the backdrop of the monolithic mansion, kissed her for the hundredth time that day.

The first nightmare came to him that night.

CPSIA information can be obtained
at www.ICGtesting.com
Printed in the USA
LVHW082221261122
733860LV00007BA/213